Little Village
Book Club

ALSO BY EMMA DAVIES

EMMA DAVIES

Lucy's Little Village Book Club

Bookouture

Published by Bookouture in 2017
An imprint of StoryFire Ltd.
Carmelite House
50 Victoria Embankment
London EC4Y 0DZ
www.bookouture.com

Previously published as *Lucy's Book Club for the Lost and Found*

ISBN: 978-1-78681-322-0
eBook ISBN: 978-1-78681-321-3

For Mum, whose light still shines

Chapter 1

It was late-night opening at the library, and Lucy Picklescott had a whole thirty-five minutes to herself before she was due back for the rest of the afternoon shift. She knew from experience that this was just enough time to cut through the churchyard, skirt the corner of the market square and walk the length of the High Street to her favourite teashop where, if he had remembered, Clive would have already plated up a plump custard slice ready for her arrival. It was her regular Thursday treat.

She was slightly out of breath when she arrived at Earl Grey's, and rather too warm; a slight flush coloured her pale cheeks. The day had morphed from dull and drizzly to blue-skied and autumnal, and Lucy's yellow raincoat was one layer too many. She shrugged it off as she reached the tearoom and pushed open the door.

Catching Clive's eye almost immediately, he waved her over towards a free table at the rear of the tearoom. Sometimes when Lucy arrived, Clive was busy in the kitchen and she was happy to wait her turn like everyone else, but if her brother-in-law was around she was treated like royalty and today was no exception. Lucy sat down and within moments tea and cake were placed in front of her. With a smile, she cast her eyes around the room; the view was so much better from the back. She pulled out a notebook and pen from her bag and laid them beside her plate, just in case inspiration struck.

The tea looked strong, exactly how Lucy liked it, and she pushed her hair away from her face before taking her first sip. She always started with her tea, drinking every drop before replacing the cup in the saucer and turning her full attention to the custard slice. This way she could savour the flavour of the pastry without interruption. She closed her eyes for the first mouthful, relishing the taste of the soft vanilla filling with its familiar comforting smell and cool, silky texture. Then came the crisp pastry flakes with their buttery finish, and a sweet hit from the icing, its stickiness lingering in her mouth. Clive was a magician where sugary things were concerned.

Lucy was about to take another bite, when she caught the eye of a young woman who was seated across from her, staring quite openly at her with a look on her face that was enough to make the hairs on the back of Lucy's neck prickle. The woman dropped her gaze, embarrassed, but not quickly enough to disguise the longing that hovered in the air between them. The face of the young woman remained downcast, eyes settled mournfully on the plate in front of her, which now held only crumbs, and perhaps a hint of regret. Lucy took in her rounded cheeks and sizeable girth and could almost see the copious cups of black coffee the woman had drunk, the breakfasts skipped, the apples eaten without pleasure, and imagine a little what it must feel like to be haunted by the hunger of a serial dieter. The woman may have just eaten a guilty treat, but Lucy guessed she had settled for something a little less sinful, and not the cake she truly desired. The one that Lucy was busy eating.

Lucy straightened, still holding her custard slice, but now it didn't look so appealing. How could she eat it knowing that another coveted it so much? She stared back down at her plate and felt slightly sick. She pushed a tentative finger against the pastry and sat for a moment lost in thought until a gentle touch on her shoulder made her almost jump out of her skin.

'Luce?' Clive's voice was gentle. 'Are you okay, love? You look a bit green about the gills.'

Almost immediately Lucy began to feel better. The sound of Clive's friendly voice brought her back to the familiar, the normality of just another Thursday afternoon. She looked up with a smile.

'I'm fine... honestly – bit tired, that's all.'

'And there was me worried my custard slices weren't up to the usual standard.'

Lucy glanced back down at her plate. 'Oh, no, they're gorgeous as ever,' she said, and she picked up the slice once more, as if to demonstrate.

Clive was still looking at her a little warily. 'Shall I bring you some more tea?' he asked.

'Only if you let me pay,' she replied. 'It's not fair to let me eat and drink all your profits.'

'You're family,' said Clive with a frown. 'That's different. And as it's my tearoom, I get to make the rules.'

Lucy knew there was no point in arguing and accepted another cup with a glance at her watch. She would need to hurry. She looked again at the pastry and sank her teeth into it. As the creamy vanilla flavour slid over her taste buds, she opened her mouth again and her first bite was swiftly followed by another, and another.

She was almost out of time as she rushed across the churchyard again. The library was still short-staffed and Lucy didn't want to be late as it would be all hands on deck for another couple of hours yet, with the arrival of the after-school crowd and the planning for tomorrow's book club meeting still to be done. She took a deep, steadying breath.

'Oh, thank God you're back, Lucy. The server's gone down again, and all the PCs have disconnected.'

She smiled at the harried face of her colleague. 'Carrie, how many times have I shown you how to reboot it? Computers can smell your fear, you know; you have to learn to show them who's boss. Come on, let's sort it out.'

★

Callum smiled to himself. He never said much, but it tickled him the way people behaved when they were using the computers. Not everyone, of course, but there were a lot like his mum and dad who thought they were the devil's work. Some of the staff at the library were just as bad. Lucy was right, you could see the fear sweep across their faces whenever the slightest thing went wrong or if someone dared asked them a technical question. Regardless, he still liked doing his work here; it certainly beat sitting at home with his laptop, trying to concentrate while his brothers squabbled.

He sat back and waited while his PC rebooted. Luckily, he had only been looking at stuff on the internet, so it was no problem, but he could hear the sighs from the people around him who feared they had probably now lost whatever they had been working on. Lucy would have to sort them all out. Their stuff would still be there, in most cases, and if it wasn't there would be smiles and apologies and a gentle reminder to make sure folks saved their work as they went along. Lucy never got cross or irritated with people, but he knew that she really didn't have the time to give them as much attention as she did. One day he might pluck up the courage to ask if he could help.

A chiming alert sounded from the depths of his bag and he bent down to fish out his phone. A pen landed on the floor beside him, and without thinking he stretched to pick it up. His fingers curled around it, slightly too late to register the movement from above him, as another hand reached out for it. Their fingers touched.

He pulled his hand up swiftly, a flush of colour flooding his face. He thrust the pen back to its owner.

'Sorry, I didn't... Sorry.'

A pretty face smiled back at him. 'No worries,' she said, before taking the pen and turning away again, back to her computer.

Callum stared at the girl beside him, at the sparkly ring on one of the fingers that had touched his. She was deep in thought, looking at an image of flowers on the screen in front of her. A large notepad lay open beside her, covered in exuberant loopy writing in lots of different colours. The dropped pen scratched across it now, in purple ink. It was cute, shaped like an owl at the top; one of those pens that had a range of different colours in it. He wanted to say something, a witty remark perhaps that would attract her attention, but even as his mind suggested it, he knew he wouldn't. It was just his luck she was already taken, but then who was he kidding? Even if she was single it would make no difference. He had never managed to come out with a witty remark in his life, and today would have been no different. He reached back down to find his phone, one eye still on the girl with the beautiful shiny hair and engagement ring – but she didn't even look up.

Chapter 2

'Odelia, Odelia!' The voice was sharp and getting sharper. Lia put down her hairbrush and examined her reflection in the bedroom mirror. She really ought to have washed her hair.

'Coming, Mum,' she called, looking at her watch. Gwen would be here any minute now.

The sound of the television was loud as she made her way downstairs, and she could already hear the strains of a beautiful classic waltz playing.

'Are you okay, Mum?' she asked, walking into the living room.

Rose was sitting in a chair opposite the fireplace, her legs stretched out in front of her, her slippers laid neatly to one side, and both socks peeled from her feet and discarded.

She stared at Lia. 'Who are you?' she asked, a raucous note to her voice.

'Mum, it's me – Lia. Odelia, your daughter.'

The older woman looked her up and down with eyes that were still surprisingly blue. She opened her mouth to argue, and then closed it again, seeming to accept what Lia had said. 'Well, someone's pinched my flip-flops again. Look, these aren't mine.'

Lia knelt on the carpet beside her, picking up a sock and gently easing it over her mother's toes. 'I'll look for them in a minute, Mum. Let's pop these back on in the meantime, shall we? It's a bit chilly today.' She glanced sideways at the television. 'Oh look, Mum, *Strictly Come*

Dancing is on. Why don't you watch that for a minute?' She finished with one sock and picked up the other, hoping the distraction would do the trick.

'I used to be a dancer, you know…'

'I know you did, Mum. You and Dad won all the medals there were going, didn't you?'

'We did. But that's because he was so handsome. And he had the lightest feet. He used to whizz me around the ballroom like I was dancing on air. All the girls were in love with him.'

'I bet they were, but you were his one and only, weren't you? His "dancing queen", he used to call you.'

'That's right… How did you know that?' Rose's voice had risen slightly again.

Lia smiled. 'I don't know, Mum, I expect you told me some time. Tell me about your costumes again… how you used to twirl and twirl, the sequins catching the light…'

'Oh, they were so beautiful. I had one, I remember, which was exactly the same colour as my eyes. The bodice was covered in tiny crystals…' Her gaze flickered back to the television.

Lia replaced the slippers and straightened up, a soft smile in her eyes. She had seen the photos, and that dress; her mum had been truly beautiful. She gently stroked the top of her mother's hair before leaving the room.

With another glance at her watch she ran lightly back up the stairs to her bedroom. Her reflection looked just as it had moments ago, and she grimaced, rooting around on the dressing table for a hairband. Ponytail it was then. She piled her hair as high as she could, pulling out two small curls on either side and fixing the rest with the band. She ruffled her fringe and puffed out her cheeks, tilting her head to one side. It would have to do; Gwen's car had just pulled up outside, and it was time to go.

Lia met her at the door. 'Thanks so much, Gwen, come in.'

The carer stepped inside, giving Lia a friendly smile. 'How are things?'

'Oh, you know. Good days, not-so-good days.'

'And today?'

'Not too bad at all. She's watching *Strictly…* again. Whoever invented that programme needs a medal. It's on an almost permanent loop some days, but, well, you know…'

Gwen narrowed her eyes. 'And how about you? How are you holding up?'

Lia touched a hand to her hair. 'Oh, I'm fine. Absolutely.'

'Well then, you get going and enjoy yourself. Your mum and me will be right as rain.' She paused for a second. 'Listen, Lia… I shouldn't really do this, but I was supposed to be with another client this afternoon and I've just had a cancellation, which means I'm free for another two hours. Why don't you take the extra time for yourself? Meet a friend, have a coffee. Go shopping – anything.'

'I can't do that,' exclaimed Lia.

'Who's to know?' replied Gwen. 'I'm not about to tell anybody, and if you don't…'

Lia bit her lip; the thought of four whole hours to herself was absolute bliss. 'Well, I must pay you – and only if you're sure.'

Gwen took hold of her arm. 'Listen, love: I'm doing it as favour, as a friend, not because I want the money. If you don't mind me saying, you look a little tired, and it will do you good.' She watched Lia's face. 'And I know you want to, I can see it in your eyes.'

Lia smiled. She had never been able to hide how she was feeling. 'You've got to promise you'll ring me if anything happens.'

'I will,' said Gwen, almost pushing her out of the door. 'Go on, go! You'll be late.'

With one final check of her bag, Lia grinned, backing off down the path. 'I owe you one, Gwen,' she called.

★

Lucy studied the biscuits on the plate and wondered if there would be enough, adding three more just to be on the safe side. She'd bought proper biscuits this time, with her own money; big chunky cookies full of chocolate chips, and some sugar-covered shortbread. The library budget only ran to custard creams and Nice biscuits, but she hoped that these luxury treats might help to break the ice.

The book club had been her idea and although two others ran locally, they were each formed from existing groups of friends and Lucy imagined it must be hard for someone new to join them. She wanted her group to be one that anyone could come along to, whether they knew each other or not. As for the reading material, Lucy was a sucker for a happy ever after, and so by and large this was what they read. She had chosen this month's title for that exact reason.

At the moment only three people regularly came to the meetings, but Lucy consoled herself with the thought that it had only been up and running for six weeks, so there was still time for it to get bigger. Just yesterday a young mum had enquired about joining and would be coming along this morning to see what it was like. The library needed more activities like this, and Lucy had a ton of ideas. It wasn't that the place was underused, more that its potential wasn't being fully explored, and Lucy was only too aware that cutbacks were looming. It didn't do to rest on one's laurels.

She looked up at the vaulted ceiling above her, not offering a prayer exactly, but recognising how she always felt in this building, as if help were just around the corner and all she had to do was call upon it. After all, wasn't that exactly why she was here? When she had first stepped foot in the place it had been like walking into the home of an old friend. There had been no need to stand on ceremony or be on best behaviour, just a comforting acceptance of everything she was. It was the same for other people too, she knew, and now that she was working here she'd do everything she could to keep that atmosphere; if the library thrived, so did everyone else.

With a final nod of satisfaction, she placed the biscuits on the table. They were all set. Ten minutes later every chair was occupied, and Lucy waited for arms to be released from coats and bags to be placed on the floor before speaking. She smiled at the newcomer.

'Hattie, it's brilliant that you came. I'm so glad you're here.' She paused to catch the eye of one or two people in the group. 'Everyone, this is Hattie, who's come to see what we're all about today. Perhaps we should introduce ourselves before getting stuck into the biscuits and then we can make a start.'

The young woman was looking around her, eyes focused a little nervously on the plate of biscuits.

'Would you like to go first, Hattie?' asked Lucy. 'Just a few words about yourself.'

Her smile was returned as Hattie pushed a length of dark hair behind her ear. 'Well, my name's Hattie,' she began, 'obviously… I've got a little girl called Poppy, who just started school a few weeks ago. I'm not from round here, though – we only moved here in the summer, so I thought that as soon as she went to school and I had a bit more time during the day I would try to meet a few people.' She looked down at her hands. 'I'm on my own, you see, so it's hard for me to get out of an evening. That's why this group is so ideal. Up until recently, looking after Poppy's been pretty much a full-time job, so I'm afraid I don't do much else now besides reading.'

Lucy nodded and looked at the woman to Hattie's left.

'I'm Lia,' she supplied. 'And reading is virtually all I do too – when I can, that is. I'm a full-time carer, you see. My mum has Alzheimer's, so this is my little bit of sanity.' She gave Hattie a sympathetic smile.

The rest of the introductions were over quickly and Lucy picked up the plate of biscuits, offering them directly to Hattie. She could tell she wanted one and was just being polite. Perhaps if she took one the others would follow suit.

'So, did you all manage to read *Precious Time*?' she asked, waiting for the answering nods. 'I'm sorry Hattie, you're at a bit of a disadvantage this time, but we'll pick the next read before we finish and then you'll soon be up and running.' She looked around the group. 'What did you all think? Thumbs up or thumbs down?'

Lia was the first to respond. 'Oh, thumbs up,' she sighed. 'It was beautiful,' she added, 'and I cried… again.'

The young lad next to her nodded vigorously. 'Me too,' he agreed. 'Well, not the crying part, but I thought the characters were brilliant. I couldn't pick a favourite, they were all so different, but so good – even the nasty one!'

'I think that's what I love about Erica's writing, Callum,' said Lucy. 'Her characters don't just introduce themselves so much as walk off the page to meet you. What about you Oscar? Perhaps not quite your cup of tea, but what did you think?'

Oscar was in his early seventies and always made Lucy smile; she never failed to be cheered up in the presence of one of his colourful bow ties. He was a regular at the library, and she had never seen him read anything that wasn't a thriller.

'It's true, I prefer my fiction a bit more masculine, but all things considered I did enjoy it. Like Lia, I could see it was a very emotional read. The start struck me as quite…' He trailed off, clearing his throat. 'Very poignant, I thought.'

'I knew I recognised the title,' said Hattie suddenly. 'Is it by Erica James? The one where the main character gives up her job and goes off with her little boy in a camper van?'

There were nods all round, and Hattie beamed.

'It has an element of pure wish-fulfilment, doesn't it?' said Lia. 'That's why I enjoyed it so much. Imagine simply taking off without any consequences and seeing where the wind takes you. And of course they all live happily ever after – that's what makes it so perfect. Isn't that what we'd all like to do?'

Lucy loved it when the discussions seemed to flow of their own accord. It didn't always happen, but she was pleased when it did. It showed the group was beginning to get to know one another better, and say what they felt rather than be polite or shy.

'I know I would,' groaned Callum, pushing his slightly too long black curls off his face. 'I've had enough of my brothers teasing me and making my life a misery. I'd take off to a remote Scottish island – provided it had an internet connection, of course – find a nice girl to settle down with, and live out my days never having to listen to them again.'

'What about you, Lia? What would you do if you could?' asked Oscar.

Lia clearly didn't need to think about it. She sat up straight, and leaned forward. 'Dance,' she whispered urgently. 'I'd want to dance.'

Chapter 3

'There'd be a dark space lit with a thousand twinkling points of lights,' continued Lia. 'Music rising and falling, silken material swishing against my legs, and I'd be twirling faster and faster, lost in the sensations that filled my head. Like a bubble of happiness rising up, a lightness of being, as if I'm on air…'

And suddenly Lucy could see just how it would be for Lia. How she must feel chained by the confinement of her life, yet lit up by her love for her mother. She could almost sense the weight of her familial duty, how worn she must feel by her endless need to be patient and longing to be released. Lucy could think of no better cure than the exquisite pleasure of a soul finding freedom as it danced.

'My mum was a professional ballroom dancer,' Lia continued. 'Years ago, mind, before I was even born; it's how she met my dad. They used to tour in the 1960s, even dancing at the Empress Ballroom in Brighton a few times. That's why I'd love to dance: for the romance of it all, the glamour, the old-fashioned elegance, and the dresses of course, all those sequins…' She gave a self-conscious laugh.

'But you must dance, surely?' asked Hattie. 'Having a mum who was a professional, I bet your house was filled with music as a child.'

Lia looked down at her shoes. 'It was for a little while, but mostly when I was very small, almost too small to remember. Then my dad left, and Mum... well, she never really danced again. She wouldn't let me either – even though I begged her to have lessons, she flatly refused. I never learned, not to this day.'

Hattie raised a hand to her mouth. 'Oh, that's so sad,' she empathised. 'But you must learn – it's never too late you know.'

Lucy saw Lia give a shrug, almost imperceptible, and she felt the wave of longing again, the sadness of an unattainable dream. Lia looked up and caught her eye.

'Maybe,' she said. 'Sorry, we're kind of getting off the subject of the book, but that's what I would do if I could.'

Lucy nodded. 'I think it's entirely relevant, Lia. That's the power of a good book, isn't it? The ability writing has to evoke such strong emotions. For me, although it's set in the modern day, it has such a nostalgic feel to it. I think it only serves to emphasise that sense of wish-fulfilment we gain from it. It upholds traditional values and morals, and sometimes that can feel like a far cry from today's society. Does the setting help, do you think? What did you all think of Deaconsbridge?'

The rest of the session passed by in lively discussion, with the addition of lots of laughter, much to Lucy's relief. They finished by choosing their next book, a tense psychological thriller, or *blood and guts* as Oscar called it. She was pleased with the way the group was bonding.

Nobody seemed in a hurry to get home, and although another customer called Lucy away almost as soon as the refreshments were cleared, she was encouraged to see Lia and Hattie still deep in conversation by the counter when she returned fifteen minutes later. Both of them had an armful of books.

'Mum used to love Emma Blair's books,' said Lia, passing across one of the books she was holding to be scanned. 'I'm not sure she really takes in any of what I read her now, but it seems to relax her, and me too, if I'm honest.'

'Well if you get stuck any time, I can recommend Charlie and Lola,' replied Hattie, smiling. 'Poppy can't get enough of them; she knows them all by heart.' She put her books down on the counter, waiting her turn as Lia began to pack hers away.

'I'll see you next time, shall I?' she asked.

'Yes, definitely. I'll be here,' replied Lia. 'Thanks, Lucy. It was great today. Bye, Hattie.'

★

Lia swung her bag from one hand to the other as she stood on the step outside the library. It wasn't particularly heavy, but it gave her something to do as she stood there. When she had left the house an hour and a half ago she had been thrilled with the prospect of some time to herself, but now she couldn't make up her mind what to do. She had thought she might have a browse through one or two of the clothes shops – there was one at the far end of the High Street that she particularly liked – but now it seemed a bit silly; frivolous, even. Actually, what it felt like was a complete waste of time. What did she need new clothes for? It wasn't as if she had anywhere to go, or anyone to see. And her mum couldn't care less what she wore.

'Are you okay?' came the voice from behind her. 'You look miles away.'

Lia looked up to see Hattie standing hesitantly on the step beside her. Her bright red coat was cheerful in the golden autumn sun. And she was smiling.

'I was,' admitted Lia, pulling a face. 'I was trying to decide what to do now.'

Hattie held onto her hair which was resolutely blowing about her face. 'Without feeling guilty, you mean?'

Lia stared at her in astonishment. She was absolutely right.

'I know, I feel like that all the time since Poppy started school. When she was at home all day I hardly had a minute to myself, but now she's at school I've suddenly got huge amounts of time to myself and I don't know what to do with it. I feel like I should be doing something useful and not wasting it, but there's only so much housework you can do! It's deathly boring, but I feel so guilty if I sit and do something I want to.'

'Stupid, isn't it?' agreed Lia. 'I never usually get any time to myself, except when Mum's asleep, but the carer who helps out so I can come to the book club is staying longer today. I've got two whole hours to do exactly what I please and I'm talking myself out of every single thing I can think of.'

Hattie grinned. 'How about a walk and some fresh air? You must feel pretty cooped up at times, and it's such a glorious day.'

Lia was flustered for a moment. 'Yes,' she said tentatively at first, and then, stronger, 'Yes, thanks, I'd like that. I do try and get Mum out as much as I can but it's often rather… fraught. Things upset her, you see.' She smiled at Hattie, both of them acknowledging the slight shyness between them. 'Where shall we go? I'm guessing you might be a regular at the swings in the park, but we could go past them, out through the field and along by the river?'

Hattie hitched her own bag up her arm a little and pulled a face. 'Oh yes, anywhere but the swings.

'Do you live in the town?' she asked once they were walking.

Lia squinted up at the sun, and nodded. 'Up by the school actually, well, past it… Where the shops are and then left. They're old council houses. I've lived there all my life.'

Hattie's eyes widened. 'Really?' she asked. 'Blimey, I can't imagine living anywhere my whole life.' She frowned suddenly. 'Sorry, that sounded really rude.'

Lia smiled generously. 'No, you're right, it wasn't exactly what I had planned either…' She caught Hattie's eye with a mischievous grin and dissolved into giggles. 'It's true. I really have lived *the* most boring life in the history of the planet.'

'Aw, that's not fair,' replied Hattie. 'It must be really difficult looking after your mum full time. Has she been ill for long?'

'About ten years altogether. But she's only in her early seventies now; she didn't have me until she was forty-one. I often wonder if that was part of the problem.'

Hattie paused momentarily before stepping out into the road after Lia. 'How so?' she asked.

'Just because she wasn't used to stopping. She was dancing from her twenties, touring with a professional troupe in the early sixties, and then later on when she and Dad got together they toured around holiday camps and cruise ships, a different one every season. Glamorous as it sounds, it must have been a hard life in many ways. When they finally decided to settle down and have me, that's when it began to go wrong. My dad left when I was four. I don't think a mundane life suited them, to be honest.'

'So, your mum was a single parent too?'

Lia nodded. 'And everything just stopped, apart from looking after me. I know she resented it, and then the dementia began to show itself from her mid-sixties I guess. She's only needed full-time care in the last four years, though.'

'That's tough,' declared Hattie, slowing her speed a little to keep pace with Lia.

'It can be,' Lia replied. 'There's only me. She has no other family, and I couldn't bear to put her in a home. Plenty of other people are in the same boat. Didn't you say you were on your own too? I know how hard it was for Mum being a single parent.'

Hattie wrinkled her nose. 'Hmm, but it's not quite the same thing as what you're going through. Children go to bed a lot earlier for a start.'

'They won't always,' countered Lia.

Hattie smiled. 'True,' she said, 'but in my case being on my own is far preferable to the alternative. My ex is a scumbag. Believe me, I'm well shot of him. It isn't easy bringing up a child on your own; there were days when Poppy was little when I'd spend hours trying to calm her crying and then would cry myself to sleep too, but at least I could provide some sort of stability for her. If I'd married her dad, that would have been impossible.'

Lia could understand that. It was hard work looking after her mum, a thankless task at times, but at least the decisions she made were her own. Things would be so much harder if she had to cope with interference from someone else. It sounded like Hattie had had a hard time, but Lia had only just met her and now wasn't the time to pry any further. 'You mentioned at the book club that you'd moved recently. Is that to be closer to your family?'

'Not exactly.' Hattie's expression was unreadable. 'I just felt I needed a change, that's all. I used to live in Herefordshire; about an hour away. But I'm still only twenty minutes or so from my sister and half an hour from my mum and dad – just in the other direction.'

'Well,' said Lia brightly, 'at least they're not so far away that they can't step in for babysitting duties every once in a while.'

This time Hattie gave a slight smile. 'My sister's pretty good, she helps out when she can, but I don't like asking too often. You know how it is.'

'Yeah, that's certainly a feeling I'm familiar with – you've made your bed and now you must lie in it…?' Lia stopped to look at Hattie; taking in the dyed black hair blowing around her face and the kind brown eyes that were ringed with a little too much eyeliner. 'We're two peas in a pod then, aren't we?' she said, wondering if she had been a bit too forward, but it felt so good talking to another human being.

Hattie gave an amused snort. 'Hardly! I mean, look at you. You're all slim and elegant, with gorgeous hair and I'm… not.'

It was true, Hattie's red coat was straining slightly at the seams, as was her bright blue blouse underneath, but Lia had never seen anyone with such a friendly smile and the most beautiful clear skin. She was a little chubby, that was all.

'I haven't washed my hair for days, I'm wearing jeans that are six years old and a tatty fleece, so you can stop that.'

The two women looked at one another for a moment, feeling the growing bond of friendship between them.

Hattie reached out her hand to open the gate into the park. 'You should learn to dance, you know, you really should,' she said.

Lia puffed out her cheeks. 'I know, a huge part of me would love to, but it's not that easy. For starters, I'd need to find more care for Mum, and social services aren't always that obliging, and—' She broke off when she caught sight of Hattie's raised eyebrow. 'I know, I know, I'm just making excuses. It's been so long since I did anything other than look after Mum, the thought alone terrifies me. Much as I'd like to, I'm not sure I'd actually have the nerve. I will think about it, I promise, but I'm going to take some convincing.'

Chapter 4

It was the time of day he liked best – early morning, with the sun just glancing across one corner of the pillowcase. They slept with the curtains open, summer or winter, but the effect was best at this time of year. Oscar always woke first, opening his eyes to see her beautiful face turned towards his. It was the first thing he saw every day and the last thing he saw at night. Strawberry-blonde curls spilled out across the pillow, and deep rosebud lips curved softly in sleep. Of course, the hair was grey now, the soft skin a little lined, but she was still the same to him as she had been when they married at the age of eighteen. And they'd said it wouldn't last.

He reached out a hand to rub a thumb across the warmth of her cheek gently. Any minute now her eyes would open and she would smile her soft sleepy smile, his name on her lips. *Hello my sweetheart*, he would say in reply. Any minute now…

He moved his head a fraction, watching as the sun tracked across the pillow. A gentle sigh stirred the air, as his fingers reached out to caress the cold wrinkle-free expanse of cotton. He closed his eyes for a second, feeling the too familiar weight that settled upon him moments after he woke. Why could he never stay in the hazy dreams of sleep? Why did the daylight always have to rob him of his memories? 'Oh, my darling, Mary,' he whispered. 'I miss you so much.'

★

'Morning Oscar!' Lucy sang, with a grin. 'You're looking especially dapper today, I must say.'

Oscar raised his hand in greeting, the gold signet ring on the little finger of his right hand glinting in the sunlight. 'Well, one tries, one tries...' he replied. He straightened up his waistcoat and checked his tie, bright-purple silk this morning. 'It wouldn't do to go through life all grey and miserable now, would it?' he added. 'And anything which puts a smile on your face, my dear, is worth it for that alone.'

'Oh, please...' muttered Rachel beside her.

Lucy gave her colleague a sharp look. 'Shh,' she hissed under her breath, moving away from the counter towards the table where she knew Oscar was headed, the evening paper from the night before clutched in her hand. She waited until he had settled himself.

'Here's yesterday's,' she said, laying the paper down on the table. 'Would you like the weekly as well?'

He looked up, a thoughtful expression his face. 'No, I think I shall do fine with just this one, thank you. And when I've had enough of that I have a fine Ken Follett to keep me company.'

'Excellent. Well, I shall leave you in peace for a bit – although it's Wednesday, don't forget, so the place will be overrun with singing children before you know it.'

Oscar smiled and shook out the paper. 'I'm quite tempted to join in myself,' he said. 'Except that I don't know any of the words. They're not like the nursery rhymes I knew in my day. Besides, I fear my pipes are a little rusty.'

'You and me both, Oscar,' Lucy replied with a grin.

Rachel was waiting for her when she arrived back at the counter, pretending to rearrange the reservation shelf.

'Don't you think it's weird?' she said as soon as Lucy was in earshot. 'I mean, he only comes in on a Wednesday when the children are here, and he could just as easily sit at the other end where it's quieter if he wants to read.'

Lucy gave Rachel an appraising look, and held her stare for slightly longer than was necessary. 'I sincerely hope you're not suggesting there is anything at all… unsavoury about Oscar. Because that would be extremely rude, judgemental and completely without any basis in truth.'

The young girl had the grace to look a little ashamed, although the jut of her chin still gave Lucy cause for concern.

'I only meant I find it odd, that's all.'

'Rachel, what days do you work here?'

'Wednesdays, Thursdays and Saturdays. Why?'

'Because it might interest you to know that Oscar comes in every Monday, Wednesday and Friday, never on a weekend. He always sits at that table where he spends approximately two and a half hours reading, I suspect because it tides him over until lunchtime, at which point he goes to the Crown for a coffee and a sandwich before his afternoon walk.'

Rachel's mouth parted just a smidge. She closed it, pursing her lips and swallowed. 'Oh,' she said. 'I didn't know that.'

'No, and the only reason I know is because I bother to talk to people, Rachel. Especially people like Oscar, who come here for company and warmth because it beats sitting alone at home. Now, if you're looking for something to do, the non-fiction returns need shelving.'

Rachel stared at her, weighing up whether she could get away with making a pithy comeback. She shrugged. 'Yeah, okay,' she answered. 'I just find him a bit creepy, that's all. I'm allowed to, you know. And he dresses weird.'

Lucy watched her walk away, then looked at her watch and sighed. Lucy had never been bothered by Rachel before, in the days when they were both just library assistants, but since Lucy had been promoted Rachel seemed to delight in making trouble. When Clare had announced her pregnancy and impending maternity leave, Lucy had been as surprised as the next person when her own name had been put forward to replace her. She could understand how Rachel felt; after all, she'd been at the library a lot longer than Lucy had. At first, she had thought her rise up the ladder was down to her degree and it was simply a matter of qualifications, but lately she had found herself becoming a little irritated by Rachel's manner, and she wondered whether Clare had felt the same. The post was only for a year to cover the maternity leave, but some days Lucy felt like it was going to last an eternity.

She could hear the approach of several loud children's voices from the hallway, and turned to log in to the computer, smiling at Carrie as she breezed past her.

'Right, that's me up, Lucy,' she said, reaching for a book on the counter. 'Wish me luck.'

Carrie loved the Rhyme Time sessions just as much as Lucy did, but the poor girl was nursing a cold, and a half-hour of energetic sing-alongs was probably the last thing she needed.

'I'll make you a big mug of tea when you're done,' replied Lucy, with a grin, to which she received a fervent thumbs-up.

★

Lucy took another bite of her banana as she prodded the teabags. It wasn't even twelve yet and she was starving. She would finish at two today, in lieu of her late-night working, so she didn't get a lunch hour, just a fifteen-minute break and then a raid of the biscuit tin when she got home. On a whim, she took down another mug and added a teabag to it. She felt a little guilty about Oscar for some reason; he wouldn't have heard the comments that Rachel made, so there was no harm done, but she had found herself glancing across at him from time to time during the children's singing and hated herself for doing so. Now she reasoned that she did so only because she trusted her instincts and wanted to prove them to herself, but instead of seeing his usual smiling face whenever she looked up, he had seemed rather sad. Perhaps a cup of tea would cheer him up.

She dropped Carrie's mug off at the counter first, as the poor girl was clearly gasping for a drink, and looked over to where Oscar had been sitting. His seat was empty.

'Has Oscar gone?' she asked.

Carrie followed her line of sight. 'Oh, I didn't see him. Odd, because he usually calls goodbye. Maybe he's just popped to the loo.'

Hmm, maybe, thought Lucy to herself, but she could feel a faint prickle of something tugging at her. She picked up the mug of tea she'd made for him and carried it over to the table. Perhaps Oscar had heard more than she'd thought, because he never left without saying goodbye; he made a point of it, in fact. Plus, he had seemed his usual chirpy self that morning, so what had changed? She directed an irritated glance back at Rachel. If Oscar *had* heard the things she'd said, then Rachel was due a firm talking-to, and Lucy wouldn't hold back.

★

'What's the matter, love?'

Lucy turned to look at her mum, the expression on her face so familiar. Even at the age of twenty-four it made her smile to see the way her mum looked at her, just like she had throughout Lucy's childhood. Every time there had been a problem – with homework, bitchy girls at school, or a boyfriend who had not turned out to be what Lucy thought – then her mum's dear face had been there. That same expression, those same words – *What's the matter, love?* – and Lucy always knew that everything in her world would come right again.

She gave her mother a weak smile. Dinner had been the usual noisy affair with her mum, dad, and younger brother, who hadn't gone back to uni yet. It was a time Lucy usually loved; sharing in the events of the day, the banter, the highs, the lows. Her dad was a primary-school teacher and always had some funny tale to tell. But tonight Lucy had been quiet, unable to join in, as if she was slightly disconnected from everyone and everything around her. And, of course, her mum had noticed.

'Is it that whatsit girl from the library again, giving you grief?' asked her mum. 'Because if it is, you can't let her get to you like that.'

Lucy gave a tired smile. 'No, Mum, it's nothing like that.' She picked up the remote and clicked off the sound on the television. Neither of them had really been watching it anyway.

'Well, I know there's something on your mind. You've got that look about you; like you've got the whole world on your shoulders.' Her mum was searching her face for clues. 'And if I know you, it won't just go away either.' She tipped her head to one side. 'Lucy…' she started a little hesitantly. 'You know I'm not being critical in asking this, but are you actually happy at the library? Because if you're not, no one will be upset if you change your mind about what you want to do. You could go back to your studies, make a career in teaching after all… No decision is ever final, is it? Your life is made up of endless possibilities.'

Lucy thought about her mum's words for a moment. She knew what she was getting at – in fact, she should probably be agreeing with her

– but the instant she had heard the words Lucy's instinct had been to deny them. She *was* happy at the library, she *did* enjoy being there – she just wasn't sure why. After all, it really didn't make any sense; ever since she was little she had talked about being a teacher like her dad. There had never been any other plan for her, and Lucy had set her sights on it with passion. She had graduated from uni with a first-class English degree, and had been all set to undertake the postgraduate course that would allow her to teach, when all of a sudden her dream had lost its shine. The job at the library was only meant to be temporary, while she worked out what she wanted to do, but as soon as she started working there it was as if she had come home. She felt like she belonged; she and the books were kindred spirits, and she could feel the magic that lay within their pages. The books had the ability to take their readers anywhere they wanted to go, could make them feel a dozen different emotions and allow them to explore new worlds. That all this could come from what was essentially a random collection of words on a page was a rare and wondrous alchemy. To Lucy's surprise, it was also a power that she yearned to master herself and, shortly after taking up her job at the library, she had bought her first notebook in which to write. It lay beside her bed most of the time, relatively untouched. She had picked it up on many occasions, her pencil poised, but the right words never came. Perhaps her desire to write was just a foolish dream. She heaved a sigh. Only time would tell.

Lucy nodded. 'I know, Mum, but it's nothing like that. I know it was a mad idea to give up all my dreams of teaching, but I love working at the library, honestly… I've just had some conversations recently that I can't get out of my mind, that's all. Nothing serious, though.'

'But enough for you to lose your usual sunny disposition. Come on, tell me about it. You know you'll feel better when you do.'

So, Lucy did. And when she had finished, there was silence for a couple of minutes; Lucy at one end of the settee, her mum at the other, between them an open box of Jaffa Cakes which, at the rate they were going, wouldn't last for very much longer. Lucy watched while her mum took another.

'So, what do you think?' she asked her cautiously. 'Am I making mountains out of molehills again? I just think I should *do* something.'

'I can see why it's getting to you; you've always been so sensitive to other people's feelings, even as a child. But as to whether you could, or should, do anything to help – now that's a different matter.'

'I'm not sure I should, but you didn't see the look on Lia's face, Mum. I don't think I've ever seen anyone want anything more. And it's such a simple thing – it's not like she wants to win the lottery or anything. All she wants to do is dance, but she's convinced herself she can't because she has to care for her mum. She's only young but her whole life is on hold.'

'A difficult place to be, feeling torn between what you'd like to do and what you know you must do. Hasn't she any other relatives that could help her out?'

Lucy bit her lip. 'I don't think so.'

'And this Oscar chap, have you even spoken to him about how he feels?'

'Not as such, no. I went to talk to him, but he'd already gone. He looked so sad, Mum – he must have heard what Rachel said, and if he didn't then something else has upset him… He's on his own; his wife died a year or so ago, and he's never mentioned anyone else. If he has any children, then I don't think they live close by.'

Her mum helped herself to another Jaffa Cake. 'Well, you know what I think?' she said. 'Being a friend costs nothing – and from what you've said that's exactly what Lia and Oscar need right now. Everything happens for a reason, and maybe if you give them a helping hand, somewhere along the line they'll help you out too, give you something back in return that perhaps you never even knew you needed. That's how it works in my experience.'

'So, do you think I should talk to them both, see if I can help in any way?'

'It can't hurt to try, can it? Helping people has to be a good idea, whichever way you look at it.'

Lucy stared at the packet of Jaffa Cakes, and took one thoughtfully. Her mum was right. What harm could it do?

Chapter 5

Lucy was worried she had missed Lia. It had been pandemonium in the library this morning; Carrie had phoned in sick and Rachel was in one of her 'Monday morning moods', which basically meant she would sit at the counter all day and find every excuse she could to stay there. Lia normally came in around ten in the morning, but Lucy was so busy sorting out the stock rotation in the children's section that it was possible that she'd been and gone without Lucy even spotting her. If she didn't catch her today she probably wouldn't see her again until nearer the weekend, and the dance courses started next week.

The day after her conversation with her mum, Lucy had fired off a series of emails to various dance schools in the local area. Not to interfere, but just so that she could let Lia have the information in case there was any way she could attend. There were all sorts of reasons why people didn't follow their dreams. She should know; she stopped herself from doing so all the time. Things moved on and then there you were two years down the line and no further forward. Perhaps this was how it was for Lia? Maybe she'd already convinced herself that her desires were just silly whims, too far out of reach to ever be attainable. But what if Lucy was able to show her otherwise? Prove to her that these things could be within her grasp after all. The emails she had sent on Lia's behalf were simply the first step.

It was gone half eleven now and Lucy gathered together the books she had been collecting, ready to box up and send on to another branch. She supposed she could always give Lia a call – her number would be on her library record – but that might seem a little pushy. Lucy had envisioned something a little more spontaneous, even if it was pre-planned.

She was almost at the stockroom door when she heard her name being called. It would seem that fate was on her side, after all. 'Morning,' she said, smiling as she turned around.

Lia looked dreadful. Even tying her hair up hadn't disguised the fact that it was long overdue for a wash. Nor did it give her face a place to hide; a face that was far too pale with dark shadows under her eyes.

'Is everything okay? You're a little later than usual this morning.'

Lia opened her mouth to speak, and then closed it again. A flicker of something passed across her face, but then she dropped her eyes and took a deep breath. When she raised them again, Lucy knew that the teeny window of time when Lia might have shared how she was actually feeling had passed. It was business as usual.

'Yes, I'm fine, thanks. I wondered if you could give me a hand with something, though, I'm a bit short on time this morning.'

'Yes, of course, what was it you wanted?'

'A new book to read to Mum. I haven't got time to look properly today, and I know you'll be able to put your hand on the perfect thing in a heartbeat.'

'No problem. Just let me pop these books in the storeroom. Won't be a sec.'

She joined Lia in the fiction section moments later, undecided whether now was really the right time to broach the subject of the dance classes.

'So, are we looking for something along the same lines as usual?' she asked.

Lia looked around her. 'Probably,' she said. 'Although the last few I read her, Mum tutted and groaned the whole time. Something a bit nostalgic or old-fashioned still appears to work best, though. She seems to make more connections with those over more modern writing.'

Lucy's brain was racing ahead of her. 'How much of the story does she understand? I mean, there's a book I'm thinking of, but it's actually a children's book. Would that matter, or wouldn't she really notice?'

'I'll give anything a go to be honest. I read Beatrix Potter once out of desperation and she seemed to quite enjoy it.'

'Right, wait here,' said Lucy, and hurried off. She plucked the book she was looking for off the shelf and stared at the cover. Perhaps...

Seconds later she delivered it into Lia's waiting hands. 'You might enjoy this too.' She held her breath.

Lia grasped the book tightly, as one finger drew a line under the title. She seemed so lost in her thoughts that Lucy doubted if she had any conscious control over it.

She sighed. 'Oh, I haven't read this for such a long time.'

And Lucy could imagine her suddenly: the young child, caught in the magic of the story, transported into the world she longed to be a part of, but which she knew she could never reach.

'This and *Ballet Shoes*, of course. I read them both over and over.' She looked up at Lucy. 'Do you know the stories?'

Lucy nodded. 'They were favourites of mine too. My friends and I used to pretend we were the sisters – I was always Posy – dreaming of a life on the stage. I mean what little girl didn't?'

Lia stared at the book in her hand. 'I'm not sure it's really a good idea...' The familiar arguments against reading it were coming now; the adult reasoning that told her the pain of remembering was far greater than the pain of allowing herself to forget.

Looking at Lia's face, Lucy could feel her own emotions threatening to get the better of her. She crossed to another aisle of shelves and withdrew a thick book. 'Take this as well,' she said, handing her a Maeve Binchy. 'This is set in the fifties – an easy story if you think *Dancing Shoes* might be a bit much for her. I am going to insist you take that one anyway, though. I think you need to read it.'

Lia stared at her, her lip trembling slightly as she flushed. 'Thank you,' she said. She looked at her watch. 'I ought to go…' she added.

'Would ten minutes hurt?' asked Lucy. 'I was just going to put the kettle on.'

She could see the indecision across Lia's face. 'No, I'd better not. We… we haven't had a good weekend you see, and I've only popped out now because Mum fell asleep and a neighbour's keeping an eye on her. She doesn't normally nap for longer than half an hour, so…'

Lucy smiled brightly. 'Good job you live in the town.'

'Er, yes.' Lia was looking a little distracted now.

'Tell you what, pop over to Rachel at the counter to have your books issued. I need to quickly print something off for you before you go, so hang on just a tick.'

She ushered Lia to the counter and went through into the back office where she did all her paperwork. Her email was already open and it only took a moment to find the message she was looking for. She printed off the attached brochure and hurried back. Lia was waiting by the door.

'I get these all the time,' she said, handing the print-out to Lia, hoping she wouldn't notice her little white lie. 'It's a list of classes offered by one of the local dance schools, and the new season starts next week… You could have a look and see what takes your fancy.'

'Oh, but I don't think I could—'

'I don't think you'd even have to pay,' added Lucy, feeling sure that Lia must be in receipt of certain benefits as a carer. Before Lia could argue, Lucy took the pamphlet back, folded it in half and tucked it inside the copy of *Dancing Shoes* that her new friend was carrying. 'I'm sure you could work something out.'

'Thank you,' Lia said. 'It's a nice thought. But I don't have anyone to go with.'

Lucy watched as the automatic doors closed behind her, her own mind ticking like an unexploded bomb. Well let's see about that, shall we, she thought to herself. Then she went back through to the office, called up the county's book catalogue and ordered Lia every single one of Noel Streatfeild's books that she could get her hands on.

★

Callum had hardly been able to believe it when the same girl he had seen the other day came and sat next to him. It was her perfume that he had noticed first – something old-fashioned, like roses, or violets possibly; Callum wasn't sure. Either way, the pen and notebook were the same. He managed a few surreptitious glances while she was working and couldn't help but notice what she was looking at: pages and pages to do with stuff about weddings. He sighed inwardly. He'd suspected it when he'd seen her ring, but the fact she was deep into planning confirmed that there was another bloke out there far luckier than him.

There was a rapid beeping noise from the computer in front of him as the screen suddenly flickered and died. He looked up as all the other monitors in the line went blank too, accompanied by a series of exasperated groans from around the room. Callum smiled to himself;

the library's server went down with an annoying frequency, but, as he got up to let Lucy know, this time it might just work in his favour.

He'd had another argument with his brothers last night. He should have walked away, but he was sick and tired of their goading. *Loser, loner,* they called him, as they pimped and preened themselves, ready for a night out on the pull. Two of them already had girlfriends and frankly they were welcome to their lot. Callum would rather be on his own than listen to the inane drivel they spouted, with their heaving chests spilling out from too-tight tops, lurid lipstick sticking to their teeth. That's what had attracted him to the girl sitting beside him. She looked like the girl next door – not literally, but she was fresh-faced, with clean-looking bouncy hair, nice clothes and a genuine smile. If she was single she'd be exactly the kind of girl he'd go for, but she wasn't; she was getting married, which meant that Callum would never dream of coming on to her, even if he did know how.

Suddenly, an idea struck: if he could think of her as just another person, with no need for silly games or flirting, perhaps he would be able to talk to her without getting flustered and tongue-tied. And if he could talk to *her*, perhaps he could learn how to talk to other people.

Lucy was on her own at the counter, deep in conversation with an elderly lady. That was one of the things he liked about Lucy; she always had time to listen to other people. It made her easy to talk to, and Callum was getting quite confident now, particularly since he had joined the book club. It wasn't the same for him, though; Lucy was *paid* to be nice to people. Admittedly, she did it much better than a lot of folk did, but it was just her job; she probably wouldn't choose to talk to him if she didn't have to.

He hovered for a moment, wondering if he could interrupt, when Lucy looked across at him and beamed a smile. She excused herself to the old lady.

'Are you okay, Callum?'

The effusiveness of her smile threw him for a moment, until he remembered what he needed to say.

'Yes, fine, thanks. But the network's gone down again, sorry.'

'Why are you apologising?' she said. 'One of these days we'll get our crummy hardware updated and then you can all work in peace. Meanwhile…' She turned back to her customer. 'Can you just give me a minute, while I reconnect this young man?' she said.

Callum blushed. 'Or I could do it, if you like… I know how.'

Lucy turned to look at the main computer behind her, clearly torn, then the telephone began to ring. With a smile and a shrug she waved him forward.

The girl was still there when he got back, staring at her blank screen anxiously.

'It won't be a minute,' he said, sitting down again. She nodded, but that was all. Callum struggled to find something else to say. He mustn't let the moment go.

'Will it all just come back up?' she said suddenly, frowning slightly. 'Only I'm useless with computers.'

Callum leaned over. 'What were you working on?' he asked.

'I wasn't working on anything,' she said. 'I was just looking at some websites.'

He smiled. 'Sorry, that's what I meant. When I asked what you were working on, I meant what program were you using? I didn't explain myself very well. It makes a difference to what gets recovered when the computer restarts.'

She still looked puzzled.

'What just comes back up,' he clarified.

'Oh, I *see*.' She smiled. 'And does the internet?'

He shook his head. 'I'm afraid not… but I can help you get it back if you like?'

At first he thought she was going to refuse, but then she looked back down at her notebook. 'Would you?' she said. 'Only I've got to get this lot sorted out if it kills me. I'm Phoebe, by the way.'

'Callum,' he replied, swallowing. 'Right, let's see where you were.' He moved the mouse and with a couple of clicks reopened an internet tab. He gave a shy smile. So far, so good.

Chapter 6

Lucy looked down at her notebook and the paltry few pages of notes she had written. She was procrastinating again and she knew it. The fact that she had other things on her mind was no excuse. She had been picking up and putting down the book all evening and was beginning to annoy herself; having a brilliant idea about what to write, then returning to scrub it all out moments later. She was going around in circles. *Either do it or don't do it*, she thought to herself, but stop dithering about. For heaven's sake, how difficult could it be? She tutted audibly and swung her legs up onto the sofa, wriggling herself further down into the cushions and flipping to the back of her notebook as she did. It was time to stop kidding herself that this had any importance and get on with something that would make a difference. She pulled off the lid of her pen with her teeth.

She knew how to go about helping Lia – at least she thought she did. Trouble was she was also aware of the old adage: you can lead a horse to water, but you can't make it drink. Just sticking a brochure for dance classes into her hand wasn't enough, however much Lia might want to go; it wasn't quite as simple as that for her. Lucy thought about Lia's situation for a moment. Lia had mentioned that she had no one to go to the classes with, and it had never occurred to Lucy before quite how isolating Lia's life must be. She thought of her own friends; how they would organise things on the spur of the moment, or drop in and out of each other's houses for a chat. What would happen to them if she were suddenly to start turning down every offer they made? she wondered. If she constantly made excuses, cancelled arrangements and had to cut short telephone conversations, how long would it be before those calls stopped coming? That was all assuming, of course, that Lia had even been able to *make* many friends. Where would she have met people if she never went out?

Hattie was something of a kindred spirit, she thought. She and Lia were both about the same age, both avid readers, and Hattie was new to the area, and a single mum. She hadn't yet made the network of friends who would help support her in looking after her daughter, so in a sense both her and Lia's opportunities to escape the house were equally limited. They had seemed to get on well at the library the other day, so perhaps Hattie might be part of the solution. Lucy made a note in her book, wondering if Hattie liked dancing too.

Then there was the question of care for Lia's mother. She was going to have to pull something very inventive out of the bag to jump this hurdle. She sucked the end of her pen, wracking her brain for any helpful nugget of information that she had squirrelled away. A few more notes were added before Lucy flipped to a clean page and added a name to the top.

Oscar. Lucy had only ever experienced real grief once before; a few years ago, when her grandfather had died. She had been tearful and missed him terribly, but that paled in comparison to the all-consuming sadness that had overwhelmed her grandma; she carried the weight of his loss around with her every day. Grief was love; that much Lucy recognised. A deep and abiding love that had suddenly found itself homeless, the object of its affection gone, leaving it behind, lingering like a lost spirit. It was a love that would change time if it could, but sentenced now only to travel back and forth through the memories that sustained it. Lucy's grandma had told her that grief carried with it longing and remorse, burning anger at times and a blanketing cloak of despair at others, but the worst thing was that it was never at peace, never still.

Thinking about her words now brought tears to Lucy's eyes, but beyond giving Oscar time to talk, Lucy wasn't sure how she could ever help him. They said that time was a great healer, but Oscar's grief seemed as raw still as it must have been when it was first created. How could she possibly begin to help him when the only suggested cure had already proved itself to be useless? Her pen scribbled across the page; time to listen was all she had.

Chapter 7

'I hope you don't mind,' said Phoebe, 'but I thought I'd better come clean and tell you what I'd done. It didn't seem fair otherwise, since you were so helpful the other day.'

Callum swallowed. 'Was I?' he said, feeling another small glow inside, but one which was rapidly replaced with anxiety as he realised what else she'd said. 'So, what do you mean by "come clean", exactly?'

'I mentioned to Gary, my fiancé, that I'd been in here to use the computers and how helpful you'd been. He knows I'm a bit of a dummy when it comes to IT, but there's so much to organise with the wedding, and he's not very helpful.'

'With computers, do you mean?'

'No, with making decisions. He just agrees with everything I say about the wedding, when once in a while it'd be nice if he had an opinion of his own, take some interest. I feel like I'm talking to a brick wall sometimes. It's his wedding too.'

Callum nodded.

'So, I just told him how helpful you'd been, and that we'd started planning some stuff and set up an email account, that sort of thing. Well, it kind of got his attention, so I laid it on a bit.'

'He's not likely to come after me with a big stick, is he?' asked Callum, only half joking, his Adam's apple moving up and down several times as he swallowed.

Phoebe laughed. 'No, don't worry. Nothing like that. He's a policeman.'

Callum could feel the colour draining from his face.

'Honestly, you've nothing to worry about. I only wanted to tell you 'cause I felt a bit bad, exaggerating things like that... Well, not exaggerating, you *were* incredibly helpful and patient...'

It would be easy to take offence, he thought, but looking at Phoebe's sunny face, she was completely without guile. She wouldn't have told him otherwise. Yes, he'd been used as a not-so-subtle prod to ensure her fiancé's interest in their wedding, but it could be worse. It had taught him quite a valuable lesson, and he filed it away neatly in the 'things he needed to know about women' compartment in his brain.

Besides which, was he not guilty of doing the very same thing? Of using Phoebe for his own gain. He had enjoyed teaching her yesterday. She was a quick learner, just inexperienced and a little unsure of herself, but she had listened to him, properly – not just paying lip service, but trusting what he said to be true. She followed his instructions and showed a childlike delight when she achieved something. More than that, she had been grateful, and Callum couldn't remember a time when anybody had been grateful for something he had done. He had gone home feeling lighter and several inches taller.

It hadn't lasted, of course. His eldest brother dumped on him minutes after he'd got through the door, but it hadn't mattered; for the entire twenty-minute walk home beforehand, Callum had genuinely felt good about himself.

'So, what is it today then?' he asked Phoebe. 'Shall we have a go at a simple spreadsheet, or do you want to do a bit more of what we covered yesterday?'

She opened her notebook. 'I need to reply to some of the emails I got yesterday,' she said, 'and then I think I can go ahead and book our wedding venue. It's after that I might need a bit of help.'

Callum looked at her radiant face, barely able to contain her excitement. 'That must be a nice feeling,' he said.

'Oh, it is!' she exclaimed, giving a huge sigh. 'There were times this year when I felt like it was never going to happen. And it's not because Gary doesn't want to get married. I just think it's all a bit… overwhelming. Big decisions, huge responsibilities, and a massive pile of money. He doesn't cope particularly well with all that.'

Callum nodded, although he didn't really understand. He'd give anything to be in that position. He'd already learned a lot himself yesterday, just looking at all the stuff Phoebe was doing. When his time for love and marriage came, he was going to enjoy every minute of it.

'Okay, whenever you're ready, just shout.'

Phoebe turned back to the screen and began to enter her login details. 'Are you sure I'm not keeping you from anything?' she asked. 'You must have things of your own to be getting on with?'

Callum thought of the endless pages of jobs adverts which he had spent the last few weeks scrolling through. He was overqualified for most of them, and those that had caught his eye would go to someone twice his age. No-one was going to pay him that kind of salary.

'Nah,' he replied. 'I'll just be on YouTube.'

★

From the doorway, Lucy smiled to herself. She had watched the pair of them together on and off yesterday, as she went about her work; she couldn't help herself. Strictly speaking they shouldn't have stayed on the computers for the length of time they did, but Lucy had used her manager status to override the settings to give them unlimited time. Callum had been a regular visitor to the library for some while now, choosing books, but more often than not to use the computers, and since he had joined the book club she had found herself drawn to his kind nature and soft voice.

She listened to him now as he gently instructed Phoebe, and mentally urged him on. He was a good teacher; he never got irritated, impatient, or worse, condescending, and when he took over the mouse or keyboard momentarily, it was always with permission. Both of them had left with smiles on their faces yesterday and it made Lucy smile too. Callum was obviously very shy but it looked as though he was beginning to come out of his shell. She had no idea why he came to the library most days, but it was obvious he had no job. He was a whizz with computers, and now watching him help Phoebe once again she began to get the first inklings of an idea. Nowhere near fully formed as yet, but certainly something to think about. She ducked back out of the computer room, added Callum to the list in her notebook and went to put the kettle on.

Half-term was always a busy time in the library. It was a few weeks away yet, but if Lucy had her way there would be a full programme of activities, for the children especially. Falling as close as it did to Bonfire Night, it lent itself to all manner of brilliant themes and this year a certain Mr Potter was definitely on the list. She just needed to find out the best way to make broomsticks.

She carried the tray of teas out to the counter, depositing two of the cups there for her colleagues and carrying the other two together with a sheaf of papers and some scissors over to the table by the children's section. She had spied Oscar about fifteen minutes ago, and now he was comfortably ensconced with yesterday's evening paper in his usual chair.

He looked up as she approached. 'I do hope you're going to come and keep me company,' he said.

Lucy smiled at his tie of choice for the day; a bright canary yellow.

'Well, I was going to ask if you wouldn't mind me sitting here,' she replied, 'so to be invited is even better. I don't want to disturb you, though; I've brought some work to do – oh, and tea as a bribe for invading your space.'

'My space?' replied Oscar, with a twinkle. 'As manager of the library, surely this is *your* space, and I, therefore, merely taking it on loan.'

She put a mug down in front of him. 'Well then,' she said, 'here's to our mutual occupancy. Two sugars, isn't it?'

He nodded. 'Alas, despite my advancing years, I am yet to find myself sweet enough.'

A sudden tug pulled firmly on Lucy's heartstrings. She didn't know him all that well, but if superficial impressions were anything to go by, Oscar was one of the sweetest people Lucy had ever met. He was always cheerful, with a smile and welcome for everyone in the library. She hoped that wherever he spent the rest of his time he had people around him who showed him they cared, even if it was just the random nod from a stranger in the street. She took a gulp of her tea and shuffled her papers.

The local primary school had a good relationship with the library and Lucy worked hard to support them. She regularly visited the school and helped with literacy projects, but this half-term would be the library's first time hosting an event for parents on behalf of the school. The head teacher had thought that holding a session for parents on the new phonics tests away from the school environment might be beneficial and Lucy had to agree. Things were always so much more relaxed during the school holidays, and even if the turnout was a little down with people being away, she hoped that those who did come would find it useful. Today's mission was to create some fun information boards that she could use to publicise the event.

She picked up the pair of scissors and began to cut out shapes from the paper in front of her, frowning in concentration. It didn't occur to her that Oscar might be watching until he spoke.

'Would you like some help?' he asked. 'I'm not so good with anything technical these days, but cutting out I can manage.'

'Are you sure you don't mind? It's a bit mind-numbing, I'm afraid.'

'As is yesterday's newspaper, unfortunately, so it would be a welcome release.'

Lucy smiled and handed over her scissors. 'I'll just go and fetch another pair.'

She returned to the table carrying a big pot of pencils as well. 'There's colouring-in too, if you want to go really wild.'

Oscar eyed the ice-cream container full of colours. 'I'm not sure I can handle the responsibility, but I'll have a go.'

'Good man.'

They worked silently for several minutes before Oscar held up a picture in front of him. 'So, I have a boat, a snail, and now a duck. Are we doing letters of the alphabet?'

Lucy looked up in surprise. 'That's very good,' she said, 'and very close. Actually, they're letter sounds.' She pointed at the boat. 'That's an *oa* sound… as in b-oa-t. This one's an *ai* sound as in snail and the duck is actually for the sound of the *qu* letters in the word quack.'

Oscar looked bemused. 'Is that what they teach children these days?'

'A bit different from when you learned to read, I bet,' replied Lucy. 'Different from when I learned, too. It's called phonics. The words are learned by the sound the letters make.'

'And does it work?' Oscar stared at the pictures in front of him.

Lucy grinned. 'I have absolutely no idea,' she said. 'But it's supposed to!'

'Another government initiative, no doubt. When I taught my children to read they just learned by repetition, there was no other way.'

'Did you have a large family, Oscar?'

He laughed. 'You could say that,' he replied. 'Anywhere between nineteen to twenty-five of the little darlings.'

Lucy's eyes widened. 'Oh gosh, you were a teacher? I never knew that!' she exclaimed.

'I was the head, actually, but I still had my own class and taught them all day, every day. Though I don't suppose we had quite so much paperwork back then.'

'But where did you teach?'

'Right here,' smiled Oscar. 'In the town, at St Michael's.'

Lucy sat forward in her seat, never imagining for one minute that this was how their conversation would go. 'But then you must know loads of folk who come in here. Blimey, I bet you taught half of them.'

'A fair few, yes. A lot have moved on of course, families do, but there's still some around… and now they have children of their own.'

'That must be so weird… Rather nice though too, I'd imagine.'

Oscar put down the picture he was still holding. 'Mostly,' he said. 'Some families are hard to forget, but sadly not always for the right reasons. It can be… painful sometimes to see history repeating itself.'

Oscar was staring out towards the door, and Lucy longed to turn around to see what he was looking at.

'There's that young lad Callum for a start, the one that comes to the book club. On the face of it he seems nice enough, but he's a prime example. One of five kids, all of them wasting their lives. Not a single drop of initiative or aspiration between then. Quite content to while away their days, drinking and smoking, one dead-end job to another, or no job at all, which is often the case. I taught his dad, and every one of his four siblings; they were all the same.'

Lucy looked up, surprised. Callum had never appeared that way to her, and she was astonished to hear Oscar talk in such a fashion.

'Some folks just don't deserve to be parents,' he finished.

Lucy looked back down at the paper and scissors she was holding. She didn't feel she could quite meet Oscar's eye, even though his voice was level and calm despite his cutting words. She knew how grumpy elderly people could be – too quick to judge the youth of today, always willing to think the worst – but Oscar was usually such a cheery soul, and seeing him now, in his dapper waistcoat and brightly coloured tie, it just didn't make any sense.

'Still, I bet you're proud as anything of your own children?'

The minute the words left her mouth she regretted them. Oscar flinched and she saw the shadow of grief cross his face once again. She'd put her foot in it. He looked so distraught part of her wished she had kept to safer subjects, but she couldn't help but feel that it would do Oscar some good to talk about how he was feeling. She'd only asked the question to see if she could get him to open up about his family.

Oscar sipped at his tea and then carefully put down his cup.

'Forgive me, Lucy,' he said. 'I've become an old man, rather set in my ways and thoughts, I'm afraid; I spoke without thinking. I'm sure Callum's a fine young man.'

Lucy blushed slightly, she hadn't intended her comment to be a rebuke either.

'I'm sorry, I didn't mean—'

'Everyone must live their lives how they see fit of course; that is after all what makes us all so wonderfully different from one another. I really mustn't let my own bitterness be my judge in such matters.' He smiled at Lucy. 'And now you must think me awfully opinionated.'

'You shouldn't apologise, Oscar. Having opinions is important. Look at me: I'm only in my early twenties, what have I got to be opinionated about? I haven't lived enough of a life yet to know what really matters and what doesn't. Mind you, I'm pretty certain it's not who gets kicked out of *I'm a Celebrity… Get Me Out of Here!*' She waved the scissors in her hands. 'Besides, you've a good many more years under your belt than me – I think a degree of bitterness is entirely normal.'

He looked at her over the top of his cup. 'Perhaps,' he replied. 'Although I suspect you're just being kind now.' He sucked in a breath. 'Normal it might be, but bitterness is still a very destructive emotion. It can suck out all the joy from things if you let it, and I think it's caused me to be far harsher than necessary on occasion; young Callum and his family are prime examples.' He stared out towards the door once more.

Lucy followed the line of his sight this time, turning back to Oscar with a quizzical expression on her face. 'I've never once thought of you as a bitter person,' she said. 'So, however you feel, you hide it well.' She could feel Oscar's indecision hovering in the air between them. He gave a soft sigh.

'Are you really sure you've got time to listen to an old man's tales?' he asked.

She flashed him a quick smile, picking up another sheet of paper. 'I absolutely have,' she replied. 'In any case, I'm working, so where's the harm?'

Oscar followed suit, picking up his own scissors once more. The smile on his face was hard to read. 'Are you sitting comfortably?'

A momentary flicker of unease ran through Lucy as she wondered whether her resolve to try and get Oscar to talk was a sensible idea, but she had already brought them to this point and there was no going back now.

He fingered the signet ring on his left hand. He wore no wedding ring, but she had seen him touch it several times already during the course of their conversation, as if to reassure himself that it was still there. She wondered whether his wife had given it to him.

'You asked me a few moments ago whether I had a large family and I'm afraid I rather evaded your question, choosing instead to tell you about my school family…'

Lucy gave a slight nod of encouragement.

'It was an important part of my life, and one which, despite my somewhat rash comments, I'm enormously proud of. No substitute for your own family of course, but, perhaps they came close, in their own way…'

He closed his eyes and swallowed, before taking a deep breath and lifting his head to look Lucy directly in the eye. 'I was a father, once,' he said, 'for a very brief moment of time. I didn't even know our child had been born until afterwards, which is odd, isn't it?' He wasn't expecting an answer. 'You'd think you'd just *know* something as important as that, wouldn't you? That your very soul would feel itself expanding into that of another. But there was nothing. It was some weeks after the birth by the time I was told, but by then of course I was a father no more. Our daughter had been given away.'

Lucy's hand flew to her mouth. 'Oscar, I'm so sorry! I never meant—'

The soft expression returned to his eyes. 'I know, Lucy, you would never pry… and perhaps I shouldn't have mentioned it now. It's not

something I speak of often, but… today just felt like the right time.'
He smiled at her. 'You're a good listener,' he added.

Lucy shook her head. 'No, I should never have pressed you. The
last thing I wanted to do was upset you.'

'We are fools to ourselves far too often,' said Oscar. 'I've carried the
weight of this around with me my whole life, and it's only now that Mary
has gone that I can see I should have spoken of it before. I thought by
never speaking of it that it would grow small and powerless, but instead
it's risen to become the monster that lurks under the bed, the stuff of
nightmares. I should be thanking you for giving me the space to share it.'

Lucy shook her head again, blinking rapidly. 'No, I've made it
worse. I can see it on your face.'

To her amazement, Oscar grinned at her. 'That, my dear, is old age,
and try as I might these saggy old features will not rearrange themselves
any other way.'

'Now you're just trying to make me feel better,' she retorted.

'As are you,' he replied.

The air around them settled as they smiled at one another. Lucy
didn't think she had ever met anyone quite like Oscar before.

'I met my Mary when we were both just sixteen years old, did
I tell you? She carried a vanilla cupcake across the village hall to
give to me and I thought I'd never seen anyone so beautiful – like a
blue-eyed angel, she was.' Oscar smiled at the memory. 'She always
laughed afterwards that it was simply because it was Christmastime
and everything looked so pretty at the dance, but it wasn't that. My
mother used to help with the refreshments at all the village hall events
so I'd been dragged to enough of them to know that no-one like Mary
had ever walked in there before. Sixteen I might have been, naïve and

inexperienced, but my heart knew when it was taken; my head had no say in the matter at all.'

'So, you must have been together—'

'Just over sixty years, all told.'

'A whole lifetime…'

'And I never regretted one second of it, not even when our baby was taken from us. They wanted to tear us apart of course, but if anything it brought us closer. I loved my Mary so much – love her still, in fact. If I have any regrets at all it's that we never got to share that love with our child. But it was not to be, and so we created a life of our own together, just the two of us.'

Lucy pushed the scissors to one side and reached out a hand towards him. 'What happened?' she asked gently.

A cloud passed across his face for an instant. 'Our parents,' he said. 'People who thought they knew better. People who could never understand that we could love and look after a child at such a young age. Of course we didn't mean for it to happen, but people didn't talk about sex much in those days, and Mary and I loved one another; we never considered what we were doing was wrong.'

'Oh Oscar, it wasn't wrong.'

He met her eye. 'No, it wasn't, but in those days it was considered a sin. When Mary fell pregnant I wanted to marry her, but instead she was taken away from me to a place where her condition wouldn't cast shame on the family. We had no say in the matter, and although I fought against it, there was nothing I could do. We weren't even allowed contact and when Mary finally returned home the baby had already been adopted.'

'But your parents thought they were doing their best for you?'

Oscar nodded. 'No doubt,' he said. 'But we married anyway, soon after, against their wishes of course, and, unsurprisingly, were left pretty much on our own.' His mouth settled into a grim line. 'It was better that way.'

Lucy didn't know what to say. The contrast between Oscar's early years and her own was stark. Her parents had never been anything but supportive; even when she made the sudden decision to give up a career in teaching they had talked things through with her rationally. They might not have understood her choice – Lucy wasn't sure she did herself – but they still allowed her to make up her own mind. Lucy was never in any doubt that she was loved and looked after. She couldn't imagine what Oscar and Mary must have gone through in their lives; living with the constant ghost of what might have been, knowing that there was always something missing. Now that was something she definitely did understand, never quite feeling whole or fulfilled.

'But didn't you ever try and find your daughter?' she blurted out, regretting her words the minute she had said them. She doubted very much whether she would ever have had the strength to do something like that.

Oscar twisted his ring as he thought how best to reply. 'We did, from time to time… in the early days, at least. But then we thought how our little girl would feel. She would be settled – with good people, they had promised us that – and to her of course her parents were just her parents, the people who brought her up. How could we upturn all that and cause her so much distress? We agreed to put it behind us and trust that our daughter was loved and cared for. It was all we could do.'

'And the potential pain in finding out was harder than the pain of letting her go?'

'Something like that.' Oscar smiled sadly, his face drawn by his emotions.

It was fear, that much Lucy recognised. The fear of the unknown, of opening Pandora's box and never knowing what you were letting yourself in for. There was truth in that old saying, *Let sleeping dogs lie*, and if she wasn't careful she was in very grave danger of waking Oscar's up; she couldn't do that to him, not after all these years of putting it to rest.

She dragged a smile onto her face. 'You're right, I'm sure she's had a wonderful life. As have you, don't you forget.'

Oscar visibly straightened. 'I have,' he said, a little of the old twinkle coming back. 'And much to look forward to... After all, not many people get to sit and cut out pictures of boats with charming young ladies, do they? I consider myself very lucky indeed.'

Chapter 8

Still reeling from her conversation with Oscar, it was half past three before Lucy really began to take in anything around her. It was only the sight of Hattie coming into the library with her daughter that snapped her out of the daze she'd been in for the past few hours. With Oscar's help, Lucy had long since finished cutting out the shapes she needed for her display. She had even gone so far as to pin them to the board, adding a heading and the posters she had already made, but it wasn't until she heard Poppy's chattering voice and saw her hand in hand with her mum that Lucy took a step back and really looked at what she had been doing.

She sighed, and started to take down the pinned shapes. The display was a mess; she would have to start again. She collected the pieces of paper together and stared at the empty board. Perhaps today was not the right time; Oscar's story had clearly affected her more than she thought. She looked across at Hattie, now sitting on the little sofa in the children's section, her daughter on her knee. Did she really have the nerve to interfere all over again?

Time was against her on this one; if what she had planned was going to happen at all, she only had a few days left to make things work. It was a simple question and Hattie would either say yes or no. If she didn't speak to her now, she might not get another chance before next week, and by then it would be too late. She looked at the poster in her hand, realising that it would give her just the excuse she needed. Her legs had already carried her halfway towards the children's section before she realised she had even made up her mind.

Hattie looked up with a smile, and then back down at her daughter. 'Poppy, this is the lady who looks after all the books. Would you like to say hello? Her name's Lucy.'

Lucy dropped down to her haunches so that she was roughly the same height as the little girl.

'Hi, Poppy,' she said. There was a shy smile in reply. 'What are you reading?'

Poppy pulled the book from her mum's lap, closing it so that Lucy could see the front.

'Hairy Maclary!' she exclaimed.

Lucy grinned at the sight of the scruffy black dog on the cover. It was a popular series of books.

'They're reading one at school,' Hattie added, 'and I noticed you had them here.'

Poppy slipped off her mum's lap and sat cross-legged on the carpet, the book on her lap. Lucy took her opportunity and handed Hattie one of the posters.

'I wondered if this might be of any interest to you,' she said. 'I'm sure it's something you'll be coming up against soon.' She waited a moment while Hattie read the details of the phonics course. 'We're holding a session here during half-term, and the children can all come along. There'll be activities for them so that mums and dads can hopefully listen more or less uninterrupted.'

'Oh, okay – thanks.' Hattie had the look of someone not entirely comfortable with the hard-sell approach.

Lucy swiftly held out her hand to retrieve the poster. 'Actually, that was just an excuse to come and talk to you. Sorry, hope you don't mind?' She stood up, flexing her legs from their cramped position.

Hattie moved over slightly on the sofa. 'Sounds mysterious,' she said, as Lucy sat down next to her.

'It's worse,' replied Lucy. 'I have a favour to ask… well, not really. I just wanted to talk to you about an idea I'd had.'

Hattie looked at her expectantly.

'I wondered if you might be able to help?'

'Go on…'

'Just that I've had Lia on my mind a bit lately—' She broke off when she saw the surprise on Hattie's face. 'The lady from the book club?' she added.

'Yes, I know who you mean. It's funny; she's been on my mind too.'

'Oh.' Lucy didn't know quite what to say.

Hattie grinned. 'Go on, you first,' she said.

Lucy took a deep breath, feeling slightly more encouraged. 'I had some brochures come through in the week,' she said, 'from one of the local dance schools. They have classes starting next week, and I thought it would be brilliant if we could somehow make it possible for Lia to go. Things are pretty tough for her at the moment and when I heard what she said at the book club it… I don't know, but it struck a chord with me.'

'I thought the same!' exclaimed Hattie. 'We went for a walk afterwards and I said she should think seriously about learning to dance. I didn't know about the classes, though. Have you spoken to Lia about them?'

Lucy nodded.

'Was she keen? I know getting someone to look after her mum is an issue for her, but I'm sure we could work something out.'

'That was my thought too, but to be honest she didn't seem that smitten with the idea. I think she's really nervous. I don't suppose she goes out much, if at all, and she did mention that she wouldn't have anyone to go with.'

'Yes, that was my impression too, and I...' Hattie trailed off, and Lucy caught the exact moment the penny dropped. 'You want me to go with her?' she asked incredulously. 'I'm not being funny, Lucy, but have you looked at me lately? I'm not really built for dancing. I mean, Lia is, isn't she? She's so elegant – I can picture her sweeping around a ballroom, her long hair piled up, the curve of her neck, skirts swaying...' She broke off and stared at her friend. 'You've just given me a brilliant idea!' She looked at her watch, and shrugged apologetically. 'I've got to go, or I won't get there today. Come on Poppy, sweetheart, time to go. We can take that book if you like and look at it later.' She turned back to Lucy. 'Would that be all right?' She stood up, taking her daughter's hand.

Lucy found herself looking up at Hattie in astonishment. 'Yes, of course.' She scrambled to her feet. 'I'll come and issue it for you.'

Moments later Lucy was staring at Hattie's retreating back in bewilderment.

'I'll let you know how I get on!' she called as she disappeared through the door.

*

Hattie stood beside the row of shops and looked up and down the street, and then, with one hand firmly in her daughter's and the other clutching a large carrier bag, she turned resolutely left.

It took a couple of tries before she got the right house, but as Lia had said, she had lived there her whole life, and while the first door

Hattie knocked on belonged to a couple who had only just moved in, the people next to them knew Lia well and pointed out the right house to Hattie.

She was a little thrown when a woman considerably older than herself opened the door, until she was offered a warm smile and asked, 'Are you looking for Lia, love?' When Hattie nodded, the door was opened a little wider. 'Come on in. I'm Gwen, one of the carers. I help look after her mum.'

Hattie stepped into the dowdy hallway, feeling her daughter tug nervously at her hand. 'I can come back another time if it's not convenient,' she said. 'I didn't tell Lia I was coming.'

Instead Gwen held out a hand towards Poppy. 'It's fine,' she said, 'no need. I was just making tea if you'd like some, or squash perhaps, and there's biscuits…' She let the sentence dangle enticingly in the air. 'Lia's upstairs, but I don't suppose she'll be long.'

She led the way down the narrow corridor, past the stairs and through to a small kitchen at the back. There was just enough room for a small table and chairs.

'Pop yourselves here a minute, and I'll go and let Lia know you've come.' She pulled out one of the chairs and Hattie had no choice but to sit down; there was scarcely room to pass otherwise. Poppy climbed onto her knee.

'Mummy, it smells funny,' she whispered.

Hattie buried her head in her daughter's hair. 'I know, sweetheart,' she murmured. 'But a friend of mine lives here, so we're not going to say anything, okay?'

Poppy nodded, and laid her head back against her mum's chest.

Hattie put her bag on the table, the only clear surface she could see. She should never have come; she hated it herself when people turned up unannounced and she hadn't had the time to tidy away Poppy's things, or the pile of ironing, but this was different. It was as if she had stepped back in time for a moment. Nothing in this house looked as if it had been touched since the 1970s: the smoke-stained ceiling, the lurid carpeted floors, the dull marked paintwork. It was everything that Lia was not, and Hattie wondered if her presence here might embarrass her new friend.

There were footsteps in the hallway and Hattie hoped that it was Gwen returning. She could make her excuses and go, saying she would catch up with Lia another time, but when the figure stepped into the room, it was Lia, wearing a dressing gown, her hair wrapped in a towel.

'Hattie! This is a lovely surprise. I thought it must be you,' she said, smiling. 'I don't think I know anyone else with young children.'

'I'm sorry, Lia. I probably should have phoned to say I was coming instead of bursting in on you like this. It was a bit of a spur-of-the-moment thing.'

Lia flicked a glance around the room, looking as if she was going to say something and then changed her mind. Instead she shrugged. 'Don't worry. As long as you can stand me looking like this, I don't mind in the slightest. I've just had the most glorious shower. Stood there for ages.' She grimaced. 'I don't always get the chance to have one uninterrupted,' she added.

Hattie smiled in sympathy. It wasn't that long ago that she had revelled in the luxury of going to the loo by herself without the company of her daughter.

'It's crazy, isn't it, the things you long for?'

Lia nodded. 'Gwen will be off soon, but at least tonight I can get into bed feeling clean. I'm usually so exhausted by the time I get there, I just fall in. The morning isn't much better either – a thirty-second blast under lukewarm water and that's the extent of my beauty routine for the day.'

Hattie glanced at the clock on the wall. She didn't have that much time either, and she wanted the chance to talk to Lia properly, without interruption. 'I brought something over for you that I thought you might like,' she said, pulling the carrier bag towards her. 'But I don't just want to leave it with you. Have you got time to look at it while I'm here? I'd like to explain why I brought it.'

Lia pulled slightly on the belt of her dressing gown, and eyed the bag suspiciously, almost as if she guessed what was inside.

'That sounds a trifle mysterious,' she said. 'But we can go up to my room, if you like? It's rather more... well, I'll show you.'

Poppy wriggled off Hattie's lap, and looked up at Lia, her eyes large. Bedrooms were where the toys usually were; at least they were in her friends' houses. Hattie smiled at her daughter's eagerness to explore. It must be a trait she had inherited from her father. Being adventurous was certainly not in Hattie's nature.

'Will Poppy be all right coming too? She won't touch anything,' she said, thinking of the trinkets in her own bedroom which held such precious sentimental value.

But Lia simply smiled. 'Of course she can... In fact, I think I might have something that Poppy would like to play with.'

The garish carpet stretched the whole length of the hallway, up the stairs and along the landing, the threads wearing thin in places. It wasn't that the house was in any way dirty, in fact as Hattie followed Lia up to her room she could see that the place was spotless, it was just very, very tired and dated. A little depressing, even. It made the sight that met Hattie's eyes when Lia opened her bedroom door even more surprising.

She stood in the doorway, rooted to the spot for a moment, doing her utmost to keep her mouth shut for fear of saying the wrong thing. In the end, she said nothing, but the snort of laughter that burst from Lia's lips let her know that her expression was something she hadn't quite been able to control.

'It's a little different from downstairs, isn't it?' said Lia, amused.

Hattie stared around her at the pale lemon walls, the thick cream carpet and the pearlescent delicacy of the duck egg blue furnishings. It was quite the prettiest room Hattie had ever seen. It was feminine, but not overly frilly or flounced, neither was it filled with accessories. Everything was calm and ordered, of the utmost taste and elegance. This was the room where Lia could, for a little moment every day, just be herself.

'It's my little haven,' she declared. 'My calm against the storm, and the rest of the house which is so pug ugly…'

Hattie couldn't help the giggle from escaping. 'It's not that bad,' she protested, 'not really.' It seemed the polite thing to say.

'It is,' said Lia. 'It's bloody awful, and don't try and deny it. But I only have so much money… and so I chose to spend it here. Some people might think me selfish, but—'

'It's not selfish, Lia,' interrupted Hattie. 'I'd say it's a necessity.'

'I like to think it stops me from rocking in my own corner,' she said, and shrugged.

There really was no point beating about the bush, thought Hattie. Gallows humour it might be, but for Lia there was probably no other way to make it through the day.

She watched as she crossed over to a small armchair in the corner of the room. She lifted up a doll that lay there and brought it over for Poppy.

'She's my Angelina Ballerina,' she said. 'I've had her since I was a little girl so she's looking a little sorry for herself now, but if you're careful you can play with her if you'd like.'

Poppy took the doll with wide eyes, cradling it to herself reverently. She smiled a shy thank you.

Hattie watched her daughter for a minute, touched at Lia's generosity. Once she was reassured that Poppy was treating the doll with the respect that it deserved, she turned back to Lia who was still standing in the middle of the room, an expectant expression on her face.

She held out the carrier bag in front of her. 'I brought this for you,' she said. 'I'm pretty sure it will fit.'

Lia eyed the bag a little suspiciously before taking it and laying it on the bed.

'It's not new, I'm afraid – it's one I made a few years ago, but it's been stored inside a cover. I never knew what to do with it really, but now I think I might have found the perfect home for it.'

Her heart began to beat a little faster as nerves bubbled up inside her. She didn't want Lia to be offended in any way and watched carefully for her reaction.

The dress was wrapped in tissue paper and it took Lia a few moments to shake it free of the folds. The instant her hands touched the soft silk her eyes widened and she hastened to uncover the deep pink roses that were peeping out. Eventually she was able to lift the material free and Hattie heard the intake of breath as she held the dress close to her in delight.

She stood up straighter, allowing the skirt to fall and settle around her, its hem just skimming her knees. Lia looked up in wonder and Hattie could see her piecing together all the possibilities this dress represented, imagining what it might look like if she were to wear it, and how it might make her feel. It was a million miles away from her dressing gown and towel, and Hattie could see from Lia's face that this was the dress of her dreams.

'You *made* this?' she whispered. 'It's... beautiful.' She looked down at the swirl of the fabric up against her and then back at Hattie. 'But why did you bring it here?'

Hattie ignored the question. 'Go and try it on,' she said.

Lia opened her mouth to protest but Hattie jumped in before she had a chance to argue. 'Go on – I want to see what you look like.'

Lia was torn, Hattie could see that. The dress was lavish, exuberant in pattern, made from sumptuous material and had about it an air of sophistication. Lia clearly didn't think it belonged inside her drab, dreary world but there was a part of her that longed to be free, and Hattie knew this was just the dress she could do it in. With a sudden grin and intake of breath, Lia whirled around and disappeared through the bedroom door, the dress clutched against her in excitement.

It had been a long time since Hattie had worn the dress, but she remembered it as if it were yesterday. Straight from the fifties in style, the deep shawl collar sat wide on the shoulders, blush pink, with cream silk rosebuds lovingly stitched in place. The sleeves dropped midway between the elbow and wrists, while the fitted bodice of cream-coloured silk with pink cabbage roses tapered to an almost impossibly tiny waist, from which a full skirt hung in soft folds that swayed as you walked. It was a dress that had once made Hattie feel like the most beautiful woman in the world, until... She pushed away the memory and focused on the bedroom door.

Lia seemed to be gone for far longer than was necessary and it took all Hattie's willpower not to hurtle through the door in search of her. Wherever Lia was, she hoped there was a mirror. She hoped she was standing in front of her reflection, eyes shining, remembering the woman inside her and what it felt like to be her. She wanted Lia to feel just like she had done all those years ago.

Eventually, the door opened and Hattie could see that it was so. Lia had taken her hair from the towel and even though it was uncombed it hung in soft waves to her shoulders, framing her delicate features. The dress fitted perfectly, its colours reflected in the gentle blush on Lia's cheeks and contrasting against her dark hair, making her skin look smooth and creamy. She stood quietly, almost nervously, scarcely believing that what she had seen in the mirror was true – but no amount of denim or fleece had been able to hide Lia's elegant frame. That was Hattie's real skill as a dressmaker: the ability to see behind the everyday and know how to bring out the beauty that lay hidden.

The tears sprang to Hattie's eyes in an unbidden rush of feeling, which was all the confirmation that Lia needed. The two women hugged, laughing and crying both, mindful not to damage the delicate dress but feeling the need to release the emotions they both felt. Lia was the first to pull away, but only to hold Hattie at arm's length, before Lia clasped her hands in excitement.

'I don't know what to say,' Lia managed. 'It's the most beautiful thing I've ever worn. I feel like...' She dropped Hattie's hands, throwing her own up as she searched for a word, *any* word which could possibly describe the merest hint of what she felt. Her face showed the myriad emotions assailing her until she slowly dropped her arms to her sides.

'I can't take this, though...' she said, her arms hanging limply as the reality of her present situation began to intrude on her thoughts. 'It's so kind of you to think of me, but really, I mean... when would I even wear it?'

But Hattie had brought the dress to Lia for one reason only. She scooped up her friend's hands again, holding them high, excitement shining in her eyes.

'A few days ago you told me how much you would love to dance but that you didn't really have the nerve. In fact, you made all sorts of excuses about why you couldn't, but you and I both know that's only because it would mean being bold and taking a chance. So that's why I've brought the dress, Lia, because you said you'd need some convincing and if this hasn't shown you that dreams can come true, then nothing will. So...' she whispered, 'it's for when you dance.'

Chapter 9

It was quiet when Lucy got in, her footsteps in the hall sounding unnaturally loud. She checked her watch but she was no later than usual. A yell up the stairs brought no reply, and it was only when she moved through to the kitchen that the reason for the empty house became clear. A note lay on the table:

Gone to get the last of your brother's bits for uni – back about seven.
Don't make tea, we'll bring in chips, love Mum xx

Lucy smiled, firstly in anticipation of the takeaway tea, but also because right now solitude was what she was craving. She flicked the switch on the kettle and went to hang up her coat.

Ever since Oscar had told her about his baby daughter, she had hardly been able to think about anything else. It seemed incomprehensible, the hurt caused to two parents, who, although young, were desperately in love and so ready to share that love with a child. Denied the opportunity, it had been the two of them against the world since the age of eighteen, never spending a day apart until Mary's death just over a year ago.

Oscar had never seen his baby daughter, but a kindly nurse at the hospital where Mary had given birth had felt pity for her and taken a Polaroid photo of the little one. The tiny black-and-white image was the only memory he had of the child he still loved, but had never known. He and Mary had always believed that time and nature would give them a second chance, but she never fell pregnant again, and it had all but broken Lucy's heart to hear the pain of loss in Oscar's voice.

It was so sad – and utterly senseless. Sixty or so years had passed; nearly a whole lifetime of love lost because another set of parents had made a decision without consultation, compassion, or understanding. They had been steadfast in their conviction that they knew best, but Oscar and Mary, and now Oscar alone, were proof that they had been wrong.

Lucy sat with the ticking of the kitchen clock behind her, tears pouring down her face, not just in sadness for everything she had heard, but in shame at her own actions. She had thought that if she helped Oscar to talk about things it might help him, but he'd spent a whole lifetime keeping his feelings under wraps and all Lucy had done was bring them to the surface once more. She wiped at her tears angrily. From now on she would keep her mouth shut – she'd done enough harm.

★

It was later than Hattie had planned by the time they got home and Poppy was beginning to get tired and hungry. Hattie had scarcely noticed, though, as she sailed down the lanes with her daughter on a tide of wellbeing, which had lasted through the preparations for their tea and Poppy's bath time, right up until the point when they were snuggled up on the sofa reading the Hairy Maclary book they had borrowed from the library earlier.

Usually Hattie's favourite time of day, even the comforting smell of Poppy's freshly washed hair under her chin couldn't dispel the first stirrings of panic. It was the right thing to do, of that she was sure. After all, why had she given Lia the dress if not to persuade her to take up dancing?

It had been so easy to get caught up in the excitement of the moment. When Gwen had popped up the stairs to check what all the commotion had been about and found her and Lia twirling each other in circles, Lia looking stunning in that dress, she offered on the spot to look after Lia's mum while Lia went dancing. So, the only thing left to consider had been who might be able to accompany her. After all, there was no way she would want to go along on her own, not when she'd hardly been out of the house in years and didn't know anybody. It had seemed the easiest thing in the world for Hattie to offer to go with her – and she wanted to, she really did, it was just that now, as her daughter sat on her lap, it was beginning to sink in what that really meant.

Once upon a time and really not that long ago, Hattie had worn that same dress. She had had the kind of life that necessitated such stunning clothes; she'd lived in a beautiful house with a beautiful man who loved her so much he had whisked her away to a desert island, and there, against a backdrop of azure sea, on sand so pale it was almost white, he had dropped to one knee and asked her to marry him. For a long time she had felt beautiful too.

He wanted a party, he'd said, to show her off to all his friends and family, a lavish celebration of what was to be the start of their fairy-tale life together. And, because he thought the world of her, he'd wanted her to plan it all and style it in the way only she could; the epitome of good taste and design. He'd bought her a single diamond to wear on her finger for all the world to see and she had known immediately the kind of dress she wanted to wear with it for the big occasion. As she'd sat down to sew she had dreamed about her future and the kind of life that had just been promised to her.

There were over a hundred guests at the party, and on entering the hotel's ballroom, hired especially for the night, her hand was on her fiancé's arm as applause rang out across the room. Amidst the whistles, claps and calls she had truly known what it was like to feel a million dollars. They had danced the night away, her dress whirling around her, the champagne flushing her cheeks a delicate pink to match her dress. And, as evening had turned to early morning, she had slipped upstairs to their room to retrieve a pair of soft ballet pumps, so that she might keep on dancing. There, against the pale damask wallpaper, she found her husband to be, his trousers around his knees, pumping hard into another woman he had pressed against the wall.

Turning on her heel, Hattie had run back to the ballroom only to realise that everyone already knew. She could see it on their faces; what she had taken for admiration and joy, she now saw was merely a polite form of pity.

Two weeks later she had found out that she was pregnant.

Still reeling from the shock of having her relationship blown apart in front of her, she'd been struck down with violent morning sickness that gripped her from morning till night. She couldn't eat or sleep as her hormones raged through her, tangling her emotions until she couldn't tell which end was up. If it hadn't been for her family she thought she might have gone mad. Her mum, like any tiger whose cub is threatened, bared her claws, protecting her from the pathetic excuses of her grovelling ex-fiancé and her so-called friends, who had suspected his appalling behaviour all along but done nothing to alert her to it. Her dad, usually so quiet and against confrontation of any sort, had also gently protected her from anything he thought might upset her.

Hattie was alone, bereft, but at least safe in her family's caring arms. Then, a few months into her pregnancy, her grandma had died. It had been a dreadful time – understandably for her mum most of all, who had been felled by grief and consumed by anger. Now, looking back, Hattie realised that that was when things began to change.

At first she'd thought her pregnancy-addled brain was imagining it – the odd hurtful comment here, a pithy remark there, but nothing that seemed to have any cause. Hattie put things down to the stress of the last few months but her mum had refused to discuss it, saying that Hattie was overreacting or just being sensitive. But as time passed it continued, and slowly but surely the closeness they had once shared evaporated and she and her mum had grown further and further apart. Although Hattie had alluded to this when she spoke to Lia in the park the other day, the truth of it was that she rarely saw her mum and dad any longer. Only her sister came to babysit now and it was a constant source of upset to Hattie that to this day she didn't understand what had gone wrong.

She had tried to keep positive about the future, after all, think how much worse things would have been if she had actually married her scumbag fiancé. At times when it felt like her heart really would break in two she knew that she had also been set free. Somewhere, some day, she would find a decent man, one who truly loved her, who would remain faithful to her as a lover and a friend and be a father to the growing bump inside her. She would never have to live a lie again. Mercifully, after her morning sickness departed as suddenly as it had arrived, the rest of her pregnancy had been a dream and Hattie had never felt so vital, so alive. When Poppy was finally born, her life, while in no way easy, felt like it had a purpose again.

For the first couple of years, looking after Poppy had consumed her days, and most of her nights too. She'd hardly had time – or the inclination, to be honest – to dwell on the state of her relationship with her mum. Motherhood may have taken her by surprise, but she was astonished by the wellspring of love she felt for her daughter and had been content to let the time go by and simply enjoy being with her. Yet as Poppy grew older and more independent, vague doubts had begun to creep into Hattie's mind. What would she do when Poppy no longer needed her every minute of the day? What would happen to her when Poppy started school? Without her family she had nothing and no-one around her, and the thought began to scare her. She'd started trying to make amends with her mother, but the wall that had been built over the years had proved hard to dismantle.

Today, for the first time in a long time, Hattie hadn't felt quite so alone. She had even felt a flicker of hope that things might be beginning to change for her. The joy on Lia's face as she had twirled around the room in her dress was all the confirmation she needed that her plan was a good one. But that dress held nothing but bad memories for her, and she wasn't sure she was ready to remember them just yet. Tonight, once Poppy was in bed, she would take out her sister's wedding gown to work on. Perhaps if she sewed all her love into this new dress, to make it as magical as she could, some of that magic might spill over and create some happier memories for their family.

Chapter 10

It was a vile evening and one which perfectly mirrored Lucy's mood. She usually loved being in the library at this time of night; when it was quiet and contemplative she felt more at one with the books and the stories around her than at any other time of the week. Sometimes, if it was really quiet and her work was up to date, she would simply sit at one of the tables with a book she had chosen at random from the shelves. She'd run her finger along the spines and stop wherever her heart decided. Many of her favourites had been found in this way, but tonight not even this would settle her.

The wind had been steadily rising all day and now the rain had joined in, battering the windows, blowing into every corner it could find, hurling in sheets across the car park. Lucy peered out the window and then back down at her watch. If it didn't stop in the next twenty minutes she was going to get absolutely soaked on her way home. The only good thing about it was that she could then legitimately run a bath, spend a good couple of hours in there and slink off to bed early with her latest read.

She picked up a couple more books and wandered down the length of the bookcase nearest to her, straightening the spines in a desultory fashion. Not surprisingly the space was quiet; a couple of college students writing essays, a gentleman browsing the crime section and Callum on the computer. Even as she glanced about, the students began to collect their things together; it was nearly seven o'clock and they had far more interesting things to do with their evening.

The table at the far end by the children's section was also empty, as it had been for most of the day – and yesterday too, when it should have been occupied, for the morning at least, by Oscar, but he had never appeared. It was the first time for as long as she could remember that he had missed a day, and as she straightened the chairs underneath the table her hand lingered on its surface for a moment as if trying to feel the words they had shared over it a few days before. But there was nothing, and Lucy could only hope that tomorrow he would return; she so desperately wanted to know how he was.

Lost in her thoughts, it took a moment for her to realise that someone was speaking to her.

'I'm sorry, Callum, I was miles away. What did you say?'

He held out a set of keys. 'I think Phoebe must have left these behind earlier. I didn't notice when she left.'

Lucy looked down at his hand, frowning.

'At least one of them looks like a door key,' he added. 'Although she left just under an hour ago. If she hadn't been able to get in I'm sure she would have noticed by now and come back.'

'Unless she didn't go straight back home, of course.'

'Oh.' Callum bit his lip. 'I didn't think of that. Shouldn't we try and get them back to her? I don't mind going, but I don't know where she lives.'

Neither did Lucy, but that was easily remedied. She was about to suggest that Callum wait a moment while she checked Phoebe's details when a thought came to her.

'I tell you what, let me have the keys, and I'll make sure she gets them back. I can just as easily pop by on my way home and if she's not in then I can keep them safe for her until tomorrow. She's bound to realise where she left them.'

There was a flicker of a smile across Callum's face but then his mouth straightened. 'In this weather?' he said.

His words confused Lucy for a moment. 'I'm sorry, I…'

'You're seriously going to go round in this weather?'

Lucy looked towards the window. 'Well—'

'On foot, when I've got a car? You don't even know where she lives – it might be right across the other side of town.' He was staring at her and he didn't look happy.

'Callum, I'm sorry, but I can't just give you Phoebe's address. It's against all the regulations. Data protection and all that.' She gave him a hesitant smile. 'It's probably better if I go.'

His fingers curled back over the keys. 'Jeez, what do you think I'm going to do to her? You're as bad as my brothers.'

Lucy's heart sank. 'It's nothing like that,' she said carefully. 'Of course it isn't, but it could put you in a really awkward position, and I'd hate for that to happen.'

'I'm not hitting on her, if that's what you think. I've been helping her plan her wedding for days – do you not think I've registered that she's getting married? In *my* book that means something.'

'Callum,' Lucy started, but he had already placed the keys down on the table and turned away. She could kick herself. That wasn't what she'd meant at all – well it sort of was, but not in the way he had taken it. She really did have a duty of care to all the library users, and it had never occurred to her for one moment that Callum's motives had been anything less than pure, but she couldn't give out addresses willy-nilly. Callum was a nice lad; there must be a way around this. She had to think quickly or he would be gone.

She followed him back to the computer room, where, as she had suspected, he was already shoving his notebook back into his bag.

'Callum,' she said rather more loudly than she had intended to. 'Listen, *I* can't give you Phoebe's address, but she can.'

His chair swung back around towards her.

'Wait here a minute, please, don't go – I'll give her a ring. You can either speak to her yourself, or if she's happy about it I can get the address.'

There was a minute shrug but Callum turned back to the computer. Lucy gave another glance at her watch, praying that Phoebe would be in. A few minutes later as she dialled the number, she saw Callum saunter over to the counter. She spoke a few words to Phoebe before handing the receiver to Callum with a smile. It was time to start closing up the library.

She had placed Phoebe's keys back down on the counter beside the telephone while Callum was talking and watched his fingers curl over them, but by the time she had spoken to the last customer to let him know they were closing, Callum had gone. She felt a little disappointed that she didn't actually see him leave.

Perhaps it was for the best that she didn't get involved. Callum might say that he wasn't interested in Phoebe but there was something about her that was attracting him. Lucy had thought endlessly about how she might help him out, but that didn't include encouraging a relationship that was wrong on every level; much better to let him make his own mistakes than make any more herself. She still felt terribly guilty about Oscar, and her attempt at helping him, too, had obviously backfired. Perhaps she needed to realise that not everything could be fixed after all.

Once outside the library she stood under the small porch for a moment, making sure that her jacket was zipped up to the top. The rain was coming down in torrents, great swathes of it moving across the car park, and it didn't look like it was going to let up any time soon. Her coat wasn't going to offer her a great deal of protection, and with no hood the rain would drip down the back of her neck in no time, but it was better than nothing, and she couldn't stay here all night. She adjusted the grip on her bag, psyching herself up to move out into the squall.

She was halfway across the car park when a sudden flare of headlights startled her. She registered the noise of a car engine starting up, and tried to pick her way over to one side as best she could, avoiding the worst of the puddles. The entrance to the car park was only narrow and unless she was happy to risk being drenched with water it would be safer if the car went first.

Water dripped off her fringe and onto her cheek and she shook her head to clear it away, wishing whoever was in the car would get a move on. She was soaked already. It was hard to hear against the roar of the wind and she almost jumped out of her skin when she felt a hand on her shoulder. She spun around as a dark shape loomed at her.

'For God's sake Lucy, get in the car!'

She stared in surprise, noticing the dark curls of the figure in front of her.

'I've been yelling at you for ages!' Callum grinned. 'Come on!' He jerked his thumb back towards his car, already racing for cover. Lucy followed suit.

She flung herself into the passenger seat as quickly as she could, slamming the door closed. Callum was holding up his arms helplessly, laughing at the sight of the water dripping off the sodden material. His shirt was wet through.

'Think I should have worn my coat,' he said, grinning.

Lucy looked down at her own sleeves which, along with the rest of her, were dripping water everywhere. She blew a raindrop off the end of her nose.

'Look what I've done to your car,' she said, horrified, but Callum just grinned even harder.

'Bit wet, isn't it? Never mind.'

'But will it be okay?'

'Sure,' he said, reaching into the pocket of his jeans and fishing out a hanky. 'Bit damp, but it's clean.' He handed it to her. 'I never knew you had curly hair,' he added. 'It suits you.'

Lucy took the hanky and groaned inwardly as she mopped at her face, trying to stem the water that was dripping off her fringe. Every morning she washed and straightened her hair. Even her own family had probably forgotten that it was curly, but soaked as it was now she knew that it had sprung into a mass of ringlets. She pulled a face.

'No – I mean it, I like it.'

Lucy shrugged; there was nothing more she could say.

'Anyway, I'm sorry,' said Callum, 'for acting like a two-year-old back there. I jumped to the wrong conclusion, I think.'

Lucy turned to look at him, and smiled gently. 'Your brothers give you a lot of grief, do they?'

Callum winced. 'And some,' he said. 'But you were only doing your job, and for all you know I might be a serial axe-murdering rapist.'

It was Lucy's turn to wince. 'Callum—'

He held out his hand towards her. 'I was just kidding,' he said. 'I know I have a huge chip on my shoulder, but there are four of them and only one of me. I get fed up with it at times... most of the time.' He smiled. 'Sorry.'

'I probably should apologise too,' she admitted. 'It's been a bit of a shit day, and I don't think I explained myself in quite the way I should have done. I'm sorry I gave you the wrong impression.'

Callum narrowed his eyes slightly. 'I noticed you weren't your usual happy self today… only because you usually are – happy I mean. It's nice. Carrie's lovely, I'm sure, but she looks terrified if you ask her anything, and Rachel's just a moody cow.'

Lucy laughed; she couldn't help herself. 'Well, thank you – I think. I shall try harder tomorrow, I just have stuff on my mind, that's all.'

Callum rubbed at the steamed-up window. 'Tell me about it,' he muttered. He turned the blowers up to full. 'I'll drop you home if you're okay to tell me where you live,' he said. 'It's the least I can do, I can't leave you here in the rain.'

She shot him a look, but his eyes were twinkling. 'In that case, I live on Greenfield Avenue.'

'Ah, the posh end of town; I might have known. I'll go to Phoebe's first then if that's okay; she's on the way. Seatbelt please.'

Lucy grinned and did as she was told.

★

The rain hadn't eased at all by the time they got to Phoebe's house, and while Lucy didn't expect Callum to be long as he hurled himself out into the weather again, it seemed only a matter of seconds before he was back in the car. He threw himself back against the driver's seat and closed his eyes for a moment, inhaling a deep breath.

'Is everything okay?' she asked.

Callum let out the breath in one huge rush. 'Yeah, but her boyfriend was upstairs and didn't sound very happy. I did a runner when I heard him on his way down for a "little chat".' His eyes were staring straight ahead. 'I mean, what is it with people? I try to do the right thing and somehow I just end up in the wrong. Do I honestly have the word "pervert" tattooed across my forehead, because I'm beginning to wonder?'

Lucy wasn't sure that Callum actually wanted a reply. She stared out the windscreen at the river of rain sliding down, before turning back to Callum.

'I don't know about you, but I don't really want to go home,' she said. 'I don't suppose you fancy a pint, do you?'

★

The pub was quiet as Lucy carried two glasses across to a table beside a traditional roaring fire. Callum had angled his chair towards it and stretched out his legs. His eyes were closed.

She smiled as she put down the glasses. 'There you go.'

He sat up immediately, an apologetic look on his face. 'Sorry,' he said unnecessarily.

'Drying out?'

'Falling asleep,' he replied. 'When I get my own place I'm going to have a real fire.'

His voice was soft and wistful, and it was an unusual comment, thought Lucy, coming from a man of his age.

'They are lovely, aren't they?'

Callum leaned forward to pick up his glass. 'Thanks for this, but I really should have got these.'

'No, no – my suggestion, my shout. Besides, have you not heard we're living in the age of equality?'

'Where chivalry is stone dead, and good manners don't matter? Yes, I had heard.'

She turned to catch Callum's eye.

'Bit too aggressive?' he said.

'Just a touch,' she replied, softening it with a smile.

'Sorry,' he said again.

She laughed. 'You really do need to stop apologising, you know… and actually as a point of view it's—'

'Soppy?'

'I was going to say refreshing… but just don't beat me over the head with it, okay?' She looked at his downcast face. 'And there's no need to apologise again either…'

He caught the inflection in her voice and looked up, realising she was teasing him. A smile spread slowly over his face.

'So, come on – tell me about your brothers.'

Callum groaned. 'Do I have to?'

'No, but then you'd have to tell me about Phoebe instead.'

He held her look. 'Okay… Well, I'm the youngest of five. My brothers and I tolerate each other but that's pretty much it, mainly because they think I'm a twat, or gay, or pathetic – or all three, actually – while I think they're all arrogant, foul-mouthed, uncaring and selfish.'

'So, who's right?'

Callum's jaw dropped, and he opened his mouth to protest before Lucy held up her hand. 'And before you answer that, let me say that I don't think you're a twat or pathetic – and I don't think you're gay, either; not that it would matter if you were, but it clearly matters to you a very great deal.'

The hand holding his glass trembled slightly as he brought it to his lips and he took several large swallows.

'Why are we having this conversation?' he asked eventually.

Lucy smiled. 'How old are you, Callum?'

'Nineteen, why?'

'Because I'm wondering why someone who's nineteen comes into my library nearly every day and yet although clearly very intelligent doesn't seem to have a job. I also wonder why, while most unemployed nineteen-year-olds I know are surfing the net for mindless crap, this chap seems to be researching the analytics of web commerce, among other things, and has now taken a young lady under his very knowledgeable wing to help her plan her wedding.'

Callum swallowed hard. 'I told you I was pathetic.'

'No, you told me everyone *else* thinks you're pathetic, and somewhere along the line you've started to believe them. What I see is someone who longs for something better but doesn't quite know how to go about getting it. I see someone who knows very clearly what he wants from his life, but somehow doesn't think he can ever attain it.'

'Ouch. And I thought you were nice.'

'Bit too aggressive?'

'Just a touch.'

She raised her glass at him. 'Touché,' she said, smiling.

Callum visibly relaxed and started to grin. 'That was very clever,' he said.

'See, I said you were intelligent. Most people wouldn't have spotted my subtle ploy but I don't hear you denying it. You do see where I'm coming from?'

'I do,' he sighed. 'So, tell me then, clever clogs: what is it I want from my life?'

Lucy stared into the fire, wondering just where the conversation was going. 'Well, I might be clever, but I'm not clairvoyant. Why don't *you* tell *me*?'

'Because it's weird.'

'Go on,' she said slowly. 'How can it be weird? Everybody wants something from their life, and underneath I think we're all pretty much the same when it comes to that.'

'Okay then,' Callum challenged. 'Tell me what *you* want from your life, and I'll consider sharing my innermost desires. But you better make it good.' He grinned at her.

Now she was on sticky ground. This wasn't the way it was supposed to go at all, and Lucy wouldn't even be able to put her own thoughts about her future into words. 'It was a general remark,' she said, avoiding his question. 'And anyway, I asked first, so that's not fair. Come on, why are you weird?'

'Because I'm too young to want the things I do. I'm not supposed to get round to thinking about these things for ages.'

Lucy frowned at him. He wasn't making a great deal of sense. 'Spit it out then. I promise I won't laugh.'

His dark eyes bored into hers for a moment. 'I want the romantic dream,' he said, holding her look. 'I want a wife, two kids, a dog, an open fire… Holidays by the sea, birthday cakes and candles, a pipe and slippers. Love, security and commitment – all of it.'

Lucy nearly dropped her glass.

'But that's lovely!' she exclaimed. 'Why wouldn't you want that?'

He stared at her. 'Because it's mad, it's a soppy fairy-tale… it's not normal.'

'Why not?'

'Because I'm *nineteen*.'

'But I thought we already agreed that you're not like most nineteen-year-olds.'

He shot her an exasperated look. 'Jesus, you don't ever let up, do you?'

Lucy sat back quietly, giving Callum some space. 'I'm sorry,' she said softly after a few moments. It wasn't fair of her to keep pressing him when she couldn't admit to her own dreams. 'I didn't mean to upset you. I guess it's difficult when you come from a home that has none of the things you want for yourself.'

'They can't see it. None of them can. My mum and dad just spend their evenings drinking and smoking. They never tell one another they love each other, we never hug – not me and them, or me and my brothers. There's just no *feeling*, nothing nice, nothing human about it all. It's all so meaningless. My brothers think it's normal to treat people that way, to shag everything that moves and not give a toss. They make fun of me because I'm different. It never crosses their minds that there might be a better way.'

'But that shouldn't stop you from believing in it, from going out and getting what you want.'

'I know, but it isn't always that easy.'

Lucy nodded. 'No, I don't suppose it is,' she said. 'But you'll get your dream one day, I know you will. It's just a matter of time.' She winced slightly at her righteous-sounding comment. Easy for her to say. Perhaps she should try and follow her own advice rather than preaching to other people. But then again knowing how Callum felt did make it easier to help him.

She took another sip of her drink. 'Can I ask you one more question, Callum? Only one, I promise.'

'Can I even stop you?' he said, but he was smiling.

'Where does Phoebe come into all this?'

Callum grinned, put down his glass and squinted up at her. 'Well, this really is the pathetic part.'

Lucy raised an eyebrow.

'She's safe – Phoebe I mean. That's how I can talk to her.'

'I'm not sure I follow?'

Callum blushed slightly. 'I don't have much experience with girls… okay I don't have *any* experience with girls. I'm a nerdy computer geek with a bunch of arsehole brothers who would make mine and any potential girlfriend's life a living hell. Believe me it's easier not to bother. And that's fine except that it's probably not going to get me very far along the road to my pipe and slippers.' He took a glug of his beer. 'The other thing I find is, as you quite rightly pointed out, my approach to… er, love and romance is not necessarily the same as many other blokes my age. It's a very cynical world we live in, and you're just going to have to trust me on this one, but if you start talking to a young girl and you're nervous and tongue-tied and generally feeling like you need a large hole to swallow you up, they usually think you're a creep, or hitting on them, or worse, and the conversation usually turns out to be not so great.'

'So, it's easier with Phoebe because she's a bit older, is that it?'

'No, it's easier because she's engaged to be married, and she knows I know she's engaged to be married, which means she isn't expecting me to be cool or flirty with her, and the fact that I'm actually helping her as well only serves to re-emphasise the fact. Ergo, I'm safe so she can talk to me, and she's safe, so I can talk to her. Simple.'

Lucy gave him a disparaging look.

'We are fulfilling a mutual need. I really need some help in not behaving like a total prat, and Phoebe has some great ideas, she just doesn't know how to go about researching them. Plus, she can barely use a computer… *could* barely, she's getting a lot better.'

Lucy picked up her own glass and drained the last of its contents, feeling her heart lift a little. 'Actually,' she said, 'I've had an idea about that. Drink up and you can go and buy me another Coke.'

Callum gave her a quizzical look but did as he was asked. The idea had occurred to her before, and it seemed as good a time as any to see how Callum felt about it. All she needed now was to work out the detail. She frowned, staring into the fire. She wouldn't be able to pin everything down, but she could flesh out the basic idea now and leave working out the rest until later.

'I think you should be the library's IT support, er, person,' she said as soon as Callum had sat back down again.

'Excuse me?' he replied.

She leaned forward to pick up her drink. 'I haven't worked all the details out yet, but there are plenty of people like Phoebe who need help with the computers and, to be honest, we don't always have the time.'

Callum grinned. 'Or in Carrie's case, the ability…'

Lucy shot him a look. 'So, what I'm saying is, how would you feel about being on call to give advice? We could run sessions maybe two times a week and you wouldn't have to do anything unless someone actually needed advice – just be there, that's all. It would be a massive help to us.'

She could see the possibility running through his head.

'And maybe in time, if it takes off, which I'm sure it will, we could even offer some structured classes one evening a week, so that you could give proper lessons.' She bit her lip. 'Only problem is that we wouldn't be able to pay you, not for the drop-in sessions anyway – you'd have to be a volunteer, but if you're going to be there anyway… and besides, just think how good it would look on your CV.'

Callum held up a hand as if to ward off a blow. 'Okay, okay!' he laughed. 'Blimey, you don't half get the bit between your teeth, do you?'

Lucy blushed. If only she could, at least where her own future was concerned. 'Sorry,' she said. 'I was getting a bit carried away, I know, but don't you think it's a brilliant idea?'

A slow smile worked its way up Callum's face. 'I do actually,' he said, 'which is why I'd love to do it. I mean, the thought terrifies me, but yeah, why the hell not?'

Chapter 11

Lia felt like she was flying, in her head at least. They hadn't learned many steps yet, it was early days, but already she could see how the movements would flow together, how they would carry her around the room, her neck arched, her arms extended. She took a deep breath, like the wind filling her sails, and stepped forwards.

The class was quite small in number, only twelve altogether, with Lia, Hattie, and one other much older chap the only singletons. They were also the only real beginners; despite the fact that the class was advertised as 'Beginners' Ballroom', everyone else had been coming for at least a term. It didn't seem to matter though and now, on their third week, Lia was beginning to, quite literally, find her feet. She wasn't entirely sure the same could be said for her friend, though.

Lia wondered whether Hattie was regretting her offer to come along for moral support. It wasn't that she couldn't dance, she picked up the steps just as quickly as everyone else, but she seemed rather ill at ease – self-conscious even. Most of the women wore the same sort of flippy skirts that Lia favoured but Hattie had insisted on a slightly longer black stretchy one, which she claimed was all she had. Coupled with a baggy tee shirt it was hard to see the lines her body was making in the large mirrors that surrounded them, and the skirt slightly hampered the movement of her legs at times. Still, she had a smile on her face – and perhaps that was the main thing.

Lia turned back to her own partner and grinned. Joe and his wife had been dancing for well over a year but now both of them had been paired with newcomers. At first Lia had worried that he wouldn't be happy with this new arrangement, but he didn't seem bothered by it and Lia was grateful for his easy-going personality; she'd lost count of the number of times she had stepped on his feet already, but he never seemed to mind. It hadn't even occurred to her that they would be dancing with partners, or more specifically, men, and Lia had felt quite faint with nerves the first time she had been put with Joe. Hattie's raised eyebrows and cheeky grin behind him did little to help.

The first time she simply held hands with Joe had aroused in her such a multitude of emotions it had pulled her up sharp. She was so used to having women around her and to suddenly find herself in such close proximity to a tall, rather solid man gave her the most vivid realisation of just how cloistered her life had become.

Joe was five feet nine; not the tallest of men, but not the shortest either, and to Lia he might as well have been a giant. Everything about him seemed huge: his hands, his feet, and the massive wall of chest that Lia couldn't even see past if he was standing straight in front of her. She wasn't used to it. The deep boom of his voice in her ear and his smell, which wasn't unpleasant in any way, but simply so very different from her female counterparts. The first time she had mentioned any of this to Hattie she had been met with shrieks of laughter, and had found out just how base her friend's sense of humour could be. Hattie hadn't meant any offence by it and on one level it had helped Lia to overcome her shyness and laugh at herself; she even felt a tiny flutter of excitement that she might one day be able to behave like any normal adult her age – but that prospect had also terrified her. The gulf between where she was now and where she might hope to be was vast, and Lia wasn't sure the distance could ever be travelled.

So for the time being she had decided simply to dance; to focus her attention on the steps, the holds, the techniques, and to ignore any other emotions than those she felt when she was dancing. Those feelings she let fill her up, imprinting them on her brain so that the memory of them might sustain her through the week until it was time for the next class. She practised in the privacy of her own room at night, letting the sensations flood through her – but only ever of the dance, the passage through space, the form her body took, the beautiful stretch of her limbs. Beyond that she was not prepared to think, or feel.

Now, she came to rest again, another circuit of the room completed. They were still practising basic waltz steps, but instead of only turning slightly through the box shapes their feet were making, their tutor had encouraged them to step wider and turn further, playing the music over and over, each time slightly faster than the last. By the end of the class, the couples were whizzing around the room and Lia had completely given in to the wordless communication from her partner that kept her where she needed to be. She had never felt more alive. She didn't know whether what she was doing was right or wrong, but for now it didn't matter; what was important was being able to move, to relax and let her body take over. There would be time for technique and intricacy – now was all about trust and learning to let go.

Hattie came to a stop just behind her and Lia caught sight of her flushed face, still smiling but with a hint of sheen to it; they had been moving at quite a pace. She giggled at something her partner said, and then blushed an ever deeper red as she caught Lia's eye and winked. The class would be ending in minutes and Lia was looking forward to their coffee together, something which had already become a tradition. No doubt she would find out then what Hattie had found so funny.

She said a polite thank-you to Joe as they dropped out of hold and moved to stand a little closer to her friend. Their tutors always had a bit of homework for them, giving them something to practise in between classes, and Lia waited in anticipation to hear what they were going to cover the following week. She beamed a smile at Hattie when it was announced that they would be learning some of the basic steps of the foxtrot; it was one of her favourites.

Class dismissed, she wandered over to collect her things, waiting while Hattie did the same, taking sips from the bottle of water she had brought along. She shrugged on her jacket and patted her pocket for her car keys.

'Oh, that was such great fun!' she laughed. 'I haven't moved at that speed since I was about six.'

'I know,' agreed Hattie. 'Only trouble is that while my mind is willing, this lump of a body has other ideas. I'm cream-crackered!'

Lia shot her a look. 'What lump of a body? Honestly, Hattie, anyone would think you were enormous the way you talk. My heart was going like the clappers by the end too.'

'Yes, we had noticed.' She laughed.

'What do you mean?' she asked, frowning gently.

'You and Joe, going nearly double the speed of everyone else.'

'We were not!'

'Yes, you were! And don't try and deny it. Anyway, I'm only teasing, you looked like you were having a ball, and I'm only jealous because if I'd have gone that fast I would have passed out.'

Lia tutted, but Hattie just grinned.

'Wait here for me?' she said. 'I'm just going to pop to the loo… Never have children,' she added, 'it does unmentionable things to your pelvic floor.'

Out of habit Lia took her phone from her bag to check for messages. There rarely were any – Gwen was as capable as they came – but she still liked the reassurance that all was well at home. She leaned up against the wall in the hallway and watched as everyone drifted past her, calling goodnight wishes as they left. She was still staring into space when a sandy-haired man shot through the double doors at the end of the corridor where she was standing and rushed towards the studio she had vacated moments earlier, yanking open the door.

'Is everyone always this late?' came the voice from beside her.

Lia looked up in surprise. 'Sorry?'

'Only I couldn't find a bloody parking space, and now I've run the whole length of the road and there's no-one even here yet.' He looked at his watch. 'Are you waiting, too?'

The question caught Lia off guard. Whether it was the directness of the words spoken or the fact that the man speaking was standing far too close for comfort, she wasn't sure, but she stammered over her reply, blushing bright red. She tried to take a step backwards but there was nowhere for her to go.

'I'm not sure,' she said.

He stared at her, wide lips slightly parted, his whole face wearing a rather distracted air. Even his hair looked agitated.

'What does that mean?' he asked.

Lia couldn't even remember what she'd said.

'The dance class…' he intoned. 'Are you waiting for it?'

'Oh, the ballroom dancing, you mean? No, that's just finished. I'm waiting for a friend.'

His eyes bored into hers, olive green under vaguely red eyebrows. He looked at his watch again. 'Shit, do you mean I've missed it?' There were freckles too.

Lia gave a small smile, wishing he would back away a bit. She cleared her throat. 'If you mean the beginners' class, yes. It's seven until eight.'

'Not eight until nine?' he queried. 'Are you sure?'

He was beginning to annoy her slightly.

'Well, I've just been dancing in it so…' She let the words dangle.

'Right,' he said eventually, after more staring, and then, 'Sorry, do I know you?'

Lia shook her head, more violently than she had intended. 'Well I don't know you, so I would hazard a guess at no.'

'Right,' he said again. 'Bugger… Okay, well maybe I'll come back next week. Seven, did you say? And you're sure?'

He shot off again down the corridor before she even had a chance to reply, nearly crashing into Hattie as she came out of the Ladies. She caught sight of Lia as she tried to peel herself away from the wall.

'The manners of some people,' she said, smiling at Lia. 'Should have tripped him up,' she added.

Lia could only agree.

'Still, I suppose when you look like that you can get away with anything much.'

Her friend was staring back down the corridor.

'Look like what? What do you mean?' asked Lia.

Hattie grinned at her. 'You don't get out much, do you? she said, amused. 'You didn't notice he was drop-dead gorgeous then?'

'No,' said Lia weakly. 'Was he?'

Hattie linked arms with her. 'Never mind, you'll learn. Come on, my turn to get the cappuccinos.'

★

The wine bar was just beginning to get a little busy by the time they got there, but Lia was able to grab their usual table while Hattie went to get their coffees. She returned a few moments later, a cappuccino in each hand, and a bag of crisps caught between her teeth which she dropped onto the table in front of Lia.

'Hey, why am I the only one eating these tonight?' she queried, having already opened the bag. For Lia, a posh coffee and a salty snack was decadence indeed, her one treat of the week.

Hattie pulled a face. 'I dunno; I just don't fancy any tonight, that's all.'

Lia gave her a rather stern look. 'Like I believe that,' she said. 'And we've more than earned it; I was seriously out of puff at times earlier.'

'Exactly,' replied Hattie a little more forcefully than intended. 'So, it won't help if I go and undo what little good I might have done by stuffing my face with crisps.' She stared down at the large round mug in front of her. 'I shouldn't even be having this. Do you know how many calories there are in one of these?'

'No, but I bet you're going to tell me.'

'About one hundred and fifty including the sugar. I'd have to walk for half an hour to burn that off.'

Lia looked at her friend's downcast face. 'I'll drink yours then if you like, and you can go and get a glass of tap water instead.'

Hattie looked up sharply to see the amused look on Lia's face.

She smiled, her shoulders dropping a little. 'Sorry,' she said. 'It's just that I saw my sister again today for a dress fitting and I've realised how little time there is until the wedding. Nowhere near enough, actually.'

'Time for what?' answered Lia with a frown. 'I'm not sure what you mean.'

'Well, she gets married at Christmas, which only gives me three months to turn myself into a size-eight stick insect. Her other brides-maids are rather glamorous, you see.'

'But you're rather glamorous just as you are!'

Hattie shrugged and took a sip of her coffee. 'I feel like I'm letting the side down...'

Lia sat back in her chair, looking at Hattie's glum face. 'You do realise how ridiculous that sounds, I hope?'

'Tell me about it,' muttered Hattie.

'Or you could tell me?' suggested Lia. 'Listen, you sat here last week and had to listen to me whinging on about the day I'd had with my mum—'

'You didn't whinge...'

'Well, whatever.' Lia gave her an exasperated look. 'You listened to me, is the main thing, so now why don't you let me do the same?'

Hattie sighed and ran her finger around the rim of her mug, collecting the stray dusting of chocolate powder that lay there. 'I'm just being silly...'

'Oh, I doubt that,' replied Lia. She held out the bag of crisps in encouragement, pleased when Hattie took one.

'I don't blame my sister for wanting everything to be perfect for her wedding – what bride wouldn't? I certainly did: no attention to detail spared, everything matching – at huge expense. She's hired a top-notch photographer and spent ages deliberating over what shots he should take, which is all fine except that I can't help thinking I'm going to stand out like a sore thumb.'

'She didn't say that, did she?' asked Lia, horrified.

'No, she wouldn't dream of it. That's what I mean when I say I'm being silly. I'm probably just being oversensitive, but it's how I feel.'

'I can understand you wanting to look nice, or feel a little more confident about yourself, but I didn't know you were that unhappy about your size.'

Hattie sighed. 'I'm not exactly. It's true my self-esteem has taken a bit of a battering over recent years, and I've put on weight which I'd be very happy to lose, but after the fiasco that was my own wedding, I don't want anything to be less than perfect for Jules. So, I'm trying to do my bit so that I look every inch as glamorous as the other bridesmaids.' She paused, taking another crisp. 'See, I told you it was daft.'

Lia's own crisp paused on its way to her mouth. 'It's not silly at all… but I never knew you were married before. You mentioned that your ex was a scumbag – is that Poppy's dad?' she asked, gently.

Hattie nodded. 'Although we never actually got married. He had pots of money too, just like my sister's fiancé, but unfortunately his brain resided in his trousers most of the time.' She coloured slightly. 'That was fine when it was me he was thinking about, but not so great when I caught him shagging someone else at our engagement party.'

'No!'

'Oh yes… It was like something out of a bad movie. Everybody knew what he was like, of course; everybody but me, that is.'

'Isn't that always the way?' Lia gave her a sympathetic smile. 'Hang on a minute, though; you said earlier that you met your sister today because you had a dress fitting. Does that mean that you were the one fitting it?'

Hattie nodded glumly. 'I've made my sister's dress and all the bridesmaids' dresses too…' She looked up at Lia. 'And that's another thing. My relationship with my mum hasn't been that easy over recent years, so I thought this might be a way of getting back into her good books. I can't have anything go wrong with the dresses, it would be a disaster. Stupid, isn't it?'

'Not stupid, no... understandable, I think. Familial duty is a powerful thing; it's not always that easy to escape its clutches, and I should know. But listen, you're putting yourself under a huge amount of pressure already. Try and lose weight by all means, but don't do it for your sister, do it for yourself instead – because it's the right thing for *you*.' She cocked her head to one side. 'Besides which,' she winked, 'that drop-dead gorgeous man that nearly knocked you flying earlier is coming to the dance class next week. Now he might well prove to be a very good incentive!'

Chapter 12

Callum had a feeling he'd been in a daze for the last couple of weeks, ever since Lucy had asked him out for a drink, in fact. Even as the thought swilled around his brain he chided himself for being so daft. Lucy hadn't asked him out – that made it sound like they'd gone on a date or something, and whatever their quiet drink in the pub had been, it most definitely was not a date. Was it? Callum wasn't entirely sure what it was, only that ever since then he'd felt like he'd been walking on air. Not even his brothers could pour cold water on his mood. For once in his life, Callum had a feeling that things might turn out to be okay; that *he* might turn out to be okay. It gave him a tiny glimmer of hope.

In many ways, their drink together had been a bit bizarre. He'd found himself telling Lucy things he never shared with anyone, and it had been uncanny the way she had been able to pick him apart. It was almost as if she'd been able to see right into his very soul, and having seen what was written there she didn't mock him, or think him stupid – instead she had offered to help. The thought was as exciting as it was utterly terrifying. And at this precise moment, he was scared witless.

Lucy had just brought him over a cup of tea and a glass of water, wishing him luck then leaving him in peace to prepare himself for the day. He glanced up at the clock, and then at his watch just to be on the safe side; the library would open in five minutes and who knew what would happen then? There was a sign above his head, and one on the back of his chair, for good measure. He even had a volunteer badge pinned to his tee shirt, but whether anyone would feel able to ask for his help was another matter.

Doing things this way initially would be helpful, Lucy had said; giving Callum a gentle introduction to being the library's resident IT guru, and giving her more time to get the classes they had planned advertised and underway. Two mornings a week he was to be 'on call' for any users of the library computers who might have a problem. Once they had established the financial support for some evening classes, Callum would lead them, teaching on a variety of subjects each week. Lucy was sure it was going to be a huge success.

The tea was still far too hot to drink, but Callum hovered the mug close to his mouth anyway. It gave his hands something to do. He didn't expect anyone to come over straight away – the computers weren't always that busy first thing in the morning – but if they did he wanted to look welcoming and approachable, even if his stomach was tied in knots. And if no-one came then he had plenty of his own work to be getting on with.

An hour and a half later and the tea was stone-cold. He took a quick swig of water, and turned his attention back to the gentleman who had appeared twenty minutes earlier, his fourth 'customer' of the morning. Lucy appeared with another cup of tea, waiting patiently by his side until a suitable gap in the conversation enabled her to interrupt.

'Try and drink it this time,' she said, smiling – and it was a genuine smile, a warm smile that made Callum feel a trifle unsteady. She turned her attention to the screen in front of them. 'Ah, the wonders of Facebook. I told you he was good, didn't I, Don?'

The man in the hot seat gave a wry laugh. 'There's life in the old dog yet,' he joked. 'Who'd have thought it, at my age, talking to my granddaughter who's halfway across the world just like she was in the same room? I won't remember a thing about how to do this when I get home, but Callum here is the most marvellous teacher. He makes it look so easy.' He shot Callum a sideways glance. 'You're going to tell me it *is* easy, aren't you?' He winked at Lucy.

Callum merely smiled. 'What did you do for a living, Don, before you retired?' he asked.

'I was a painter and decorator, why?'

Callum paused, just for a second. 'Because, as far as I can see, hanging wallpaper in a straight line looks like torture, but I bet once you know how to do it properly it's easy, right?'

Lucy laughed, catching Don's eye. 'See, I told you he was good,' she repeated.

The rest of the morning passed in much the same fashion, with Callum having very little awareness of time moving on. The only thing he was aware of was a growing sense of something inside of him that almost made him laugh out loud; it was such an ordinary thing, but something he had never felt in his life before. He had excused himself to go to the toilet at one point and, as he stared at himself in the mirror over the basin while washing his hands, he wondered if this new-found feeling showed on the outside. He had to guess that it did, and this made him smile even wider. It was a nice surprise, discovering that he really rather liked people. He liked talking to them, he liked hearing about their lives; the little snippets of information that made one person different from the next. He liked seeing how they approached things, how this became so clearly an extension of their character, but more than that he understood that the way he interacted with them was different as a result, and this thrilled him more than anything. It made him feel normal. So far, he had only spent one morning in his new role, but something had changed inside him, and he wasn't about to give it up.

Lucy popped her head around the door to say that she was now taking her lunch break; a cue for his session to end. He removed his badge, and slowly peeled the notices off the wall and his chair with a smile, laying them carefully on the desk beside him. His head was stuffed full with ideas and although his own stomach was grumbling, there was no way he was having a break just yet; he had too many things to research first. His fingers found the mouse beside the computer and he opened another internet tab.

The clearing of a throat behind him broke into his thoughts. He turned to see Oscar standing behind him, an apologetic look on his face.

'Forgive me,' he said. 'I know the session is over for the morning, but I rather wondered if you might still be able to help me.' He glanced towards the door. 'Only, it's a bit delicate.'

Callum stared at the face in front of him and smiled as encouragingly as he could. 'What can I help you with?' he asked.

There was another check of the doorway. The voice dropped to a whisper. 'I'd like some help finding out some information, but I'd rather than Lucy doesn't see me.'

'Lucy?'

'Yes, only I think I upset her before and so perhaps it's best if she doesn't know I've been to you for help.'

Callum didn't think he had ever seen Lucy upset. 'I see,' he replied. 'I'm not sure I understand why my helping you would upset her, though. I mean, this was her idea in the first place.'

'Apologies, I'm not explaining myself very well. May I sit down?' Oscar indicated the empty chair next to Callum with a nod of his head. 'I think you've misunderstood.' He paused for a moment while he settled himself. 'It's not the fact that I'm asking you for help which might give offence, but more the nature of the thing I'd like to discuss.'

'I see,' said Callum again, frowning gently, 'although if this… something delicate involves Lucy, perhaps I'm not the best person to ask.'

'No, no, it doesn't involve Lucy per se, it's rather more that I'd like you to find out some information for me. Information that relates to a conversation I've had with her recently about something very sensitive from my past. I'd like to do some initial research before I let Lucy know I'm taking it further. I'm not sure I should be following this up at all, to be honest, or if I'm ready to deal with what I might find – and that's why I'd rather Lucy didn't know for the moment. She's a lovely girl and I don't want to worry her for no good reason. Does that make sense?'

'Partly,' replied Callum slowly, 'but perhaps if you explain what it is you're trying to find out I can show you where to get the information from. That might make more sense. Computers can be powerful research tools if you know how to use them properly and where to look. I can certainly show you how to do that. That way you don't even need to tell me all the details if you don't want to.' He looked up at Oscar's face to see him shaking his head.

'I'm afraid I'm a bit too long in the tooth for all that. What I'd like is for you to do the research for me. Could you do that? If I tell you what I want to know… it might take some time, but I could come back and you could tell me what you'd found.' There was a pleading look in his eye. 'I could pay you,' he added.

Callum held out his hand to try and allay the sense of urgency he could hear in Oscar's voice. 'I wouldn't dream of it,' he replied, pulling his notebook towards him and taking the cap off his pen. 'I'd be very happy to help, so if I promise not to say anything to Lucy, why don't you tell me what you'd like me to do?'

Oscar smiled, finally. 'Thank you,' he said. 'Now we'd best be quick.' He tapped the top of the page in Callum's notebook. 'So, here's what I'd like you to find out.'

★

It was gone two o'clock before Callum finally sank his teeth into a sandwich. He'd even gone out and bought one from the deli on the corner of the market square, not something he had ever done before. Usually he just walked slowly past the window, eyeing up the enticing display of cakes, breads and cheeses. Today he had pushed the door open with no thought to the cost. He had earned this treat, and that made it all the more worthwhile.

His mouth was still full when Phoebe plonked herself down at the computer next to him, so although he made smiley eye contact with her, he had to chew in an exaggerated fashion to convey his inability to speak straight away.

'It's okay, don't rush,' she stated. 'I'm not meant to be talking to you.'

A piece of chicken caught in Callum's throat and it took a moment for his spluttery coughing to dislodge it, even longer for him to swallow the rest of the food in his mouth. He stared at her in disbelief.

Phoebe stared back, her look almost a glare until a few seconds later her face broke into a sunny smile. 'Good job I'm going to ignore the jealous twat then, isn't it?' she said, laughing.

Callum felt his stomach settle back into place. 'I take it we're talking about Gary?' he asked. 'Is that... I mean... is that why you haven't been in for ages? I was wondering why.'

He received an appraising look. 'Do you honestly think I'm so under his thumb that one click of his fingers and I do what he says?' She pretended to pout. 'Nah, I haven't been in because I've been working double shifts, not because he *forbade* me to come in here.'

Callum smiled weakly. 'And *did* he forbid you to come in here?'

'Well, he tried,' grinned back Phoebe, 'but I told him to stop being such a prat.'

'Jesus, all I did was bring back your keys,' he said. 'What would he have rather I had done? Left you standing on the doorstep?'

'Ah, but I wasn't, was I?'

'No... but I didn't know that!'

Phoebe made an emphatic gesture with her finger. 'That's exactly what I told him,' she said. 'And I told him that Lucy had offered to bring the keys round but that she didn't have a car and you did, and given the vile weather I could hardly insist that Lucy walk over.'

'What did he say?' Callum's eyes were round.

'Nothing much, he just harrumphed for a bit and sulked in the kitchen. I got my own back of course, when he came wheedling round to me, looking to have make-up sex. I went to bed and read instead.' She smiled, triumphantly.

'Is that a thing?' he whispered. 'Make-up sex?'

'Yeah, you know when you have an argument and then... well, make up afterwards.'

Callum, who didn't, wished she would keep her voice down. 'I never meant to cause any problems,' he said. 'Is everything all right?'

Phoebe winked at him. 'I'm looking at wedding stationery today,' she said. 'Do you want to give me a hand?'

'Of course. And actually, I've been thinking about all this – websites and online commerce, that kind of stuff,' replied Callum, pulling his notebook across so that it rested between them. 'When we're done, could you help me out? I've had an idea, but I want to know what you think.'

When Lucy looked in on them at the end of the afternoon to let them know they were closing soon, their heads were still bent together. She smiled.

Chapter 13

'So, you're all set for tonight, then?' asked Lucy, knowing that the moment she said it Lia's head would fill with thoughts of the sheer exuberant joy of dancing.

They were just finishing up another book club meeting, and Lia's eyes flashed as she passed Lucy her book. 'I am.' She grinned. 'Although, I think that this week Hattie might be looking forward to it rather more than usual.'

Hattie rolled her eyes. 'Oh please, would you stop? Otherwise, I'm going to be so embarrassed when I get there that I'll probably do something completely cringey. All I said was that he was very good-looking. I'm definitely not interested in any romantic entanglements just now.'

Lucy lifted her eyebrows. 'Oh?' she said. 'That sounds like a story if ever I heard one.' She looked between the two women. 'Come on, one of you tell me.'

'Don't you dare!' said Hattie to Lia, grinning. 'Besides, neither Callum nor Oscar will be remotely interested…'

'Says who?' joked Callum. 'I'd love to know.' He smirked at Oscar.

Lia leaned forward and whispered. 'There's going to be a new man at the dance class tonight, who apparently, according to Hattie, is drop-dead gorgeous…'

'He was! I mean he is. How did you not notice, Lia? You've got eyes, haven't you…?'

Lia groaned. 'Would you listen to her? See what I have to put up with? I only didn't notice him because he was standing so darn close to me, I was too busy trying to keep him out of my face and off of my feet.'

'Excuses, excuses.'

'He was also really quite rude…'

'Ah…' said Lucy, looking at Hattie. 'So, do we think he's one of those mean and brooding types? Underneath it all he has a heart of gold, and all it takes is the love of a good woman…'

'I sincerely hope so, for Lia's sake,' replied Hattie with a wink. She picked up a plate of biscuits from the table in front of them. 'I do apologise Oscar – what are we like?'

'Enchanting,' he replied. 'Although I admit that your conversations are somewhat beyond my scope of experience. Things were very different in my day.' He held out his hand for the plate. 'My turn to wash up, I believe.'

Hattie smiled as she passed it over. 'Come on, I'll give you a hand. We'll leave Lucy and Callum to convince Lia of the error of her ways. I bet our mystery man will be lovely.'

'Oh, go on with you,' said Lia. 'We both know he's going to turn up and be just like he was last week: abrupt, in your face, and probably with raging halitosis. I bet I get partnered with him…'

★

And of course, that's exactly what happened. One or two absentees meant a change in the normal line-up of dancing partners and, as the mystery man hovered nervously at the edge of the studio Lia could feel the tutor's eyes rest on her for just a smidgen too long. She had known exactly what was coming next and it took all her willpower not to let out a groan as she pasted on a fake smile at the woman's suggestion.

'Lia, I know you haven't been with us for all that long, but as you've been doing so brilliantly you'll be just the person to help, er… this gentleman along.' She turned to him. 'I'm sorry, what did you say your name was?'

The man cleared his throat. 'It's… well, you can call me Jay,' he replied. He gave Lia a hesitant look that seemed to be both an apology and a plea for help at the same time.

Lia smiled again, not because she wanted to, but because it was the way she had been brought up. It would probably only be for one class, after all; hopefully everyone would be back next week and normal partners could be taken. She took a step to one side, edging closer to the newcomer, and noted that he did the same. There was no point in being petulant about it, she decided. If he was here, he was here to dance and really that was the only thing Lia cared about. She'd been a total beginner too not that long ago, and everyone had to start somewhere. She looked to their tutor for guidance.

'Just pop to the side here for a moment Lia, and we'll have a chat first, once everyone else is underway, so we can see the best way to proceed.' She held her arms up to attract the attention of the rest of the class and Lia was left nervously waiting while she gave her instructions to everyone else. She could feel the intensity of Jay's gaze, but she was reluctant to make eye contact in case he saw it as a sign to invade her space in the same manner as last week. When she finally did risk a glance, he was staring down at his shoes. He looked rather lost.

'You made it then,' she whispered, all at once feeling rather sorry for him.

His head shot up as he gave her a puzzled look.

'Last week?' she prompted him. 'You came at the wrong time.'

She saw the click of recognition in his eyes. 'Oh, that was you,' he said. 'I thought I'd seen you somewhere before. Yes, my secretary got the timings muddled up.'

There was something about his words that seemed familiar, but perhaps it was just the pattern of speech itself, slightly jerky. He was still looking at her, his pale-green eyes quite intense.

'Yes, you said that last week too, that you'd seen me before.'

'Did I?' He smiled suddenly. 'Well this time, it's true!' His lips were pale too, surrounded by a smattering of tawny freckles. He looked down at his feet again. 'Was I rude?' he asked. 'Only, I'm sorry if I was. I think that was the day my secretary got quite a few things wrong – I'd been chasing my tail from morning till night, if I remember rightly.'

Lia wasn't sure quite what to say. 'You seemed a little harassed,' she said.

The wide smile came again. 'Ah… so I was rude. Again, I apologise.'

'It's okay,' she replied. 'It doesn't sound as if it was entirely your fault. Does your secretary often get things wrong?'

He rubbed a distracted hand through his hair. 'Not often, no. To be fair it wasn't really her fault either; she wasn't feeling at all well and then my father shouted at her for putting sugar in his coffee by mistake. I don't think she was having a great day either.'

'It doesn't sound like it.' Lia paused for a moment. 'Now it's going to sound like I'm being rude, but isn't it a bit odd getting your secretary to arrange a dance class for you? It's not really a work thing, is it?'

He held her look for a few seconds, the ghost of a smile playing around his lips. He opened his mouth to speak and then closed it again, the amusement fading as quickly as it had come. 'It's a long story,' he said eventually. 'And boring.'

Lia took the hint. 'Well now, it's a new week, and more importantly, the chance to forget about everything else but dancing for a while. What could be better?'

The nod of agreement she was hoping for didn't materialise. Instead the genial expression of a few moments ago was replaced by one of almost steely determination.

'And yet again I find myself having to apologise, because I doubt very much whether this hour is going to be fun for you at all. I've never danced before and I'm fairly certain I will do so appallingly badly.'

Lia smiled to try and diffuse the tension she could feel growing. 'You never know, you might be a natural. Besides, a willingness to have a go is all that's really required. The rest can follow later.'

'Now you're just being kind. Completely misguided of course. I know what my body is capable of and it generally does the opposite of what I intend, so forgive me if I don't share your enthusiasm.' He dropped her look and the conversation was over.

Lia looked down at her own feet, feeling as if she had said something she shouldn't have, but as she replayed the words in her head she couldn't work out what. Perhaps Jay was as poor at conversation as he claimed to be at dancing?

She felt a touch on her arm as their tutor came across to speak to them both. Hopefully she would have firm instructions for them; Lia was beginning to think it was the only way she was going to get through this.

★

Jay wasn't so much a bad dancer as a rather wooden one; reasonably competent, but with little feel for the music or the mood of the dance they were trying to perform. He moved through the series of steps like a puppet on the end of a string, going in the right direction but with each movement distinct and separate from the last. Nothing flowed, and that included the conversation. At one point, he stopped her in the middle of a tricky sequence to wholeheartedly apologise once again, before restarting with his tongue sticking out in concentration. Lia had tried to offer encouragement. He was obviously very nervous, and understandably shy, but as each suggestion she made was largely ignored, she found it increasingly hard to lighten the mood. She was relieved when the end of the class drew near. Her arms ached from being held in too stiff a pose and she felt none of the fluid lightness that always cheered her while she danced. She felt almost cheated, as if a precious evening had been wasted.

She had caught Hattie's sympathetic look on several occasions as she flew past, this week paired with one of the more accomplished dancers and literally being swept off her feet. It made Lia's mood drop even further to see the enjoyment on their faces – and she realised that that was what was the most puzzling thing about Jay; he didn't even appear to *like* dancing, the class seemingly a chore for him, as he concentrated furiously to commit the steps to memory, rather than the wonderful joy it was for her. Why bother coming when you felt like that?

Lia dropped out of hold quickly, crossing to the side of the room, where she pretended to be looking for something in her bag. Hattie joined her after a moment, coming close to her side.

'Was that as bad as it looked?' Hattie whispered, keeping an eye on Jay, who was still standing self-consciously in the middle of the room.

Lia nodded, a pained expression on her face. 'He seemed okay to begin with, but then he just clammed up and I got Mr Wooden Puppet instead. My bloody shoulder's killing me!'

'He does look a bit serious, but he probably—' She stopped suddenly. 'Shh, he's coming over.'

Lia rummaged in her bag again, her back to the room. She fished out her water bottle, even though she wasn't remotely thirsty, feeling the heat from Jay's stare burning a hole in the back of her neck. She turned around, unscrewing the cap of the bottle.

'Ah, that's better,' she said to no-one in particular, taking a swig of water.

'Perhaps I could buy you a drink?' said Jay. 'To say thank you,' he added.

Lia nearly dropped the bottle. She looked at Hattie for help, mentally begging her friend to get her out of this one, but Hattie was ignoring her, eyes fixed on Jay, smiling.

'Oh,' said Lia. 'I'm not sure if… well, what I mean is that Hattie and I normally go for a coffee afterwards. You know, a bit of a girly treat…'

'I could buy Hattie a drink as well,' he replied, his smile totally disarming.

Hattie was still grinning, and Lia knew she was going to get little help from her friend. Then she held out her hand and looked pointedly at Lia for an introduction.

'I'm sorry, I don't know your name,' she said.

Jay took her hand, giving an amused smile. 'Well now,' he said, 'it's a little embarrassing.'

'His name's Jay,' said Lia, helpfully.

The green eyes swivelled in her direction. 'It's not, actually,' he answered. 'Some people call me Jay – as in, you know, the letter "J" – simply because it's easier, less… open to judgement?' He paused, sighed at their bemused faces and then continued. 'It's Jasper.'

Lia was aware of Hattie trying to stifle a giggle out of the corner of her eye, but she couldn't seem to move herself, pinned as she was under Jasper's scrutiny. He held her look for a few seconds more before dropping his gaze to the floor. She could see him swallowing, and there it was again; the unease, the uncertainty, that were so at odds with his earlier charming smile.

Hattie let out the giggle. Whether she was intending to or not, it broke the tension. Not for the first time Lia wondered why she couldn't be more like her friend. Hattie had a way of putting people at ease that she had never had.

'Blimey!' she exclaimed. 'Your parents really didn't think that one through, did they?' she said, totally without guile. 'Never mind, we won't hold it against you,' she added, giving a theatrical wink, which made Lia blush and Jasper laugh.

'That's settled then. Where shall we go?'

Lia sighed. There was no way she could do this. 'It's a really kind offer, Jasper,' she said as gently as she could, 'but I'm afraid I don't think I'd be much in the way of company tonight. I've got a headache threatening, and besides, I have to get back home.' She flicked a glance towards her friend. 'Sorry, Hattie, I hope you don't mind.'

She received a slightly quizzical look, but really Hattie would be much better off without her. 'Don't let me stop you two going, though – really.'

Two heads turned towards her, but Hattie was beaming. Lia turned to smile at Jasper to confirm what a wonderful idea this was, only to find his expression more serious again. He held out his hand rather formally.

'I wanted to say thank you, Lia. You've been perfectly lovely when I suspect I've been nothing of the sort and have rather ruined your enjoyment tonight. Will I see you again next week?'

Lia took his hand and gave a feeble smile. She hadn't a clue what to say and was desperately trying to think of something that wouldn't sound like an encouragement when Jasper gave her hand a final squeeze.

'I hope you feel better soon,' he said, then turned to Hattie and ramped up the smile. 'Right then, shall we get going?'

Lia bent down to pick up her bag, smiling at them both as they turned away from her.

'See you next week,' she said as lightly as she could, the memory of Jasper's eyes burning into her brain as she watched his retreating back.

Chapter 14

Hattie could scarcely believe her luck. She'd never tried her hand at matchmaking before, but this was all falling into her lap rather nicely. Jasper *was* gorgeous and she'd checked his left hand on at least twenty occasions now, and there was definitely no sign of a ring. If there was anyone who deserved a fine male specimen in her life it was Lia, and if she'd read the signals right, Jasper was certainly interested. The opportunity to turn the tables and have a little chat with him on her own was too good to miss.

She watched his back at the bar as he waited to be served, musing over the direction her evening had suddenly taken. Another woman on the other side of the bar looked up with interest and Hattie smiled to herself; Jasper was certainly attracting a fair amount of attention, and who could blame anyone? A slightly drizzly, cool autumn evening in the local wine bar wasn't generally the time or place to see such exotic creatures. With his beautiful eyes and perfectly chiselled jaw, she might have given him a second look herself had her circumstances been different, but with Poppy still so young she had no desire for a relationship just yet; it wouldn't be fair. Perhaps even more appealing than Jasper's looks was the way he seemed to be so completely unaware of the appraising glances thrown in his direction. He was making his way back to her now, a cup of coffee in each hand, his lips pursed in concentration.

Hattie listened to him chatter away in nervous excitement for at least fifteen minutes, until he casually leaned forward and rested a hand on his freckled chin.

'Have you and Lia been friends for long?' he asked.

She suppressed a smile; so, she had read him right. She took another sip of her coffee and stared into his olive green eyes that twinkled at the mention of Lia's name.

'Not at all, really, no,' she replied. 'I've not long moved into the area, you see,' she continued, wondering how much else to add and then deciding that there really was no point in hiding anything. 'I'm a single mum, and Lia and I met through a book club at the local library. She's her mum's carer so doesn't get out much either and we just sort of hit it off.' She smiled. 'The dancing is her thing, though, really; I'm just along for mutual support, although I will admit it's a lot more fun than I thought it was going to be.'

Jasper nodded. 'I've yet to be persuaded about the fun part, but I'll take your word for it,' he said. 'Actually, I feel rather bad that Lia got lumbered with me tonight,' he added, looking up at Hattie. 'The ballroom is not my natural habitat and although I tried to act as if I was enjoying it, I think Lia sussed me out rather quickly. I hope I didn't upset her too much. Was the headache real, do you think?'

Hattie's normal instinct would have been to deny any subterfuge on Lia's part, if only to make Jasper feel a bit better, but perhaps it was time to put him straight about Lia's real motives – that way she might even get to learn his, also.

'I suspect it was what you might call a political headache,' she replied. 'Not so much that Lia herself didn't want to come out with you, but being the generous soul she is, rather more that she thought I might enjoy being alone in your company.'

Jasper stared down at their respective hands; both cradled around their mugs on the table. They were only inches apart from one another. He gave a soft sigh, and swallowed. 'Oh, I see...' And then, 'Sorry.' He gave a rueful smile. 'You must think I'm awful.'

Hattie smiled benevolently. 'Not really,' she said. 'Lia's agenda is no different from mine. And besides, the coffee is rather good here.'

The smile lit up his face this time. 'You're a good soul, Hattie,' he said, 'but when I saw Lia again this week, there was something about her which caught my attention, and I really can't explain it. The trouble is that I haven't got much time, and I really need her help... In fact what I probably need is your help, too...'

Hattie pushed her mug towards Jasper. 'I'm a good listener,' she said.

★

Two hours later and Hattie paused before she turned the key in her front door. She had texted her sister to say she would be later than usual, but she couldn't have left any earlier even if she had wanted to; both Jasper and the story he had told her were complex and fascinating and she could have listened to him for hours. Families were strange things, she concluded as she dropped her bag on the hall table and opened the living room door.

Her sister was sitting on the sofa, a magazine on her lap. 'Good evening, was it?' she asked, arching her eyebrows as she flicked a page over.

Hattie grinned as she bustled through the room and on into the kitchen. She turned on the light, heading for the kettle. 'Yes, thanks,' she called through the door. 'And not what you're thinking. I just went for a drink after with some people from the dance class. It made a nice change actually,' she added. 'You know, some adult company.' She certainly wasn't about to tell her sister that she'd been for a drink with Jasper – she'd be teased mercilessly. Besides, it hadn't been like that at all. 'Have you got time for a coffee, Jules, or are you rushing off?' She stuck her head around the door.

Her sister put down the magazine and looked at her watch. 'I won't, thank you, no. We've got an early start tomorrow, haven't we? And I'm not as used to you at getting up early.'

Hattie's heart sank a little. She, Jules and her mum were off to London in the morning, to pick up Jules's wedding rings. It should be a wonderful day out, but she couldn't help feeling a little apprehensive about the trip. She hadn't been out with her mum for such a long time, and this was Jules's special day so she would hate for there to be any unpleasantness.

Jules took one look at her sister's face and got up from the sofa. 'It'll be fine, Hattie,' she said, coming into the kitchen and giving her a squeeze. 'Mum knows how important this is to me, and she's been warned to be on her best behaviour. I know she's particularly stressed at the moment, but even Dad has chipped in this time, and you know him – anything for a quiet life. Don't worry, we're going to have a lovely day.'

Hattie smiled, but she still wasn't entirely convinced. 'Okay then,' she said. 'I'll let you get off. Was everything with Poppy okay?' she asked, knowing that it would have been. There was no need to even wait for the reply. 'Listen, I'm busting for a wee, do you want to see yourself out? I'll meet you tomorrow at the station. A quarter past nine we said, didn't we?'

As soon as she heard the front door click she made her way back down the hallway. She didn't need the loo and she didn't really want a cup of coffee either so instead, pushing thoughts of tomorrow out of her head, went to sit on the sofa to hug the thought of her conversation with Jasper to her for a little while longer. It was so exciting, she couldn't wait to see Lia's reaction when he told her. It wasn't until she was brushing her teeth a little later that she wondered whether giving Lia's address to Jasper might have been a little rash.

Chapter 15

Hattie had argued that they should have booked tickets, but, as usual, no-one had listened to her and now they hadn't even managed to end up sitting together. The train was busy and as they'd walked up the aisle searching for seats her mum had pulled Jules into a spare pair, leaving Hattie to continue looking alone. Now she was squashed into a space three rows down from them, trying to accommodate her legs around the large holdall belonging to the woman sitting next to her. She pulled her headphones out of her bag, resolutely stuck them into her phone and wished she'd never agreed to come.

She'd had a day like this herself when she was in the throes of organising her own wedding. A girly day out with her mum and sister, which she remembered being filled with laughter and excitement; a rite of passage on her way to becoming a married woman. Apart from collecting Jules's rings, they would be taking afternoon tea at The Ritz and visiting a specialist haberdasher so that Jules could pick out some lavish adornments for her dress. It should be a lovely day for all of them, but try as she might Hattie still couldn't rid herself of the notion that her mum would have preferred it if she'd stayed behind.

Sorry I couldn't get to sit with you, she texted. *But can't wait to see your rings! Xx* She clicked send and waited for Jules to reply.

Almost immediately a text pinged back. *Me neither! I hope I luuurvve them. Pity Ryan isn't here with us, but having you and Mum is the next best thing xx*

Hattie smiled and settled back into her seat, chiding herself. Perhaps it was going to be okay after all.

At one time in her life, London had been a familiar place for her. She and her fiancé had often come up for the weekend to attend parties, the theatre, or some opening of a show that he had managed to snag tickets for. They shopped and dined, moving about with an assurance that only truly came to those who believed they were entitled to it. But now, too many years had gone by and Hattie had lost her self-confidence. She had also lost her taste for that kind of lifestyle; it seemed shallow and meaningless now. And, although it had hurt at the time, her break-up – along with the birth of her daughter – had taught her what was important in life; family, love, friendship, honesty and integrity – not how much you earned or the size of your house. Jules and Ryan were spending a huge amount of money on their wedding, just as she had, and at times it sent warning bells echoing through her head; she couldn't bear for her sister to make the same mistakes she had.

Hattie pushed the thoughts away. Jules was a different person from her and she shouldn't forget that. More importantly, her relationship with Ryan seemed to be a good one, and if she wasn't careful Hattie ran the risk of appearing critical of them, which was not her intention at all. This was Jules's special day, she reminded herself, and she would do all she could to help make it one.

★

Hattie's heart sank as she linked arms with Jules and followed her mum through the door of the Bond Street jewellers. She wanted her sister to be treated like royalty but the snooty reception they received as they entered the quiet room was far from welcoming. The rings were stunning, she couldn't deny that, but they were in and back out onto the street again within minutes and the whole thing felt a little flat to her. She felt rather sorry for Jules, that her special moment had been so disappointing, but she needn't have worried – Jules burst out laughing seconds later.

'Thank God we're out of there! Did you see that woman's face when my stomach gurgled?' she exclaimed. 'Remind me never to eat that many jelly beans on the train again.' And as if to illustrate her point her stomach gurgled again, causing Hattie to clutch her sides in an agony of laughter. Even her mum joined in, and it was several minutes before they were able to move on.

The good humour lasted right through the rest of their shopping and their afternoon tea. They had such a good day Hattie had almost forgotten that things between them had ever been difficult until about an hour before they were due to catch the tube to the train station. The haberdashery shop was vast and Hattie wished she had more time to stare open-mouthed at the array of dressmaking equipment and bolts of the most exquisite material she had ever seen. But Jules was on a mission, and it soon became clear that the vision she had for her wedding dress was morphing into something far beyond what she and Hattie had originally discussed.

Hattie's heart filled with dread as Jules moved over to a huge mahogany counter displaying beads, sequins and crystals of every shade and size, and imported gems of every colour.

Jules ran her hands through a pile of Swarovski crystals, greedily. 'This is just what I want, Hattie. See, I told you they were beautiful.'

Everything inside Hattie sank. 'Gosh, they're very… bling,' was the best she could say when all she wanted to shout was, *No, please no – what are you thinking?* Hattie had been working night and day to make Jules's dress from the finest, sleekest mulberry silk. They had chosen the final design together after looking at numerous ideas that Hattie had supplied and she had given a lot of thought to how the dress would look, how it would flatter and accentuate Jules's figure. Sewing crystals of that size onto it would cause the material to pucker and distort, ruining the line and totally destroying the elegant gown Hattie had created.

She looked over at her sister's face, which was filled with excitement and wonder, and it was suddenly obvious that the dress Hattie had designed for her wasn't what she wanted at all. What on earth was she going to do? She looked anxiously to her mum for help, only to find her rolling a crystal around in her palm with glee.

'Oh Jules, these are going to look stunning. What do you think, Hattie?'

Hattie's stomach twisted as she took the bead from her mum, holding it up towards the light as if to see it better. It *was* beautiful. On the right dress they would look stunning, but sadly that wasn't the dress currently laid out in Hattie's spare bedroom. She tried desperately to think of something to say that wouldn't sound too negative.

'They are gorgeous, Jules, but have you seen the price?' As excuses went it was a pretty good one. The beads were several pounds each, and she would need hundreds of them.

'Yeah, I know how much they cost. But I don't want my friends thinking I'm a cheapskate just because my dress is handmade.'

Hattie could feel the heat rising up from her toes. She knew Jules didn't mean it the way it sounded, but she couldn't help feeling hurt. Apart from the hours spent on it, Jules's dress was a unique creation, and Hattie had poured everything she could into it. She opened her mouth to reply, but before she could speak, her mother's cold voice came between them.

'Don't you like them, Hattie?'

'No, it's not that, it's just—'

'Only you've got that look on your face.'

The breath caught in her throat.

'And before we know it you'll say something which will really upset Jules.'

Hattie stared at her mum in horror, tears welling up out of nowhere. That was so unfair. There was a shocked intake of breath beside her.

'For goodness' sake keep your voice down, Mum,' hissed Jules. 'And you promised!'

The look between them was implicit and Hattie understood exactly what had been said behind her back before they had even arrived in London.

Her mum sucked in her cheeks. 'Well, honestly – I knew she'd do something to upset you, and now she has.'

'I haven't done anything!' protested Hattie. 'I didn't say I disliked the crystals – just pointed out that they're a bit on the expensive side, that's all.'

'And what's wrong with that?' Despite Jules's caution, her mum wasn't finished yet. 'Why can't Jules have what she wants? You did, I seem to remember.'

Hattie dug her nails into the palm of her hand, trying to keep calm. The last thing she wanted to do was have an argument today. 'I didn't say that either, Mum.'

'No, but you implied it. Anyone would think you were jealous. Just because your wedding never happened, don't go pouring cold water over Jules's dreams.'

Hattie bit her lip, beginning to tremble. 'I've always been the first to admit I made a lot of mistakes over our wedding. I got so caught up in everything having to be the best there was that I forgot what was important about getting married. I know that Jules isn't going to make those same mistakes, but I can't help feeling the way I do. I'm just trying to help.' She gave her sister a beseeching look. 'Of course you can have what you want, Jules.'

It was the only thing she could say under the circumstances, but she felt her heart sink even further. The beads would ruin the dress, and Hattie so desperately wanted it to be perfect for her sister.

Jules smiled, reaching out to touch Hattie's hand. 'I know how difficult this is for you,' she said, 'but you really mustn't worry. The beads *are* expensive, more than I thought to be honest, but just think how they'll look.'

Hattie nodded mutely. There was nothing she could do but agree. Somehow, she would just have to find a way to give Jules what she wanted, even if it meant starting the dress again. Her mind was already thinking of possible solutions when her mum made a derisive noise in her throat.

'See, it's obvious you don't like them! You could at least pretend, for Jules's sake.' She narrowed her eyes. 'You always think you're better than us, don't you? That's what the problem is, isn't it? You're right and we're wrong!'

Hattie's hand flew to her mouth, and she turned to Jules as the first tear rolled down her cheek. 'I'm so sorry, Jules. I'll be outside.'

She wasn't sure how long she stood on the pavement, trying to avoid the curious looks of passers-by as she stared into the distance, heaving with silent sobs. She had tried so hard to convince herself that nothing was wrong and, as the day had gone along, she had almost started to believe it. But now her mum's hurtful words had left her reeling and she couldn't understand why she'd even said those things.

A gentle touch on her arm made her jump.

'Come back inside, please?' Her sister's voice was soft.

Hattie looked into her eyes, but she couldn't speak. She shook her head.

Jules sighed. 'Listen, I've spoken to Mum. She knows she was in the wrong.'

'Then why say it, Jules? I just don't get what I'm supposed to have done. Can you imagine how it makes me feel, knowing that she thinks so little of me?' She wiped her chin.

'It's not that, Hattie, it's just that...' She trailed off, squeezing her arm again. 'Listen, come back inside and we can talk about it. Otherwise I'm not sure what we're going to do.' She passed Hattie a tissue. 'Please?'

Hattie dabbed at her eyes and cheeks, trying to pull herself together. This wasn't fair on her, but it was also supposed to be Jules's special day and right now she looked wretched too.

She gave a weak nod. 'Okay,' she began, screwing up her courage. 'But can I just say something first? Just to you.'

Her sister held her look for a moment before rolling her eyes. 'Oh,' she said abruptly as the penny dropped. 'So, you *didn't* like the beads then.'

'No, I loved the beads, Jules,' Hattie replied, 'but... I'm sorry, I just don't think they're right for your dress. I can't pretend otherwise, but I've got some suggestions, which I think might work even better. If we go back inside I can show you, but I wanted you to know that... first.'

Jules raised an eyebrow, a flash of disappointment crossing her face, but then Hattie saw her nod in understanding. 'I'll back you up,' she said, lifting her chin a little, 'as long as you tell me I'm still going to look gorgeous.'

Hattie returned her soft smile. 'Promise,' she said, taking her arm and following her back inside.

Their mum was still standing by the counter examining the trays of beads and crystals.

'Right,' said Jules in a business-like manner. 'Hattie has explained what the problem is with the beads – and I agree with her.' She flashed a smile. 'So, I'm not having any more silly comments; we need to listen to what she has to say.'

Hattie's mouth dropped open in surprise. She risked a glance at her mum, relieved to see a slight dip of her head. She swallowed, composing her thoughts, knowing she had to get this right.

'A good dressmaker works with the person, not the dress. A bad dressmaker can easily make an elegant person look frumpy, a thin one look fat, or a sensual one have all the allure of a brick...' She smiled at her sister. 'Sometimes you get lucky. Sometimes you get to design for someone who is all those things; elegant, with an enviable figure and who positively exudes sex appeal – that's you, Jules, in case you haven't worked it out. I want you to have the dress of your dreams, because you're my sister and you deserve to look stunning, but you have to trust me. The design I created for you will make you look amazing, because it will define and emphasise all of your best features. You don't need huge sparkling beads to get people's attention, however beautiful they are—'

'Because I'll look like a dumpy, ostentatious tart!'

Jules's explosive giggle made Hattie jump. She frowned, but then caught her sister's infectious grin. 'Yes!' she agreed, the previous tense atmosphere dissolving in an instant, leaving gales of laughter in its place.

'Oh, stop,' said Jules, clutching her sides a few moments later. 'My mascara will be all down my face!' She was almost bent double. 'Can't I have just a teeny bit of bling, though?' she asked in a fake whiny voice. 'I'd really set my heart on it.'

Hattie grinned at her sister's expression. 'Of course, but it's got to be subtle. It's much more effective that way anyway,' she replied, thinking on her feet. 'Do you know what would look stunning? Seed pearls, tiny ones, worked onto the front bodice – not covering it, but enough to catch the light and add interest. Every now and then I could add a tiny crystal, just to oomph it up a bit.' She groaned. 'It will take me hours, but...'

'But would you do it? For Jules?' Her mum's voice was soft.

'Of course I would, Mum. We're family; I'd do anything to help.'

Her mum gave a slight nod. 'This is important to you, isn't it?'

'Oh, Mum, it is! I can't begin to tell you how much. Not just because Jules is getting married...' She stopped, wondering how much she should say, knowing that this was the perfect opportunity to reach out to her family. 'My dressmaking isn't just some sad hobby I do because there's nothing else in my life – I want to really make a go of it. Now that Poppy's at school, I'd like to make it into a proper business, something that will support us – but mainly because it's something I love doing and care passionately about. And I'm pretty sure I can make it work.'

Hattie studied her mum's face, and finally saw the beginnings of a smile there.

'I'm sure you will,' she said. 'I think that's a very good idea. And I like the idea of the seed pearls, too. Just as long as Jules is really happy with them.'

Jules beamed. 'Oh, I am,' she said. 'I really am. They're going to look stunning.'

'And so will you, Jules,' replied Hattie, 'I promise.'

Chapter 16

The park was always glorious, to Oscar anyway. It didn't matter if there was sunshine or rain, a carpet of snowdrops under the trees at the far end, or blowsy sweet-smelling roses in later summer, there was always something to gladden his heart. It was a skill that Oscar had become particularly adept at over the years: the ability to find comfort in something new each and every day. Whether it was some sight or sound that filled him with joy or enriched his knowledge, or a kind word or deed that made him feel better, they were all like sparkling diamonds laying a trail through what would be otherwise dark days. As time went by, finding things to be grateful for had become a habit and a necessity. It was a good way to live, and today was no different.

The air was mild after a dry week of late autumn sun, and the paths that threaded their way through the park were littered with fallen leaves; golden, russet and ruby, all dried, all waiting to be kicked and crunched by feet, both little and big. Oscar scuffed at the path as he walked, smiling as he watched a squirrel race away with an acorn. Up ahead, a mother and her small child were doing just the same, the child's pink wellingtons bright in the low sunlight. As they kicked their way through the piles of leaves, bending every now and again to pick up armfuls and throw them high into the air, the wind blew the child's shrieks of laughter straight through Oscar's heart.

His optimism was something of a smokescreen; something he and Mary had developed as a way of getting through their days so that they did not dwell too heavily on the love that was lost to them. It helped enormously, but it never really took away the pain; even on days like today, filled with wonderful sights and sounds, the bittersweet ache sat inside Oscar like an old friend.

He slowed slightly as he reached the section of path that would take him past the playground and around the bend by the seats to the little kiosk that sold ice-creams in the summer. From here, a swing gate would take him out onto the leafy lane that ran parallel to Fish Street, and only a few minutes' walk from the library. He was later than usual, deliberately so. He had arranged to meet Callum just as soon as Lucy had gone to lunch, and nerves skipped through him as he anticipated what the young lad might have to tell him.

He also felt rather guilty about concealing his search from his favourite librarian. It wasn't that he thought Lucy would disapprove of his decision. In fact, given the way their conversation had turned that day, he was sure that she would fully understand. But she had encouraged him to talk and he didn't want her to feel bad for unlocking a part of him that he had kept a tight hold on all these years – not until he knew the outcome. He had no idea what the search would uncover and it made him feel relieved and terrified in equal measure, but for now it was a burden he must carry alone.

During their early life together, he and Mary had often discussed what might have become of the child they lost, but as the years passed and Mary failed to fall pregnant again, it became a subject they avoided; neither one of them had wanted to spoil their otherwise joyous marriage. They compensated. They found happiness in other things, and in time it was a topic of conversation that was never returned to. Now Oscar was alone again and Lucy's gentle encouragement had given voice to his feelings. He was ready to open up that wound in his heart once more – and there was no going back.

The library was quiet when he arrived and he took up his usual position, where he could read with an uninterrupted view of the counter. If he leaned forward he could also see through the door into the computer room and, as he settled himself in his seat, he noticed Callum's dark head bobbing as he spoke with someone. His hand reached to touch his cravat as he caught sight of Lucy across the room. He had chosen its bright yellow colour deliberately, and he beamed a smile in her direction, pleased when she turned and raised a hand in greeting. Business as usual, he bent his head to his book and began to read.

When, at last, he heard Lucy call to her colleague that she wouldn't be long, sailing through the door with her handbag tucked under her arm, Oscar leaped from his seat and slipped into the chair beside Callum, his heart beating fast. Callum was still tapping furiously on the keyboard as Oscar cleared his throat and Callum's fingers stilled.

'My wife used to be able to type like that,' Oscar commented. 'And I could never figure out how she managed it without looking.'

Callum smiled. 'I learned to touch-type years ago,' he replied. 'Got fed up with my brain going faster than my fingers could.' He shrugged. 'It's just habit. Once you know how, you don't even think about it.' His eyes strayed to the door. 'Has Lucy gone out?' he asked.

Oscar nodded. 'Just this minute,' he said, 'but she told a colleague she wouldn't be long.' He looked at Callum expectantly. 'I'm sorry to rush you,' he added.

Callum curled his fingers around his notebook. 'No problem,' he said. 'This won't take long. It's pretty straightforward really.' He turned to a few pages previously. 'There seem to be two options,' he continued.

'The first would be to look up the adoption records yourself. I've found the site where you can do this, and although it might take a while to narrow things down, with the detail that you've got I'd be optimistic you'd find something.'

Oscar nodded. 'Yes, Mary was meticulous in recording what she knew at the time of the birth. Even at that age she had her wits well and truly about her.'

'After that, it's a paper trail really... but most of the stuff you can find out from the internet. If you have the adoptive name, addresses, et cetera, most people can be found relatively easily...' Callum trailed off, dropping his eyes for a moment. 'Well, they can if you know how,' he finished. 'You'll only have a problem if your daughter has registered for no contact.'

'I see,' said Oscar slowly. 'I presume that means that her details are withheld?'

'Exactly. And neither you, nor any intermediary acting on your behalf, can contact her if that's the case.'

'But we wouldn't know that until we find her details... That seems a little like winning a battle but losing the war.'

Callum pulled a face. 'It does, I'm afraid. But, to use another analogy, we shouldn't ever let our fear of striking out prevent us from playing the game.'

Oscar studied the face of the young man in front of him. He was so much like his father in looks, but underneath, so very different.

'Wise words,' he commented. 'Babe Ruth, I believe. Are you a baseball fan?'

Callum laughed. 'No, not at all. I just have a crop of inspirational quotes available for any occasion.' He dropped his voice. 'It helps when you have a family like mine.'

'I see,' replied Oscar, wondering if he should enquire further, then decided not to pry. 'You mentioned there were two options?'

'Yes, sorry. The other thing you can do is use an intermediary to help find your daughter – charities usually, who operate a tracing service for reuniting families. It's a slightly... softer option.' Callum let his last words hang in the air.

'Softer?'

There was a nod. 'Look, it's none of my business, but I know first-hand that families can be odd things. Sometimes I think I'd be quite happy to find out that I'm adopted... What I mean is: we don't get to choose our family, adopted or not, and there's never any guarantee that family relationships will be happy ones. There's no way of knowing how your daughter feels about her adoptive parents, or her birth parents; hell, she might not even know she *is* adopted.' He paused, looking at Oscar seriously, but gently. 'Whichever way she finds out you want to get in contact, it's going to come as a massive shock. These intermediaries act as a buffer, they can broach the subject with her gently and neutrally, give her the details little by little if she wants them. Smooth the way and all that.' Callum tipped his head on one side, regarding Oscar with a wisdom far beyond his years.

Oscar sat back in his chair, myriad thoughts running through his head; surprisingly, the most immediate were not about his daughter at all.

'You know, I taught both your parents once upon a time,' he said. 'And I'm happy to say that you are nothing like them.'

Callum's mouth dropped open. 'I knew you looked familiar when I met you the first time,' he exclaimed. 'You were head teacher at St Michael's, weren't you? Or Old Man Smallwood, as my dad called you. Sorry, no offence.' He grinned. 'Were they terrible?' His smile grew even wider. 'They haven't changed much.'

'Forgive me,' said Oscar. 'Perhaps I shouldn't have mentioned it, and I know it's quite wrong of me to make such judgements, but—'

Callum put out his hand to forestall any further comment. 'Don't apologise. That's the nicest thing anyone's said to me in ages. I'm made up to find someone who actually agrees with me that being a layabout is not a career choice. Like I said: funny things, families.' He beamed at Oscar before glancing over at the clock on the wall. 'What do you reckon, then?' he said. 'I can go ahead and make some enquiries on your behalf, if you'd like?'

Oscar took a deep breath. His answer could well change the course of the rest of his life.

'Or you might want to think about it for a bit,' prompted Callum. 'It's a big decision. You could take a day or two and let me know?'

'I feel rather as if I've been thinking about it my whole adult life,' said Oscar, 'but it's the fear of how I'll cope if it goes wrong that makes me cautious. That, and old age.'

Callum raised his eyebrows, looking at Oscar with a kind expression. 'Can it hurt much more than it already does now?'

Oscar may have been a teacher for most of his life, a thousand facts and figures his to impart, but he had learned a thing or two today. He nodded gently, a soft smile creasing his face. 'You're absolutely right,' he agreed. 'Let's do it.'

Chapter 17

There were days when Lia could cry with frustration. Most of the time she was able to keep her mum moving along, to find diversions that, however small, were enough to prevent her from becoming fixated with something, but sometimes her mother's dementia took an unpredictable turn and there was nothing she could do about it; the two of them became locked in a vicious cycle that seemed never-ending. Tonight was one of those nights.

Lia put down her sandwich and breathed deeply, trying to keep calm, as getting agitated often only made things worse. If she pretended to her mum that everything was under control, sometimes Lia even began to believe it herself.

Rose's strident voice was plain to hear, even in the kitchen. 'I said I wanted a drink,' she shrieked. 'Where are you? Where are you?'

Lia rushed down the hallway, crossing the living room to the small table that sat beside her mum's favourite chair and picking up the full mug that was already there.

'Sorry, Mum, I'm here now, and I've brought you a nice cup of tea – look.' She held out the mug. 'Have a sip now before it goes cold.' The mug had already been on the table for the last ten minutes or so and was rapidly cooling.

'Don't be so silly. I'll burn myself. For goodness' sake put it down!'

Lia did as she was told. There really was no point in trying to explain. Instead, she picked up a book from the floor. 'I borrowed this from the library, Mum,' she said showing her the cover. '*Dancing Shoes.* I thought I could read it to you later – would you like that?'

Rose gripped the book with withered hands. 'I used to be dancer, you know,' she replied.

Lia smiled. 'I know you did, Mum. I tell you what, why don't you have your cup of tea now before it gets cold, and then we can start if you like.'

The blue eyes turned towards her. 'Oh, bless you, you are a dear. How did you know I was thirsty?' She handed Lia back the book and picked up the mug, draining the contents in one go. 'Just how I like it,' she said.

'I'm going to pop to the kitchen for a minute, Mum, but I'll be right back. Wait here for me, okay?' She laid the book in her mum's lap. With any luck, she might be able to snatch a few more minutes and finish her sandwich or, if her mum dropped off to sleep as she sometimes did after her tea, Lia might have a chance to do the washing-up instead of leaving it until later.

She was almost at the kitchen when the doorbell rang. She checked her watch, but it was a bit too early for Gwen's last visit of the day. It was tempting not to open the door at all, but Lia had tried that once before and the caller had simply rung again and again, upsetting her mum in the process. It was better that she dealt with it.

The front door had a tendency to stick. Especially if, like today, it had rained, making the wood warp even more so Lia had to yank hard to get it open. Jasper nearly fell off the doorstep in surprise.

He was unrecognisable in his suit and tie. Lia's first thought was that he had come to sell her something. But on closer inspection, after she had recovered from the initial surprise of seeing him, she registered that his tie was loosened and the suit rather rumpled. Then she noticed the flowers hanging limply by his side. What on earth was he doing here? And how the hell had he found out where she lived? She reached for her hair, desperately trying to remember if she had brushed it. Words were completely beyond her.

An agonising few seconds passed as both of them stared at each other, until eventually Jasper raised the bunch of flowers towards her. 'They're roses,' he said. 'Not red… I thought that would be too… but these are a nice pink.'

Lia had a sudden vision of Jasper's secretary on the phone to the florist, but she batted it away. 'Yes, pink,' she agreed, dumbfounded.

'They're meant to say sorry,' he continued. 'I'm meant to say sorry,' he corrected himself, 'for the other night.'

Lia looked him up and down, his cheeks almost the same colour as the flowers. She should invite him in, she thought, but her mother… how could she explain? She couldn't, it wouldn't be fair.

'I should put them in some water,' she said. 'Thank you.' One ear was already turned towards the living room, listening out for her mum. Jasper was hovering. 'Would you like to come in?' she asked, heart sinking, willing him to say no.

Jasper looked at her and then at his feet, as if coaxing them over the threshold. He looked up with a sudden smile. 'Yes,' was all he said.

Stepping into the hallway, he looked around slowly despite Lia's best efforts to usher him away from the dowdy hallway. It didn't help that the only part of the house that was remotely presentable to guests was her bedroom – she certainly was not about to let Jasper in there.

'Come down to the kitchen,' she said. 'I can make us a drink, if you'd like.' Her stomach gave another lurch. That was the last thing she wanted to do but somehow the words had just slipped out of her mouth. With any luck he would refuse.

'That would be lovely, thank you,' he replied. 'You must say if I've come at a bad time,' he added, looking at her intently. 'Hattie mentioned that you care for your mum…'

Lia stared at him. 'Hattie?' What on earth had Hattie to do with anything? She was about to question him further when her mother's voice called out from the living room.

'Frank, is that you? Frank?'

Lia sighed and gave Jasper an apologetic smile. 'I'm sorry, I should go…' She indicated the open doorway with her hand, expecting to see him at least nodding in understanding as he prepared to wait for her. Instead, to her horror, he took a step to one side as if making to move past her. She mirrored his movement, blocking his path.

'I'm sorry,' she said again. 'She's not too good today. Some days she's more with it than others and—'

'Who's Frank?'

Lia's heart began to beat even faster. She didn't have time for explanations. If she didn't manage to distract her mum soon, the situation would escalate and she would have a devil of a job trying to calm her down. She realised her mother must be reacting to the sound of Jasper's voice; so few men, so few strangers, had been inside this house in the past few years. She held out a hand towards him.

'Please, could you just let me go and talk to her for a minute? Wait here.'

Her mum's voice sounded again, even louder this time. 'Frank, where are you?'

Lia's head swivelled between Jasper and the open doorway. Her mum would appear any second now and then, whether he wanted to or not, Jasper would be drawn into their lives and there would be nothing Lia could do to stop it.

'Who's Frank?' asked Jasper again, more urgently this time.

'My dad,' she all but hissed. 'But he left us when I was four. The Frank she remembers could be from any time in the past. Please, just wait here.'

'Will she remember this?'

'What?' Lia replied, getting more and more frustrated. 'Why does that matter?'

Jasper laid his hand gently on her arm. 'If I pretend to be Frank, will it matter? Will she remember later on, is what I mean. Will it hurt her?'

Lia's head was filling up with information she didn't have the capacity or time to process. She just wished he would stop talking so that she could go and deal with her mum, in her own way, just like she always did. She gave him a pleading look. Why couldn't he see how difficult she was finding this? 'No, but I don't want—'

'And your mum's name?'

'Rose, but I—'

Jasper's gaze suddenly shifted from her face to somewhere over her right shoulder, and she felt her heart plummet. A shuffle from behind her confirmed her fears. Her mum was up.

'You're late!' came the accusation.

Jasper's face lifted into a smile as he stepped past her.

'Rose, my darling,' he said. 'I'm so sorry. The traffic was dreadful.'

Lia whirled around just in time to see Jasper kiss her mother's cheek. What on earth was he doing?

'But I'm home now, so never mind.'

'Well your dinner's ruined. Half past six, I said.'

'I know,' Jasper crooned. 'I'm sorry.' He took her arm. 'Why don't you come and sit down and you can tell me all about your day. Has Lia been all right?'

Rose's face softened. 'We made daisy chains,' she said. 'It's been such a beautiful day. And then after lunch we were even able to get her little tea set out and have a picnic for her dolls on the lawn.'

'I wish I could have been here,' replied Jasper.

Mutely, Lia followed them both into the living room. She stared at Jasper's back, utterly bemused. The radio was still playing softly in the background; a programme of songs from the musicals.

'And wouldn't you know it, they're playing our favourite, Rose; listen. I always did love this song.'

He lifted her arm as if to swing her round – and to Lia's amazement her mother turned, taking Jasper's other hand and pulling him towards her. For a split second Jasper looked like he had bitten off more than he could chew, but as Lia watched, his face relaxed again and he slid an arm around her mum's waist, moving his feet into the position that he had been taught only recently. He took a tentative step forward and Rose followed his lead, moving into a gentle waltz that circled them slowly around the room. Lia couldn't remember the last time she had seen her mum dance.

After a moment Rose audibly sighed and lowered her head against Jasper's shoulder, her eyes closed as she swayed in time to the music. Jasper slowed his steps, lowering his arm so that both their hands folded in against his chest. He closed his eyes, dropping his chin against the top of her head.

Lia wiped her fingers under her eyes, chasing away the tears that suddenly sprung up from nowhere. She had never seen anything so beautiful, and she didn't want to miss a second of it. For all that Jasper was dressed in a suit and tie and was forty-odd years younger than her mum, somehow, he had slipped into her world and they looked every inch like her mum and dad would have done all those years ago.

The closing strains of the violins faded out as the song came to end and Lia held her breath as the radio DJ began to talk once more. Jasper made no move to pull away.

A few more seconds ticked by until Rose herself lifted her head. 'Oh Frank, you always did know how to show a girl a good time.'

Jasper smiled. 'Anything for my beautiful Rose,' he whispered. He gently straightened up, taking Rose's hand and leading her over to the chair by the fireside. 'Shall I get us a drink?' he asked, as he slowly lowered Lia's mum into the chair. 'A glass of sherry perhaps, or some tea?'

'A glass of sherry would be wonderful,' she replied, her eyes already closing.

Jasper held her hand a little longer before laying it softly in her lap. He stood looking down at her and Lia couldn't quite see the expression on his face, but she could tell that he needed a moment before he turned and faced her again. To be honest she was grateful too; she hadn't a clue what she was going to say to him.

Eventually he straightened up and began to back away slowly as if fearing the floorboards might creak and disturb her. When he drew level with Lia he lifted his head slightly, flicking the smallest of looks at her before dropping his head once again and moving past her to the doorway. He seemed suddenly very awkward and for the second time within a matter of minutes Lia found herself staring at his back.

She followed him from the room to find him standing in the hallway in much the same spot that he had occupied earlier. The flowers she still held were growing heavy in her hand as she stumbled over what to say.

'Thank you—'

'I'm sorry—'

Their words collided as they both opened their mouths to speak again and then closed them.

Lia grinned first; her cheeks she knew were still wet with tears. 'I'll put the kettle on,' she said.

The tension in the dim hallway suddenly popped like a bursting balloon and Jasper looked up at her properly for the first time, a wide smile stretching the freckles on his cheeks. His hand moved to touch his forehead and he peeped through his fingers. 'I really didn't intend…'

'No, it was wonderful…'

They stared at one another again, before Lia blushed bright red. 'Really,' she said, 'I want to thank you. I've never seen Mum like that – not for years.'

Jasper's head dropped again. 'It just seemed like the best thing to do… under the circumstances. But I probably shouldn't have… It could have gone horribly wrong, and I…'

'But it didn't… and you tried, at least… Most people just look like they want to run away.'

'The thought did cross my mind, but you looked so… and it was…' He smiled again and looked up at her through thick eyelashes. 'I'm not explaining myself very well, am I?'

Lia laughed. 'No, but neither am I. Come on, I need that cup of tea. Perhaps that will help.'

'We're British so I should jolly well hope so.'

If Jasper had appeared unfazed by both the state of her house and an impromptu dance session with her mother, he was just as accepting of the state of her kitchen, which was cluttered, untidy and still held the remains of her half-eaten sandwich. He came to stand behind her.

'I can make the tea,' he said, 'if you want to put the flowers into water.'

For the second time that night Lia smiled at him gratefully. 'The cups are in there,' she said, motioning to the cupboard above the kettle. 'I'll just get a vase.'

By the time she had undone the packaging and placed the blooms in water, Jasper had already set down two mugs on the table.

'Was that your supper?' he asked with a look at her plate.

Lia pulled a face. 'Ruined, like yours,' she said with a wry smile, 'but I'll get something later, don't worry.'

'Ah yes. I wonder what I was having?' he replied with a grin that suddenly slid off his face. 'I should probably explain why I'm here,' he added, 'before you think I'm mad. You probably already think I'm very rude.'

Lia looked at his face for a moment. The traces of embarrassment were still showing in his eyes. 'I'm just grateful,' she said. 'Whether you're a madman or not, I've never seen my mum respond to anyone like that before. I did wonder what on earth you were doing to start with but, all things considered, I'd say it turned out very well.'

Jasper pulled his mug a little closer. 'That's very kind,' he said. 'Although, when you hear why I came over you still might change your mind.' He gave a slight glance back towards the kitchen door. 'Are we all right to talk for a minute? I realise now, of course, how stupid it was to come unannounced.'

Lia glanced at her watch. 'Mum's carer will be here soon to settle her for the night, but she's likely to doze for a bit. I should spit it out if I were you, before that changes.' She cocked her head to one side. 'Or before I do decide you're a madman.'

Jasper gave a quick nod. 'Well, the first thing to say of course is that I haven't been stalking you – but I *have* been talking about you. With Hattie, when we went for that drink the other night?'

'Go on.'

'And she probably shouldn't have, but she gave me your address. We'd had a bit to drink by then,' he added, 'and we were getting on really well. I'd somehow managed to persuade her that I'm actually quite a nice chap.'

Lia laughed. 'Some friend she is…'

'I think she thought at first that I, well… you know, was trying to chat her up.'

'Why weren't you?' asked Lia. 'She's gorgeous.'

Jasper thought about her words for a moment. 'Yes, I suppose she is,' he replied. 'I'm really not very good at that sort of thing.'

Lia tried to hide her smile. Well, that made two of them.

'And I confess I did have an ulterior motive, which when I explained it to Hattie made perfect sense – except that now I'm not so sure. I don't want to give you the wrong idea.'

'And what idea would that be?' Lia couldn't help herself. She knew it was cruel to tease him, but for some reason she suddenly felt in a ridiculously good mood. 'Jasper,' she said with a smile, 'despite the fact that you brought me flowers, and flirted outrageously with my mother, I'm under no illusion that your visit here tonight was for romantic purposes. And please don't make a show of trying to deny it, otherwise you'll only be digging yourself an even bigger hole, and this time I shall let you fall in. Perhaps now might be the time to explain why you're really here?'

Lia had never seen a man look quite so pathetically grateful, but then Jasper had one of those faces, just like hers, that could never hide what he was feeling. Even his freckles seemed to be in on the act.

'I rather think I deserve to be left in the hole, actually,' he said. 'For days in the burning sun with nothing but a dry crust. I really couldn't have been any ruder if I'd tried, and there's absolutely no reason why I wouldn't be here with romantic intentions, except…'

'Except you're not,' finished Lia.

Jasper groaned. 'I'm not exactly making this easy for myself, am I?'

'Jasper, I'm only teasing…' She paused for a moment, sucking in her cheeks. 'I probably shouldn't be saying this, but to be absolutely honest I wouldn't know what to do with you even if you *were* here to ask me out…' She risked a peep at him, but his gaze was levelled at the table. 'I look after my mum twenty-four-seven. I don't get out much, and I don't have the time or the inclination for… relationships… or whatever you want to call them. I think it might make things easier for us both if I just come right out and say it, to save any confusion or misunderstanding.' Jasper was still looking at the table. 'Although I am very grateful for your help tonight,' she added, trying to soften the effect of her words.

She shuffled in her seat, knowing that it wasn't just the wooden chair that was making her feel uncomfortable. For goodness' sake, she might as well just hang a sign around her neck proclaiming to the world what a sad old spinster she was. It was all very well being shy and inexperienced when it came to members of the opposite sex, but she had managed to sound both ridiculous and pompous in one fell swoop.

Jasper cleared his throat, his olive eyes making only the briefest of contact with hers. 'Good, he said. 'I mean, you're welcome, and really I agree. Much better to be honest about these things from the start.' He nodded emphatically, eyes still focused about two inches from the table top. 'So… I'll just ask you then, shall I? About the thing I came here for?'

Lia looked up, slightly alarmed to feel a pang of disappointment ripple through her. She nodded her assent.

'It's a bit of a long story, so I'll try to be as brief as possible, but I need a girlfriend. Not a real one, just one who can dance. And I need her in about eight weeks. I was rather hoping that you might be able to help me out.'

Chapter 18

'There you go, Callum – I told you there'd be plenty. Go on, help yourself to more while you still can.'

Callum took the dish of roast potatoes from Lucy and smiled. He already had three on his plate, but she could see he'd happily eat several more. He'd looked anxious, bordering on terrified, when he'd first arrived, but was beginning to relax a little as Lucy knew he would. Her family had a knack for making people feel at ease, and a big get-together for a roast was about as relaxed as it got.

She had invited him yesterday evening, quite out of the blue, as she'd been preparing to lock up the library. It wasn't until she had bustled past Callum for about the fourth time with a chair under each arm that he had jumped up, insisting that he should help.

They had chatted as they worked, polite chit-chat at first, until Lucy had asked him what he had been doing during the day. His outpouring of energy and enthusiasm was instantaneous, and as she listened she realised that she wanted to hear more; in fact, something about the way Callum spoke made her feel as if she could listen to him for hours. Before she knew it, she had invited him round for tea.

He'd only been here for half an hour and had already stirred the gravy for her mum, been reminded to call her Val, not Mrs Picklescott, met her sister, Hannah, and her husband, Clive, and was now sitting opposite Lucy at the table with the biggest plate of food in front of him he had probably seen in weeks. Lucy's mum took roast dinners very seriously.

So far, everyone had behaved themselves, but there was always the possibility that someone would make a toe-curlingly embarrassing remark. Lucy thanked her lucky stars that her brother, Mark, was away at uni, because he was usually the prime culprit. She cringed as she thought back to the last time she had brought a boyfriend home... not that she did that very often... and of course Callum wasn't her boyfriend either... She swallowed, and prayed that no-one had got the wrong idea.

She thought back to their conversation in the pub, when Callum had shared his dreams for the future, and she wondered if that was what he would be thinking about now as he waited patiently for the gravy to be passed around the table. Would he be picturing his own life, sitting at the head of the table with the other four chairs occupied by his own children and their partners? It was what fascinated her about Callum; he was so terribly unsure of himself, and yet so driven and determined. She half hoped a little of that might rub off on her...

'Right, come on everybody, no standing on ceremony or the food will get cold.' Her mum smiled warmly at everyone around the table. 'I hope you're okay with chicken, Callum?'

He only managed a nod, his mouth was so full of food, but after a moment of rapid chewing he was able to smile, swallow and say, 'I can't remember the last time I had roast chicken. It's perfect, honestly. And very kind of you to let me come around at such short notice.'

'Well that's our pleasure. We've heard so much about you, after all. Lucy has been telling us how clever you are, haven't you, love?'

Lucy gave a nod in his direction, making him blush into his roast potatoes.

'Oh,' he stammered. 'I'm not sure what to say to that.'

'I said you'd be far too modest as well,' Lucy added, 'didn't I, Mum? And I was right. It's been brilliant having you helping out, and people are really beginning to feed back to us how wonderful you've been.'

Callum stared at her. 'Have they?' he gulped.

'Of course they have! And it's made it so much easier for me, not having to worry about whether the PCs are going to crash every two minutes – let alone having to stop to find emails for people, or help them to print pictures and stuff. The library's IT resources are great to have, but they can take a lot of time too.'

'Most people are like me, I reckon,' said Clive. 'Totally clueless when it comes to computers. I never learned how to use them I guess, and now I don't seem to have the time to figure it all out.'

Callum paused, a forkful of green beans halfway to his mouth. 'It's a confidence thing, mainly. People are always afraid to push this button or that button and find out what it does. You never learn that way. I've pretty much taught myself over the years... but perhaps that's just me – a bit of a nerd, I'm afraid.'

'Nothing wrong with being nerdy,' said Clive. 'I've been there. When I was fourteen I started making cakes. You can guess how well that went down with my mates. They were talking about football and sneaking off for a crafty smoke behind the bike sheds at school and I was looking up recipes and talking about how to get the perfect rise on a Victoria sponge.'

Hannah beamed at him. 'But your mum thought you were an angel.' She laughed. 'Although it's possible she was the only one. I'll admit when we were at school I always thought you were weird. It wasn't until you wooed me with your profiteroles and almond croissants that I began to see the advantages of having a boyfriend that was a bit handy with a rolling pin.'

Callum returned her smile. 'Perhaps I won't give up just yet then, although I'm not sure that the lure of a perfectly formulated spreadsheet will have quite the same effect.'

'Oh God... yeah, I see what you mean.' She laughed.

Lucy dug her sister in the ribs. 'Oi, don't be cruel. Callum's been working on some brilliant ideas for his own business, actually. I thought you might be able to give him a few tips, Clive. You know, on how to get started and the like.'

Clive took a sip of water, regarding Callum with interest. 'You any good with websites?' he asked.

'Brilliant,' Callum replied succinctly, with a sideways glance at Lucy.

'Right, well, after this lot and a rather sumptuous tarte Tatin courtesy of *moi*, I reckon you and I should have a bit of a chat, don't you?'

Lucy beamed at Clive, glad that he had taken up her prompt.

★

The rest of the meal passed in a riot of conversation. It all seemed so easy, thought Callum, whose family gatherings were always fraught with snide comments, disagreements and coarse language. Tonight was proof that other families did seem to be able to enjoy one another's company without viciously teasing and talking over one another. Lucy's family teased one another, but it was affectionate and full of fun. To anyone else, her family might seem ordinary, but to Callum they were extraordinary indeed.

He had offered to wash up as soon as the meal was over, but Val wouldn't hear of it and he had been banished to the living room along with Hannah, who was a nurse and had been on her feet all day.

Lucy's dad had appeared too, towards the end of the meal, apologising for his lateness due to a parents' evening that had overrun. The minute he sat down Val had placed a plate of warmed food in front of him with a kiss and a smile. Callum had never been happier; he was full to the brim, the cushions on the sofa were soft and inviting and the family cat had just come to settle on his lap, soft paws kneading his thighs. He would have dropped off to sleep had Hannah not started to talk.

They had been chatting for a few minutes before Callum realised that they were alone and he was talking to a woman he'd just met like they'd been friends for years, all his usual awkwardness and shyness gone. Perhaps, he wondered, he had been talking to the wrong people all his life. Hannah seemed genuinely interested in his plans for his new venture into e-commerce, and Callum enjoyed sharing his ideas until her husband joined them twenty minutes or so later.

It was the idea that was the thing, according to Clive; the absolute conviction that your idea was sound, and the commitment to put it into practice. Everything else was just organisation. He seemed impressed by what Callum had found out so far about the mechanics of starting up a business and was quite happy to share his own experiences of what had, and hadn't, worked well for him. Not everything had gone according to plan, and at times things had been far from plain sailing, but Clive had never doubted that his business would be a success; it was simply a matter of time. Now his hard work was repaying him, not just financially, but in satisfaction.

Satisfaction. Callum mulled the word over in his head. It sounded good. It sounded like something that he wanted in his life, and best of all, it sounded like something that could finally be within his reach.

Before he knew it, it was nine o'clock, and he and Clive had been talking non-stop for a matter of hours. Clive seemed so interested in what he had to say that Callum had found himself opening up about his plans without really thinking; from his own ideas about start-ups and online shops, the conversation had naturally turned towards Earl Grey's. Clive was quite keen on the idea of having his own website for the tearoom, but had absolutely no idea how to put it together. He had some vague thoughts about what it should look like, and the things he might like to include on it, but beyond that he was open to suggestions. Callum was more than happy to oblige.

He really ought to have been going, but the relaxed atmosphere in the room was hard to leave and Callum didn't want to think about returning home and pushing open his own front door. He knew from experience that his shouts of hello as he walked through into the hallway would go unanswered. It was time, though; he didn't want to outstay his welcome. Reluctantly, he ushered the cat to one side and stood.

Lucy was on her feet first, smiling at Callum and thanking him for coming over. Thanking *him*, when surely it should be the other way around? He would never be able to thank her enough. She and her family had opened his eyes to a way of living that he had hitherto only dreamed of and, if that wasn't enough, they had also given him the courage to pursue his dreams. He thanked Clive profusely for his advice, promising to get in touch within a day or two with some designs for his website.

Lucy's mum looked up from the corner of the room and put down the paperback she had been reading.

'Are you sure you won't stay for a hot chocolate, love? We usually have one about this time.'

Callum shook his head. It was tempting, but he had to go home some time; it was probably best not to delay it any longer. The disappointment would only feel greater if he did.

'I won't, thanks,' he replied. 'I'm honestly still full up. I don't think I could manage anything else.' He beamed a smile at her, wondering whether he ought to kiss her cheek goodbye. 'It's been lovely, though, meeting you all.'

'And you, Callum. You're a wonderful young man, and don't let anyone tell you otherwise. Now, if you're going to be showing Clive some designs and things in a day or two, why don't you come over for lunch again on Sunday? That way, you don't have to rush.'

Callum looked from Lucy to her mum and back again, but Lucy didn't look at all dismayed by the idea and her mum was smiling broadly so he bit down his apprehension and said instead, 'Would that be all right? I'd love to.'

He hardly remembered any of the journey home, feeling rather surprised when he turned into his cracked concrete driveway. All the way back he had replayed his conversations with Lucy's family over and over again in his head, and even though he tried to convince himself that he had got it all wrong, he fairly floated up the stairs to his room. The television had been blaring from the front room, the table in the kitchen littered with metal bottle tops from the beers that had been consumed during the evening, but he didn't even bother shouting hello. In his room, he pulled his laptop out from under the bed. He had a future to build.

Chapter 19

Hattie pursed her lips together, trying to hold onto the hem of the dress that kept slipping through her fingers as well as a mouthful of pins. If Jules's bridesmaid didn't quit wriggling around, Hattie thought she might just go ahead and stick a pin in her leg anyway, just for the hell of it. She knew it was simply excitement, but it didn't help. She'd been at her mum's house for two hours and, apart from anything else, Poppy was getting bored and her noise level was rising. It was putting Hattie more and more on edge.

Her mum hadn't been unwelcoming, but this was the first time they had seen one another since their recent trip to London, and Hattie still felt as if she were treading on eggshells to some extent. The remainder of their trip that day had ended amicably enough –Jules had been lovely to Hattie about the change in design to her dress and, if she was disappointed at all, she hadn't let it show. Her mum, too, had gone back to being on her best behaviour – but it still left Hattie with questions about the outburst and the reason behind it unanswered.

She tried to focus on the task in hand; to her delight the dresses had not only fitted perfectly but looked utterly gorgeous, even if she did say so herself. Jules's two bridesmaids shrieked with glee at their reflections in the mirror, but somehow Hattie couldn't help feeling that her mum's comments had more to do with how beautiful the girls were themselves, rather than with Hattie's dresses. 'Don't you look ravishing?' she had said, not *Doesn't the dress look ravishing?* And, 'Your waist looks so tiny!', not *How clever you are to cut the dress to emphasise her best feature?* Hattie knew she was being petulant, but she'd give anything to hear an unreserved compliment, just once. Jules had done her best to bolster and support her, but they were in her mum's house, on her territory, and Hattie could see that even Jules was a little jumpy.

A loud squawk from Poppy broke into her thoughts as her mum's raised voice could be heard through the open living-room door. Moments later her tearful daughter came rushing to Hattie's side. Hattie released the material she was holding and gathered Poppy to her, swiftly removing the pins from her mouth at the same time.

'For goodness' sake, Hattie – I told her not to play with the buttons and now they've spilled all over the floor!' her mother cried.

Hattie clamped her jaw together. 'Well then, Poppy and I will pick them up again in a minute – won't we, Pops? She just likes playing with them, Mum. I used to when I was little, don't you remember? It's not as if there's any real harm done, is there?'

She could feel her mother's displeasure prickling the back of her neck, but she refused to turn around and engage with her.

'Come on Poppy, just sit here for Mummy for a minute, and then I promise we'll be done. There might be time to stop off in the park for a play on the swings before we go home. And, if you're really good, we could even have an ice-cream.'

'You know, perhaps spoiling her the way you do might be the reason she misbehaves so much.'

Hattie whirled around to face her mum, her patience finally snapping. 'Or, it might have something to do with the fact that we've both been stuck here for two hours on a Sunday afternoon, when we could have been out having a fun time together, which is what we'd usually do.'

She yanked on the hem of the bridesmaid's dress she was holding. 'Now jolly well stand still and let me get this hem straight and then you can take it off.'

There was an awkward giggle, which only served to infuriate Hattie even more, but she said nothing, deftly pinning the fabric as quickly as she could. She had hoped that she might be able to try on her own dress today, but there was no way she was going to stay a minute longer than was necessary. She blinked hard, trying not to let the tears that were threatening succeed. Her mum never used to be so hard on her, so critical and short-tempered. She had wracked her brains searching for a reason to explain it, but always drew a blank. Since her mum refused to discuss it, there was little she could do but try and try again. She was exhausted. She had spent too many hours working long into the night to finish the dresses in time, and she really didn't think she could cope with a showdown now.

Twenty minutes later, Hattie began to gather her and Poppy's things together, the dresses now packed carefully away for their final alterations. She knew she couldn't go on like this, that she needed to have a heart-to-heart with her mum at some point in the near future, but not today; it was time to focus on Poppy. She hugged Jules goodbye and, with a promise to give her sister a call soon, took her daughter's hand and left.

★

The day had grown somewhat overcast by the time they reached the park, but the wind had dropped and it was still a mild day. So far, October had been kind to them, and Hattie prayed that it would continue; there was nothing worse than not being able to get out of the house when you had a small child, and the thought of the looming winter was not a pleasant one.

As usual, Poppy made a beeline for the swings. Now that she had the hang of doing it by herself, the challenge was to go higher and higher. It set Hattie's teeth on edge from time to time, but she knew that she must let her daughter test her own capabilities. Today there was a spare swing beside Poppy and Hattie squeezed her bottom onto the seat, trying to pick up the same pace as her daughter. For a few seconds they swung in time with one another, laughing as they whooshed through the air in sync, but Hattie's weight advantage was no match for the laws of physics and her swing soon dropped out of rhythm. She waved at Poppy each time they passed each other, her legs working furiously to keep up with her daughter's effortless swing. Before too long they were both in fits of giggles.

'Someone's having fun.'

Hattie turned her head at the sound of Lia's voice from beside her. She caught sight of her just for a second before she flew past her once more, long enough to see that she wasn't alone.

'Hello,' she called. 'Hang on! Now I've got this thing going I'm not sure how I'm going to stop it.' She straightened her legs out in front of her, hoping the drag might slow her down. Eventually, it slowed enough for Hattie to catch her feet on the ground and bring herself to a complete halt. She was still laughing, more so when she tried to extricate herself from the seat, which seemed to have glued itself to her bottom.

'I am *so* not the right size for this now,' she said, rubbing at the side of her thighs.

'Brave, though,' replied Lia, smiling. 'It looks terrifying from where I'm standing.'

Hattie moved forward to greet her friend.

'This is my mum, Rose,' added Lia. 'Say hello, Mum. This is a friend of mine, Hattie, and that's her daughter, Poppy.'

The old lady beamed at them both. 'Have you seen any daisies?' she asked.

Lia gave Hattie a pointed look. 'We've been trying to find some to make daisy chains with,' she explained. 'But it's not really the right time of year.'

Hattie smiled. 'Oh, that's a shame. How about conker-collecting? The kids have had most of them, but there's still some about over by the path to the river. Chestnuts too, I think.'

'How about that, Mum? That sounds like a good idea. You love the colour of conkers, don't you?' She smiled at Hattie gratefully. 'We've been having a lovely walk this afternoon, but I think Mum's beginning to get a bit tired now.'

'I know the feeling. My legs are worn out from all that swinging. Would you like to come and sit down on the bench, Rose? We can watch Poppy swinging, if you like.'

As if to emphasise the point her daughter put on a turn of speed and went even higher. Hattie tried not to let her anxiety show.

Lia pointed. 'Do you remember how we used to come here after school, Mum? I think I was still in the junior school then. There was a massive slide too, much bigger than the one there is now.' She held her mum's hand. 'I went down so fast one day I shot off the bottom, do you remember?'

Her mum turned to her, bright blue eyes searching her face. 'I do!' she said. 'You screamed the place down.'

Lia laughed. 'I'm not surprised. Come on Mum, let's go and sit, shall we?'

Hattie watched her friend closely but she seemed quite relaxed. Perhaps today was a good day; she hoped so. She wasn't sure how long they would be able to stay on the bench but Rose seemed quite content at the moment just to sit and watch the world go by. It must be odd, she thought, for Lia to bring her mum here, back to the park she used to play in as a child, their roles reversed. Too much of today had made Hattie feel like a child again; seeking affection, fighting for her mother's approval.

She looked across at her daughter playing so innocently on the swing. Perhaps it was simply that, in the years before Poppy was born, Hattie had been too preoccupied with her own life – her fiancé, her wedding, her busy social calendar – to notice that anything was amiss with her family. Or were the difficulties she perceived confined only to more recent times? She tried to remember back to the period before Poppy arrived, but her memories of that time eluded her.

She felt a gentle nudge to her arm. 'Penny for them?' said Lia.

Hattie's attention snapped back to the present. 'Oh, sorry. I was miles away.'

'I can see that. You were staring at Poppy, though. Is everything all right?'

Hattie blushed, caught out. 'I was just thinking about mother-and-daughter relationships,' she said. 'Bit complicated sometimes, aren't they?'

Lia tucked a strand of hair behind her ear. 'They're certainly that. Although, why do I get the feeling you're not talking about you and Poppy?'

Hattie pulled a face. 'Sorry, I shouldn't be talking like this. It's just seeing you with your mum, and how things are for you… it's hard, I can see that, and yet I know you'd do anything for her. Whatever she does, you still love her, you still care for her to the best of your ability. I feel the same way about Poppy. I get this ferocious wave of love for her sometimes – when I see her doing something she adores, when she's happy and carefree – and I think I'd do anything to keep her that way. I can't contemplate a time when that might be different, but I dunno…'

A sudden gust of wind blew a handful of leaves across the grass in front of them and Lia watched them wistfully for a moment. 'Love is complex, isn't it? Sometimes, when I've had a really bad day…' She turned to look back at her mum, lowering her voice, 'I could happily throttle her, and yet other times, I'd walk over hot coals if it would make her better. One minute she can be yelling abuse at me, and then the next she does something so gentle, so tender, that it wipes out all the bad things in an instant. I suppose, at the end of the day, she's still my mum and I'm still her daughter, even if she can't always remember that. There's a bond there that ties us together, that weaves its way through everything that we do or say.'

Hattie nodded, thinking about Lia's words for a moment, recognising that essentially she felt the same. And yet why could she not seem to regain that relationship with her own mother? Why had things changed so much? And perhaps more importantly, what had happened to change them? She let her gaze wander back towards Poppy; she would hate it if anything ever came between them. It was clear to her now that she owed it to herself and her mum to try and put things right; ignoring things wasn't the answer after all. The easy way out, but cowardly too. She took a deep breath and turned back to Lia with a bright smile.

'Sorry. I'm being rather maudlin, and it's such a lovely day. Ignore me. I've been over to my mum's this afternoon with my sister to do the final fittings on the bridesmaids' dresses and… let's just say it wasn't a great afternoon. However, it is still a beautiful day and I'm determined to enjoy it now.'

'I don't mind talking about it, Hattie, if you want to.'

Hattie smiled back at her friend. 'Another day perhaps. Besides which, I've just remembered that I owe you a huge apology.'

'Whatever for?'

'Ah… well I think I might have accidentally given Jasper your address. I didn't mean to, but we'd had quite a bit to drink and he was so…' She broke off at the sight of Lia's face. 'He's been to see you, hasn't he?'

Lia nodded, a rather stern expression on her face. 'He has…' she said, ominously, 'and I'm afraid I pretty much threw him out. Not that I blame you at all, Hattie, please don't think that. I can see that he's very charming when he wants to be, but what a blinking nerve! Do you know why he wanted to see me?'

'Well that's why I gave him your address actually. I know it's a bit unusual, but I thought it would be such a lovely thing to do. Nerve-wracking yes, but wonderful at the same time. Didn't you think so?'

Lia stared at her, blinking. 'Well I know I'm a bit old-fashioned and things have probably moved on a lot, but I still don't think you can just waltz over to someone and tell them you need them to be your girlfriend. Not for real, but at a specific time on a specific date, like you're booking an appointment to have your hair done. If I wanted a boyfriend – not that I do by the way, but if I did – I'd rather like to choose one myself, and at least be wooed, not commanded to take up the post.'

Hattie did a double-take. 'He wanted *what*? He didn't say anything about wanting a girlfriend. Jesus, that's a bit forward.'

'I know. I don't know what he said to you, but he turned up with a bunch of roses, flattered my mum and got her wrapped around his little finger and then when I asked him what he had come around for he suddenly went all coy, saying that he thought I'd got the wrong idea. When I told him I didn't want any kind of romantic entanglements right now, he said he didn't either. He did, however, want a *fake* girlfriend, and he thought I could be it. Charming! That made me feel really good about myself, I can tell you.'

Hattie was just about to reply when a thought struck her. 'Hang on a minute. Something's not quite right here. Did he not mention the dance to you at all, and the whole family thing…?'

Lia frowned. 'No… well, he said something about needing someone who was able to dance, but that was hardly a compliment; he could have loitered outside the dance class and picked anyone.'

Hattie shook her head. 'But that was what we spent so long talking about that night – this big dance he's got coming up; how his career depends on it, how he's beholden to his family even though he hates being in that position… Ring any bells?'

Lia was shaking her head. 'He didn't mention anything like that.'

The two women stared at one another in confusion, until Lia gave a slight grimace. 'Although, to be fair, I maybe didn't give him the chance to say any of that… I sort of asked him to leave…' She bit at her lip. 'Did I jump to conclusions, do you think?'

'Possibly…' admitted Hattie. 'Although it sounds like the idiot didn't explain himself all that well.'

Lia sighed. 'Tell me what you know,' she said, with a glance at her mum.

Hattie sucked in a breath, trying hard to remember the details of that evening. 'So, basically, his family are like mega-important business people,' she began, 'and every year they have this big charity bash on the day before Christmas Eve, which raises thousands of pounds for the local community. Well, as Jasper put it, it helps to assuage their consciences for the other eleven months of the year when all they do is trample over other people. Anyway… this year he's been charged with the task of organising this event, knowing that at the end of the evening there will be a big fuss made and he'll be welcomed into the company's arms as a new partner.'

There was a groan from beside her. 'And this affects me how?'

'Because at the start of the event, which is really posh – did I mention that? – there's a formal dance, which is kicked off by whichever member of the family has organised the event and they do this solo thing that "opens" the evening and sets the tone, blah blah blah. Jasper's other family members are all married, so when it was their turns, they already had partners.'

Lia put her head in her hands. 'Oh my God… And that's what he wants me to do? Pretend to be his girlfriend and then dance in front of a whole crowd of people? He must be joking. What on earth would make him think I'd want to do anything of the sort…?'

Hattie made a small noise in her throat. 'Erm, that might be my fault,' she whispered. 'I know how you love to dance, and you're doing so well… Besides, it will be amazing. Think what it will look like. And so close to Christmas: thousands of sparkly lights, champagne, huge Christmas trees all covered in decorations… And oh, the dresses! Think about all the wonderful dresses…' She stopped suddenly, looking up at Lia. 'You're not really buying this, are you?'

It was clear that Lia didn't know quite what to say. 'I can see why you thought of me and I'm not saying it wouldn't be lovely… it's just not my cup of tea, that's all. I would love to be able to dance properly, but whenever I picture it there's only ever two of us, just me and a mystery partner in a huge empty ballroom… and no-one else.'

Hattie leaned across and took Lia's hand. 'I'm so sorry,' she said. 'I think I've made a complete mess of this. It's just that when Jasper told me about it he sounded so anxious, so desperate and helpless. I know he's very good-looking and charming with it, but I honestly didn't think he was trying anything funny. He genuinely seemed distressed. I would never have given him your address, otherwise.'

Lia squeezed her hand. 'I know that, Hattie, and none of this is your fault. In fact, to be fair, I rather think I jumped to conclusions. I certainly didn't give Jasper a fair hearing. Perhaps I owe him an apology, or at least the opportunity to explain properly.'

Beside her Rose was beginning to fidget. 'I think I ought to get going, but...' she paused for a moment, her head on one side, 'did Jasper say he would be at the class this week?' she asked. 'Only, perhaps—'

'Oh, yes, he'll be there,' replied Hattie, with a knowing smile.

Chapter 20

Lucy looked up from her notebook. 'Sorry, Oscar, I was miles away. Is everything all right?'

She was standing behind the counter, the only staff member on duty while Rachel was at lunch, and using the time alone to surreptitiously fill a few more pages with her exuberant handwriting. After Callum had gone home the night before she had been suddenly struck by an idea, which now that it had come to her demanded to be acted upon; she couldn't get the words down quickly enough.

Perhaps it had been listening to Clive and Callum chatting away about their businesses that had set her thinking – watching them revel in doing the thing they loved, day in day out. The two of them had been like small boys discussing their football heroes, talking nineteen to the dozen, and interrupting each other as their voices rose and fell in excitement. It was a long time since she had felt that way, but finally putting pencil to paper felt so good, she didn't want to stop. To her amazement she hadn't even noticed Oscar approach and had no idea how long he had been standing in front of her.

'Oh, fine and dandy,' he replied. 'Same as always, although I'm not sure the same can be said for you, my dear.'

He'd been late today and looked a little jumpy, but Lucy had been so busy she hadn't had the opportunity to talk to him properly. On the odd occasion when she had glanced in his direction she wasn't absolutely convinced he was reading the book in front of him, even though he was pretending to. Standing in front of her now, she could feel the waves of anxiety radiating from him.

Lucy gave him a quizzical look. 'And why wouldn't everything be fine with me, Oscar?' Surely he hadn't been able to see what she'd been writing.

'Only that you look a little tired. I've been watching you this morning; rushing around as usual, hardly stopping. In fact, I don't think I've seen you have a cup of tea since I've been here. It must surely be time for you to have a break?' He looked pointedly at his watch. 'We can't have the captain of the ship going down, you know.'

'Well, that's very kind of you,' replied Lucy, somewhat perplexed. 'But I'm honestly okay. I'm taking my lunch a little later today, that's all. Rachel has a dental check-up and so is having a bit longer than usual, but she'll be back in a few minutes.' She smiled. 'At least, she should be. If she isn't there'll be hell to pay.'

Oscar nodded his approval. 'Well, in that case I shall stop fussing,' he said. 'But you make sure you take your full time, won't you?'

He smiled again – a little awkwardly, thought Lucy – before raising a hand as if to wave and ambling back to his seat. She watched him go, deep in thought. It was an innocent enough conversation, and not totally unusual, as Oscar was a kindly soul. But why did she get the feeling he was trying to get her out of the way?

True to her word, Rachel returned shortly afterwards, and it only took Lucy a matter of moments to grab her coat and bag before heading for the door. She deliberately looked in Oscar's direction to give him a thumbs-up that she was leaving, but his head was bent resolutely to the paper. She smiled to herself and walked out the door.

She had only just reached the edge of the car park when she realised that she had left her letter behind and, tutting, retraced her steps to the library. It was tempting just to leave posting it until the next day, but she didn't want to run the risk of it arriving a day late for her friend's birthday. With any luck, she could sneak back in and out without anyone stopping her to ask something. She glanced into the IT room as she passed down the hallway and, as she did so, became aware of familiar voices – one of which she expected, but the other taking her completely by surprise.

Callum and Oscar were huddled around a computer screen, deep in conversation. Surprising as it was, Lucy thought it was rather nice to know that the members of the book club met each other outside of their meetings, though she remembered that Oscar had been rather scathing about Callum's family. Lucy had no desire to eavesdrop but she hesitated just for a moment; something was different here. All morning Oscar had seemed uneasy, preoccupied, and, she noted, even though he had answered her when she had asked him how he was, he had immediately deflected the question back to her. And now, he was listening to Callum with an eagerness that she found all the more intriguing; his shoulders were still a little hunched, but to her eyes he looked excited, rather than anxious. And something else too – something in the way that he looked at Callum, drinking in his words and leaning in. Lucy thought for a moment how best to describe the emotion she saw there, and then she realised what it was: fleeting and uncertain, but very definitely hope.

She retrieved her letter from her locker in the staffroom and headed back outside once more, resolutely staring down the hallway as she did so. She had grown used to the change in Callum over the last few weeks as their friendship had developed, but now here was Oscar, also looking much happier about things. Whatever had caused this change was obviously Callum's doing, and that made her more pleased than she could say.

Since she had first invited Callum around for tea, the invitation had been extended several times over, and he was now a more or less permanent fixture at the Picklescott dining table. He and Clive got on like a house on fire, and in return for help with his business plan, Callum was building Earl Grey's a brilliant website.

Sometimes Lucy sat with them, but not always. She much preferred to sit back and watch them, her pencil dancing over the page of her notebook from time to time. It was not the fact that Callum's confidence was soaring that most fascinated her, or the pleasure she gained from seeing him step closer to realising his dreams for running his own business – it was the fact that although whenever he arrived he brought a little of the burden of his home life with him, he always left looking so much lighter and taller. It was her family that Callum came for, of that she was certain. It was the feelings of warmth they gave him that he lapped up, like a cat basking in the heat of a fire, its limbs stretched out to luxuriate in the feeling. Callum was learning what the word 'home' really meant.

★

'How can she still live in the same county? That doesn't seem possible, after all this time.'

Callum smiled at Oscar. 'But you've lived here all of your life. Why shouldn't she? Not everyone moves around incessantly, you know.'

The old man shook his head in wonder. 'But I expected her to live in the Outer Hebrides, at least. I never dreamed for one minute that she would be close to me.' He scratched the end of his chin. 'Do you think she's been here all the while? That I might even have seen her one day, and never known? That Mary and I might have bumped into her in the supermarket and glanced into her basket idly wondering what she was having for her tea…?'

Callum took in a breath. He laid a hand gently on Oscar's arm, part in sympathy, part in warning.

Oscar turned to look at him full on. 'I know; I'm getting ahead of myself here.'

'I just don't want you to get hurt, Oscar. There are no guarantees, and it's still very early days.'

The look on Oscar's face when he discovered that his daughter had been found had almost reduced Callum to tears. He would have loved nothing more than for it to be the joyous reunion that Oscar dreamed of but, like a lot of things in life, it wasn't that simple. Callum would have to be very careful how he imparted the information he'd received to Oscar; the outcome would very much depend on how he handled things. For now, Oscar only needed to know that the charity had found his daughter, and that she was alive. The other details could wait. It was best if Oscar got used to things, one step at a time.

'So, what happens now?' Oscar asked. 'I know there are still things that need to be verified, but if she wants to meet me? They can arrange that, can't they?'

'I think it's best if we take their advice on what might be the most appropriate way forward. The email just asked us to get back in touch with them once we've had a chance to think about the next step. We should do exactly that, and take it from there.' He turned back to the computer screen. 'Why don't you take a day or two to think about it?' He took in Oscar's startled expression. 'I know you've probably thought about nothing else for a long time, but there will be no hiding from what *might* happen, so you need to be sure you're ready for what *could* happen.' He smiled in sympathy. 'I'm sorry if you think I'm stalling you, but I think it's for the best.'

Oscar gave a wry smile. 'Read minds as well, can you?' He scrutinised Callum's face for a moment. 'But I do understand what you're trying to do,' he said eventually. 'And I thank you for it. You always think that making mistakes and taking rash decisions is the prerogative of the young, don't you? But I can see that I'm quite capable of doing the very same myself.' He twisted the signet ring on his little finger. 'So, I will be patient and take your kind and thoughtful advice. As much as it pains me to have to wait that long, I'll contact you again at the end of the week and let you know whether I'm going to follow this up.' He sighed. 'I've waited this long, another couple of days won't hurt, will it?'

Callum nodded. 'I think it's the right decision,' he said, 'I'm here all week. Why don't you pop back in to see me on Friday, and we can take it from there?'

Oscar got slowly to his feet. 'Right you are, young man,' he said, placing a hand on Callum's shoulder. 'And, thank you.' He dipped his head in farewell as he made his way from the room.

He would need to speak to Lucy about this now, thought Callum. It had gone too far for him to handle by himself and Lucy would know what to do, he knew she would. He felt the burden of the responsibility pressing heavily on his shoulders. He'd do anything to have this all work out for Oscar, but sadly it would be out of his hands soon. He glanced at his watch, wondering if Lucy was back from her lunch yet. He was just about to go and look for her when someone plonked herself onto the seat next to his in a whirl of energy.

'Hiya!' she said.

Callum grinned broadly; he hadn't seen Phoebe for weeks. 'You look well.' In fact, Phoebe looked like the proverbial cat that got the cream.

She gave him a surreptitious wink. 'I am well,' she said. '*Very* well. All thanks to you, of course.'

'What have I got to do with anything?' he asked, genuinely puzzled.

To his surprise, Phoebe blew him a kiss. 'Perhaps I should be your manager and hire you out to other women whose boyfriends have gone off the boil,' she said with a grin. 'You've worked wonders.'

Callum swallowed. 'Have I?'

'Oh yes,' came the quick reply. 'Gary is now well and truly "engaged", if you know what I mean… in every way. Who knew that a teeny bit of competition would work such wonders in the bedroom? Our sex life has gone through the roof! It's just like it was when we first got together.'

Callum flicked a glance around the room, blushing furiously. What if someone heard her?

He leaned forward. 'For God's sake, Phoebe, keep your voice down… and for Christ's sake explain – I haven't got a clue what you're talking about.'

She sat back suddenly in her chair, staring at Callum as if seeing him for the first time. She grinned again. 'Sorry, I didn't explain myself very well, did I? I'm a bit excited.'

'Yeah, I can see that,' muttered Callum. 'I take it the wedding preparations are going well?'

Phoebe held out her hand with its bright red polished fingernails, turning it this way and that so that her ring caught the light, flashing little pinpoints of colour around the room. 'I can't give you all the credit,' she said, 'I acted my socks off too, if the truth be known, but whatever the reason, you helping me out with all of this made Gary realise that we're not married yet, and if he wanted to keep me, he was going to have to get his act together – and that's exactly what he's done.'

Callum frowned. He wasn't sure he liked what he was hearing. 'But I haven't done anything, Phoebe. What has any of this got to do with me?'

'Well, only that me dropping your name into conversation every two minutes has worked miracles, that's all. A little bit of the green-eyed monster and all that.' She grinned at him. 'And you needn't look like that, I made sure I was really blasé about it, you know, like there couldn't possibly be anything between us, and that I could never fancy you. I even made out that you were a bit soppy like, you know.'

'Jesus, thanks Phoebe.'

'No, no, I don't mean it, you know I don't, but just so that Gary wouldn't get completely the wrong idea. Enough to make him think that maybe he shouldn't take me for granted, you know, that other people might find me attractive… To be honest, I think we were both as bad as one another. We've been together quite a while now, and the wedding preparations seemed to drag on. It had all got a bit boring, I suppose. Now we're all fired up again. It's made us realise that what we have is special.' She smiled brightly at him. 'There's nothing for you to worry about.'

'Really?' asked Callum weakly. 'Are you sure about that?'

'Don't be daft.' She laughed. 'Gary's a pussycat.' She tapped her fingers on the keyboard in front of her. 'So, how are you, anyway? Still working on your business ideas?'

Callum swallowed, trying to unglue his brain sufficiently to make sense of what Phoebe had been saying. There was something really not right about all of this, but Phoebe looked so happy he was reluctant to ask her for more details. In the end, self-preservation got the better of him.

'I've put together a few ideas, yes,' he said tentatively. 'In fact, I wanted to have a chat to you about some of them, but maybe now's not the right time. I can't see Gary going for it, not now he's probably baying for my blood.'

Phoebe's head swivelled around to look at him, her ponytail swishing to one side. 'Why would he be doing that?' she asked, surprised. 'He's totally cool about you and me.'

'Phoebe, there is no you and me.'

'Exactly!' she exclaimed. 'Honestly, Callum, it's the oldest trick in the book. All I did was mention a few times how much help you'd been sorting out stuff for the wedding, and then when I'd got Gary's attention I showed him what we'd done, all the things I learned. He knows there's nothing between us, and he was chuffed to bits with all the computer stuff I can do now. All I did was show him the possibility of what might have happened if I fancied you, but seeing as I don't, it's okay. You don't mind, do you? I know you don't fancy me either.'

Callum wasn't exactly sure what he thought. He knew that Phoebe's words were meant to reassure him, but strangely they were having the opposite effect. In fact, his stomach was churning.

'No, I don't mind,' he said slowly. 'Listen, Phoebe, I haven't had my lunch yet and I'm starving. I'm just going to pop out for a bit. You don't need my help now, do you?'

Phoebe had already turned back to the computer. 'Nah, I'm good,' she replied.

The day outside was a little cool and it only took a minute for Callum to realise that he should have brought his jacket with him. A weak sun was trying to break through the clouds, but a cool wind was blowing across the car park and Callum could feel the hairs on his arms begin to rise. He blew out his cheeks, wrapping his arms around himself as he leaned up against the wall beside the library steps. He wasn't sure what had just happened inside but it didn't feel right.

He supposed he should be happy. His relationship with Phoebe, if you could call it that, had only ever been about trying to help her out. He had enjoyed their conversations; she was easy to talk to and, as the weeks had gone by, he had felt quite comfortable in her company. Couple this with his IT duties in the library and he was beginning to think he had got this whole 'talking to people' thing down to a fine art – or at least to a point where people didn't think he was a complete prat. He knew that Phoebe had dropped his name into conversations with Gary before, she had already mentioned it, so why did it feel different this time? Why did he feel like he had been used?

The answer, of course, was staring him in the face: because it was so very different from how he felt about Lucy. He'd wanted to help her too, to relieve the burden that the library's never-ending IT problems caused her, but instead of taking what he had to offer and then dismissing him once she'd got what she wanted, Lucy had set about helping *him*.

He'd been a complete idiot over this whole business with Phoebe. He had thought he'd been so helpful with her wedding planning, but really he'd just been a handy accessory in her plot to make her fiancé jealous. It hadn't helped that he'd been captivated by all the images he had seen of people in love; the romance of it all, a desire to experience all the things that were missing from his own life and that he so desperately wanted. Something had changed. Now he didn't feel quite the same as he had those few weeks ago, and Phoebe and his silly business ideas were no longer what he needed to make him happy. It was time to get real.

He shivered suddenly as his stomach gave a loud growl of hunger. First, he needed to find something to eat, and second, he needed to know what to do about Oscar.

Chapter 21

Lia could feel the nervous excitement fluttering in her stomach. What would they learn today? Would she be able to master it? Usually, as soon as she took her partner's hand, she would relax into the rhythm and movement and all her anxieties would fade away. Today, though, the nerves were proper nerves. The last time she had seen Jasper she had been blunt to the point of rudeness.

In the days leading up to the class, she had replayed in her head the conversation she'd had with Hattie in the park. The more she thought about it, the more she realised that she had jumped to conclusions over Jasper's behaviour, and never given him the opportunity to fully explain his very unusual request. Perhaps she had made a terrible mistake and the flowers, the charm and the anxiety were all genuine. He had acted with a gentleness and real generosity of spirit towards her mother, and those things were hard to fake.

The room was beginning to fill up around her, and Lia caught Hattie's eye as she glanced around. It was three minutes to seven and there was no sign of Jasper. Already people were beginning to join up with their usual partners, and Lia hovered anxiously by the tutor, wondering if she should resume her former partnership with Joe. It would be perfectly understandable if Jasper didn't come, and even if he did, it would be perfectly understandable if he didn't want to dance with Lia.

A loud banging of the double doors at the side of the room made her look up, along with everyone else. Jasper. Lia smiled. She had fallen for it herself before; those doors were half the weight they looked and swung wildly if you gave them too much of a shove. Jasper's hasty entrance into the dance hall had caused a lot more of a scene than he'd intended.

For a moment Lia thought that he was about to turn on his heels and leave but, after a lengthy pause staring at the ground, he set off determinedly in her direction. She took a step back, quite alarmed by his pace, only to watch him stalk straight past her without so much as a nod. He approached the tutor, taking her arm and bending his head low to hers in urgent conversation. The tutor's head rose and quickly scanned the room. Lia moved forward, hoping to catch her eye, but her gaze settled upon an older woman across the room. Lia didn't know her name but she was an accomplished dancer.

She couldn't deny the disappointment she felt. It was what she had wanted, but now that it looked like she was actually going to lose her opportunity to dance with Jasper again, she felt deflated. This shouldn't be how it ended. She might not want to be Jasper's date to the charity ball, but she could at least help him to get there; she owed him that much. To her surprise, she found her arm on his even before she knew what she was going to say. He looked up, startled and a little embarrassed.

'Hello again,' she said simply.

Jasper nodded, his eyes raking the floor. 'I'm sorry,' he said. 'I thought it best if we didn't—'

'Dance?' suggested Lia.

'Speak,' finished Jasper at the same time.

'Oh.'

'I had no wish to make you angry,' he said, 'but it seemed I failed in that regard also.'

Lia could hardly deny it. 'Perhaps,' she acknowledged. 'But then I also failed to give you a fair hearing, which was the very least you deserved.'

Beside them the tutor sneaked a glance at her watch.

Lia pulled Jasper to one side. 'How about we dance?' she suggested. 'And the rest we can get to as and when the opportunity presents itself. That is, unless you'd rather…'

He looked up, a soft curve settling on his wide mouth. 'No, I'd rather dance with you. Shall we?' And with that he led Lia out onto the floor.

It was different this time. Jasper still danced with ferocious concentration but even Lia could see the huge improvement in his technique. He moved with a light placing of his feet; quick, decisive, and assured. In fact, on several occasions she realised that she was the one wrong-footed; Lia felt every note when she danced, but this sometimes came at the expense of her technique. Jasper, on the other hand, danced like he was following a series of technical drawings, in need of a bit of colour to bring them to life. As they swept past one of the large mirrors in the room, her heart thudded with the realisation that if they could each impart to the other a little of their individual flair, they could be very good indeed.

She laughed. 'Have you been practising?' she asked.

Jasper's brows knitted together in a frown. 'I don't have much time,' was all he said.

'Ah,' she said, acknowledging his situation. 'Why don't you come back to mine for a coffee after the class, and this time I'll let you explain.'

★

'You're an only child, aren't you?' he asked as Lia placed two mugs of tea on the table. 'So you know the weight of expectation placed on you to carry forward the family line, heaped on you alone because you've no other siblings to dilute it?'

'Well, I'm not sure there was ever any expectation placed on me, at least not in the sense you mean.' She cocked her head to one side. 'There was certainly expectation of another kind…'

Jasper's olive eyes regarded her solemnly from across the table. 'How so?' he asked.

Lia picked at a scratch on the table surface. 'Only that my mum's never been what you'd call a strong person. She didn't cope well when my dad left, and although I was only a young child, I learned to be self-sufficient pretty quickly. Mum soon became reliant on me, too – even before she got ill. And now she depends on me entirely.'

'I think I may just have qualified for the most insensitive idiot of the year award,' said Jasper with a grimace. 'Honestly, I think I deserve to be thrown out again. Shoving my petty problems in your face is the height of selfishness, given what you cope with on a daily basis.'

'Only because your desire not to let your family down is so strong. I wouldn't say that was selfish. I can see how trapped you feel, how tied down you are by your sense of duty to your family. That's a feeling I know well. I didn't give you the opportunity to explain before, but now's your chance. I'm not promising anything, but I'd like to understand why this is so important to you.'

Jasper fiddled with the buttons on his shirt. 'Have you even heard of us?' he asked.

'No, but then that's hardly surprising. I hardly step foot out the house, and big business is not exactly my forte.'

'No, mine neither… and that's the problem, I guess,' replied Jasper. 'I love my family, but not what we do. I never have done. My dad was born to it, as were his brothers and his father before him. But where they all walked the walk and talked the talk, I stumble my way through the days with a very patient secretary who just about manages to keep me from making a complete arse of myself.'

'But just because you're family, it doesn't necessarily follow that you have the same skill set – surely they must see that?' Lia studied his face. 'It's no crime to want to do something different. I'm sure they'd understand.'

'They'd accept it if they had to,' said Jasper, running a hand through his hair, 'but I'm not sure they'd ever understand it. They live, eat and breathe the family business, and they think everyone wants a taste of it… except for me, that is. I think it's poisonous.'

Lia stood up, crossing to a cupboard. 'Would you like a biscuit?' she asked, reaching in to take down a packet and placing it on the table. 'So, what do they do then? Why don't you like it?'

'They trample all over people,' Jasper replied bluntly, reaching forward to take a cookie. 'Of course, they dress it all up so that it looks nice and appealing. Businesses fail for all sorts of reasons, but often it's because there's a weak link. So, they go in as "consultants", under the guise of saving them, when in reality they're only there to make money by exploiting their failings – and by putting stress on the weakest link until it breaks, they're the ones who get to come to the rescue. By rescue, I mean selling off component parts of the business, sometimes all of it, and coming out looking like the sun's shining from every orifice. They make people think our presence in their company was what they wanted all along, but really they're there to destroy it.'

'Oh.' Lia swallowed. 'That doesn't sound quite so appealing.'

Jasper sighed. 'I'm being melodramatic.' He squinted up at her. 'But some days that does feel like what we do. That, and putting on a good show.'

'Is that where the charity ball comes in?'

Jasper looked at her for a moment, a gentle frown on his face. 'No… it was a metaphor,' he said, 'like when—'

'I know what it was,' said Lia with a grin, which faded as she took in his expression. 'I was just trying to… you know… well, lighten the mood a little, make a bit of a joke?'

Jasper was staring at her.

'Not a very good one, admittedly,' she muttered.

She heard a loud crunch as Jasper bit into his biscuit. He chewed determinedly. 'You see,' he said, 'that's my problem. I take it all too seriously.'

Lia dunked the last of her own biscuit into her tea, throwing it into her mouth before it disintegrated. 'So, what makes you *un*serious?' she asked. 'Something must do.'

For a second it was as if she had turned on a light. Jasper's face cleared in an instant, brightened by a sudden smile.

'Well yes, there is something,' he acknowledged. 'Something that's more important to me than anything – and that's the plan. That's what I'm going to do when I quit.'

'And?' she queried. 'What is it?'

He touched the side of his nose, infuriatingly. 'You'll laugh,' he said. 'So for now all you need to know is that after the charity ball, after the dance, I intend to make it happen. *For now…*'

'You want to go out with a bang?'

Jasper pulled a face. 'Sort of,' he said. 'I want to go out without having made a fool of myself, or my family. I want our reputation to be upheld.

I want the ball to be the success it always is and for everyone to see my promotion to partnership. It's important that people see our strength, our unity; anything less would weaken our position in the market.'

'And afterwards?'

'Afterwards, I let them down gently. I give them time to come up with some plausible excuse for my leaving that will allow them to save face. An illness perhaps, I don't know.'

Lia could feel the air around her go still. 'This is really important to you, isn't it?' she said eventually. There was no need to wait for a reply. 'But I'm really not cut out for this sort of thing, Jasper. I can help you to dance, we can learn together, but I don't think I could ever get up at some fancy ball and dance in front of hundreds of people. I'd die of embarrassment.'

'You'd be amazing.' He looked down at the table for a moment. 'I have money, Lia,' he added. 'For things; a dress, shoes, jewellery, whatever you wanted... if that would help.'

A rueful smile pulled at the corners of her mouth. 'We'd need to practise,' she said. 'A lot.'

'Whatever you say.'

'In your spare time...'

'Of course. Whenever you want.'

She was about to say something else when a sudden thought hit her. Her hand flew to her mouth. 'What am I saying!' she exclaimed. 'How can I possibly do all this? Who's going to look after Mum?'

Jasper looked panic-stricken. 'I could come here,' he said. 'And whatever care Rose needed, I could pay for... Your mum would be well looked after, and you'd still be on hand if there was a problem.' He glanced around the room, thinking on his feet. 'We could use the dining room. Push the table and chairs back against the wall?'

'It's barely big enough.'

'It's a start.'

Lia searched his face. She wanted to say no. She wanted to find reasons why it couldn't possibly work, but, oh… how she wanted to dance too. There were tiny flutterings at the edges of her mind – glimmering images of what it might be like to dance, over and over again, her feet a whirl, her hair flowing behind her as she spun faster and faster…

'Come on Thursday,' she said. 'About seven.'

Chapter 22

'Callum, I'm so sorry. The day just ran away with me, one thing after another. Are you okay?' He gave her an unconvincing nod. 'Listen, I won't be much longer, are you all right to wait? You could go home if you want to, and I'll meet you there.'

Callum stared at her, jolted by the sudden realisation of what her words meant to him. When Lucy said 'go home' she was talking about *her* house; he no longer made the distinction between Lucy's and his own, but more importantly neither did Lucy. When had that happened? he wondered. He narrowed his eyes, taking in the soft golden curls of her hair, which she now no longer straightened each morning. It looked natural, more gentle, and it really suited her. Her face wore the length of her day, tiredness darkening the delicate skin under her blue eyes and flushing her cheeks. He felt the urge to reach out a hand to soothe her, and swallowed hard as emotion churned within him for the third time that day.

'We could get chips or something?'

Her voice was prompting a reply, but Callum could only nod, struck dumb in the moment.

'Or a takeaway of some sort, I don't mind…'

He dragged himself back to the conversation. 'No, chips are fine. I could go and get them if you like, while I'm waiting. Do you want the usual?'

Lucy considered his question, pursing her lips together. 'I think it's going to have to be,' she said. 'And don't forget—'

'I know, plenty of salt and vinegar.' Because that was another thing. He *did* know what her usual was. He *did* know that she liked plenty of salt and vinegar and that when the food was on her plate she would liberally cover everything in brown sauce too. Just as he knew that she covered roast dinners in gravy and puddings in custard, and that she had spoonsful of pickle in her cheese sandwiches. Lucy couldn't abide dry food.

He logged off from the computer and picked his jacket up from the back of the chair, shrugging it on. It had long since got dark and the evening air had a definite nip to it. He gave a smile and fished in his pocket, checking for his wallet.

'I won't be long,' he added. 'I'll meet you outside, shall I?' He didn't wait for a reply, knowing that it wouldn't take Lucy long to cash up and close down the library for the day, but also anxious to get a little fresh air.

★

The tea-time rush had been and gone and Callum was served quickly; chips and two pieces of steaming fish just out of the fryer now nestled in his arms. The smell of the vinegar was making him salivate and he picked up his pace as he turned the corner of the road to walk back to the library. The lights were still on as he approached but he knew that Lucy would appear any minute now. He crossed the car park to meet her by the door, but as he walked, deep in thought, it took a good half a minute to realise that someone else was already standing there. A tall, fit-looking bloke with close-cropped dark hair.

'Can I help you?' Callum asked, fearing that Lucy would get the fright of her life opening the door to find someone other than him on the other side.

The man's face, dark with designer stubble, turned towards him. 'I was wondering if I'd missed you, but I guess not,' he said. 'You must be Callum,' he added. 'Not many blokes with poncey curly hair around these days.'

A ripple of anxiety passed through Callum. He was used to caustic remarks from his brothers, but not from complete strangers. Particularly ones who were a lot bigger than him.

'Callum it is then,' the stranger added. 'Or you'd be keen to tell me otherwise, wouldn't you? 'Cause, yeah, you've read it right: I do look like I'm about to give you a pasting.'

Thus far in his life Callum had managed to avoid being thumped. He'd come close once or twice, but his brothers had taught him that taking the line of least resistance was usually best. He wasn't big on machismo, and until recently had assumed most people thought he was a loser anyway, so standing up for himself was never very high on his list of priorities. Tonight he felt a little different, though. Tonight, Lucy was about to step through the door and see something she really shouldn't have to see. Whoever this clown was had nothing to do with her, and Callum couldn't run the risk that she might get hurt herself. If he was going to get a thrashing there probably wasn't much he could do about it, but the very least he could do was take the fight elsewhere and put Lucy out of harm's way. Still clutching his fish and chips tight to his chest, Callum took a deep breath – and ran.

The questions crowding his brain would have to wait; his only concern was putting distance between himself and the muscle man. He needn't have bothered; his small stature was no match for the long legs of whoever it was with an axe to grind, and it was only a matter of seconds before he was jerked backwards by the scruff of his neck, his jacket twisted into the fist of the man chasing him. He was pulled roughly into his chest and then spun around to face him, both arms held fast in an iron grip.

'Fucking coward!' the man spat. 'Stand still, you little runt.'

Callum did as he was told, the hot chips burning his skin through their paper and the thin material of his tee shirt.

'Fancied your chances, did you?' The man shook Callum hard. 'Big man, eh? Not so big from where I'm standing... Phoebe was right, no reason why she'd fancy you. I mean, look at you – pathetic.' He let go of Callum's arms with a shove, his face drawn into a sneer.

The penny dropped. There were a million and one things that Callum could say – probably *should* say – but at that precise moment he reasoned that none of them would do any good. He sighed, letting his shoulders drop.

'Gary, I presume?' he said with a resigned air. 'Fiancé of Phoebe, the girl I've been helping in the library. The one planning her wedding...'

'Yeah, that's right. The girl who's marrying *me*, not you, sunshine. Got it?'

'The policeman...?'

'Yeah... which is the only reason why my hand is not currently round your throat...'

'You're a real charmer, aren't you?'

Gary took a step closer so that his face was only inches from Callum's.

'Don't get smart. I might not be able to touch you, but I can still make your life a real misery if I want to. It'll be your word against mine. Nothing you can do about it. Believe me, it's not worth it.'

Callum held up a hand. 'Yeah, I believe you. And you're right, I'm worthless scum, not the sort that Phoebe would fall for at all. I mean, look at me compared to you.'

Gary's brows knitted together as he tried to work out whether he'd just been insulted.

'You've got nothing to worry about, mate, believe me,' Callum added.

The car park suddenly dimmed as the library lights were switched off. Gary threw a glance towards the building.

'Yeah, well – I'd better not have. If I ever catch you sniffing around—'

'You won't!'

A finger was pushed into Callum's chest. 'Well then, you'd better piss off, hadn't you, before I change my mind.'

Callum managed to point a finger at the only car left in the car park. He took a step towards it. 'I'll just…' He could hear the beeping of the library alarm setting itself. 'Only, the librarian's coming,' he added, beginning to fish in his pocket for his car keys. He drew the bunch of keys out, peering at them in the dark and trying to decipher which one was for the ignition. When he looked up, Gary was gone.

★

Lucy pulled her coat around her as she locked the library door. It wasn't that she felt cold, more that it had been a long day and her tiredness was suddenly catching up with her. She longed for the comfort of home, and the salty tang of her fish supper, which, with any luck, would be waiting for her in the car park along with Callum.

She looked around for his familiar figure, expecting him to be standing close by the door, as usual. The smile was already on her face, but it fell as she spotted him by his car. He was staring into space, looking beyond the car park into the lane at the bottom, their dinner clutched tight to his chest. Even in the dusky light she could tell there was something wrong. Perhaps it was the way he was standing, or the expression on the half of his face that was towards her, but something felt different in the space that separated them. She took a step closer.

'Callum?' she called.

To her relief, he turned immediately, his face clearing and a smile replacing the tight lines of his mouth.

He waved a hand in greeting. 'Come on,' he replied. 'The chips are getting cold.'

Lucy needed no second invitation; she was starving. She climbed into the car next to him, settling her bag in the footwell and reaching for her seatbelt. Automatically, she turned to take the food from Callum as he sought to get the key into the ignition. He must have been waiting longer than she thought; his hands were so cold they were trembling. Eventually, the engine roared into life and Callum turned up the heater to full.

'Sorry,' she said. 'I didn't realise I'd taken so long.' She reached out a hand to touch his. It was like ice.

'Yeah… no… it's okay.' Callum shook his head. 'Sorry, I was miles away. What did you say?'

Lucy gave him a sideways glance, before shifting slightly in her seat. 'Only that I'd taken longer than I thought… You're cold?' she said, frowning gently. 'Callum, is everything all right? You seem a bit… odd.'

'Odd…' he repeated. 'Yeah, I'm that all right. Odd… stupid, that's me. I can think of several more words as well.'

This time she took his hand, pulling it off the steering wheel and twisting his fingers into her own. He offered no resistance. It was hard to know what to say; ten minutes ago he'd seemed fine.

'Callum, what's happened?' she asked. 'Have I done something wrong?'

Immediately his head swivelled round, his eyes seeking hers. 'No!' he said, almost fiercely. 'Nothing like that. Not you.'

'Then who, Callum?' she asked, picking up on this clue. 'Who's upset you?'

He opened his mouth to speak, and then closed it again. 'Not here,' he whispered, after a moment. 'Let's go home… please.' He pulled gently at his hand and Lucy released it, watching as he put the car into gear, but his face was turned resolutely to the front.

'Okay,' she replied. 'We'll eat, and then you've got to promise you'll tell me what's been going on. Maybe you'll feel better once you've got some food inside you,' she added hopefully.

She thought she saw a slight nod, and then they were pulling away, out onto the lane and through into the High Street. They sat in silence the whole way home.

The house was almost in darkness when they arrived, just a single light burning in the living room. Lucy stuck her head around the door to let her mum know they were home. She looked up from the bundle of yarn on her lap.

'Oh, hello love. Everything okay?'

'Yeah fine, but we're starving. I brought chips home. Do you want a cup of tea?'

'Got one, love, thanks. You go and eat.'

Lucy escaped, glad that the house was almost empty. It would give her a chance to talk to Callum, and if Lucy couldn't help, her mum would; she was great at giving advice. It struck her then, how much Callum had become a part of her life at home. He chatted to her family as if he had known them for years, and seemed just as happy in their company as he was in hers. Now that she thought about it, she realised how important this was to her. There had been times in the past when things had been very different – with Lucy's last boyfriend for example. Not the same thing of course, but seeing how easily Callum had slotted into their lives was in stark contrast to the way she had always felt so on edge bringing Pete back. She smiled to herself. Her mum didn't always say as much, but she was an excellent judge of character. The thought brought a sudden flush to her cheeks.

By the time she got back to the kitchen, Callum had already laid the table and put the plates out, ready to dish up. He was just fetching the sauce from the cupboard as she moved past him to flick the kettle on.

'Blimey, I'm hungry,' she remarked as she began to unpeel the paper around the fish. She smiled when she saw that Callum had asked for it to be wrapped separately from the chips; that way the batter stayed crispy.

Callum came to stand behind her, inhaling deeply as the vinegary smell was released. 'Yeah, me too.' He smiled, reaching past her to take down mugs from the cupboard and set about making two huge mugs of tea, delivering them to the table only seconds after Lucy had laid out the food.

For a few moments, nothing further was said as they chewed steadily. Callum took a big swig of tea, closed his eyes and sighed.

'Better?' she asked.

'Much,' he said. 'Thanks. I think I was hungrier than I realised.'

'That doesn't let you off the hook though,' she added, waving her fork at him. 'It wasn't just hunger back there in the car park, was it?'

Callum grinned. 'Nope,' he said. 'And now I feel like a complete prat as well.'

'What? As well as odd and stupid?'

He gave a groan. 'Don't tease me, it's bad enough.'

Lucy swallowed, looking at him intently. 'Come on, tell me.'

For a minute she thought he was going to clam up on her again, but then he laid his knife and fork down. 'I was in shock, I think. Phoebe's boyfriend had just had a go at me in the car park. I thought he was going to beat the daylights out of me, to be honest.'

'What, Gary? Why?' she said, surprised. 'Anyway, I thought he was a copper?'

'He is,' agreed Callum. 'Apparently that's the only reason I'm still in one piece.'

'So, even though he's a policeman, he's still the sort that goes around threatening people, is he? What a total thug.'

'I think he thought he had just cause.'

Lucy narrowed her eyes. 'Jealousy? I saw Phoebe in the library earlier, didn't I? What did she have to say? Does she know what he's like?'

Callum speared another chip. 'No, and I'm not about to bloody tell her. She's on her own with this one, I'm afraid. She thinks they're madly in love, and now that she's dangled me in front of him like a carrot, he's suddenly become Mr Absolutely Wonderful and can do no wrong.'

'What do you mean, she dangled you like a carrot?'

'Well, it's my fault of course, but I honestly didn't think I was doing any harm. All the time I was helping Phoebe with the wedding, she was dropping not-so-subtle hints to Gary to make him jealous.'

'So, that worked well then.'

'Yeah, *too* well,' replied Callum ruefully. 'I don't have a huge opinion of myself, but I feel totally played if I'm honest. I guess it's just one I'll have to chalk up to experience. I got it wrong. It wouldn't be the first time I've misjudged someone's character.'

'Only because you naturally look for the good in people, and well… Sometimes they're not.'

'And sometimes I'm an idiot.'

Lucy heaved a sigh. 'Will you stop that!' she exclaimed. 'Honestly, Callum, you've done nothing wrong. You were trying to help someone out of the goodness of your heart and they've both behaved badly. It sounds to me as if they're well suited. She's a manipulative… whatnot… and he's an out-and-out thug.'

Callum took another sip of tea, watching the liquid settle back in the cup. He stared at it for a moment or two, before clearing his throat.

'Thank you,' he said, softly, looking up at her suddenly. 'For not misjudging me, I mean,' he added. 'Most people would have assumed there's no smoke without fire when I mentioned what Phoebe's boyfriend had done… and probably think that Gary was justified in wanting to thump me. After all, I have been spending rather a lot of time with her.'

'Yes, but you're friends, that's all. There was nothing in it. We're friends and there's nothing…' she stopped suddenly. 'I mean, any of your mates would know that you'd never do anything inappropriate. You're nice, Callum. You're generous, caring, have a great sense of humour and I…' she stopped again. 'Well, why wouldn't I believe you?' She shoved a huge chunk of fish into her mouth and began to chew.

'Don't stop,' he said with a grin. 'I was beginning to quite enjoy that!'

Lucy blushed. 'I just meant that you have all these good qualities that you never give yourself credit for, but perhaps other people do. Not people like Gary and Phoebe, obviously, but… other people,' she finished.

'Like you?' asked Callum, trying not to laugh.

'Yes, me, okay?' she replied, sticking out her tongue. 'You know what I mean. Stop teasing me.' She could feel her insides doing strange things that had nothing to do with her dinner, but at least Callum was looking better – and feeling better, hopefully. 'Seriously, though,' she began. 'Gary's not going to cause a problem for you, is he?'

'I shouldn't think so. I practically fainted when he had me by the scruff of the neck; he could see I'm not going to give him any trouble. He just wanted to make a point, that's all, and I'm very good at keeping out of people's way when I want to. Neither he nor Phoebe will have any cause to talk to me again, I can guarantee it.'

Lucy nodded. 'Was that what you wanted to talk to me about earlier? At the library.'

'No, something else entirely… only I'm not sure whether I should.'

'Only one way to find out,' she replied, pushing a chip into a pool of sauce.

Chapter 23

It was hard for Callum to know where to begin. He probably should have spoken to Lucy about Oscar way before now, but the old man was so keen to keep their conversations from her for some reason. Perhaps he had already spoken to her about his daughter and Lucy had advised him not to try and find her?

Callum was anxious not to do the wrong thing here, and he certainly didn't want to upset either Lucy or Oscar, but at the present moment in time he was finding it difficult to see how he could avoid breaking his commitment to one of them.

'How well do you know Oscar?' he asked eventually.

'Oscar? Well, outside of the book club I chat to him most days he's in the library, but it's small talk mostly – I wouldn't say I know him well.' She paused for a moment. 'I saw you together today at lunch, didn't I? Have you been helping him on the computers?'

Callum pulled a face. 'In a roundabout way,' he said. 'Although, probably not in the way you think.' He ran a hand around the back of his neck, massaging the muscle there, which was beginning to ache. 'The problem is, though – I don't think I'm supposed to talk you about… this particular thing. Oscar thinks it might upset you. But I really could do with some advice, and that means telling you, doesn't it?'

'I guess so.' Lucy shrugged. 'But what could Oscar and you be talking about that would upset me…?' She stared at Callum. 'Unless…'

'What?' asked Callum, hoping desperately that Lucy's response would mean *he* didn't have to spell it out.

'Well, there is something we've spoken about but it's a very private thing, and, poor Oscar; I've never seen someone so upset. I don't think he'd really ever spoken about it with anyone before, so it was like he was feeling it for the first time; such an awful raw grief.'

She looked up at him and he was startled to see tears welling in her eyes.

'It was horrible,' she added. 'He was so sad, even after all this time. This… thing happened years ago.'

It couldn't be anything else, reasoned Callum. They had to be talking about the same thing. His eyes softened as he looked at her face, so distressed by the thought of what Oscar was going through. Without thinking he reached across the table and took her hand, just as she had done for him earlier.

'He had a daughter,' he said quietly.

'Yes,' she whispered back. 'One who was taken from him and Mary at birth. Oh, Callum, they had so much love to give, but they were never able to give it – and now Mary's gone, and it's too late.'

He squeezed her fingers gently. 'No, Lucy,' he said. 'It's not too late. We've found her. We've found Oscar's daughter.'

Lucy sat up straight, her astonished eyes searching his. A tear glinted at one corner, which she impatiently brushed away.

'How?' she asked, but then almost as soon as she said it, nodding in understanding as she put two and two together. 'That's what you've been helping Oscar with,' she said. 'Oh my God, Callum – thank you so much. Is he going to see her?'

Her face was suddenly so excited that Callum felt awful. He smiled at her reassuringly, wanting to keep the smile on her face, but knowing that she would see through his expression in an instant. And she did; the hand not clutching at his flew to her mouth.

'Oh no, what's happened?'

Callum stared down at his plate, the last congealing chips now forgotten. 'I had an email,' he explained, 'from the charity we contacted to try to help find Oscar's daughter. It confirmed that they'd been able to locate her, but they also warned that the lady had placed a "no contact" note on her file a few years ago.'

Lucy frowned. 'What does that mean?'

'It means, that if at some point in the future someone came looking for her, she has no desire to be found. In other words, she did not want her details passed on to either of her birth parents.'

'I was so scared for Oscar that something like this might happen if he ever tried to find her. I can't believe that it can end like this though. Isn't there anything that Oscar or you can do?'

'Well, the email said that Oscar should think about what he wanted to do. He could either accept that his daughter doesn't want to be contacted, or the organisation could contact her to double-check that's really what she wants. In some cases when a "no contact" note is placed on the file, adoptees still change their minds; over the years circumstances change, feelings change – but there are no guarantees. Once they've given their decision, it's final. The birth parent "shouldn't underestimate the emotional distress that this could cause", they said, and they're supposed to think very carefully before asking them to go ahead and make contact.'

Lucy nodded. 'So, what has Oscar decided?' she asked, anxiety written across her face.

Callum held her look before dropping his gaze. 'He doesn't know about the no-contact thing,' he said quietly. 'I didn't tell him. I couldn't.' He looked up again into Lucy's understanding eyes. 'How could I, Lucy? He'd just found out his daughter was alive. How could I tell him that she didn't want to see him? It would break his heart. Again.'

'Oh, Callum,' said Lucy, and she moved her other hand to cover his in silent understanding.

Chapter 24

Hattie lifted the bags carefully from the back seat and, holding them aloft, gingerly closed the car door; it would be just like her to slam it and catch the edge of one of the dresses – and that would be it, she'd have to start all over again. Grease, mud and silk were never going to make a good match.

Satisfied that she'd skirted that particular hurdle, she picked her way up the path to her sister's house and pressed the doorbell with her elbow, the weight of the dresses heavy in her arms. She should be looking forward to this evening – a celebration of weeks of hard work, making her forget her aching back and tender fingers in an instant – but although Hattie was thrilled to bits with the end results of her labours, she was terrified of what Jules might think.

She was just about to ring the bell again, when the door was flung open and Jules stood there beaming at her.

'Oh, God, I wasn't sure if you were coming!' she gushed.

'I'm ten minutes late, that's all.' She laughed. 'Of *course* I'd be coming.' Hattie wriggled the bags in her arms, trying to get a better grip. 'Well, can I come in or not? These weigh a ton.' She moved past her sister, wiping her feet carefully on the mat and treading onto the pale carpet with a prayer. 'I'll just take my shoes off, shall I?' she said, turning to deposit the bags in Jules's arms.

A few moments later the precious cargo was laid out onto the settee and Hattie was looking around the room. She was pleased to see that Jules had brought the large standing mirror down from her bedroom and switched on all the lamps as well as the lights. It probably wasn't ideal, trying on her wedding dress at night, but there was no other time to do it; Hattie's babysitter was getting booked up with early Christmas parties. At least the artificial light would make the beadwork sparkle.

Jules had already slipped out of her jeans and was now pulling her top carefully over her head. Hattie had insisted that she wear her hair up; she wanted to be able to see the curve of her neck and how well the cut of the dress flattered her shoulders.

Finally, her sister stood before her and Hattie was ready to lift her creation over her head and settle it around her.

'Close your eyes,' she said. 'Until I tell you.'

She buttoned up the back of the dress, pleased that it closed easily while still remaining close to the skin, just how she had designed it. She checked the fall of material at the back before moving to the front and adjusting the sleeves slightly. She stood back to give it one last objective look and breathed out a slow, steadying breath. It was perfect.

'Okay, you can open your eyes now – but no peeking. Just pop your shoes on and then you can turn around.'

Her sister did as she was told, holding on to Hattie for support.

'And now, slowly turn around and look in the mirror…'

For a few horrifying moments, Jules said nothing. Then one hand moved to gently touch the bodice of the dress, as if making sure it was real. Her eyes were full of tears as she turned to Hattie.

'I never thought…' she began. 'It's so, so beautiful, Hattie. I don't know what to say.' She stood gazing at her reflection, shimmering in the light.

Hattie let out her breath. 'Do you like it?' she asked softly. 'Really? You're not just saying that?'

'I never thought I could look like this,' whispered her sister. 'Not in a million years. I love it, I absolutely love it!'

She gave an excited whoop of delight, suddenly remembering that she could move, and she turned this way and that, admiring the dress from every angle, her face beaming.

'You're a total genius! After what you said, I thought the beading would make me look frumpy, but it doesn't. I've even got a proper waist!' She whirled to face Hattie. 'Thank you so much!' she gushed. 'It's incredible. I don't know how you did it.'

Hattie looked at her sister's face and saw some of her own relief echoed there too. It suddenly struck her how anxious Jules must have been about this whole thing too; it wasn't just her. Jules was caught up in the madness of organising a wedding, where the pressure to compete was so easy to become entangled in. She looked more relaxed than Hattie had seen her in weeks and she realised, rather belatedly, that Jules had been anxious too. She'd trusted Hattie with a huge responsibility. What if she'd hated her dress? How could she have possibly explained that to her sister? If she had bought one from a shop she wouldn't have had to worry – but she hadn't. She'd chosen *her*. Hattie felt her own tears beginning to well. The thought hadn't even occurred to her. She was so busy feeling sorry for herself about how things were with her mum, that she never even stopped to consider how Jules must have been feeling. She moved forward to take her sister's hands.

'You look just how I wanted you to, Jules… truly beautiful. You don't know how much it means to hear you say you love it.'

'And I do, sis, I really do.' She raised a hand to her eyes. 'Oh God, look at me, I'm a wreck.'

Hattie's own tears spilled over and she fished in her pocket for a tissue. 'You and me both,' she grimaced, handing Jules a tissue too. 'And for God's sake, don't cry all over the dress.'

'I won't. I even left my mascara off, just in case,' laughed Jules. 'You know what I'm like!'

They both stood side by side for a few minutes, staring at the mirror. Hattie's aching back and sore fingers were indeed forgotten as they gazed at the beautiful dress. With its wide neckline and tiny capped sleeves, the bodice accentuated curves Jules didn't really have, while hundreds of tiny seed pearls shimmered in the lamplight, and every now and again a flash from a strategically placed crystal – just enough to create intrigue and admire, but without detracting from the sheer elegance of the gown. Hattie felt a profound peace wash over her as Jules's fingers reached for hers again.

'I don't want to ever take this off,' she said, 'but I know I've got to. Would you help me out, so we can pack it away safely?'

Hattie smiled. 'But not for long,' she replied. 'Just think of that. Only a month to go. And we've still got time to do another fitting if we need to, just to check that all's still okay.'

Jules nodded. 'And I've threatened the bridesmaids with all sorts if they put on any weight, or lose any, for that matter.'

'I should still be able to sort it out if they do, don't worry.'

Jules gave her reflection one last look before turning back to her. 'Thank you,' she said. 'I mean it, Hattie. What you've done for me is amazing, and I don't think I've properly said so before.' She dabbed at her eyes with the tissue. 'Come on, let's see you in your dress before I start crying all over the place again.'

Hattie hadn't expected to be trying on her outfit as well. As far as knew she was bringing all the bridesmaids' dresses to Jules's for safekeeping until the wedding day and, barring one last check for any final tweaks, that would be that. She suddenly felt rather shy, stripping off in front of her sister. Her underwear was a rather tired white from repeated washing and definitely more utilitarian than the silky wisps that Jules favoured. Having just seen how beautiful her sister could look, it would surely only serve to accentuate her own shortcomings. But Jules was looking at her expectantly and she didn't want to spoil the mood by being petulant.

The bags holding the dresses were all named and it only took a moment to find hers. With Jules's help she slid it over her head, the deepest midnight-blue silk feeling cool against her skin.

Together they stared at her reflection in the mirror.

'Oh,' was all Jules said, but it summed up Hattie's reaction perfectly.

'I must have put the wrong one on,' she said. 'Hang on...' She checked the other bags laid out on the sofa, but according to the labels she had indeed taken the one bearing her name.

Jules was frowning. 'But you can't have, surely... None of the others are... Well, they're not as big...' Her voice trailed away, partly in embarrassment and partly in confusion.

Hattie stared at her and then looked down at the gown, which hung from her body loosely. By rights it should be closely fitted, the fabric cleverly tucked to accommodate her ample bosom, and falling in a way to disguise her wide hips, but today the dress was hanging limply, shapeless and ill-fitting. She slipped the material down over her hips, twisting the bodice around until she could see the neckline at the back, the place she always put a few stitches as she worked to identify whose dress was whose. There was no doubt about it; this was definitely hers. Besides which, the others were all smaller than hers; there was no way she'd get into any of them.

'You've lost weight,' said Jules, with a grin. 'Look at you!'

And Hattie did look: at her stomach, which now lay flat beneath her ribcage; at her boobs, which nestled inside of her bra instead of trying to escape from it; and at her bum, which might just have less wobble to it than before. She poked an experimental finger at her thighs and lifted one leg to look at the gentle curve of her calf and the slender ankle.

'Holy cow!' she exclaimed. 'I have an' all.' And she thought back to the countless evenings of late, where she had sat and sewed instead of mindlessly eating biscuits while she watched the television. She thought of the dance classes and all the practice she had done with Lia, now able to keep up with her instead of having to stop every ten minutes or so for a breather. How she had run around chasing Poppy in the park only the day before yesterday without even getting out of breath.

With the dress around her ankles, she waddled over to the sofa, rooting through the bags until she found the one she was looking for. Sharon was a ten going on twelve, but not quite as tall as Hattie, and not quite as much up top, but still…

It fitted pretty much perfectly – in fact if anything it was slightly too loose – and Hattie's heart gave a leap. She could scarcely believe her reflection in the mirror. It was a very long time since she had looked like this, and best of all she hadn't really tried or noticed it happening. That was the real reason she was so chuffed to bits, because she suddenly realised that her life had turned a corner. She was no longer the sad stay-at-home mum, with hardly any friends and nothing to look forward to. She was no longer the person who quietly ate away her misery, alone in front of the TV. Instead, she was fired with an energy, with a passion that she hadn't felt since she was much, much younger.

Her dressmaking success was filling her head with ideas, and the possibilities it suggested for her future stretched out in front of her like glittering stepping stones across a stream. Not only that, but she was enjoying the company of others again, and in Lia and Lucy had found the meaning of friendship once more. She had taken a risk moving here when she did, but now, after only a few short months, things were definitely taking an upwards turn. She turned back to Jules.

'What do you think?' she asked.

'I think you look beautiful,' Jules replied without hesitation. 'The colour is perfect – it really suits you. I'm so glad I took your advice. The midnight-blue and silver theme is going to look absolutely stunning, and if we're lucky enough to get snow as well…' Her sister beamed at the thought of their sparkly winter wedding.

'Well, I can't do anything about the weather,' replied Hattie, smiling. 'But I do think it's going to be very special, snow or no snow.'

She looked at Jules's generous smile. Perhaps this evening might be the time to broach the subject she had been so worried about bringing up. 'I don't know about you, but all this excitement is making me thirsty. Any chance of a cuppa, Jules?'

She grinned. 'Yes, me too. I'll put the kettle on… In fact, it seems a bit ironic now, but I bought a cheesecake as well – I thought it would be nice to have a slice.'

Hattie returned her smile and nodded enthusiastically. When they were younger it had become a habit for them to meet up a couple of times a week to gossip – usually about work or boyfriends, but always with coffee and cheesecake. The fact that Jules had thought of doing this now said more to her than her words ever could.

'Yes, come on, I think we deserve it,' she said. 'Now that we've both seen how beautiful we are, a teeny pig-out on cheesecake won't hurt.' She let Jules help her out of the dress and returned it carefully to its bag, then pulled her jeans and jumper on with a smile, this time noticing how loose they were against her hips.

Jules's kitchen was three times the size of her own, stylishly designed with none of the debris that accompanied motherhood. The cheesecake was already waiting in the middle of the table, and Hattie could feel herself salivating.

'It's lemon-and-ginger,' said Jules, handing her a cake slice. 'And don't be stingy with the portion size.'

Hattie didn't need a second invitation.

She sat back, waiting for Jules to bring the drinks to the table. It was difficult to know where to begin. Tonight was the perfect opportunity to talk to her sister about her worries but it was also a very special night and she wasn't sure it was fair to alter the mood. But she didn't have to; Jules broke the ice for her.

'Things have been pretty pants just lately, haven't they? Between you and Mum, I mean.' She handed Hattie a mug. 'And don't try and deny it because it's a difficult subject – I know they have.'

Hattie wrapped her hands around the warmth of her mug. 'I just don't know what I'm supposed to have done wrong, Jules… It's like she's blaming me for something all the time, and things never used to be like this. I'm sure they weren't. I don't know, but I'm not imagining things; I know I'm not.'

Jules looked at her, a pained expression on her face. 'No, you're not,' she said. 'And I haven't exactly helped, have I? Or been honest with you, either. I should have told you the minute I found out, but Mum was so upset and I—' She stopped suddenly. 'I'm so sorry, Hattie. There really is no excuse.'

Hattie looked up sharply, taken aback by the sudden admission, and bubbles of apprehension began to rise in her stomach. This was beginning to get way bigger than she had imagined. 'Go on,' she said slowly.

'The thing is, it isn't as if it was your fault. You weren't to know when you said those things – and in fact if you'd known the truth you probably wouldn't have said them at all. It's really not fair – and for goodness' sake it was years ago – but Mum's being so stubborn about everything, she's making it a whole lot worse. In fact, lately I think she's lost the plot altogether.'

Hattie shook her head. 'Jules, you're not making any sense. What on earth are you talking about? And what am I supposed to have said?'

'I'm not supposed to tell you, Mum made me promise, but I can't bear to walk up the aisle with this still hanging over our heads. I'm only sorry it's taken me so long to do something about it.'

'Jules!' Hattie almost shouted, anxiety rising like a tide in her throat. 'What have I done?'

Chapter 25

'Does this mean your young man is coming again today?'

Lia blushed. 'How many times, Mum? He's not my young man, he's just a friend, that's all.'

'But you're courting, aren't you?'

'We're dancing, Mum, that's all.'

'Dancing, my eye. In my book that's still courting.' She turned to the man standing beside Lia. 'What do you say, Christopher?'

Christopher laughed. 'I couldn't possibly comment, Rose, but I think it's high time you allowed me to beat you at snakes and ladders again – come on.' And with that he led Lia's mum away, throwing a smile back at Lia over his shoulder.

She watched them go, a soft expression on her face. A month ago, she would never have believed all this was possible, but the change in her mum had been as dramatic as it had been welcome. In fact, it was scary how fast things had moved since Jasper had first suggested that he help find someone to look after Rose while they practised, and in Christopher he had found the perfect carer. A man in his forties, he had an instant and profound rapport with Rose. He was gentle and considerate, with a wicked sense of humour that Rose loved, but more than anything he had the ability to enter the world that Rose inhabited, even when it differed vastly from reality, and they made their time together an adventure.

The first week that Jasper had appeared for their 'lesson' Lia had cleared out the dining room in advance, relegating to the garage the table and chairs that she never used and pushing the old sideboard and bookcase into a corner. Just these small changes transformed the room into a big enough space for them to dance. It wasn't ideal, but it would work. They had been a little awkward with one another to start with, made nervous by the informal setting, but after half an hour or so they had begun to relax. So much so, that a sudden voice from the doorway made them both jump out of their skin.

'Arms higher, young man!' it commanded. 'You're leading your lady, not cavorting with her.'

They had both whirled around to see Rose standing in the doorway, an intense expression on her face.

'Carry on,' she said, waving her hand at them. 'It wasn't all bad.'

Lia didn't know how long her mum had been watching them, but from that moment on she did so whenever they danced. Every now and again she became her younger self again, the professional dancer turned teacher, and barked instructions gleefully across the room – although later on she sometimes seemed to have no memory of it at all. Lia was astounded and delighted that watching she and Jasper dance unlocked something within her mother that allowed the old Rose to surface.

Lia's only concern was that all this was costing Jasper an inordinate amount of money, but he wouldn't entertain any discussion on the subject, saying that this was the price they had negotiated for Lia's help with his dancing and that was all there was to it. It was clear he was a wealthy man, but he drank tea out of Lia's motley collection of mugs and sat at her scratched table just as happily as if they were eating in the finest restaurant. It seemed to matter little to him, and for that also Lia was immensely grateful.

Today, Jasper arrived shortly after Christopher and, although he greeted Lia in a cheerful manner, as they started dancing she could see immediately that he was preoccupied. She continued in their routine for a few minutes more before pulling him to a halt.

'Was that as bad as it felt?' asked Jasper with a grimace.

'Like a duck trying to ride a horse,' replied Lia, laughing. She looked at Jasper's serious face and then poked him until he too began to laugh.

'Dare I ask which one of us was the duck?'

Lia giggled. 'No,' she replied. 'But stop looking at your feet – you know the steps. And you're doing that counting thing again.'

'Was I?' Jasper groaned and rubbed his neck. 'Sorry Lia,' he added, 'I just can't seem to switch off today. It's been a tough week and I've had my ear well and truly bent about how the planning is coming along for the ball. I know there's only just over a month to go; I don't need my family reminding me every five minutes.'

Lia smiled in sympathy. 'And it's your day off. You could probably do with the rest.' She took hold of his hands again. 'It will be all right, you know.'

Jasper pulled her into hold. 'Shall we try it one more time?' he said, straightening up and attempting to find the right line.

For a moment, Lia started to compose herself ready to dance but then she suddenly pulled away.

'You know what – I've had a better idea.' She dropped his hands, looking at her watch. 'Ages ago you told me there was something that you were going to do when you quit your job, something that meant more to you than anything. You also said I would laugh at you, but if I solemnly promise not to, is it something you can show me?'

Jasper searched her face for a clue as to what she was up to. 'Possibly,' he said, 'but I'm not sure what it's got to do with anything.'

'Just that you said it was what relaxed you… and I think we need a break from all this; we're just going round in circles.'

Predictably Jasper's head dropped towards the floor.

'I know you're worried about wasting time, but I honestly think it will do you good. You need to unbend a little bit… if you don't mind me saying. We could afford to take a couple of hours out, couldn't we?'

She could see the indecision written on Jasper's face, but she also knew that he had come to the same conclusion as she had.

'Well, I suppose it is the weekend,' he agreed. 'And I don't imagine Christopher will mind – he's on time-and-a-half, after all.'

'Oh, I didn't mean—'

Jasper held up a stern hand. 'Nuh-uh,' he said. 'None of that. I'll just pop and have a word with him. Go and get your coat… and something warm.'

Twenty minutes later and they were still driving. Lia had her coat, scarf and gloves laid out on the back seat, ready for wherever they were going. Jasper wouldn't tell her exactly where that was, only that it was 'the other side of the hill'.

'Are we nearly there?' she asked. 'Only… I didn't really want to put you to all this trouble, I just thought…'

Jasper's only reply was a huge grin.

Lia had no choice but to sit back in the luxurious seat and relax. The scenery was certainly stunning, and it was ages since she'd been able to go on a drive like this. They had turned off the main road some ten minutes ago, and Lia had no idea where she was exactly, but for now she was happy to let the miles slip by.

'Are you ready for this?' asked Jasper a little while later and Lia sat up straighter as he turned the car between two huge brick pillars.

'Why, what is this place?'

'You'll see,' he said, driving on.

They crossed over a cattle grid onto a smooth expanse of tarmac, which made its way through an avenue of trees before sweeping in a wide arc to arrive in front of what could only be a rather exclusive country hotel. A huge stone portico stood guard at the top of a flight of stone steps, flanked by an array of manicured bay trees and bushes. Above, rose a beautiful red-brick house, its arched windows spreading out on either side – too many for Lia to count.

Jasper brought the car to a halt just shy of the steps, and by the time Lia had undone her seatbelt he was already out of the car, pulling her door open for her.

'Come on,' he urged. 'If we're quick we might even make feeding time.'

Lia glanced at her watch. It was indeed approaching lunchtime, but she was struck by Jasper's odd choice of words. Had he brought her here for a meal? She took his hand and clambered from the car.

He ran lightly up the steps and was inside before she was even halfway up. She crossed the threshold behind him, tentatively closing the door behind her as she tried to stem the sharp intake of breath.

She was standing in a marble-tiled hallway, its ceiling high above her, mahogany pillars standing like sentinels at each corner. To her right, an enormous staircase with marble steps and balustrades as tall as her rose majestically, while a huge panelled gallery surrounded her.

At first, she couldn't even see Jasper, but then she spotted him casually leaning against a pillar at the far left-hand side of the room. A grin split his face from ear to ear. As soon as he saw that she had spied him, he beckoned her forwards, disappearing through a mahogany door. With a backwards glance, she followed him.

'Jasper, wait a minute!' she called. '*Now* where have you gone…?'

Ahead of her another door opened and Jasper's head appeared. 'Come on!' he called, holding out his hand as he waited for her to catch up.

She grabbed hold of it, knowing that the moment she did so she would be whisked away once more. She scarcely had time to register the grandeur of the room before they were rushing along a narrow corridor, under an arch and through a swing door, stopping finally in the biggest kitchen she had even seen in her life. It was only when Jasper threw his car keys into a copper dish, resting on a huge dresser, that the penny finally dropped. She tugged at his hand.

'Hang on,' she panted. 'Please. Stop a minute.'

She looked at Jasper, standing in the middle of the space, and then at the room itself, which, now that she was focusing on it, was obviously somewhere he was very much at home.

'You *live* here?' she asked incredulously, her voice rising by several octaves.

Immediately Jasper dropped his head, half looking at her from under his lashes, almost shyly. It was something he did whenever he felt unsure of himself, but which gave him a rather endearing look. It was an expression that she was getting pleasantly used to. His eyes scoured the skirting boards.

'It doesn't make any difference...' he said, trailing off.

Lia waited for him to finish what he was saying, realising after a few moments that he wasn't going to.

He held out his hand again. 'Come on,' he repeated, 'or we'll miss it.' He gave her a quick smile and lifted her hand in his, looking just for a moment as if he was about to kiss it. Instead, bizarrely, he looked down at her feet. 'You'll need some boots,' he added. 'Mine will be a bit big, but they'll have to do.'

★

Ten minutes later Lia found herself standing on top of a wide grassy hill, bordered on one side by a stand of trees, and on the other a steep slope as the ground dropped away into the distance. They had followed the track up here from the house, but she could still see it in the distance. The Land Rover that had brought them up here must have been older than she was, and what it lacked in comfort it made up for in sheer dogged determination as it crawled up the steep embankment. They had come to rest alongside another ancient farm vehicle and, as Lia clambered out, she noticed a man some distance away, a pair of binoculars to his eyes. Asking her to stay where she was, Jasper made his way over to him.

The wind was bitter and beginning to make her eyes water, but there was something so timeless about being in this wild space. She could imagine how beautiful it would look on a summer's day, but even now, with the bare scruffy bleakness of approaching winter, she could see that it was a place to feel free, completely unencumbered from the stresses and strains of daily life. She wondered if this was why Jasper came up here. It occurred to her then that this was probably his land, and she turned to look back at the house. There was no way on earth that it made no difference, whatever Jasper said.

As she watched she became aware of a distinctive cry, high above her. She might have lived in a small market town most of her life, but surrounded by beautiful Shropshire countryside, she was no stranger to the distinctive cry of buzzards. Except that as she listened now, she realised this couldn't be a buzzard. The cry was not a single note, but more a series of linked swooping notes, almost akin to a shepherd whistling for his sheepdog. As it continued the two men came hurrying back towards her.

'We're just in time,' said Jasper, slightly breathless, although from excitement rather than anything else. 'Can I introduce you, Lia? This is Dougie, my estate manager.'

A rough hand was held out towards her. 'Please to meet you, Miss,' he said.

'Lia here is the one who's been helping me with my dancing.'

'Oh aye, I reckon that's a bit of a tall order.'

Lia smiled at the man, who could have been anywhere between his forties and his seventies. 'He's very good, actually,' she said. 'Although he needs to… well…'

'Stiff as that gatepost there, I shouldn't wonder,' sniffed Dougie. 'Not surprising as 'im's always in those fancy suits.' He snorted with laughter. 'Still, not long now, lad – you're gonna show 'em, aren't you?'

Jasper made a curious noise in the back of his throat and handed Lia the pair of binoculars. 'Something like that,' he muttered. 'Keep your eye on the line of trees.'

'What am I looking for?'

'You'll see.'

Almost as soon as she raised the binoculars, four huge birds broke cover of the trees, swooping to land on the slope of the field in front of them. They were far too fast for her to follow and she lowered the glasses to orientate her vision.

'What are they?' she asked, open-mouthed as she watched them take off almost instantly, loud cries accompanying their swooping flights.

'Red kites,' he replied. 'See the distinctive colouring underneath, almost chestnut-red with vivid white patches, and bright-yellow talons?'

'They look huge!' she replied, entranced by their effortless flight.

'Well, they have a wingspan of about two metres, so yes, pretty huge.'

She watched them for a while longer before switching her gaze to Jasper himself, and finally she understood. His feet were planted firmly apart as he stood motionless beside her, the wind ruffling his hair and buffeting the front of his jacket, but he seemed not to notice. Instead, he was at one with the wind and sky, face upturned, a smile lighting up his face as his eyes followed the kites this way and that. Here, Jasper was in his element – not sitting around a table in a boardroom or shaking the hands of suited businessmen, but here, out in the field, where no-one ever came except him, and Dougie, and the birds.

'Numbers of kites are on the increase in Shropshire, but they're still not that common. We've got quite a few breeding pairs now, and I'm hoping to set up a proper feeding station. People will come from all over to see them.'

'People?' asked Lia, surprised. 'Why would you want people here? I'd have thought you'd want to keep this all to yourself?'

Jasper laughed. 'Well, within reason… but there's plenty of room for all of us. This is a bit extravagant for just one person, don't you think? No, I'd like to get some hides up, maybe think about accommodation as well.' He tapped his head. 'I'm still planning it all out, but I'll make it happen… one day soon.' He turned away from her again, eyes on the sky once more.

A sudden strong gust of wind caught at Lia and nearly overbalanced her. She put out a hand against Jasper to steady herself, the sudden contact making her blush for some reason. She went scarlet as he pulled her in closer, rubbing her arm.

'Bit fresh, isn't it?' He nodded at Dougie. 'We'd best go down,' he said.

She immediately thought of her mum back at home. Even with Christopher's very competent care, she felt awkward about leaving the house, and she really had no idea what time she would be home. As if reading her mind, Jasper glanced at his watch.

'We'll grab a bite to eat, shall we, and something warm to drink? I'll give Christopher a call and let him know what we're up to.'

Lia could only nod, but she felt suddenly very out of control. She was used to taking decisions and, lovely though Jasper was, it felt odd doing things at someone else's behest.

They said their goodbyes and left Dougie to his duties, Jasper promising to catch up with him later.

'What did you think?' asked Jasper once they were settled in the Land Rover again. 'Perhaps you can see why I love it?'

'It's beautiful,' she agreed. 'And it must be the most amazing place to live… I can't imagine what it must be like, but I can see how it makes you feel. You seemed rather different when we were up there.'

'Less uptight?'

'At home, I think… yes, definitely, you looked at home, at one with the place.'

'I was lucky enough to be able to buy it several years ago, but it was purely by chance that I spotted the kites. Since then I've taken on Dougie to keep things ticking over for me; he doesn't always say a lot, but he shares my love for these amazing creatures, and I wouldn't be in a position to even think about throwing in the towel with the family firm if it wasn't for him.'

'It must make you very happy,' surmised Lia, looking at his face as he kept his eyes on the narrow track.

'It does,' he agreed, with a slow intake of breath. 'And what makes you happy, Lia? I mean, *really* happy?'

Lia thought for a second, surprised by the answer that popped into her head. She couldn't say that, though, so she chose a different word.

'Dancing,' she said. 'That, and when I see Mum as she used to be. It doesn't last long, I know that, and I know she isn't getting better, not really, but...'

Jasper risked a sympathetic smile at her. 'There's always hope,' he said.

Lia shook her head. 'No, she won't get better. I understand that, but these past few weeks have helped her enormously, and I only have you to thank for that.'

'No thanks required,' he replied. 'You're a special person, Lia; it's very easy to help you. In fact, I consider it a privilege.'

The air in the car grew suddenly warm and Lia was grateful to see the array of buildings come into view once again. She wasn't sure quite what to say, so instead she said nothing, running her finger along the edge of the forest-green scarf Jasper had lent to her along with the boots. It was beautifully soft.

Chapter 26

The kitchen was blissfully warm after their exposure to the wind on the hillside and Lia sank gratefully into a small armchair, wiggling her toes, which felt like blocks of ice. Jasper was busying himself with an expensive-looking coffee machine, which, she was told, made gorgeous hot chocolate too.

'Will a sandwich do?' he asked. 'Bacon? Or sausage, perhaps?'

'Sausage I think, if it's not too much trouble.'

'With onions, I hope?'

'Of course!' She smiled, her mouth beginning to water at the thought. Her sandwiches, when she could be bothered to make them, were usually just cheese and pickle. This was a real treat and made more so by the fact that someone else was doing the cooking. She sat back in her chair, idly watching Jasper at work.

'You can go and explore if you like,' he said, his back still to her. 'I don't mind. Just open and close all the doors and you'll soon get the gist of it. I'm not really good with the whole guided-tour thing, but you might like to have a wander by yourself.'

Lia, looking around the kitchen in awe, had been thinking just that, and she wriggled forward in her chair.

'I'm not even sure I could make it back to the hallway,' she said, trying to remember the rooms they had come through.

'That way,' pointed Jasper. 'Follow your nose and you'll be fine. And if you get lost just shout, I'll hear you.' He turned back round to face her. 'Oh, and when you get to the room with all the bookcases, pay particular attention.'

Lia gave him a puzzled look. 'Okay,' she said slowly, heading for the door.

It was an odd sensation wandering through the rooms in someone else's house by herself. Part of her, the polite, well-mannered part, didn't want to be nosey, but the other part was intrigued by this snapshot into somebody else's life and wanted to shamelessly snoop at every little detail. It did occur to her that perhaps this was why Jasper had suggested she go by herself – almost as if he wanted her to see these things that made him who he was but without him having to explain anything to her. She knew him well enough to know that he wouldn't be at all comfortable with that.

His love for his family was clear to see. Photographs covered the walls in two of the rooms; one was obviously an office and the other a much more informal sitting room, where she could see that Jasper spent most of his time. There were more personal possessions here than in any other room and although it was meticulously tidy, like the others, she could imagine Jasper sitting here of an evening reading, perhaps with a glass of wine. One or two of the rooms were very grand indeed, and had rather an austere air about them, but this one, despite having the same ornate panelling to the walls and intricately painted ceilings, was furnished much more simply; a mixture of the traditional and modern. She pushed open a door, gasping when she saw what was ahead of her: she had obviously found the library.

For a moment, she felt just like she was in a stately home. The ancient books had lent their particular smell to the space, and mingled with the scent of old polish it was like stepping back in time. She circled the room, awestruck by the rows and rows of leather-bound volumes that filled a whole series of inset, floor-to-ceiling bookcases. It was some minutes before she remembered Jasper's words to her. She could see nothing unusual about the room – in fact it was almost symmetrical, with shuttered windows down one side and doors at either end. Most of the rooms she had ventured into had interconnecting doors and must have been located along one side of the grand hallway, and this seemed to be no different. She strode across to the door on the other side and pulled it open, expecting to see another room. Instead, she was surprised to find a deep cupboard, stacked full of chairs, of all things. She closed the door again, thoughtfully.

It wasn't until she crossed the floor to look out the window that she realised her mistake. The view of the rear garden was wide and to her right, jutting into the space, was a vast pair of bay windows, each set with three huge panes of glass. They must belong to the room next door, and, if the previous arrangements were anything to go by, there should be a door into it from here. She crossed the room once more, this time examining the wall next to the cupboard.

She chuckled when she found it. The only thing that gave it away was the slightly bigger gap between two sets of bookcases, bookcases which were exactly the same width as the doors… There was no obvious handle so she pushed at the outer edge and was rewarded with a bit of give on one side. As she released the pressure, some sort of spring-loaded mechanism forced the door open. Carefully, she pulled it towards her, and peered beyond into a small corridor, which, she realised, exactly matched the dimensions of the cupboard. At the other end of the corridor was another door – presumably into another room.

She walked forward. Her mouth dropped open as she passed through the door and peered beyond, eyes raking from ceiling to floor, across the vast space and back again, taking in the sweep of the imposing architecture, the delicacy of the ornate detail. She'd never seen anything like it. The ballroom stretched away from her, huge arched bay windows extending down an entire wall, allowing light to flood in, onto the mahogany floor. The opposite wall was wood-panelled with sunken marble frescos and in the middle an enormous fireplace jutted out, its centrepiece a huge figurehead with pale marble skin, its hair gleaming with brushed gold.

Lia lost herself in thought for a minute, captivated by the idea of her swirling passage across the space – seeing the flash of the mirror at the far end and the jade ceiling with its intricate plasterwork overhead as she twirled, crystal chandeliers leaving a trail of light across her eyes as she moved faster and faster, the music sounding out the beat of her heart. Here was the room her dreams had taken her to. She hurtled back to the kitchen.

Jasper was plating up two rounds of sandwiches as she burst in.

'You found it then?' he asked.

'You swine!' Lia laughed. 'Why didn't you tell me you had a ruddy ballroom here? Talk about an unfair advantage. And not just any ballroom either, but one fit for royalty.'

'It is rather special,' he agreed, his eyes dancing in tune with the expression on her face. 'I'd like to say something profound about it being the reason I fell in love with the house, but alas, the ballroom and my new-found desire to dance are entirely unconnected.'

'Well, I don't care,' Lia declared. 'I'm taking you in there for a spin whether you want one or not.'

Jasper pushed her sandwich across the counter towards her. 'Come on, let's eat first. I haven't slaved over a hot stove for nothing. We can argue the toss later.'

Lia joined him at the huge island unit in the centre of the kitchen and pulled out a stool to sit down. Her sandwich was about an inch and a half deep, and the sight of the golden onions peeking from its sides brought a rush of saliva to her mouth. She was suddenly starving.

Beside her, Jasper took a huge bite, and was about to go in for a second when he broke off, catching her eye.

'Oh, I rang Christopher, by the way. You're not to worry, everything is just as it should be. They've had a lovely morning, making Rice Krispy cakes, among other things.'

Lia swallowed hard, a lump of bread caught in her throat. She had completely forgotten about her mum. She placed her sandwich back down on the plate, tears coming from nowhere. How could she have been so thoughtless, so selfish? She was too busy being swept away by the life that someone else led, that's what it was. A grand house and a few birds had been all it took to make her forget her responsibilities and behave like a giddy schoolgirl. Her mum was *her* responsibility, not Jasper's, and she would do well to remember that.

She pushed her plate away and was about to stand when she felt a strong grip on her arm.

'No,' said Jasper bluntly. 'Sit down.' He was watching her intently as his hand slipped down to grasp hers. 'Don't do this to yourself, Lia,' he said. 'You deserve so much better than this. You've done nothing wrong... except allow yourself to be who you really are for an hour or two. Not Lia the carer, or Lia the dutiful daughter, but instead the Lia who loves the feel of the wind in her hair, or the young princess who dreams of a life beyond the castle walls and who'd give her eye teeth to be at the ball. You've come to life in the last couple of hours – don't let guilt persuade you you're not worth it.'

Lia wrenched her hand away. 'Have you quite finished?' she demanded, her embarrassment showing itself as anger, flushing her cheeks bright red. 'How dare you think you know me – what I want, what I think. Just because you feel duty-bound to your family, too, don't think I'm just like you... because I'm not.'

Jasper looked at her, quietly and calmly. There was something in his eyes that Lia couldn't quite fathom. 'Regardless,' he said, 'when you've calmed down I think you might find that we have more in common than you suspect. You think I'm being preachy, but I'm not. I'm just telling it like it is, Lia. I've not only been there and done that, but I have the tee shirt in every size, colour and shape imaginable... and, I'm trying to be a friend.'

She stared at him, her mouth struggling to form words from the tangle of thoughts in her head – thoughts she was already beginning to suspect would tell her that Jasper was right. But she didn't want to acknowledge them; she couldn't acknowledge them, because if she did, where would that leave her? What would it mean for her? She didn't have a huge pot of money like Jasper did, or a big house in which to chase her dreams. She had to be Lia the carer and Lia the dutiful daughter because the other Lia simply didn't exist, and never would.

'Please eat your sandwich,' said Jasper softly. 'And if you really want to, I'll take you home straight after. Just tell me one thing: earlier today you said you wanted me to show you what it was that made me different from who I usually am, the thing that relaxes me. Why did you want that?'

Lia looked up in surprise. She had completely forgotten that. Despite herself, she could feel the corners of her mouth curving into a wry smile.

'Because you dance like a duck trying to ride a horse,' she said. 'Your body thinks it's a duck and therefore there's no possible way it can either ride a horse or dance for that matter. You have all the technical stuff down but you don't *feel* the music – you don't let it fill you up and work itself right down deep inside, so deep that it becomes a part of you so that when you dance the music comes spilling out too. People want to see the music, Jasper, not your arms or legs moving through a routine. Your body needs to feel the rhythm and become part of it. In fact, it must *be* the music.'

'So, I need to relax, to feel like I do when I'm up on the hill?'

'Partly…' she agreed. 'But it's more than that,' she added, nibbling at the edge of her sandwich. 'Think about how you feel when you watch the kites and why that relaxes you.'

The taste of the sweet onions rolled over her tongue and she took a bigger bite, chewing slowly while she waited for his reply. She saw the moment when he found the answer for himself.

'They're so at one with the sky,' he said. 'Huge birds and yet they glide and soar as if they're weightless.' He broke off suddenly, his own emotion catching at his throat. 'I imagine that's what freedom must feel like.'

Lia leaned forward. 'And that's how you must dance,' she whispered. 'Let go. Feel the music around you like air.'

Jasper nodded, his hand reaching out once more to take hers. 'Shall we?' he said.

It was different the minute they stepped foot onto the floor. Jasper pressed a button on his phone and the whole room filled with the rich sound of the piece they had been dancing to. He turned up the volume.

Lia smiled. 'Don't watch your feet,' she said, marvelling at seeing them reflected in the huge mirror at the far end of the room. She took his hand and laid her other gently on his shoulder waiting for the cue in the music, and then she stepped out to follow his lead.

Three and a half minutes was all it took for them to find the freedom they both so desperately craved. The music soared above them, taking them higher one minute and then swooping them down to the ground the next, as they moved around the ballroom in effortless flight. At times, Lia felt as if her feet were hardly touching the ground, and as her own inhibitions relaxed she became aware of another sensation. Strange though it was to her, she let herself be open to it. By the time the music faded, the boundaries between her and Jasper were blurred and indistinct. She was as much him as he was her, and as they came to a stop she rested her head against his chest.

They stayed that way for several minutes, catching their breath, calming their emotions to the point where they were able to speak once more. Lia could feel Jasper's heart beating through the thin fabric of his shirt, a sensation she could never remember feeling before, and it suddenly struck her what it was to be human.

'Not a duck in sight…' she murmured and felt a ripple of amusement pass through the muscles in Jasper's stomach.

He pulled away from her, holding her at arm's length as if to see her better.

'I didn't just imagine that, did I? Please tell me I didn't.'

Lia shook her head. 'You didn't,' she replied. 'That was the most real thing I've felt for a long time. See, all it took was something special to unlock it—'

'Or *someone* special…' he said. 'You've taught me a lot today, Lia, and not just how to dance.'

She laughed, trying to lighten the poignancy of the moment. She didn't think she was ready to deal with all that it implied just yet.

'Go on with you. It was there all the time…'

'But you saw it, didn't you? You saw the thing that was within me and knew that you could make it come alive.' He raised a hand to her cheek, leaving it there for just a moment, a soft look of query on his face. 'I wish I could do the same for you, Lia… Perhaps I can, if you'll let me.'

She pulled away, slightly unsure of what to say. Jasper couldn't change anything, even if he wanted to. Her mum was never going to recover and it was better that she stopped deluding herself. Like Jasper had said, perhaps she did want to flee the castle walls from time to time, but that's all it was – a fairy-tale wish.

'I can't,' she replied. 'I promised my mum I'd care for her, always, and that means at home, in the place where I grew up, where she feels safe.'

'But have you thought what you're going to do, Lia? When the time comes, I mean; when your mum becomes too ill for you to look after her. What happens to you then?'

Lia looked up into his eyes. 'I don't know,' she whispered fearfully.

Chapter 27

Callum hadn't moved from his spot in the IT room all Friday, but Oscar never came. He and Lucy had planned what they would do and say, but the day crawled by and the opportunity never arose. It was almost as if Oscar knew it would be bad news. And now it was Monday and the book club was due to meet in half an hour; Callum didn't think he'd be able to look Oscar in the eye.

He was about to go and speak to Lucy again when Oscar's distinctive shape filled the doorway, and Callum felt his heart sink. How could he tell him here, in this very public space, that his daughter didn't want to see him? He could see that Oscar was expecting to talk to him, but folks would be gathering for the meeting soon and Lucy would be busy. He smiled a welcome; there wasn't much else he could do.

'My apologies,' said Oscar. 'I was struck down by the most ferocious head cold on Thursday and I confess I didn't feel well enough to come along on Friday. Of course, I couldn't ring to let you know of my absence. That would have… well, you know.' And he tapped the side of his nose. 'I'm much better today. I thought we might just have time to discuss things before the book club starts.'

Callum shifted uneasily in his seat. 'I'm glad you're feeling brighter,' he said lamely, 'although Lucy mentioned that she wanted a quick word with you before the meeting… Something about the next choice of book?' He grimaced slightly. 'I'm not sure that will give us enough time, although… Perhaps I should go and find her and then she can chat to you about whatever it is and we can take it from there. It might save us from getting interrupted.' He flicked a glance towards the door, praying that this might get him off the hook.

Oscar sat down beside him, watching his face carefully. 'You know, one thing about being a teacher,' he said, 'is that you develop a very keen ability to spot when someone is being economical with the truth. I've seen that look on many a boy's face in the past.'

Callum immediately dropped his gaze.

'Just as I can see it on your face now… And, perhaps if you look properly, you can see it on my own face, too…' He regarded Callum's surprised face sadly. 'I'm afraid I did what you young people call "bottling it",' he added. 'I was perfectly well on Friday, just as I am today in fact, but I had begun to dwell on my fears, convincing myself that it was all too good to be true and that what I had originally thought would be a simple conclusion to the matter could not possibly be. Now, of course I can see that I was right to doubt things.' He patted Callum's arm. 'And so, now I must apologise as well because I can see I've put you in the most awful position these last few weeks. It was selfish of me; I should have undertaken these enquiries on my own.'

Callum was horrified. 'No, don't say that; you mustn't be sorry. I'm glad I was able to help you, if only so that now you're not facing things on your own.' He ran a hand across his face. 'I should have told you last week what the email really said, but I just couldn't bring myself to do it, not when you'd only just learned how close your daughter was all this time. It seemed the cruellest thing, and if I'm honest… Well, I wanted to get some advice too.'

'Advice?'

Callum nodded sheepishly. 'I wasn't sure how to handle this by myself... and Lucy's a very good listener.' He dropped her name gently into the conversation. It was best if Oscar knew everything after all.

He pondered this information for a moment. 'I see,' he said slowly. 'Yes, I can understand how that would make sense. She seems to me to be a very lovely young woman.'

'She is,' replied Callum, holding Oscar's look so that he could see how much he meant it. 'Perhaps I shouldn't have told her, but if I'm honest I feel happier that she knows. Lucy cares about you a great deal, Oscar – she cares about everybody and I know she wants to help. We just didn't want to tell you like this...'

Oscar gave a soft smile. 'I see. And what exactly are you telling me, Callum? Is this the end of the road?'

'Not necessarily...'

'Go on.'

'But there are no guarantees, I wouldn't want you to think—'

'Whatever it is you have to say is fine, Callum. Hope is a fickle friend, I know that – but better than none, and I have prepared myself for the worst. If that is all you have to offer I must accept it, and yet... There still remains a possibility, however small, and it is this that I cannot ignore.'

Callum nodded, and took a deep breath. 'Your daughter asked for no contact from her birth parents, and a note has been placed on her file accordingly.' Oscar's face remained impassive. '*But*, this request was made some years ago, and given that, the standard response is for the search organisation to enquire if these wishes still stand. It's not unusual for people to change their minds once they know someone has been in touch.'

'I see. And I'm to choose, am I? Whether I want to quit while I'm ahead, or go for broke and run the risk of having my hopes dashed one last, and very final, time.'

The tension surrounding Oscar was palpable, like an overinflated balloon. One more breath would be all it took for it to burst. Callum swallowed.

'That's pretty much the size of it, yes,' he said.

A pause.

'I'm an old man,' said Oscar eventually, 'and I will never have the opportunity or the strength to do this again. I have enjoyed a lifetime of love from a woman who has meant more to me than words could possibly express, and one I know I will meet again, in time. If that is all I'm to have then I will still die a happy man, but I'm not planning on going anywhere for a good few years yet, and if there is any possibility that I might get to meet my daughter, finally, after all these years, then I must take it. Otherwise I risk taking regret with me to the grave – and for Mary's sake as much as for my own, I'm not prepared to do that.' He stood slowly, straightening his waistcoat as he did so. 'May I leave these last instructions for you to follow up on my behalf?'

Callum nodded, finding it hard to speak around the lump in his throat.

'And perhaps, if you would be so kind, you could pass my apologies to Lucy for missing the meeting. I think a spot of fresh air would serve me better today.'

He tipped his head in grateful farewell and walked from the room, leaving Callum utterly devoid of speech and close to tears.

★

Lucy looked around the book club, from one member to the next. Understandably, Callum still had his head bent, but Hattie too looked rather dejected. Along with Lia, she was usually one of the most vocal in the group, but today she had hardly said a dozen words the entire time she had been there. In fact, out of them all, only Lia looked animated – indeed quite literally as if she was dancing on air. Lucy lowered the book she was holding to her lap.

'You know, the one thing about running your own book club is that you get to make the rules,' she said, pleased to see heads turning to her with interest, 'and so I've decided for today to ditch the literary discussion because I can see that Lia is bursting with excitement, and I, for one, am dying to get the gossip.' She gave Lia a beaming smile. 'Come on, tell us what's got you all fired up. Whatever it is will be far more interesting than what we've been reading.'

To her delight, Lia returned the smile, leaning forward and drawing the group in. 'Oh, I've had the most amazing weekend,' she breathed. 'You'll never believe it when I tell you, but Jasper took me to his house and he has an *actual* ballroom it in, replete with wooden floor, mahogany mirrors at least fifteen feet high, and the biggest marble fireplace you've ever seen!'

Lucy's was not the only jaw that dropped.

'You went to his house?' asked Hattie. 'But Lia, that's… That's like a whole other level. You dark horse, you!'

Lia blushed. 'Hattie, honestly! It wasn't like that at all… Well, maybe it was a teeny tiny bit…' She snorted with laughter. 'I don't know what's the matter with me.'

'I do!' giggled Hattie. 'Most people call it lust.' She stopped then, raising a hand to her mouth. 'Am I even allowed to say the word lust in a library?'

'You most definitely are,' replied Lucy, grinning. 'Come on then, Lia, don't leave it there. Spill the beans.'

She watched as Lia sucked in a breath, trying to steady herself, her eyes still dancing with her memories. Lucy was also aware that, beside her, Callum had seemed to wake from his stupor. He would be hanging on Lia's every word, of that she was certain, but without Oscar present he was now the only male in the group and as such was probably feeling a trifle embarrassed at the undisguised glee with which the three women were discussing Lia's relationship with Jasper. And what about her own motives? Lucy was thrilled for her friend; Lia was really opening up and watching her bloom – there was no other word for it – gave her a huge sense of delight, but she also knew that she would try to commit her every word to memory; they were far too precious to waste.

'Well,' began Lia. 'It's a bit of a long story really…'

'The best kind,' urged Hattie. 'Start at the beginning.'

The words rolled out of Lia in one almost continuous sentence. Apart from the odd interruption from Hattie, who wanted more details on all the more salacious aspects of her story, it was as if a dam had been breached in Lia's reserve and the outpour was unstoppable. When she got to the part about Jasper's house, there was a collective intake of breath at her description of it, but their excitement was nothing compared to that on Lia's face as she relayed what had happened on the hillside and her subsequent eureka moment while teaching Jasper to dance.

It was at this point that Lucy suddenly realised what was missing; in every previous conversation they had shared about dancing, Lia's words had been coloured by the acute longing that she felt. Today, though, that longing was no longer there and Lucy realised that Lia no longer yearned to dance because she *was* dancing. She was feeling exactly as she had dreamed she would for all those years. Lucy had to cough to hide the sudden swell of emotion that rose within her.

By the time Lia had finished, Hattie all but clapped, her hands clasped together in excitement. 'Does this mean that you're going to dance at the ball?' she urged. 'Because, if it does, I'm going to make you the most amazing dress you've ever seen!'

'But you've already given me an amazing dress, Hattie,' protested Lia.

'That didn't answer my question,' she replied pointedly.

Lia screwed up her face. 'I must be mad,' she confessed, 'but yes, I've said I'll dance.'

'I knew it!' Hattie screamed, launching herself out of her seat and throwing her arms around Lia. 'Oh, I'm so happy for you.'

Lucy suddenly felt as if she were witnessing everything from a slight distance, a bit like watching a film, and it gave her the most peculiar feeling – not altogether unpleasant, but one that sent tingles down her spine, nonetheless. She turned to look at Callum, only to find that he was regarding her intently, and she quickly looked away as the thoughts that had been swirling inconclusively around her brain solidified into a single truth.

She felt her cheeks grow hot and was relieved when Hattie alerted her to the fact that their time was up. Usually, the others stayed to help clear away the refreshments, but today Lucy insisted that she do it herself. She needed some space and time to think and the few minutes she would have alone doing the washing-up might be the only opportunity she had for a while. She hugged both Lia and Hattie and said goodbye, promising to catch up with them soon, and gratefully closed the kitchen door behind her.

She turned on the hot tap and watched as the jet of water turned the washing-up liquid into a mass of bubbles. She let her mind quieten as she stared at the iridescent patterns forming in between the suds, only reaching to turn off the tap once the water was in danger of overflowing the bowl. She plunged her hands into it, feeling the heat calm her. She didn't know why she was feeling this way, but the turn of events in Lia's life seemed extraordinary and Lucy was rather overwhelmed.

Mindful of the time, she added the mugs to the water and began to wash them. At any moment Rachel would stick her head around the door to 'politely' enquire how much longer she was likely to be. She often did this, and it irritated Lucy no end. She had a reply ready on her lips when she heard the door open, but was surprised to hear someone else's voice.

'Sorry, is it okay for me to come in here?'

Lucy placed the mug she was holding onto the draining board. 'Of course,' she replied as evenly as she could. 'Is everything all right, Lia?'

The huge smile was still in place. 'I just wanted to say a special thank-you,' she said. 'To you, in particular. I mean, if it wasn't for you encouraging me to take up dancing, none of this would be happening right now. You found the course for me, got Hattie to come along – even found those wonderful books for Mum to read… It's all a bit scary, but nothing like this has ever happened to me before.' She came further into the room. 'I can't thank you enough.'

And before Lucy knew it Lia had flung her arms around her.

'Oh, now I've dripped water all down the back of your coat,' said Lucy, trying her best to keep her wet hands away from Lia's back.

'I don't care,' she declared. 'What's a little water between friends? And you've been such a good friend, Lucy. I can't believe how much you've done for me. Hattie as well, but if you hadn't started it all off, well… I know that none of this might lead anywhere, but even if just a few dances are all, then at least I'll have had those. That, and the best few weeks ever. It's given me a glimpse of what life should be all about, that there are choices and things I can change. I've never felt this way before.'

Lucy stared at her. She had been feeling so horribly guilty, so overwhelmed by the enormity of what she had done and the worry of it all going catastrophically wrong, but here was Lia, ecstatic, elated and thanking her. So maybe she had helped, after all. And if she had helped Lia, could she still help Oscar and Callum? Or even, maybe, herself…

Chapter 28

At first, Hattie had been buoyed by the joy of hearing Lia so happy. Her steps had been light, her mood cheerful as she thought of the delight on Lia's face and the excitement in her voice. But before she had even got to the end of the road she felt her mood begin to darken again as she remembered why she hadn't been at all happy when she left the house this morning…

Did seeing someone else's good mood automatically highlight the fact that your own was considerably worse, or was it just that the issues Hattie was struggling with were too awful to simply fade away as soon as something better came along? Without even thinking, she opened the gate and entered the park. There were a few hardy souls there, but it was not a day for lingering, and the folks she did see were walking with purpose. She hadn't intended to stop until she saw a lone figure seated on the bench nearest the play area. Oscar didn't look like someone who wanted company, but she couldn't pass by without saying anything.

'I missed you at the book club today,' she said. 'I wondered, perhaps, if you weren't feeling very well. There's a hideous flu bug doing the rounds.'

Oscar looked up, taking a moment to focus on her face. He smiled, a little sadly she thought.

'Not unwell, no. Just a trifle out of sorts.'

'Well that makes two of us then,' she said, plonking herself down on the bench next to him. 'I wasn't looking forward to having to be jolly either, as it happens, but Lia had some lovely news about her and Jasper – and the dancing of course – and it cheered me up a bit.' She pulled her coat around her, tugging the sleeves down over her hands. 'Trouble is, now I feel flat as a pancake again. Perhaps it's catching?'

'It's a melancholy sort of day,' Oscar replied, raising his eyes heavenward.

'Cold too. But it's not that – not in my case anyway.'

'Mine neither,' admitted Oscar. 'I always thought when I was younger that things would be so much simpler in old age. All life's problems solved or healed by the passage of time, but now I find the reverse to be true. I had more energy to deal with things then, less time to dwell on what might have been.' He turned to Hattie and smiled. 'Always live your life in the present, my dear,' he said, 'and never put off doing something that's important. In my experience, these things rarely go away. You learn to live with them, or they fade and you can pretend they're not really there, and then one day you'll be as old as I am, and find yourself still wrestling with them.'

Hattie stared at Oscar, horrified. 'When will I ever learn not to open my big mouth?' she said. 'I'm so sorry, I didn't mean to upset you.'

To her relief, Oscar fixed her with a cheery smile. 'Not upset, my dear; resigned, perhaps? Hoping against hope that I haven't left things too late.' He glanced at his watch. 'And fortunate that the landlady at the Crown has a very fine steak pie for me, which I shall shortly be eating before a roaring fire.' He waved a vague hand in the direction of the town. 'You could join me, if the thought's not too unbearable.'

Hattie pulled a face. 'Do you know what, Oscar? On another occasion I think I'd like that very much, but I've just realised that I have somewhere I need to be. Are you sure you'll be all right?'

'Of course, but what about you?'

'Me? I'm going to take your very good advice.' She grinned at him. 'Enjoy your pie!'

She hurtled out of the park. She was still a good ten minutes away from home, and she would have to pick up Poppy from school later, but she wanted to give herself as much time as possible. She hadn't known what she was going to do until she'd spoken to Oscar, when it suddenly all became very clear indeed. She had a feeling that it was going to take a while, though ...

*

Her mum lived about half an hour's drive away, only ten minutes away from the house where Hattie grew up as a child. When her grandma died her mum and dad had replaced the bay-fronted semi she had always loved with an ultra-modern new build on a select development that Hattie hated. In fact, it was around that time her mum had eschewed anything that reminded her of her life as a child and, although now Hattie knew why she had done this, she still couldn't understand it. It felt like a betrayal to her, a symptom of her mum's misplaced and misguided anger. Hattie wasn't optimistic that she would be able to make her change her mind, particularly when Jules had already tried, but she was damn well going to try.

She was halfway there when she wondered if she should have called ahead first. Her mum didn't work on a Monday, but there was no guarantee that she would be in. Of course, had she called, there was also every possibility that her mum wouldn't want to see her. The thought sat unpleasantly in Hattie's stomach; she had been on the receiving end of her mother's hurtful behaviour too many times in the past, when all it would have taken was an explanation, which Hattie was convinced she deserved. At the very least, she should have been given an opportunity to defend herself, but all these things had been denied her.

★

It wasn't even Thursday, but Clive needed only to look at Lucy's face as she walked urgently through the door of Earl Grey's to know that only pastry of the highest order would be sufficient.

It was a quiet day and Lucy smiled gratefully at Clive as she pulled Callum towards the rear of the tearoom to sit down. She had just about forty minutes of her break left, but that would be enough. That was the wonderful thing about Callum; she never had to explain herself at length, because he always seemed to know what she was thinking – sometimes better than she did herself. Today though, he had plenty on his mind too.

'Go on, you first,' she said when they were seated. 'What happened with Oscar?'

She listened quietly while Callum retold the events of that morning. She had heard the story briefly of course just moments before the book club had started, but now she could see why Callum was so distraught.

'It wasn't so much that he was upset,' said Callum, 'I anticipated that, but he's just such a gentle man and expects so little, it's heartbreaking. He has a little hope, and that's all… and I'm so… angry, that we can't give him more. How could anyone not want to have Oscar in their life?'

'But his daughter doesn't know him like we do,' Lucy replied, gently. 'She'll have her reasons for not wanting to see him, and they could be based on anything – her own relationship with her adoptive mother, for example, her upbringing, or her own prejudices. What they won't be based on is the knowledge of what a lovely man Oscar is.'

'But that's so unfair!'

Lucy held his look for a second before nodding sadly. 'There must be something we can do,' she said. 'Oscar has lived with this pain most of his life, and now, he's going to suffer all the more, at a time when he should be able to enjoy his retirement. I know he's lost Mary, but he has years ahead of him yet.' She lowered her head. 'I want to help him so much, but by getting him to open up about all of this I feel like I've condemned him to live out the rest of his days feeling nothing but sadness. I should have left him alone.'

Callum sat back as Clive placed a tray on the table between them.

'But the distress Oscar's been carrying over the loss of his daughter isn't new, Lucy; he's been lugging around that hurt his whole life. You've given him the courage to finally do something about overcoming that loss and, more importantly, given him hope when there was none. Surely that's better than no hope at all?' He picked up the teapot and began to pour.

Lucy knew what Callum had said was true, but it still did nothing to assuage the guilt she felt, or her sense of helplessness. Once the tea was poured, Callum sat back once again but didn't reach to taste it. Clearly, he was waiting for her to tell him the truth about how she was feeling, but Lucy was finding it hard to admit that to herself, so how could she possibly do so to Callum?

Fortunately, he mistook her silence for shyness. 'I know why you're feeling guilty,' he said. 'Because you think you're responsible for everything that's happened, and because you think you were wrong to interfere. But what else could you have done, knowing how unhappy Oscar – *and* Lia – were? I don't see how you could have ignored it, and besides, you're forgetting that everything is turning out wonderfully well for Lia – and we don't yet know what's going to happen with Oscar.' He reached out across the table to take her hand. 'I think what you've done is incredibly kind and caring. Be brave, Lucy. We're not at the end yet, and when we get there, even you might be surprised by the outcome.'

Lucy stared at him. Now, what was that supposed to mean? She was just about to question him further when Clive appeared at her elbow.

'Sorry, Luce, can I interrupt for a minute? I need to pick Callum's brains about this website. It's probably me, but...'

Lucy waved an airy hand. 'No, you go ahead, Clive, it's fine, honestly.'

Callum flicked her an apologetic look. 'Do you need me to come and have a look?' he asked.

Clive pulled a face. 'Would you mind? Only I've tried to load on this week's specials and they're not appearing.'

Lucy watched as Callum followed her brother-in-law into the office, realising she was grateful for the time it bought her. She wasn't entirely sure what was meant by Callum's last comment or, more to the point, she suspected she *did* know, she just wasn't quite ready to admit to it yet.

She eyed the pastry, which still lay invitingly on the plate. An innocuous custard slice, just like the one that seemed to have started her on this whole rollercoaster of a journey. Normally, she wouldn't have thought twice about eating it, but today it seemed to have acquired a rather strange poignancy. She tutted crossly. *Oh, for goodness' sake*, she thought. *Get a grip on yourself, Lucy*. And with that, she picked up the cake and sank her teeth into it.

She was mid-mouthful when Callum reappeared, looking even more sheepish. 'Sorry, Lucy, Clive's got himself into a right pickle. I said I'd hang on for a minute to sort him out. Is that okay? We can talk again later.'

'Hmm,' she mumbled, tapping at her watch and swallowing hastily. 'I ought to get back anyway. I'll just finish this.'

Callum grinned. 'Just don't eat mine as well, or there'll be trouble. I'll see you later.' He moved to go before changing his mind and turning back to her. 'Just give it time, Lucy,' he added. 'I'm convinced that's all it needs.'

★

He stared at the computer screen as if deep in thought. Clive wasn't in a pickle at all – Callum could rectify the issue in all of three clicks of the mouse – but for some reason the images were dancing in front of his eyes and he couldn't focus on what he was seeing. Beside him, Clive shuffled in his seat.

'Go on then, tell me what idiot thing I've done,' he said, scratching his head.

Callum dragged his thoughts back to the present. Half an hour ago he was thinking about Oscar, or, to be more exact, he was thinking about Lucy thinking about Oscar and how preoccupied she seemed to be. Now, he was just thinking about Lucy.

He turned slowly to Clive, trying to come up with a response to his question, but his thought processes were running interminably slowly. The irony of his situation was not lost on him; if he were a PC he would turn himself off and then on again to try and remedy things, but in his case a stern talking-to was going to have to suffice. He gave himself a shake.

'You're going to have to tell her, you know,' said Clive, peering at the screen. 'Because the longer you leave it the harder it's going to be. Plus, if I know my sister-in-law she's just as bad as you are.'

Callum's mouth dropped open like a fish.

'And don't try and deny it either; we've all been there, mate. I recognise the signs. Just get it over and done with and then you can both start enjoying it.'

'Erm,' stammered Callum. 'I'm not quite sure I follow...'

Clive winked. 'Yes, you do, mate. Lucy,' he said pointedly. 'You do fancy her, don't you?'

'Do I?' gulped Callum. 'I hadn't really thought about it,' he lied.

'So, answer me this then. Do you, or do you not, find yourself wanting to talk to her at every minute of the day, even when she's not there? Do you feel instantly better when she's in the room? Do you find yourself looking at things and thinking *Lucy would like that* to yourself? And is the purpose of pretty much any conversation to get her to smile because you can't wait to see her eyes light up when she does?' He paused to give Callum an amused look. 'Because if the answer to any or all of those questions is yes, then you've got it bad, just like the rest of us.'

Callum didn't think he needed to reply. How on earth did Clive know all that?

'Is it obvious?' he whispered, 'I mean, will Lucy know?'

Clive looked at him in exasperation. 'Dur...' he said, smiling. 'Lucy feels the same way, you muppet... She just hasn't quite worked it all out yet.'

God only knew what colour his face was, but Callum couldn't begin to worry about that – he was too busy trying to calm his heart down, which was currently beating at ninety miles an hour. Clive seemed so certain of himself and the thought caused a bubble of happiness to burst inside Callum's chest. He hadn't yet been sure of his feelings. He had even wondered whether it was simply a case of wishful thinking – Lucy was the only girl he had ever been remotely close to – but Clive's words had confirmed everything he needed to know. More than that, because something else had been wandering through his thoughts of late: when Clive said that Lucy hadn't worked it all out yet, Callum knew without a shadow of a doubt that he was wrong. Because Lucy *did* know. She had known all along.

Chapter 29

Lia breathed in the cold air gratefully. They had been dancing for what seemed like hours and she was beyond hot. She could feel Jasper's guiding hand in the small of her back and this alone was enough to make her temperature rise a few more degrees. Since that day in the ballroom at his house it was as if a key had suddenly unlocked something within them both. Jasper had found some balance in his life; no longer was he so uptight and anxious about things, but instead had learned to relax and express himself with real feeling and emotion. His dancing had improved tenfold. For Lia, the change was just as dramatic – and it was also terrifying.

Before her mum had become ill, there had been a time when she had considered herself a young woman with a future ahead of her, excited and open to the possibility of sharing her life with someone. There had been the odd boyfriend, nothing serious, but there had always been the hope that, one day, these things would happen for her. In the last five years or so, she had lost that hope. Lia, the young woman with the beautiful chestnut hair, smiling eyes and an elegance that belied her years, had been replaced by a duller version; a Lia who wore shapeless clothes, whose hair was tied up out of the way and whose eyes had lost their shine through the loss of her dreams.

Now, it was as if every nerve ending had awoken, each muscle and sinew alive to the sensations that were flooding her body. She heard colour in Jasper's voice, saw the sound his words carved through the air and felt their texture as they settled upon her skin. She didn't think she had ever been so aware of another person, and the feelings he aroused in her were brand new and utterly terrifying. She both loved and hated them at the same time.

Tonight had been the final dance class of the year and there were now only three weeks to go until she and Jasper appeared together in front of the huge crowd at the charity ball. As Jasper led her outside, the streets sparkled with the glow of Christmas lights from the houses opposite. There was a sense of expectation growing in the air around them, a mounting excitement that was down to the season and the close of the year but also, for Lia, what lay beyond. The dance was to be the great finale to so many things in her life, and the thought fizzed inside her like sherbet on her tongue.

There had been an intense look in Jasper's eyes tonight and at times she had totally forgotten they were surrounded by other couples. Had she imagined it, or had his touch lingered just that bit longer than usual? Was the pressure of his hand against her back just that little bit lower than it had ever been before? To Lia, though, it hardly mattered whether these things were true; the one thing she *hadn't* imagined was the way they made her feel.

The house was quiet when they arrived, the lights in the kitchen off and those in the living room dimmed low. Usually, the television would be on and, as they passed down the hallway, Lia could see Gwen's head beside her mum's on the sofa, her soft lilting accent just about audible. Lia smiled as she watched them; her mum had been much calmer of late, and her concentration so much improved that reading to her had become a real pleasure again. She wondered whether Gwen was working her way through *Dancing Shoes* one more time. Jasper flicked on the kitchen light and automatically made for the kettle as Lia shrugged off her coat, hanging it over the back of a chair.

'I'll just nip and see if Gwen and Mum would like anything,' she said, torn between her desire to continue her evening with Jasper and her responsibilities.

Even though it wasn't late she could see that her mum was already dozing, and Gwen looked tired too. She had a sudden pang of guilt at the thought that Gwen was doing extra shifts to help Lia out, and had probably done a full day's work before she'd even arrived. It wouldn't be fair to keep her any longer, now that Lia was home.

'Is everything okay?' she whispered.

There was a grateful smile. 'Fine,' she replied. 'I'm not quite sure what was going on earlier,' she added, 'but all's well again now. Just got a bit confused, that's all, more so than usual, and I've no idea what triggered it. She couldn't tolerate her usual TV so we switched to reading instead.' She looked down at the book in her hand. 'I haven't read this since I was a child – I'm quite tempted to stay and finish it.'

'Well, you can if you really want to,' replied Lia, 'but I should get home if I were you.' She didn't need to tell Gwen how tired she looked. 'I can sort Mum from here.'

'But I haven't got her ready... Sorry, we got a bit carried away, and she's falling asleep now.'

'Don't worry, I can do it. I might give her bath a miss and get her straight to bed if she's that tired.' She smiled at Gwen's expression. 'Honestly, you've done more than enough for me. Go home and spend what's left of the evening with your own family.'

Jasper offered to help, just as she knew he would, but he accepted her refusal with good grace, understanding her desire for time with her mum without the need of an explanation. This quiet period before bed was often when Lia felt closest to her mother and Jasper knew when to withdraw. It didn't stop him from lingering slightly longer than usual on the doorstep, though, and his goodbye seemed to carry the weight of all that Lia was feeling herself. Still, tomorrow was another day, she reminded herself, and Jasper wasn't going anywhere.

She tiptoed back into the living room and lowered herself gently onto the sofa beside her mum, picking up the copy of *Dancing Shoes* and resting it on her lap.

'Hello, Mum,' she whispered, leaning in against her.

Rose's eyes had been closed and Lia had wondered if she was asleep, but to her surprise, they flickered open and she smiled.

'Lia.' She took her hand, squeezing it for a moment. 'Have you been dancing? I waited up for you.'

'I have,' she said. 'I've only just got back.'

The blue eyes rested on hers. 'I thought you had. Your cheeks are all pink and you look very pretty. Frank always says he loves me best when my cheeks are flushed like that. We went dancing tonight, too.'

'Did you?' asked Lia. 'I bet you had a lovely time.'

'Oh, we did… and don't you dare tell Mum, but he kissed me too, bold as brass.'

Lia smiled. 'Well, the cheek of it! But I won't tell, don't worry. Your secret's safe with me.'

'You're a good girl,' she replied, squeezing Lia's hand again. 'I might go to bed now that you're home though.' Her mouth opened wide in a yawn. 'I'm so tired.'

'Well that makes two of us. Come on then, let's go up, and once you're in bed I'll bring up some cocoa, how about that?'

★

She knew the minute she woke that something wasn't right. She had been tired herself when she climbed under the covers and, despite the huge number of things rushing through her brain, she had fallen asleep almost instantly. At first, she thought that a noise had woken her, but as she lay there staring at the ceiling, heart pounding, she realised that it couldn't have been a noise after all – what had woken her had in fact been the opposite: the complete absence of something that ought to have been there. She hurtled down the hallway to her mum's room.

Her mum had gone to bed as promised, gently and without protest, soft words on her lips and a smile in her eyes. Lia never dreamed for one minute that the light would go from them so soon, but the very moment she entered the room she knew her mum had gone. Her sweet smile had slipped away into the quiet spaces of the night while Lia wasn't looking. She pulled aside the covers and lay down gently on the edge of the bed, cradling her mother to her one last time as she waited for the dawn.

She wondered afterwards whether she should have done more, whether in the small fragments of time before it all went mad she should have checked whether anything more could be done. But, no. A massive brain haemorrhage, the doctor said when he arrived; one final stroke of bad luck that had carried her away from Lia for good.

She hadn't known who else to call at such an early hour, but Jasper had been calm and reassuring, knowing instantly what to do and who to call: the doctor and the local undertaker. The undertaker took her mum away, gently persuading her that she was better off at the funeral home. How could she be? *This* was her home. This was where she belonged. With Lia.

Jasper would have rushed to her side if she'd let him, but he seemed somehow too solid, too male in this house of women, and so instead she turned down his offer and sipped at the hot, sweet tea, which he had said would be good for her, and dressed herself in yesterday's clothes. There was only one other person who could comfort her now, someone who would take a single look at her and understand exactly how she was feeling and what she needed.

'Lucy,' she'd said softly in response to his question. 'I'd like Lucy to come.'

Chapter 30

'Jasper rang me,' explained Lucy a little breathlessly. 'I came as soon as I could.'

She stood on the doorstep without a clue what to do. How on earth could she possibly be of comfort to Lia when she had had so little experience of life, or more importantly death, before? She felt totally out of her depth, and almost ashamed of her inability to help when Lia needed her the most.

Because Lia had no-one. No brothers or sisters, no other parent with whom to share the grief. In life she, and she alone, had been there to care for her mum, and so it was in death. Only Lia could make the decisions over how to carry her memory forward. Her other relatives were scattered, scarcely seen, her mum's illness keeping them at bay. It was a huge burden for Lia to bear and one that was written across her face. Instinctively, Lucy held out her arms, folding Lia's mute body into hers.

The tears didn't come straight away, but Lucy could feel them building, could feel the tension in Lia's body as she fought to stay in control, fearful of what would happen once she let go. Eventually, with a huge intake of breath, she felt Lia's first sob shudder against her shoulder. From then on it was all Lucy could do to hold onto her friend, her slight frame shaking violently as her grief exploded from her. They clung together, rocking, Lucy's own tears falling onto Lia's hair until gradually, like a storm rolling past, the intensity lessened, the ragged breathing eased and a washed-out calm took their place.

'Do you know what the very worst thing is?' said Lia, a little while later as they sat in the living room, Lia holding a copy of *Dancing Shoes* in her hand. 'It's that her life has suddenly become so very small. I want to shout out to the world that she's gone and make them listen, make them acknowledge that her life had meaning. I want to scream at them that she was huge, that she was so very important that they cannot just carry on as if nothing has happened. But there's no-one to tell. If there's no-one to listen, then she's just gone – her life over in a blink, like she was never really here. So utterly, utterly tiny in the vastness of everything.'

'But to you, she was the world,' replied Lucy. 'She was a whole chunk of universe that surrounded you and everything you did, and she'll never be unimportant or small if you remember all the million, gazillion things she was.'

'But what if I forget? What if I stop remembering?'

Lucy looked at her friend's pale anxious face. 'You won't,' she said, 'you can't, because she's inside of you, Lia. She is you, and you are her, and that's the way it will stay until the day *you* die.'

Lia nodded slowly, eyes brimming but seeing the truth of Lucy's words and finding some small measure of comfort in them. 'That's a nice thought,' she said, and Lucy had to turn away as her own eyes filled with tears again.

She'd never had to think like this before; to explore what death might look like, or to consider the possibility of a pain so vast and all-consuming that it might never leave. A few days ago, Lucy had seen Lia happier than she could remember her being, but now her life had turned once again and become something else. She thought back to her conversation with Oscar all those weeks ago. Love was at the heart of everything; the most wonderful of emotions with the biggest capacity for hurt. Oscar's daughter wasn't dead, but he had still grieved for her as if she were, and it was only the thought of that love now that was keeping him going, giving him hope. Lucy knew without a doubt that the same would be true for Lia; above all the hurt and pain she was currently feeling, she must never forget what it was to love someone like that.

She placed a hand on the book which Lia still clutched.

'Have you got photos of her?' she asked. 'From when she was dancing? I'd love to see them.'

Lia looked surprised but she nodded and crossed the room to a bookcase which stood in one corner. She lifted down a wicker basket and brought it back for Lucy to see.

'I used to get this lot out for Mum sometimes,' she said. 'In the early days of her illness. It seemed to help then. There's medals and all sorts in here, not just photos.' Lia lifted out a blue-and-red striped ribbon to show her. 'For a long while, after my dad left, she wouldn't have anything to do with this stuff. She said it was a part of her life that was over and there was no point dwelling on it. It was all up in the loft, though – she hadn't thrown any of it away.'

Lucy took a photograph that Lia handed to her. It was a rather stiff and formal picture, clearly taken at a competition. Two dancers stood side by side, medals around their necks, while two judges, Lucy supposed, flanked them on either side.

'Were these your parents?' she asked, looking at the black-and-white photo.

Lia nodded. 'It's hard to see the detail, but my mum had the most beautiful dresses. That one was one of her favourites – bright blue.'

Lucy looked at the diminutive figure. 'She looks tiny next to your dad.'

Lia peered closer. 'Yes, it's funny. I don't remember them ever being so different in height, unless my dad was standing on a box, of course. They did things like that in photos back then. When you think about it, they should have looked quite odd when they danced, but they didn't; they were beautiful together, so graceful.'

'It's easy to see why you're such a great dancer,' added Lucy, smiling. 'You're so like your mum.'

'Am I?' Lia took back the photo. 'I never thought so, but she had chestnut hair too, so I guess I do to some extent. That's why she loved that dress I think; she had bright green eyes as well, and the colour really suited her.'

'And your dad?' asked Lucy.

'Oh, dark is all I remember. Eyes like coals, but always smiling, twinkly.'

Lucy watched as Lia studied the photos, a smile playing over her face as the memories came flooding back, just as she hoped they would. 'It's so sad that your mum stopped dancing,' she said. 'I understand it up to a point, but to give all that up must have been heartbreaking.'

Lia sniffed. 'She loved my dad, you see. That's what it was. It broke her heart when he left and I think the thought of ever dancing without him was just too much to bear. He was the one, you see – her perfect lead – and no-one could ever match him.'

'And is that how you feel about Jasper?'

To Lucy's horror the tears began to well again.

'I don't know now,' said Lia, sniffing. 'I thought so, but not any more... how can I? Not when I've let my mum down so badly.'

Lucy looked around the room as if suddenly realising that Jasper wasn't there and thinking very much that he ought to be.

'Lia, how could you have possibly let your mum down? You've done everything you could for her, and you said yourself how much better she's been over the last few weeks. That's down to you – you and Jasper.'

She had hardly finished the sentence before Lia shook her head violently. 'No,' she said. 'I got it wrong. It's like these photos. Once upon a time I was convinced that they were helping her. She would become more animated, lucid for longer periods of time, and she would talk about other memories too. But then, after a while, it made her more agitated. She got so distressed, and I realised that all the memories did were highlight what she had lost. They made her sad in the end, not happy.' Her face was full of anguish as she looked up at Lucy. 'I've been kidding myself these last few weeks, because I so wanted to believe that things were getting better, but in fact all I've done is forgotten what these memories did to her.' She brushed angrily at her eyes and threw the photograph back in the basket.

Lucy could have kicked herself. She had thought that by encouraging Lia to revisit these happy memories of her mum it would help her to realise that they would always be with her, and for a time it seemed to be working – but now she had gone and put her foot in it. She should have realised that something was up after her strange conversation with Jasper that morning, or at least when she got to the house and found Lia by herself. Something didn't fit. Jasper would want to help Lia right now, to comfort her, but Lia had pushed him away. Lucy passed across another tissue.

'What happened, Lia?' she asked gently. 'Have you and Jasper had an argument?'

Lia plucked at the tissue she was holding, wiping her nose against the back of her hand instead of using it.

'No, that's just it,' she said between sniffs. 'We've been getting on so well that we even… well, we could have… in a little while…'

Lucy frowned. 'Lia, I'm not sure I follow.'

Lia stared at her. 'You know… kissed… and then…'

'Would it have been so very wrong if you had?'

'Of course it would!' retorted Lia, her voice raised. 'I spent so much time away from Mum, when I should have been here. Think how much worse it would have been if… So, I pushed him away earlier, on the phone. I couldn't bear to see him.' A tear escaped and rolled down her cheek. 'Sometimes I'm so selfish, I disgust myself.'

Lucy flinched at the harshness of her words; Lia didn't deserve to punish herself this way, and if Lucy was any kind of a friend she couldn't stand by and watch her.

'Your relationship with Jasper and losing your mum are two different things, you know, Lia. It might not seem like it now, but happiness and sadness can exist side by side. You have room in your heart for both, and you mustn't let your grief confuse the two. Don't push Jasper away when you need his love and support – now more than ever.'

Lia raised her chin. 'I don't need him,' she said stubbornly. 'He took me away from my mum when she needed me the most, and I was stupid enough to let him, following my own selfish whims when I should have remembered what I was supposed to be doing.'

'Lia, he didn't. He brought you and your mum a lot of happiness over the last few weeks. No-one could have predicted this would happen; you told me the doctor said so himself. If anything, dancing has made you more able to cope with things so that you enjoyed the time you had with your mum all the more. Last week you told me your mum had come alive of late and think how wonderful it is that at least she had that before she died.'

'But my mum and I did perfectly well without anyone else, and… and…' She suddenly realised what she had said and her face crumpled. 'Lucy, what am I going to do? I've pushed Jasper away now too. There's just me now.'

Chapter 31

The vicar smiled benignly at the gathered group as Hattie seethed, quietly. In one corner of the church stood a vast Christmas tree that twinkled under the church's overhead lights. It was traditionally garish in a riot of clashing colours and, while Hattie approved wholeheartedly, she knew she would have to soothe her sister's ruffled feathers at some point. When Jules had orchestrated the arrangements for her winter-themed floral decorations, she obviously hadn't factored in the likelihood of being upstaged by a gaudy fifteen-foot tree.

It was not this, however, which was making Hattie so upset. The wedding rehearsal was nearing an end and, while she was keen to make everything as near perfect as possible for Jules's frazzled nerves, there was no way she was leaving tonight without confronting her mum.

Her mum hadn't been home the day Hattie had gone to see her, or the two times after that, and although her dad had been there on one occasion he wouldn't discuss it, saying it wouldn't be fair if her mum wasn't present. Honestly! He even went so far as to say he understood how she was feeling, but his assurances that he would speak to her mum and ask her to call on Hattie had obviously fallen on deaf ears, because no further contact had been made. Ever since, her emotions had swollen to the point where it would have taken little for them to erupt, probably quite spectacularly. She just wanted to talk to her mum, to explain what she had meant all those years ago, but her mum's point-blank refusal to discuss it was heartbreaking – and felt unfair, not to mention hurtful. Hattie baulked at the injustice of it all – but she wasn't prepared to let tonight's occasion stand in the way of resolving the issue. Her mum could be as stubborn as a mule at times, and with Jules's wedding so imminent, and Christmas right behind it, she couldn't afford to leave it any longer. After all, now it wasn't just her relationship with her mum that was at stake.

The original plan had been for them all to go back to Jules's house for a meal after the rehearsal. However, five minutes ago, as the vicar had been explaining what would happen at the wedding when they went through to the vestry to witness the signing of the register, she had heard her mum whisper to Jules that she had one of her headaches coming on and might have to give the meal a miss. It was political, Hattie was sure of it. She knew she didn't see as much of her mum as Jules did, but she wasn't aware of her suffering from headaches in the past. Her dad wasn't looking too chuffed at the announcement, either.

She should have been paying attention to what the vicar was saying but she found her mind wandering back over the conversation she'd had with Jules at the final dress fitting and it was all she could do to keep a composed look on her face. The more she thought about it, the angrier it made her feel. It wasn't just her mum affected by this – it had shocked Hattie to the core. What hurt Hattie more than anything was the fact that her mum had kept it from her all these years, like an embarrassing illness that had been allowed to fester over time, and all because of some innocent comments that Hattie had once made – Innocent because she would never have made them if she'd known the truth about her mum. Of course, her mum had totally misinterpreted them and, worse, never given Hattie the opportunity to explain. It was no wonder they found themselves in the situation they were in now.

Finally, things seemed as if they were being wrapped up. Jules and Ryan were beaming from ear to ear and shaking the vicar's hand and, despite her turmoil inside, Hattie could still feel a thrill of excitement for them; it was less than a week until their wedding. She fell in line with the other bridesmaids and followed them back up the aisle as they went to collect coats, gloves and scarves, muffling themselves up against the bitter chill outside.

Her mum and dad were the first out into the quiet lane and Hattie hurried to catch up with Jules. She hated having to do this.

'Is Mum really not coming back to yours?' she asked.

Jules looked at her fiancé for guidance and Hattie could see the anxiety on her face, even in the dim light.

'I know you need to do this, Hattie, but does it have to be tonight?' She kept the smile on her face and her voice low.

'Jules, you get married at the weekend – when else am I going to get the chance? I can't come to your wedding and not have her talking to me; that would be awful… for all of us.'

Jules sighed. 'I know she owes you an explanation, and she was wrong to take offence over what you said, but do you still think she's wrong about the other thing too?'

'Don't you?' Hattie countered. 'Think what it might mean for us, Jules, and for any children you might have. Family is the most important thing in the world.'

'I know. It is.' Jules squeezed her hand and looked out into the night beyond the church door. 'Go on, Hattie, go after her. I'll make your excuses and we'll still have a nice evening.'

Hattie flashed her a quick smile and hurried down the path from the church. Her mum and dad were just pulling away from the kerb, and as Hattie climbed into her own car, she prayed they were going straight home; it was just around the corner.

It was her dad who opened the front door, his initial smile of delight fading into sheepish understanding as he worked out why she was there.

'It's probably not a great time, love,' he said. 'Your mum's not feeling too good.'

'That's rubbish, Dad, and we both know it. I know you're sticking up for her, I wouldn't expect anything less, but are you going to let me in, or what?'

'Hattie, this is very hard on your mother – it's very hard on all of us.'

'But it's not right, Dad,' she protested.

Her father took a step backwards, an apology in his eyes. 'I know,' he said quietly. 'Look, come in, but your mother doesn't want to discuss it and I can't force her to. We have to respect her decision, love.'

'And I do, Dad. I understand how hard this must be for her, but she's had five years to get used to the idea – I've only just found out. I will respect her decision when she's discussed it with me like an adult instead of keeping me in the dark because she misunderstood some comments I made years ago. Comments which, I might add, I would never have made if she'd told me the truth at the time. That wasn't fair. I should at least be able to explain now.'

'It's all right, Bob, let her in.'

Hattie stared down the hallway at the sound of her mother's voice. Her head was just poking around the living room door.

'Mum, I'm not here to make trouble, honestly.'

'I know you're not, love.' She paused for a moment, looking at her feet. 'Your dad had a word with me.' Her mum took a step into the hallway. They could only have been home a couple of minutes and yet her mum had already kicked off her shoes and replaced them with fluffy slippers. They looked rather incongruous with the smart skirt she was wearing.

'I was scared, Hattie,' she said. 'I didn't know what to think about any of it at the time. I still don't. It was all such a shock, and I know I reacted badly, but when you said those things, I, well…'

'What, Mum?' Hattie had moved past her dad and was now only a couple of feet away from her. She could see that she was trying to hold back tears.

'I thought it meant you didn't love me, too.'

Hattie covered the distance in seconds, pulling her mum to her as if she were the child. 'Oh, Mum,' she said, close to tears herself. 'How can you think this is about not loving someone, when it's exactly the opposite? Your mum loved you so much…'

She glanced back at her dad, who was still hovering by the front door.

'I'll go and put the kettle on,' he said, and Hattie flashed him a grateful smile.

'Come on, Mum,' she said, holding her arm and guiding her back towards the living room. 'Let's go and sort this out once and for all.'

If a room could be said to reflect someone's personality, then this one summed up her mum perfectly. Everything about it was uptight, striving for perfection, careful and measured, playing it safe. Where Hattie's rooms were colourful and chaotic, alive with colour and texture, her mum had chosen muted shades of coffee and cream and everything matched. There were accents of gold, but no other colours, either in the soft furnishings or the few personal possessions that were allowed in the room. It was quite possibly this preference for order, thought Hattie, that was the reason why her mum had been knocked for six by recent events; every aspect of her life was planned and executed so carefully, she simply couldn't cope when anything unexpected came along.

It certainly wasn't a room for lounging in, and by the time her mum had perched on one end of the stiffly upholstered sofa, Hattie could see that her guard was back in place, shutters raised against any potential unpleasantness. It made Hattie want to shake her.

'Why didn't you tell me you were adopted?' she began straight away. 'You told Jules, why not me?'

Her mother pursed her lips. 'Because of all that silly business with your wedding. It wasn't the right time.'

Hattie could feel her shoulders begin to tense. 'That "silly business", as you put it, was the night I caught my fiancé with someone else. The night my heart was broken into a thousand tiny pieces. Was I supposed to just ignore it?'

'I didn't say that,' replied her mum, chin jutting out, 'but it *was* quite hard to talk to you – you were in such a state.'

The anger hit Hattie with full force. Her mouth dropped open as she stared at her mother's impassive face. 'Is it any wonder?' Her words were like little chips of ice. 'I thought I was the luckiest girl alive the night of our engagement party; I certainly felt like the happiest. My whole life was ahead of me, all my hopes and dreams were about to come true. And instead of it being the start of our lives together, the man I loved with all my heart, and who I thought loved me, swapped our future for a mindless fuck.'

Her mother's hand shot to her face. 'Hattie!' she exclaimed.

'What? That's what it was. His very words, if I remember rightly. Then days later, when I'm still reeling from the shock, I find out I'm pregnant. The fact it wasn't planned isn't something I'm particularly proud of, but it was still something that should have been one of the happiest times in my life, full of wonder and love, and he even took that from me.' She wiped away a sudden tear angrily. 'Except that he didn't, not really, because you know what I discovered? That even when my whole life had fallen apart and I thought I'd been left with nothing, I found something so strong, so powerful, that it gave me the strength to go on. I thought you, of all people, would understand how special the love you have for a child is, and that nothing can come between it.'

'I thought I did too,' her mum replied, bitterly. 'But how wrong could I have been? My mother was a coward – my real mother that is. She never even bothered to fight for me.'

'You don't know that! Things were different back then. I was lucky, I had a choice, but maybe she didn't. Maybe she spent every day of her life thinking about you, hating that she'd had to give you up.'

'Don't you think I haven't thought about that, Hattie? Every day since I found out I was adopted – and just when I thought I was beginning to understand things, you open your mouth and rub my nose in it!'

Hattie swallowed back the bile that filled her mouth. She wanted to scream how unfair it all was, but she knew she had to take some of the responsibility for her words too. She softened her voice.

'Mum, I would never have said those things if I knew you were adopted. I was an emotional mess too, you know. Finding out I was pregnant sent my emotions through the roof, and then Grandma died only a couple of months afterwards. I never meant to hurt you – how could I, when I didn't know? I said those things because I suddenly realised that the little life growing inside of me was depending on me for everything and I was determined not to let her down.'

'You told me that adoption was a hideous thing to do!'

Hattie hung her head. 'Yes, I did, Mum,' she said wearily, 'because I had a *choice*. Because I was lucky and had a loving family around me who I knew would support me – *were* supporting me. Under those circumstances giving my baby up for adoption would have been the wrong thing to do, that's all I meant. I could have got rid of her; sometimes during the really tough times I even wondered whether I made the right decision, but Mum, Poppy is the best thing that's ever happened to me, and she's only here because of you… and Dad and Jules. For the first time in my life, I realised what it was to be totally responsible for another life. That the tiny person growing inside of me only ever had me to fight for her, to care for her, to love her. How could I refuse her that?' Her voice caught in her throat. 'Mum, everything I felt then was because of how you'd brought me up and loved me. You taught me what was right from wrong. I only turned down adoption because I *could*, don't you see that? I could never have coped all those months if it hadn't been for you, looking after me, standing up for me. I felt loved and although my world had fallen apart, you made me feel like everything was going to be okay, just as you always had. I said those things to show you how grateful I was, how lucky I felt to have you all around me, not the other way around.

'Your real mum may never have had that choice, however much she wanted to. Don't hate her for that, just because her circumstances may have been different from mine… And don't hate me because you misunderstood what I said, because you'd just given me the greatest gift a mother could ever have: you allowed me to love my daughter just the way you loved me.' And with that, she burst into tears.

It had felt like years since her mum's arms had encircled her, but the moment they did, it was as if those years had never been.

'Hattie, I'm so sorry… I didn't realise. I never thought…'

'I'm sorry, too...'

Hattie wasn't sure how long they clung to one another, as their tears of both sorrow and happiness turned their noses and faces red, and made their shoulders damp. At some point the seat beside Hattie dipped as her father came to join them, his arms lending strength to them both.

'I thought your grandma was a coward too,' her mum confessed. 'For all these years I felt like she'd taken away something from our relationship but now I realise why she did what she did.'

'Grandma knew she was dying, didn't she?' Hattie guessed.

'She did, and I blamed her for all the times when she could have told me but didn't, her death robbing me of the chance to talk to her about it, but now I think I see why.'

Hattie nodded. 'She loved you so much, Mum. It didn't matter to her that she'd adopted you – she rightly thought of herself as your mum, and the idea of that ever changing was too awful to contemplate. She wanted to remain your mum the whole time she was alive and not suddenly become something else in your eyes. Some people might think that's selfish, denying you the knowledge all those years, but I can see why to her it made perfect sense. She wanted to protect you – like only a mother could. By leaving you that letter in her will, she ran the risk of spoiling your memories of her forever... But I think she trusted that you'd come to the right conclusion; that you'd know that she'd only ever done what she did out of love.'

'And it took you to show me that.' She smiled at Hattie, her carefully styled blonde hair now tousled. 'I've been so stupid,' she added with a rueful smile. 'You'd think I'd know better at my age.'

'Mum, we're all capable of making mistakes, however old we are. The trick is in recognising them and doing something about them before they wreck our lives any further.' She gave her mum's hand an encouraging squeeze. 'Have you thought any more about what you might do now?'

She could see the look that passed between her parents over her head.

'About the letter from the adoption agency?' her mum said. 'Is that what you mean?'

'I'm sorry, Mum. Jules told me, only because I—'

'I know. I've been horrible to you these last few weeks since the agency contacted me, and I shouldn't have tried to colour Jules's judgement too. You don't need to apologise, sweetheart. I should have told you all about this years ago – when Grandma first died, in fact, but... well, it was just the timing of it all... And then, somehow, the years just went by and I was able to forget the things you said and move on. It's only since the whole issue of adoption got stirred up again recently that those old feelings resurfaced. If I'd have acted properly back then, things wouldn't have festered like they have... I'm so sorry, Hattie. And now one of the biggest decisions of my life is facing me and I even kept that from you, when what I should have done was share it.'

She sat up a little straighter, her hands smoothing her hair and rubbing at her face. 'Now I know that this isn't a decision for me to take on my own after all. These are my parents, Hattie, but they're also your and Jules's grandparents. I think we should talk about this together, like a proper family.'

Hattie broke into a smile. 'Mum, I think that's a brilliant idea.'

Chapter 32

'Give me twenty minutes,' whispered Jules. 'I've been trying to get rid of Ryan's parents for the last half hour. I've done coffee and mints, even made hints about having to get up early in the morning, but they don't seem to be in a hurry to get back to the hotel.'

'Take it as a compliment,' replied Hattie, smiling at the exasperation in her sister's voice. 'At least they're not making snide remarks about having their son come back home so he can have some "proper" food.'

Jules laughed. 'I'm almost beginning to wish they would,' she said. 'They'll be wanting to move in at this rate.'

'Just tip us the wink when the coast is clear. As long as you're sure it's not too late.'

Hattie could hear the smile in her sister's voice as she answered. 'No way, I've been waiting a long time for this.'

She clicked off the call and turned to face her mum, who was waiting anxiously behind her. 'All sorted,' she said. 'We can go in about half an hour. And, Mum… stop fussing, your hair looks lovely.'

Now that the reality of what they were about to discuss was beginning to sink in, Hattie could see her mum's nerves begin to flower. She was adrift; for the first time in quite a few years she wasn't fully in control and she was unsure how to deal with this new sensation.

Hattie couldn't imagine what it must be like to face the decision her mum was about to make. Of all the people in your life, your family were the ones you took for granted – and whether you got on with them or not, parents were parents. Of course, she wasn't naïve enough to think that everyone had this luxury – she was well aware that some folks didn't have the great start in life she'd had – but for the majority of people it was something they never thought about.

It also made her realise what a happy childhood she'd had. Things had got a bit emotional with her mum back there for a few minutes, but everything she had said was true. She had always known that she was loved, and though the last few years had felt a little rocky, she'd been aware even then that her mum and dad would have been there for her if she really needed them.

What must it be like to question that love? She wasn't sure how she felt about the fact that her grandma wasn't her real grandmother – but then again, she absolutely *was* in every way that mattered. How strange to think that now there was another person out there who, with one word from them, was waiting hopefully to fulfil that role. If Hattie's head was buzzing, what on earth must her mum be feeling?

She turned to her dad and took the coat he was holding out, helping her mum shrug her arms into the sleeves. Whatever else happened in the next couple of hours, they must help her mum find a way through the chaos and confusion, which surely was filling her head right now. Her safety net had gone, and it was up to them to help her back down to the ground.

★

Half an hour later it was clear that Jules's guests had only just left. The coffee table in the living room was littered with glasses and a couple of mugs, and virtually every surface in the kitchen held serving dishes, platters or stacks of plates and bowls. Hattie realised with a rush of saliva to her mouth that she had not yet eaten, and with a look behind her swiped a profiterole off one of the platters and shoved it into her mouth whole. A satisfying squirt of crème pâtissière filled her cheeks as she chewed.

She was about to start clearing things away when she realised that someone was standing behind her. She swallowed hastily.

'I thought I'd give Mum and Jules a bit of time together,' she said to Ryan, not quite meeting his eyes. 'And I don't know how long we're going to be, but you and Jules won't want to tackle this lot when we're gone, will you? Can I help tidy up?'

Ryan grinned. 'You must be starving,' he said, causing colour to flood Hattie's cheeks. 'Bugger the washing up – I'd stay and polish this lot off if I were you.' He picked up his own profiterole, winking at her as he too popped one in his mouth.

'I'm so hungry,' she admitted. 'Sorry. But these are gorgeous. Did Jules make them herself?'

Ryan sidled past her to the sink. 'Don't tell anyone, but she found a chap locally that makes them for parties and whatnot. They're really good, aren't they? Only trouble is, I think Jules catered for twice the number she needed.'

'Well, the three of us not turning up at the last minute didn't help, did it?'

Hattie found herself being scrutinised. 'Understandable,' said Ryan. 'Did you and your mum get things sorted?'

'I think so,' she replied. 'It's early days but I feel better than I have done in a long while.'

'Good.' He smiled at her. 'Jules has been really worried about you. I think she's found it all a bit difficult – like she was stuck in the middle?'

Hattie returned the smile, knowing that what Ryan said was true. 'I know, that's the stupid thing… This could have been sorted out ages ago, if only everyone had been honest and got together to discuss it. Still, that's families for you,' she said. 'You're not regretting marrying Jules I hope, now that you know what you're letting yourself in for?'

'Not a chance.' He grinned. 'My family are just as bad at times, too.' He scratched his chin. 'I do think you all need some time together, though… which is why I'm currently on kitchen duty.' He waved his arms at her. 'So, go on, shoo – go back and join them. I'm going to put the kettle on, make a big pot of tea and leave you all to it.'

Hattie smiled gratefully, feeling that another piece of the jigsaw had just fallen into place. She had always liked Ryan, but in truth she really didn't know him that well, and given her own disastrous wedding plans she was anxious that her sister didn't repeat her mistakes. Tonight's conversation with Ryan had put her mind firmly at rest.

She was about to say something to that effect when he suddenly came forward to kiss her cheek.

'I just wanted to say as well, you know in case I don't get a proper chance on the big day… but having you make all the dresses for Jules has meant the world to her. I hope you know that. Of course, I haven't seen hers yet, but the bridesmaids' dresses are totally gorgeous, and I can't wait to see Jules on Saturday – I know she's going to look amazing.' He gave her arm a squeeze. 'So, thank you.'

Hattie could feel her eyes begin to prickle. Today really was turning into the most emotional of days. But it felt good. In fact, it felt bloody marvellous.

Her mum and Jules were sitting side by side on the sofa when she returned to the living room, and her mum immediately patted the seat beside her.

'Come on, love,' she said. 'I need you to hold my hand too.'

★

If she was being absolutely honest with herself, Hattie would have had to say that disappointment was the emotion that slightly got the upper hand. She had thought about it all the way home, even though she was dog-tired and most of her brain felt utterly scrambled. She understood her mum's point of view perfectly, though; in fact, if it were her in that situation, she would have done the same. It was just that there was a part of Hattie that was always hopeful and open to possibility. There were two people out there somewhere, who desperately wanted to meet her mum, and therefore probably her too, and now she would never get the chance to know what they were like.

Replaying the last hour and a half in her mind, it was clear to Hattie that even by the time they got to Jules's house, her mum had all but made up her mind not to meet her birth parents. Hattie had had a part to play in that; if it hadn't been for her, and the things she had said tonight, her mum might have gone on believing that the woman she called Mum was a coward, and a selfish one at that. Instead, she finally understood why her adoption had been kept from her – that it had been an act of love from a mother to a daughter, and she didn't need to think beyond that. In the end, it had seemed a simple decision; things were okay in their world right now and that's the way they would stay.

Hattie pushed open her front door, relieved to hear only the soft sound of the TV from the living room. Poppy was obviously tucked up in bed and fast asleep and, as soon as Hattie had paid the babysitter, that's right where she headed too.

It was only some twenty minutes later, as she drew back her duvet cover, that she realised with a start that her mobile phone had been switched off since the wedding rehearsal. The babysitter hadn't mentioned it, but the thought that she would have been unreachable if her daughter had needed her filled her with guilt.

A series of beeps echoed through the room as she plugged her phone in to charge, and she automatically glanced down at the display, thinking that her mum or Jules perhaps were wishing her goodnight. Instead, she saw that she had missed three calls in the last two hours. She frowned as she quickly scanned the details, surprised as she noted the number. Why on earth would Jasper be calling her at this time of night?

Chapter 33

It was bitterly cold, or maybe that was just the way Lia was feeling; she hadn't felt warm for days. She pulled her cardigan around her and folded her arms across her chest. It didn't seem to matter how many clothes she wore, and even the central heating made little difference. She frowned, wondering whether it was even on, but she really couldn't be bothered to get off the sofa to check. She picked up the TV remote that was lying beside her and clicked off the television.

She had absolutely nothing to do. She was burying her mum tomorrow, but today still stretched ahead of her like a vast empty desert. She shook her head angrily. It wasn't a desert at all, it was cold for goodness' sake. It was... it was... she slapped her hands down on the cushions... all utterly pointless. Even her thoughts had been reduced to meaningless clichés.

The house was clean. She had watered the plants. The beds had been stripped and the washing hung in damp swathes over the banisters. She had chosen hymns, prayers and music and written down words to say. She had called people and told them her mother was dead. She had organised a buffet for people coming to the funeral and she had done everything that people had asked her to. Countless decisions over the flowers, the handles on the coffin, the number of people who would carry it, and the pattern that would go on the order of service. They were things she had no right and no desire to be thinking about, but finally, they were all done. Perhaps now people would stop talking at her. She laid her head back wearily on the sofa and closed her eyes.

It could have been anywhere between five minutes and three hours later that she became aware of the doorbell ringing. She was tempted not to answer it but she had tried that, and all that happened was that her phone started ringing instead – and when she ignored that, too, there were anxious taps on the window and shouts through the letter box. So many endless visits. Lucy had been the first, of course, followed by Hattie, and Gwen too. Jasper had called round once, but after she'd asked him to leave he'd resorted to sending Christopher to check up on her. After that, it was just Lucy who came, or Callum, or Hattie, or Lucy and Callum together. She got up with a sigh and went to answer the door.

Jasper looked awful. She had no idea what she, herself, looked like, but she didn't think he had slept in days. It puzzled her at first, until she realised why.

'Your family giving you a hard time, are they?' she said. Usually a comment like this would have had Jasper's head hanging from his shoulders, or at the very least his eyes grazing the floor, but to her surprise today all she saw was a slight tightening of his jaw line. His eyes remained on hers, their usual olive-green colour darkened with tiredness and something else she couldn't quite discern…

'Lia, I've never been anything other than honest with you so yes, they are giving me a hard time. So is my secretary, if you want to know, who is almost having a nervous breakdown on my behalf. That's not, however, why I'm here. Can I come in?'

She stepped to one side.

'Have you eaten today?'

Lia stared at him. She had done nothing *but* eat. Everyone who came made stuff, or brought stuff. Sandwiches, soup, casseroles, and tea, endless cups of tea.

'Yes,' she replied wearily, 'I've had—'

'Only I didn't think Lucy or Hattie had been round yet today.'

How on earth did he know that? She looked at her watch, trying to work out what day it was. She really couldn't remember whether she had seen anyone or not, but it was only eleven so she supposed she couldn't have. Besides, what difference did that make? She was perfectly capable of getting herself something to eat and drink. She opened her mouth to reply but Jasper had already moved past her down the hallway. She shut the front door with a bang.

The kitchen was just how she had left it, spotless, and she glared at Jasper as he plucked a loaf of bread from the side and started to cut huge doorsteps from it. He rammed the bread into the toaster and flicked the switch on the kettle with his other hand. He was obviously in a hurry.

'Jasper, I can do that for myself, you know, and you clearly have somewhere else you need to be. Despite the fact that you've been checking up on me every two minutes, I am capable of looking after myself. I also asked you not to come here, so why don't you do us both a favour and leave? Because I don't think I can cope with you banging around my kitchen.' She placed her hands on her hips. 'I can't cope with your anger,' she added. 'Or your pity.'

He whirled around to face her, eyes blazing, and she flinched, waiting for the explosion of rage that was about to come her way. Instead, just when she thought she couldn't hold her breath any longer, he lurched past her and strode down the hall. She realised a second too late that this wasn't what she wanted at all, and the tide of sorrow that hit her almost took her feet out from under her. She grabbed onto the back of a chair to steady herself, the tears that were never far from the surface already pouring down her face. She braced herself for the slam of the front door as Jasper left and the knowledge that she had lost him for good, but her heart was pounding in her chest and she struggled to hear over the roaring that filled her ears. She lifted her head slightly.

'I couldn't go,' said Jasper, leaning against the door frame, his own eyes filled with tears at the sight of her. 'A part of me wanted to. I probably should have, but I couldn't.'

He moved forward until he was standing beside her, his arms dangling by his sides. 'I don't know what you want from me,' he said. 'I wish I knew. You infuriate me at times, but I can't leave you. Every minute I'm apart from you it's like there's this deep, dark hollow inside, and I so desperately want to stay with you, Lia. Don't make me go.'

She could see one of his arms twitching and she knew it wouldn't take much to have them both surround her, taking away her pain. She took a step towards him, her hand outstretched. 'I won't,' she managed, 'I don't know what I want from you either, except to be here.'

Seconds later his hands were in her hair, his mouth grazing her cheek. 'We'll work it out,' he murmured, 'I promise.' Behind them the toaster popped with a satisfying clunk that neither of them heard.

★

Jasper scraped the last of the jam out of the jar and spread it onto the slices of toast that already dripped with butter.

'Now I feel guilty,' said Lia. 'I know you need to be anywhere but here.'

Jasper gave her an exasperated look. 'It's true,' he said. 'I've cancelled two meetings to be with you, and I'm not sure my secretary is ever going to speak to me again. It's a good job that Christmas is just around the corner so I can buy her an embarrassingly expensive present to make up for it.' He finished making the toast and handed the plate to Lia. 'However, much as I feel bad for dumping her in it when she's really a very nice person, I actually don't give a flying fuck about the meeting or the people I was meeting with.' He gave her a stern look. 'The same can't be said about you.'

Lia bit into a thick slice of toast. It was honest to God the best thing she'd ever tasted, and she realised she was ravenous. She also realised something else.

'I can't dance, Jasper,' she said in a rush. 'At the ball, I mean. I know I said I would, but I can't, not now.'

Jasper looked up. 'I know,' he said. 'It's okay.'

'But it isn't though, is it?' she replied. 'Not really.'

His eyes were still soft as they met hers. 'I think my family have got used to me not holding with tradition. I'm leaving the firm; I guess in the end it doesn't matter much how I go.' He licked his lips. 'There'll still be a ball of course, and all the lavish celebrations that go with it – just not me performing the grand opening dance.'

'And not me, either.'

'No.' He was quiet for a moment. 'I've hired a kind of circus act thing instead. I'm not really sure what they do actually – human juggling or something.'

Lia smiled ruefully. 'Your secretary organise that, did she?' she said. 'At great cost, no doubt. I'm surprised you managed to get anything so close to Christmas.'

'Well, I expect she must have promised to sleep with the whole troupe. She's very loyal, my secretary.'

He was teasing her, at least she hoped he was. 'So, money really does buy you everything?' she quipped in reply.

The smile dropped from his eyes. 'Not everything,' he said sombrely, 'but it can dig you out of a hole when you need it to.'

Part of Lia wished she had one of those right now. Somewhere dark and bottomless she could climb into. 'I'm sorry,' she said.

'Me too,' replied Jasper, taking another bite of his toast. 'I didn't mean to fall in love with you, Lia,' he added.

Lia's breath caught in her throat. She took a shaky breath. 'I didn't mean to fall in love with you, either.' There, she had said it. The fluttery words that had been dancing about her head for weeks were out, finally gone from her body. The relief was enormous. It was the first time she had ever said that to anyone – and she was inordinately pleased that it was to Jasper. The trouble was, she still didn't know what she was going to do about it. And, by the look on his face, neither did he.

'It was just meant to be the sort of transaction I deal with every day. A service, if you like.' He studied her face. 'I'm aware that sounds arrogant and uncaring,' he said. 'It's not meant to. But that's the way I've lived my life, Lia. It still is, to some extent. Perhaps it was part of the process; learning to be different again, learning to be me, but somewhere along the way, your smile and your laughter became a part of me.' He was quiet again, struggling for the right words. 'Actually, I think what did it, over everything, was your positivity. That ability you have to find joy in the simplest of things. I've never known that before, even up on the hill with the birds, I never knew that was what I felt until I was with you. It made me realise it's something I never want to lose.'

Lia's eyes filled with tears again. 'And it made me realise what it is to share that joy with someone,' she said softly. 'But Jasper, I don't know what kind of person I'm going to be when… when all of this is over. I can't be the same, how can I? Everything I was before is gone. The way I was, with you, with everyone, belonged to the Lia who looked after her mum, but now that she's not here any more, I'm going to have to find a new Lia. I'm just not sure how she's going to turn out... or how long it's going to take her before she knows what she is.' She sniffed, reaching for the tissue that Jasper automatically handed her.

He nodded gently. 'I can wait,' he said, but Lia shook her head.

'No, that's not fair,' she said. 'Don't make me promise.'

'I won't,' he replied. 'But I will wait.'

Lia had no answer for him this time.

They sat for a few silent moments until Jasper leaned forward slightly. 'After tomorrow I won't ask anything of you, but would you do something for me, one last time?'

Her nod was so slight she wondered at first whether he could even see it, but he drew her hand closer to him and she knew that he had.

'You mustn't be on your own tomorrow, or tonight. Will you let me stay? Look after you, be with you so that you won't feel so alone?'

She smiled a grateful smile through her tears. 'I'd like that,' she said sadly.

★

She slept on the sofa for most of the afternoon, waking with a start around four, thick-headed and far too hot under the blanket she had pulled around her. At first, she had dozed with her head in Jasper's lap. He said he didn't mind but when she woke for the first time she insisted that she move, and now he sat quietly at the other end of the sofa, head bent, reading. She threw back the cover, which made him jump.

'Ugh,' she grumbled, 'now I feel awful.'

He smiled. 'A temporary feeling, it'll pass. You look much better; the sleep will have done you good.'

She licked her lips. 'My mouth feels like the inside of a cage.'

Her legs bounced as Jasper got up suddenly. 'Too much information,' he said with a grin. 'I'll go and put the kettle on.'

He was only gone about a minute before he returned. 'I've had a better idea,' he said. 'I think we both could do with some fresh air. It's relatively early, so why don't we go for a walk? We can pop in somewhere for a drink too.'

Lia smothered a smile. 'My coffee getting to you, is it?' she teased. 'Don't bother to answer that,' she added, remembering the look on his face as he tasted her instant offering. She sat up and swung her legs over the side of the sofa, gently placing them on the ground as if testing their ability to hold her. After a moment she stood, wobbling slightly. 'I'll go and sort myself out,' she grimaced. 'I imagine I look rather less than lovely right now.'

She all but dragged herself up the stairs, her body not yet willing but her mind knowing that Jasper was right. She needed to get out of the house, and now that the idea had been put in her head she wondered why she hadn't thought it for herself. She closed her eyes briefly as she passed her mum's bedroom door, and carried on down the hallway.

The air outside was clean, untainted by emotion, and Lia sucked it gratefully into her lungs, feeling it spread through her like a cooling balm. Jasper took her hand as she walked out onto the path and it seemed to fit, as if it had always been there. She was glad of his solidness beside her.

As she pushed open the garden gate onto the street she blinked at the swathes of lights which blazed up and down the road; optimistic fairy lights that adorned windows, hedges, and trees – both indoors and out. They took Lia by surprise, partly because they alluded to the simple passage of time, which no longer seemed to hold any relevance for her, but also because they seemed so incongruous. Why was the whole world not in mourning? How was the world turning without her, when surely it should be stuck fast? She felt affronted by it at first, mocked by the joy that shone out into the night, when all she could see ahead of her was darkness. But, as they neared the town and the profusion of lights grew greater, she started to find it strangely comforting; an assurance that, whatever happened in the world, nothing was powerful enough to halt the seasons from turning. It gave her hope that perhaps there would be something for her, after.

Jasper was quiet beside her, perhaps lost in his own thoughts, or possibly mindful of hers. Since they had spoken earlier in the kitchen they had not revisited the subject of their relationship, and it had given her time to breathe, to simply exist in her own space with no demands on her, other than his presence. He was right; she didn't want to be on her own, but neither did she want to be told how to feel or what to think. She needed these last few hours before tomorrow to prepare herself mentally for what was to come, and the only way she could do that was by herself.

She shivered slightly as they turned the final corner before the High Street, a keen wind cutting across them for a moment before they passed once more into the shelter of the buildings. Strings of bright lights crisscrossed the street, multi-coloured, swaying gently, and all along both sides of the road the shops were each lit up with their own decorations. It was a cheery, welcoming sight.

'Drink first? Or shall we walk?' asked Jasper as they drew level with Earl Grey's, and she smiled at his supposedly innocent remark.

She checked her watch. 'They'll be closing soon, so a quick drink I think,' she said. 'I could just check with Clive that all's well for tomorrow too, couldn't I?'

Jasper didn't reply, but then he didn't need to. He opened the door for her, and followed her in.

There were only two other customers still lingering, and Lia hesitated, unsure whether it was fair to sit down now, when the tearoom would be closing shortly. But no sooner had she thought it than Clive appeared from behind the counter.

'You look freezing!' he exclaimed. 'Come and sit down and I'll get you something to drink.'

Lia glanced at Jasper. 'Only if you're sure that's okay. I didn't realise it was quite so late.'

Clive waved an airy hand. 'It's no problem, come on, sit. What can I get you?'

He reappeared a couple of minutes later with two steaming hot chocolates, placing them on the table and then sitting down himself.

'Now, is everything all right for tomorrow? If you want to change anything just say, otherwise I'll go with what we planned, and you won't need to worry about any of it.'

Lia was grateful for his business-like approach. Having him cater for the post-funeral gathering had been Lucy's idea of course, and it made perfect sense. He was kind, but not gushing, and had even come out to the house to make the arrangements. Lia had liked him instantly.

She smiled. 'That wasn't why we came in really, but I'll leave it to you, Clive. What we discussed sounded lovely.'

He called a thank-you across the room to the couple who were just leaving before turning his attention back to Lia. 'Right you are, then,' he said. 'I'll be here for a bit yet, so can I tempt you with anything else? I've got some whopping Chelsea buns left, or if you fancy something savoury I can rustle up some soup and a toastie perhaps. Vegetable and tarragon?'

It sounded exactly what Lia needed, but she was far too polite to agree to his suggestion. 'Clive, we mustn't keep you, that's really very kind, but—'

He got up suddenly and went over to the door, swiftly turning over the sign. He fished in his pocket for a bunch of keys and with a deft movement locked the door as well.

'Now then,' he said, returning. 'Does that make you feel better? I'm holding you captive for the time being, and like I said I'll be here for a bit yet, so having you two stay makes no odds to me.'

'The soup and sandwich sounds like a wonderful idea,' said Jasper firmly. 'Thanks Clive.' He picked up his hot chocolate and slurped the cream from the top, his eyes fixed on Lia. She followed his lead.

It was strange sitting in the empty tearoom eating their food, but oddly comforting. The streets outside still danced with light, but were almost deserted. The workers had gone for the day, and the last-minute shoppers had followed them, no doubt hurrying home to get their own dinner. It was like being in a warm cocoon and, thought Lia suddenly, exactly where she wanted to be.

The soup was thick and flavoursome, the cheese toastie tangy and crisp, with grilled cheddar bubbling from its edges. Clive had retreated to the kitchen after first extracting a promise that they would stay as long as they liked, and for the last ten minutes or so they had both eaten steadily. Clive had turned some music on and the soft sound wafted out into the room. Christmas crooners, but it suited the atmosphere perfectly.

'That was very kind of Clive,' remarked Lia, some minutes later. 'It's only just occurred to me why he's here,' she added. 'How stupid am I?'

'Not stupid at all,' replied Jasper, although Lia could see that he had long since guessed that Clive's work for the evening was only just beginning. Clive had told her that everything would be made fresh for the funeral gathering tomorrow and he obviously meant it. 'He's Lucy's brother-in-law, isn't he?' Jasper asked.

Lia nodded. 'Hmm. You can see they're related. I don't know any of Lucy's other family, but I'd be willing to bet they're all as lovely as she is. I've got high hopes for Callum joining them too.'

Jasper gave her a quizzical look. 'Callum?'

'He's from the book club,' Lia explained. 'And he's been helping Lucy out in the library too. Now I think him and Lucy are, well, you know...'

Jasper still looked blank.

'Well, they're together... At least I think they are, and if they're not they should be. I've never seen a couple so in tune with one another.'

She could have kicked herself the minute she said it; the last thing she wanted to do was to bring up the subject of relationships again, hers or anyone else's.

Jasper had chosen that particular moment to take another bite of his toastie but she saw the instant her words hit home. There was a definite pause in his chewing before he carried on. The fact that he ignored it almost made it worse. How much more could she torture the poor man?

She sat in silence, fiddling with a crust on her plate, scarcely aware of her surroundings.

'Would you like to dance?' asked Jasper.

Her head shot up. 'What?'

'Would you like to dance? I've always loved this song.'

She stared at him, mute, trying to make out the music.

He had put down his sandwich and was staring at her intently. She nodded slowly, rising to her feet.

The space between the tables was tiny, but enough for Jasper to pull her to him, one arm around her waist, the other enfolding hers against his chest. He laid his cheek against the top of her head and together they moved slowly, silently with the music.

'Merry Christmas, Lia.' His voice was barely a whisper, the words lost in her hair.

'Merry Christmas, Jasper,' she whispered back, raising her head from his shoulder and closing her eyes. His lips were soft on hers and his hand rose to cradle the back of her neck, brushing gently against her cheek.

His voice was hoarse when he spoke again, his fingers still woven through her hair, caressing her neck. 'You're trembling.'

'I know… I'm afraid…'

'Of me?' he asked gently, pulling back slightly.

'No,' she breathed. 'I'm afraid of living.'

'Oh, Lia…' His thumb brushed away her tear. 'In the midst of life, we are in death,' he murmured, 'but you mustn't ever, ever, be afraid to live…'

And then he kissed her and she was lost all over again.

Chapter 34

Lucy put the phone down and burst into tears. 'I'm sorry,' she sput-tered, 'but that's the best news I've had all day.' Callum looked up from his laptop, startled.

'It's okay.' She flapped her hand at him. 'I'm fine. It's just with everything else that's been going on… Oh, that's just lovely…'

Callum didn't look at all convinced. 'Are you sure, only, you're crying, and—'

'They're happy tears,' she interrupted him. 'That's what I do when I'm happy.'

'Right…' said Callum slowly, shaking his head. 'I'll try and remember that.'

That made Lucy smile too, the fact that Callum's thoughts about her were stretching into the future.

'So, are you going to tell me what the good news is?' he asked, trying to stifle a smile.

Lucy scrubbed at her eyes. 'That was Clive on the phone,' she said. 'You'll never guess who he's just had in the tearoom?'

Callum rolled his eyes. 'Just tell me Luce, I'm never gonna guess. We'll be here all night.'

She leaned forward, a little excited now. 'Jasper and Lia. Dancing. Together. What do you think of that?'

'Dancing?'

'Yes, apparently. Slow-dancing to a Christmas record. Clive said it was one of the most touching things he's ever seen.'

'Why would they be dancing in the tearoom?' He scratched his head. 'Lucy, try and remember that I couldn't actually hear your telephone conversation. What on earth are you talking about?'

Lucy grinned, all trace of her tears gone now. 'Clive's working late at the tearoom tonight, preparing the buffet for the funeral tomorrow. He was just shutting up shop when Jasper and Lia came in for a drink. Well, you know Clive, he made them something to eat and said they could stay for as long as they liked... Anyway, he put on some Christmas music while he was working and when he popped back through a little while later to collect their plates they were slow-dancing in the middle of the room.'

'And?'

'How can you ask me *and*? I think they might be together after all. Oh God, I hope so. I won't feel quite so much like it's my fault if they are.'

There was an audible tut. 'For heaven's sake, Lucy – how can Lia's mum dying possibly be your fault?'

'You know what I mean,' she pouted. 'I still feel responsible for all of this.' She looked down at the lines she had written in her notebook. 'You know, with Oscar as well. They were both on the verge of being so happy, but now...'

Callum had been trying to turn his attention back to his laptop. He sighed. 'Listen, we don't know how things are going to pan out for either of them. So, the only thing we can do is be there for them if they need it. And tomorrow, Lia definitely will need our help. It's great if Jasper's going to be on the scene too, but things won't end for Lia tomorrow. In fact, it's only the beginning.'

Lucy bit her lip. 'They're weird things, beginnings,' she mused, looking up at Callum. 'In that they always follow an ending... So, in fact an ending is never really the end at all, is it?'

'I guess,' replied Callum. 'And that's as opposed to a beginning, a middle and an end.' He gave her a pointed look, flicking his eyes to the notebook in front of her. 'Are you ever going to tell anyone about that? Or better still, show it to someone?'

Lucy pulled the notebook to her, defensively. 'No,' she said. 'Why would I?'

'Only, I can't see the point of it otherwise. Why do you do it?'

She looked down at the words on the page, thinking for a few moments. 'Because it's just something I do, that's all.'

Callum gave a wry smile. 'Okay,' he said. 'Just you keep thinking that then. After all, there's no need to consider that it might possibly lead to something else, is there? Perhaps a new beginning all of your own? I mean, there's nothing wrong with it, but you weren't planning on staying at the library forever, were you?'

'Don't you bloody start,' she muttered. 'I've had enough of Rachel, trying to depose me by any possible means. That's her latest trick.'

'She still giving you a hard time then?'

'And some. Her latest tactic consists of rubbishing our jobs at every available opportunity. How it's a fruitless career, how in fact there are no job prospects at all, and that anyone would be mad to try and carve a future out of it. Of course, she doesn't mean it at all, she'd give her eye teeth to be manager, and if Clare doesn't come back from maternity leave they *will* have to think about a permanent replacement.'

'Well let them think about it. Lucy, you'll have done the job for the best part of a year by then. That would put you in a very good position if you wanted to be considered.'

Lucy pulled at her lip. 'I know, it's just that…'

Callum gently closed the lid on his laptop and shuffled his chair closer to her. He sat back, folded his hands in his lap and fixed his eyes on her face. And waited.

'You can admit how you're feeling, you know,' he said after a few minutes of watching Lucy squirm, 'because you know I'm going to sit here until you do.' The skin at the side of Lucy's finger had almost formed a callus where she'd been holding a pencil, and she picked at it where the edges of the skin were rough.

'Lucy…?' There was a warning note to Callum's voice.

'Okay,' she huffed. 'Stop nagging me. It's just that I've tried for so long to keep from acknowledging any of this that I'm finding it really tough to admit to it. And now there's all this other stuff too.'

'What stuff?'

'Well, I used to think that things were quite simple and then I found myself becoming involved in what was happening in other people's lives, and I've realised just how complicated life can be – how you can be set on a particular path one minute and then something comes along which prompts a life-changing decision. Like, Lia for example, or Oscar. It's made me realise what a journey life is, but also that for the last few months I've stopped being a driver and become a passenger; almost as if I'm waiting for something… Trouble is, I'm not sure what.'

Callum looked at her, weighing up her words. 'Perhaps there's something about yourself that you haven't acknowledged yet, something that you need to understand before you can move on. I've been on a pretty steep learning curve myself lately and I've realised quite a few things about my life, too – about what I want. Ask yourself how you feel about everything in your life right now; maybe that will give you the answer.'

She stared at him, suddenly realising what he had said. Of course! Her thoughts hadn't been just about Oscar, Lia and Hattie, they'd been about Callum too. All those weeks ago when they'd sat in the pub, Callum had confided in her the things he wanted from his life, and from that moment on his life had begun to change so that now… She swallowed. Now when she looked at him she saw a very different person than the one who had been sitting beside her that night. Now she saw someone who… And then she stopped, and swallowed again as both of her trains of thought collided. She hardly dared to ask the question.

'So how do *you* feel?' she asked. 'What's changed for you over the last little while?'

She had expected Callum to perhaps blush a little, or at least to look a little reticent. Instead, his mouth widened in a huge grin and his eyes reflected a light that hadn't been there before, as he very deliberately held her look.

'Oh, that's easy,' he said. 'You, of course.'

'Ah.' It was all she could think of to say.

Callum maintained the grin. 'Or, if you want more details, the fact that I felt a totally worthless nobody – shy, insecure, with no confidence to speak of – and now I don't. I was antagonised by my brothers, largely ignored by my parents, and now I've found what it is to be a proper family. I've been welcomed into your home as if I'm one of you, by people who take a real interest in what I have to say and who've shown me how simple things like eating a meal together, or playing Monopoly, or talking about their day, are so important. More than that; these things become our lives, they make us who we are. They are loving and nurturing, happy and supportive and there's nothing whatsoever trivial about all that.'

He paused to take an even bigger breath. 'And, a few months ago, I thought that love was fireworks and not being able to breathe, indefatigable lust and something that changed you totally as a person. I've learned now that if you're really lucky, love grows out of a friendship that you never want to lose, it brings colour and meaning to everything you do – sometimes with fireworks, yes, but more often in the quiet, small things. Far from changing you, love takes the person that you already were and makes it into a better version of you.' He smiled mischievously. 'The only thing I was right about was the indefatigable lust.'

'Oh.' Lucy blushed furiously, her heart suddenly going like the clappers. 'So, what are we going to do now?'

'Well, I'm going to start putting the plans for my business into action, and—'

Lucy pushed at his arm. 'I wasn't talking about our bloody jobs!'

Callum grinned. 'No? Oh well, then I don't know about you, but first I'm going to check if the lady in question feels the same way as me. Then, when she indicates that she does and that she has no objection, I'm going to kiss her.' He gave her an enquiring look. 'I should have done this weeks ago.'

It really was the strangest thing, thought Lucy as his lips met hers, because ten minutes ago she'd had no inkling that her evening would turn out this way. She had only been concerned with how Lia, Oscar and everyone else had been feeling and how the complexities of the last few months were playing out. The pages in her notebook were filling up, but apart from trying to identify her part in all of this, she had never directed her thoughts to her own situation and how that was changing.

Now, it was as if she was reading her own character's story in a book and she had just reached the plot twist; the part where the reader slaps their forehead and mutters, 'Of course, how did I not see that coming!'

More than that, though, it was as if Callum's touch was dragging her deeper and deeper within herself, to the heart of what really mattered. All of her vague thoughts and hopes crystallised into a clear and perfect vision of how she wanted her future to be. If she were to look up, she wondered, would she see this longing rising around her, like a plume of coloured smoke? She could feel herself smiling, because that was something else she knew… It would be green, of that she was certain, because green was the colour of hope.

'Well I'm glad you're smiling,' said Callum, who was grinning from ear to ear. 'I did wonder whether I was about to get slapped.'

'No, definitely not slapped,' murmured Lucy, pulling him closer again. 'Do that once more,' she added, 'I just want to be sure…'

She pulled away eventually, a little breathless. 'Did you feel that?' she urged.

'Well, I felt something,' Callum replied, a very obvious twinkle in his eye.

Lucy blushed. 'No, I didn't mean that, although…'

Callum winked at her this time. 'So, has the penny dropped? Have you finally figured it out?'

The notebook still sat on the table in front of them, and Lucy pulled it towards her, opening it at the page on which she had last written. A page that showed part of the chapter she had been working on. She stared at the words, then she flicked backwards a few sheets. She sat back thinking of the drawer in her bedroom that held at least ten other notebooks, and which between them formed the book she had somehow started to write.

'What do you mean, have I finally figured it out?' She looked back up at Callum's smiling face. 'Are you telling me you knew that's this is what I should be doing? Why didn't you tell me, you swine!'

Callum grinned. 'Because you needed to work it out for yourself. You needed to see your place in all of this – not as someone who was helping everyone else along their journey, including me by the way, but as someone on a journey of their own.'

'The weird thing is, now I can see my desire to write has been there all the time, staring me in the face. Every now and then I would glimpse it out of the corner of my eye, but I refused to turn and look at it properly, to acknowledge that it even existed. I think I've been so busy getting caught up in what everyone else was yearning for that I didn't stop to think about what I wanted. Maybe I felt guilty about giving up a career in teaching, I don't know…'

'But now you're ready to let it into your life?' Callum's hand took hers.

'Oh yes,' replied Lucy, 'now I'm ready.' She could see the blank pages stretching ahead of her, filling with her words, bringing colour and life to the stories that she wanted to tell. The thought made her happier than almost anything. Almost…

'It's not the only thing I'm ready to let into my life, though,' she said, leaning forwards once more. 'There's something else very special, too.'

Chapter 35

The view from her bedroom window was the same as it had been for every one of Lia's thirty-two years. But come tomorrow, things would be different. Today, she would say her final goodbyes to her mum – and that altered everything. As she stared down into the street, she wondered how this new world would look. At least the weather was being kind.

Even so, it was cold in the bedroom and Lia held the mug of tea to her in comfort. It was the first of many she would undoubtedly drink during the hours ahead and, while a part of her wished for time to stand still, another wished for an end to the day so that she could climb back into bed and hide from everything, losing herself in the oblivion of sleep.

She had been aware of Jasper's presence at times during the night, conscious of the thin wall that separated them as he lay in the hastily made up spare room, but she had slept, much to her surprise, until his soft knock this morning and a welcome drink. She had risen and put on the dress that Hattie had given to her. It was bold, bright and utterly beautiful, just the sort of thing her mum would have loved to dance in and therefore the perfect thing to wear.

The day went as well as could be expected. Jasper didn't leave her side, his unobtrusive and undemanding presence, and gentle care of her exactly what she needed. He spoke to people when she had no words, organised them when decisions were beyond her and, as the morning became the afternoon, she could feel her face begin to unstiffen from its taut veil of dried tears.

Now they were back at her house and the kind neighbours and acquaintances that had come to pay their last respects had gone. There was just Jasper, Lucy, Hattie, Callum and Oscar left; five firm friends crowded into her tiny kitchen, and she felt safe, cocooned in the warmth of their closeness. There would be a time soon when Lia would want to be on her own, but not yet.

The kettle was coming to the boil again. More tea, but it was a comforting routine, part of the ritual of friendship, and today, more than any other day, they were all prepared to drink gallons of the stuff if it helped Lia. She looked around at their generous faces and realised that, apart from Oscar, they had each taken their turn in her kitchen this week – making drinks, preparing meals. They had got her through it and she realised suddenly that, from now on, they would be a part of her future too.

Hattie was deep in conversation with Lucy and Callum. Maybe Lia had imagined it, but there had been a touch here and there between the latter two that spoke of a new closeness. Or perhaps, thought Lia, it was just the happiness that shone out from both their faces. She tuned back in to the conversation when she heard her name.

'But you must be thrilled!' Lucy was saying to Hattie. 'From what you've said, there's going to be masses of people at the wedding, and they'll all be wanting to know who made the beautiful dresses. Even if you only get a couple of bites it will be worth it. Word of mouth is the best advertisement. I mean, look at Lia today; apart from being the most inappropriate outfit I think I've ever seen anyone wear at a funeral, she looks amazing.'

Jasper cleared his throat pointedly and Lia blushed.

'I know we said I should wear this when I dance, but now I'm not going to; it just seemed… fitting to wear it today.'

'And I'm honoured, Lia, I truly am. If that dress has helped you at all, then my job is done,' said Hattie.

'But like Lucy said, when people get to see what you're capable of, it'll hopefully be a job that goes on and on.'

Hattie grinned. 'I know, and my sister has promised to sing my praises at every opportunity; a couple of her friends are getting married soon and they'll all be there. If I can get one or two commissions I can update my sewing machine and buy some other bits and bobs I'll need. Then I'll be all set to go. The best thing, of course, is that it will all work so well around Poppy.'

She fingered the neckline of the beautiful shift dress that Lia knew she had made.

'I don't know why I didn't think of turning my dressmaking into a business before.'

'Things often have a time and place all of their own, I find, and you know instinctively when the moment is right,' said Lucy.

'Plus,' Lia cut in, 'you look absolutely gorgeous, and whether you realise it or not, that's given you masses of confidence.' She reached out a hand towards Hattie. 'I mean, look at this dress,' she added. 'You would never have worn something so slim-fitting before and even though you didn't need to lose any weight, the confidence it's giving you is rippling through other areas of your life.'

Hattie looked down at her dress, clearly thinking about Lia's words. 'I think I've finally become unstuck,' she said. 'Freed from all those things that were holding me back. Things I didn't even know I was stuck to.' She pulled a face. 'Like Poppy's dad, for one. I thought I was over him when really I've been letting him and his actions tell me I'm rubbish for years. You start to believe it after a while.'

Callum nodded, a knowing smile on his face. 'You do,' he said. 'It's a trap I've fallen into myself, but if you're lucky, something, or someone, comes along to change all that.' He looked pointedly at Lucy, and Lia felt a surge of happiness. It made her hugely relieved that she could still feel such a thing.

'You've obviously found what it is that sets you on fire,' added Callum. 'There'll be no stopping you now.'

Hattie blushed gently. 'I hope so,' she said. 'I feel it's time I stopped treading water.' She dropped her head a tiny bit. 'There's another reason,' she added – somewhat shyly, thought Lia. 'Just something that's given me some hope for the future, which is daft really, considering, and harder still to explain why, but the thought of it all makes me feel… optimistic – a little excited, even.' She looked directly at Lia. 'I've told you a few things about my family, haven't I? How cold my mum has been over recent years?' She looked at the group and then back at Lia, fingers touching her mouth. 'I'm not sure I should tell you this really, but I don't suppose it matters—' She stopped suddenly, pulling her brows into a frown and then, 'No, actually – it's nothing to be ashamed of; that was part of the problem all along… You see, my mum was adopted; she found out just after I fell pregnant with Poppy, when the woman I thought of as my grandma died. I told her I could never give Poppy up for adoption – but only because I had the luxury of choice and didn't know about Mum's situation, but she took it the wrong way…' She paused again. 'Anyway, none of that much matters now. The thing is that my mum's real parents have come forward, and while she doesn't want to see them just yet, one day I might get to meet my real grandparents, and I'd love that for Poppy too. My granddad died when I was quite young, but I always had such a special relationship with my grandma. Nothing will ever change how I feel about her, but it would be wonderful to have that all over again…'

Lia looked up sharply, suddenly aware that the room had gone very quiet. Hattie sensed it too, a sudden flush of colour tinting her cheeks. 'Oh, God, I'm sorry. Listen to me rambling on. You don't want to hear all about that family stuff, I—'

It was Lucy who came to her rescue, moving between them all to give Hattie a warm hug.

'I think that's wonderful,' she said, pulling away with a generous smile on her face. 'You're right, it is a lovely thought, but, more than that, your family has been through some tough times. That you're managing to put those things behind you now can only be good.'

Lia could feel her eyes begin to prickle again, but she went forward to hug Hattie regardless. 'Lucy's right,' she said. 'There's nothing more important than family, is there?' She flapped a hand at her face. 'Just ignore me if I start blubbing again, but isn't that why we're all here today? To celebrate a life and to rejoice that it was here at all? What is it someone said…? *Don't cry because it's over, smile because it happened.*'

Oscar got to his feet, his sombre black suit enlivened by a deep-purple waistcoat and bow tie. 'Hear hear, young lady!' he said. 'Hear, hear!' And he raised an imaginary glass to her. The bubble of tension in the room dissolved in an instant.

'Oscar, that's a fine idea,' said Jasper, stepping forward. 'We need a drink! Now, is everyone okay with tea, or do we think we might manage a glass of something stronger?'

Lia looked at the clock on the wall. 'It's five o'clock somewhere,' she said. 'There's wine in the fridge, Jasper – and for God's sake, please everyone; sit down and help me finish this mountain of food!'

They all stared at the table, which was heaped with the remains of the wonderful buffet that Clive had made. Hattie pulled out a chair, as did Callum, followed rapidly by Lucy, who patted the one next to her. Jasper plonked a bottle of wine amid the bowls and dishes and stood at one end of the table. He motioned for Lia to take the other, and she sat down, laughing, with a small curtsy.

'Come on everyone,' she said, 'dig in.'

No-one needed a second invitation and the conversation flowed once more.

'It's just like my first book club meeting,' said Hattie. 'Do you remember? Where everyone talked about wish fulfilment and what they longed for. At the time, I didn't say anything because I didn't know what I wanted, but you did, Lia, and you got your wish to dance after all. You will keep it up, won't you?'

Lia gave Jasper a tentative smile. 'I will,' she said. 'It might take me a while to get back into it – the next few months are going to be tough – but I will. I don't think I could live without dancing now.' She paused for a moment, flicking another glance at Jasper. 'In fact, no-one knows this yet, and it will take me an age to get good enough to be able to do it, but one day I think I'd like to teach people to dance.'

Jasper laid a hand over hers. 'That is absolutely the best idea I've heard in ages,' he said with conviction, and Lia beamed.

'And what about you, Oscar?' added Hattie. 'What will the new year hold for you, do you think?'

Oscar steepled his fingers theatrically. 'I should much rather listen to what you young people have up your sleeves. At my advanced age, I'll just be happy to make it out alive.' He directed a look at Callum. 'This chap here, for example, has some pretty remarkable talents. I'd like to know what you've decided to do?'

Lia didn't think she had ever seen Callum blush so red before. It was a good sign.

'Well, I...' He scratched his head. 'I'm going to enjoy getting to know Lucy a whole lot better.' He winked to a low whistle from Hattie. 'And then I'm going to start up my own business in IT consultancy, amongst other things designing websites for people trying to get their own businesses off the ground.'

Oscar nodded, just like a proud father. 'I'm delighted to hear it. You have a bright future ahead of you.'

Hattie elbowed Callum gently. 'Mates' rates?' she asked with another wink, which set them all off laughing again.

'I had a good feeling about you two,' said Lia, beaming at Lucy. 'I'm so happy for you, and no-one deserves it more. If it hadn't been for you encouraging me to follow my dreams I'd never have learned to dance, or met Jasper...'

'And I wouldn't have lost weight and found my mojo again,' added Hattie.

'I'd still be festering at home letting my brothers take the piss at every opportunity, whereas now...' Callum flashed a cheeky grin at Lucy.

Oscar cleared his throat. 'And I wouldn't be delighting in the company of a wonderful group of friends, who make me feel younger than I have in years.'

Lia raised her glass towards Lucy. 'There you are then,' she said. 'You started all of this, Lucy, you've helped us all along the road – but what about *you*? What's the one thing you long for the most?'

'If she doesn't say me, I'm going to be very disappointed,' said Callum, pausing for effect. 'Under the circumstances I'll let her off – but only because I *do* know what she wants, and it's almost as good.' He sat back, grinning at her. 'Go on, Luce – tell everyone.'

Lucy screwed up her face. 'Oh, this is so embarrassing…'

'No, it isn't,' countered Callum. 'I think it's wonderful, and so will everyone else.'

Lucy looked hesitantly around the room.

'Go, on,' Lia urged, 'tell us what it is.'

Lucy took a visible breath. 'It's something I've been doing for years – not properly, just little bits here and there, but these last few months… I dunno; it feels a lot more important now – like an itch I can no longer bear not scratching.'

'What is it, Lucy?' asked Hattie eagerly.

'I want to write,' said Lucy simply. 'I mean, I *am* writing, I have been, but it's what I want to do now, properly, more than anything.'

Hattie clasped her hands together like an excited child. 'What, books, you mean? Stories? Like we read in the book club?'

Lucy nodded, her eyes shining.

'Isn't it brilliant?' said Callum. 'I told you.'

Lia found a huge smile on her face, again. It was just about the most perfect thing she had heard. 'You should write about us, Lucy,' she said quietly. 'Just listening to us all here today, and hearing what we've all got planned – there isn't anyone who could tell our story better than you.'

'But I couldn't do that!' protested Lucy.

'Why ever not?' said Lia. 'If we all agreed – and I for one would definitely agree.'

'Yes, so would I!' added Hattie. 'Although only if you make me a size eight with big boobs!'

'I'd like to be a foot taller,' said Callum.

'And of course, I'd be a devilishly handsome cad with a twinkle in his eye,' finished Oscar.

Lucy laughed. 'But you already have a twinkle in your eye, Oscar.'

'Well then,' he replied. 'You're halfway there already.'

'I don't know,' said Lucy, fidgeting slightly. 'I'll think about it.'

Chapter 36

Oscar placed the glass of port carefully on the table beside his chair. It was only early, perhaps too early, but it was a Christmas Eve tradition and one that he still carried out. He rarely had alcohol in the house now – living alone it was too much of a temptation. It would be far too easy to succumb to its false friendship, to believe the promises it made, and he had no desire to see out his time in a daily attempt to erase those memories he no longer cared for. Alcohol was no great discerner and he knew that the countless good memories would be lost to it also.

He looked steadily at the chair on the opposite side of the fireplace. 'They were happy years, Mary, were they not?' he said. 'And for the most part I never wanted anyone but you.' He shook his head gently and frowned. 'I don't know, perhaps you were right after all. Maybe it *is* better never to allow possibility to sweet-talk you, to dangle hope in front of you like a carrot before a donkey.' He frowned again and picked up the newspaper from the arm of the chair. 'Yes, perhaps you were right.'

He shook the paper open, casting his eyes down the columns until he found what he was looking for. He didn't enjoy many of the festive programmes that television had to offer but the carol concert from King's College was something he never missed. He had over an hour and a half to wait, though, so perhaps he should enjoy a slice of the

Christmas cake he had stashed away in his cupboards. That, and a good book should pass the time quite nicely.

Ten minutes later he picked up the last remaining chunk of marzipan from a plate at his side. The book remained unopened on his lap, but he turned his attention to it now, replacing his glass on the table and lifting the pages to where a bookmark had been inserted previously. He stared at the words until they blurred in front of his unseeing eyes. A heavy tear splashed onto the page. He brushed it away, angrily. Why couldn't he just leave things alone? Accept that it was over, and move on with his life. He knew he was being foolish, and that a wise man would drink his port and read his book, but Oscar's heart was not prepared to give up just yet – not when there was still a little hope.

He closed his book again and stared once more at the chair where his wife had always sat. 'There's not much I've asked for over the years, but we always prayed for a little Christmas miracle, didn't we, Mary? Perhaps this year…' He gave a sad smile and pulled himself to his feet.

★

She would be out, of course, thought Oscar. At this time of night on Christmas Eve, Hattie and her little girl would undoubtedly be somewhere else, listening to carols or visiting family, but as he picked his way carefully down the road to her house, he looked at the lit-up windows he passed and prayed.

He almost didn't do it. His hand rose from the pocket of his heavy tweed jacket and hovered somewhere in mid-air before he finally screwed up the courage to ring her doorbell. His heart began to beat wildly and he leaned against the porch as he waited.

A burst of warm air, heavy with the smell of oranges and spice, was released into the night as the door opened, and suddenly there was Hattie, laughing and smiling at something just said.

'Oscar!' she exclaimed, pulling him in with her smile. 'Poppy said it was Father Christmas, but I told her it was far too early!' She leaned towards him, lowering her voice. 'You're not, are you? Only the mince pies aren't cooked yet.'

Oscar looked past her to the brightly lit kitchen beyond, where her daughter was perched on a stool at the table.

'I'm sorry, I didn't mean to interrupt,' he said, taking a step backward. What was he thinking, coming here on Christmas Eve?

But Hattie just grinned. 'You're not,' she said. 'Please come in and save me from a very overexcited five-year-old. I hope you like tinsel.' She led him down the hallway.

'Poppy, this is Oscar, a friend of mine. Come and say hello… only mind your sticky fingers.'

The little girl climbed down from her stool, her tinsel 'crown' slipping down over her eyes. She smiled shyly, moving forward until she was standing directly in front of Oscar. She looked him up and down. 'I like your tie,' she said suddenly, with a grin. 'It's like the man's on the television.'

'We've been watching cheesy Christmas movies,' said Hattie, holding out her hands. 'Shall I take your coat? It's a bit warm in here.'

Oscar began to unbutton his jacket. 'Only if it's not too much trouble,' he said. 'I wasn't sure if you'd be in.'

Hattie rolled her eyes. 'Ah, Billy No-Mates, that's us,' she said, still smiling. 'We usually go to my sister's or my mum's, but Jules is on her honeymoon, and Mum and Dad… Well, it's been a bit trying the last few weeks so Dad's whisked her off for a last-minute turkey-and-tinsel break. They did offer for Poppy and me to go too, but trying to keep a five-year-old entertained in a hotel room over Christmas didn't sound like fun. So, I figured we'd have a brilliant time on our own. Isn't that right, Pops?' She smiled at her daughter and then looked back at Oscar, more carefully this time. 'Would you like a drink of something?' she asked.

She was obviously wondering why he was here, and in truth Oscar had no answer to that question. Where would he start? He shouldn't be here. He should leave this little family to their happy activities and go back the way he had come, keeping his selfish questions to himself.

'Oscar, is everything all right?'

He started at her words, pulling himself back from his thoughts and fixing a bright smile on his face. 'Yes, of course,' he said. 'I just…'

Hattie glanced back at the table, which was covered with flour. 'We've nearly finished here,' she said. 'Why don't you come and sit down while we spoon in the last of the mincemeat, and then madam here is going to get ready for bed while they cook. I'll make a drink too.'

Poppy scampered back to the table and picked up two sticky teaspoons. There was mincemeat right the way up the handle, and Hattie grimaced slightly as she picked up the jar, tilting it at an angle so that Poppy could scrape out the gooey filling, tongue sticking out from between her teeth as she proceeded to drop spoonsful of the mixture into the waiting pastry cases.

'We won't win any prizes for presentation,' said Hattie, 'but I hear the reindeer aren't that fussy.'

Oscar chuckled at the numerous dollops of mincemeat that lay around where they were working. 'In my day, the reindeer had carrots,' he said. 'Times seemed to have changed.'

'Oh no, they get carrots too,' replied Hattie, 'and Quality Street.' She smiled at Poppy. 'Well, they're going to need a lot of energy if they're going to fly around the whole world in one night.'

Poppy was nodding her head up and down. 'Yes, they are,' she said solemnly.

Five minutes later and they were done. Hattie peeled off her daughter's apron and lifted her carefully, arms outstretched, towards the sink, where she put her hands under the running tap to get the worst of the stickiness off. It was obviously a well-rehearsed routine.

'Right then,' said Hattie. 'Proper wash and then PJs. And I mean a proper wash. Father Christmas will not be coming to little girls who haven't cleaned their teeth.' She gave her daughter a kiss and set her back down on the ground. 'Go on, off you go.'

She turned back to Oscar, grinning. 'Don't you just love it?' she said.

It made the breath catch in his throat.

'Now, where were we?' Hattie stood with her hands on her hips, surveying the drifts of flour, lumps of pastry, sticky mincemeat and general chaos that surrounded them. She shrugged. 'It can wait,' she said. 'Tea or coffee, Oscar?'

Oscar looked at her sunny face, flushed pink from the heat of the kitchen, or possibly just the spirit of Christmas. He couldn't do it.

'I'm sorry,' he said. 'I shouldn't have come. You have much to do and precious time to spend with your daughter—'

'Oscar, I have time to spend with my friends too, especially on Christmas Eve, so none of that "I must be going". Come and sit down... Although just mind where you put your arms or you'll get covered in flour!' She stood pointedly by the kettle with a mug in her hand.

'Thank you.' Oscar smiled. 'I'll have tea please – two sugars, I'm afraid.'

The drinks underway, Hattie picked up a cloth from the sink and began to rinse it under the hot tap, coming back to the table to scoop the debris away.

Oscar sat as directed and watched her for a moment. She was a wonderful mum, who clearly delighted in her daughter's company. A young woman who was doing the best for her child under what must have been very difficult circumstances at times. And now, here she was, on the verge of trying to make a successful business to support both herself and her daughter. If Oscar were her father he would be very proud indeed… or even if he were her grandfather. He cleared his throat.

'Hattie, there's something I rather hoped I might discuss with you,' he began, 'although I confess my timing leaves a lot to be desired. The subject matter is also… Perhaps "difficult" is the right word?'

'Oh?' Hattie's head swung up to look at him as she stopped what she was doing. 'That sounds a little ominous.'

Oscar smiled as warm a smile as he could manage. 'It's not meant to be, my dear, trust me, but I cannot think of any way other than to simply say it.'

Hattie sat down on the stool with a thump, the dishcloth still in her hand. She watched him for a minute. 'I don't think I've ever seen you looking quite so serious, Oscar, but in the short time I've known you, you've never acted with anything other than the utmost respect for other people. Whatever you want to say is fine with me.'

Oscar gave one last smile before he opened his mouth to speak.

'I think you might be aware that I lost my Mary just over a year ago, and it seems to me now almost inconceivable the amount of time that's passed since we first met. We were eighteen and desperately in love, and even though it was more usual to marry young then than perhaps it is now, this went against us from the start. Our parents considered us incapable of loving each other as much as we did and, in my darker moments, I lay the blame for our naïvety at their door. When Mary fell pregnant she was taken from me, and as soon as our daughter was born she too was whisked away, out of sight from judgemental eyes and gossiping tongues, as if she was something to regret and hide from the world.'

Oscar struggled for a moment, swallowing. 'We would have called her Susan.'

Hattie reached forward to cover his hand with hers. He could see in her eyes that she knew where this was leading, but she held his look, allowing him the time and space to tell his story.

'I considered myself the luckiest man alive when I got my Mary back. I don't think I could have survived if I'd have lost her too, and so we married, against our parents' wishes. But although we had the happiest of marriages, we were never blessed with any more children.'

'Did you ever try to find her?' asked Hattie gently.

Oscar hung his head. 'No. Mary couldn't bear the thought of finding her and having the possibility that we might lose her all over again. We built our lives around each other, and that's the way we stayed.'

Hattie remained silent. It must be hard for her to know what to say, thought Oscar.

'I talked about my mum when we were at Lia's the other day.' Her voice was hesitant. 'Are you here because you want my help to find Susan?'

Oscar couldn't blame her for going for the easiest option to swallow, but now he didn't know how to reply. The silence began to lengthen uncomfortably.

'I see,' said Hattie quietly. 'I should have guessed, really. What other explanation could there be for you coming here?' Her hand still covered his but she sat up slightly, causing it to move a little. She looked down at it. 'But my mum has said she doesn't want any contact. What makes you think it's her?'

She was being protective of her family, of course she was, thought Oscar. He would expect nothing less. But he was committed now, he had to push this as far as he could go or forever wonder if he could have done more. He looked up into Hattie's dark eyes.

'Hope,' he said simply.

It was too much. He saw the tears spring into her eyes almost immediately. She was a mother; she knew how it felt to contemplate the thought of losing a child because her darkest fears had taken her there.

'Oscar, I can't,' she whispered, a tear spilling down her cheek. 'We all agreed. My mum's been through so much and I have to respect her decision, however much I would love you to be right. What if she does find out who her real parents are, and it's not you, what then? She'd be opening herself up to something she never really wanted.'

'I know.' Oscar's voice cracked, as much for the distress he was causing Hattie as for the final sliver of hope he saw evaporating before his eyes. His journey was at an end, he could go no further.

'I'm sorry,' he added. 'I hope you understand, I had to ask.' He held the edge of the table as he got to his feet. 'I really am very sorry, I didn't mean to upset you.'

Hattie wiped her eyes. 'Oh, Oscar, you haven't upset me. I just wish I could help, but I—'

Oscar held up a hand. 'My dear girl, you've been kindness itself letting me sit here and ramble on.' He looked around the kitchen. 'Now, if I'm not much mistaken, you have mince pies to bake and a little girl to enjoy Christmas with. You take good care of one another.'

Hattie came from behind the table and threw her arms around him, hugging him tight for a minute. 'Oscar, it's Christmas! I can't bear the thought of you by yourself like this. Won't you stay? I never did make you that drink. Poppy and I will just be playing board games later and it's so much better with three.'

'No,' said Oscar firmly. 'I've outstayed my welcome, and I think it's best if I go. Perhaps my coat, if I may?'

He waited while Hattie went to fetch it, struggling to keep himself together. He had thought that by talking to her he might be more able to cope with his daughter's decision, but now he didn't want to face the truth. The reality wasn't enlightening, or comforting; it didn't provide a means to move forward. It was just final. The end. Oscar's heart could take no more.

He was close to tears as he allowed Hattie to give him one last hug. Her face was filled with concern but he was unable to meet her eye. Pulling away, he gave a smile that was more of a grimace and turned towards the door.

'Oscar?' The warmth in Hattie's voice was calling him back but he was reluctant to stop. 'If we were to find out that my mum *is* your daughter, that would make me your granddaughter, wouldn't it?' There was a gentle tone to her voice that tugged on the invisible line between them. 'And in the blink of an eye our relationship would go from being one thing to something else entirely…' Her voice was wistful now. 'But that would be all right. It would be encouraged because we'd be family…'

Oscar couldn't resist and he turned back to face her.

'And I'm wondering why that one tiny piece of information should make all the difference to how two people behave when their whole lives have been spent apart. That doesn't make sense; it's not like a switch that you can choose to turn on or off.'

He frowned gently. 'Well, put like that, it does sound odd, I admit, but I imagine it's not something that would happen overnight. It would be about getting to know one another first, trusting each other, growing a friendship. I would never seek to presume—'

'Oscar,' interrupted Hattie softly. 'We already have all that, so let me ask you: suppose I had just found out that you *were* my grandfather, would you be leaving now? Or would you be staying a while, before returning again tomorrow to spend Christmas Day with us?'

Oscar stared at her. His heart was trying to get him to believe something that could never be true, but his head was saying he mustn't listen. 'My dear Hattie, it's a kind thing to say, but we don't know that I'm anything of the sort.'

'But you might be. And you didn't answer my question.' Her face was flushed pink as she spoke. 'Would you still be going?'

'Well, I…'

'Even if you knew that given the choice of anyone in the world who I'd want to be my grandfather, I'd choose you without a second thought?' She smiled at him, a full-on beam that lit up her whole face.

Oscar's heart felt like it was about to burst with happiness. 'No, I'd stay,' he said. 'Of course, I'd stay.'

Hattie came towards him, her arms outstretched. 'Then let's get your jacket off again. It's the time of year for miracles, isn't it? That's what I always tell Poppy, and that if we believe in them hard enough, one day they might even come true.' She kissed his cheek. 'And for now, we can just pretend. Happy Christmas, Gramps,' she whispered.

★

Just under a mile away, Lia sat on her mum's bed. Moments ago, there had been tears running down her face, but the shock had dried them rapidly. On her lap, she still held the freshly laundered nightie that she had been about to put away in a drawer when she had found the notebook.

She had never seen it before, but it was new and of good quality. She'd wondered where it had come from until she saw what was written inside, and she realised that her mum must have asked either Jasper or Christopher to buy it for her.

Inside were pages and pages of lists. One contained her own name, written over and over; another, their address. A page further on held details of her mum's favourite blue dress that she danced in – the writing shaky, the details added and then crossed out as she sought to remember. There were names of dances – the foxtrot, Viennese waltz, rumba and cha-cha-cha – and on one page even drawings of feet, numbered, Lia now knew, in a sequence of steps.

She stared at the pages, turning them this way and that. The sudden realisation brought fresh tears to Lia's eyes; her mum *had* been improving over the last few months, and more than that she had felt it herself. The notebook was a way of trying to cling on to the memories she knew to be true, of remembering who she was and her life and everyone in it. It was so desperately sad to see how she had tried to capture these tiny moments of lucidity before they faded forever. Lia hugged the book to her. Out of all the things her mum had tried to remember, it was her dancing that she never wanted to forget. After years of denying how important it was to her life, in the last few months of that life, she had allowed herself to remember what had made her truly happy.

Lia had been wrong when she told Lucy that the memories made her mum worse; they hadn't at all. They had made her better, happier, than she had been in years. She opened the book again, eyes shining, and turned the pages in wonder, reading and smiling. It wasn't until she got to the last few entries that the breath caught in her throat. On one page her mum had written *Lia dance lessons*, underscoring it several times over, and on another was written only one word: *Jasper*.

She clutched the notebook to her, touching it to her lips as a wave of emotion swept over her. She lurched up from the bed, her mum's nightie falling to the floor. She stopped then and picked it up, sniffing hard as tears rolled down her face, and gently she placed it on the bed. 'Thanks, Mum,' she whispered. 'For everything.'

Eyes swimming, she raced down the stairs and into the kitchen, snatching up her phone from the table. She pressed the home button to bring the screen to life, Jasper's text still visible – a text he had sent to her earlier in the day, and one that she had read a hundred times over. She could hardly see it for tears but she knew it by heart now, anyway. It was a line from a song by The Byrds they had danced to recently.

Underneath it Jasper had written: *The seasons turn Lia, and I will still be here waiting. Take time, Lia, as much as you need. Merry Christmas, Jasper x*

She raced around the house, snatching things at random, looking at her watch every few minutes. Even though she had all the time in the world, she now couldn't bear to waste a single second.

The lights were turned off one by one, until Lia was ready, standing in the hallway, trembling, with one hand on the door. She took a deep breath and pulled it open, smiling as she closed it gently behind her. Then, walking out into the deserted streets, she gave one final look at the darkened house, climbed into her car and drove towards the twinkling lights ahead of her. Jasper's house was only about half an hour away, and if she was lucky there would still be time for one last dance before bed.

★

By contrast, Lucy's house was full of people and the noise level had been steadily rising all evening. Her brother, sister and Clive had been making cocktails for the last hour or so. It was the same every year: her mum became increasingly merry on sherry during the afternoon as everyone helped to prepare the mammoth lunch they would all devour on Christmas Day. It was a time that Lucy loved, and more so this year because she had got to watch the look on Callum's face, which radiated with happiness. He had even tried his hand at making sausage rolls, much to Clive's amusement, but now they had left the rest of the family to it and escaped to the relative quiet of the living room.

Without thinking, she picked up her notebook from the table beside the sofa and turned to the last entry, rereading the words she had written there earlier this morning.

'Well,' said Callum, grinning. 'Have you given everyone the ending they deserve?'

Lucy tapped her pen against her teeth. 'I think so,' she replied. 'Yes, I have.' Then, much stronger now, 'In fact, it all turns out wonderfully.'

Callum sighed and reached for the box of After Eights. 'But what about you?' he asked. 'I hope you've given yourself a brilliant future?'

Lucy caught the twinkle in his eye. 'What, about *us*, you mean?' she said, leaning into him for a kiss. 'Of course, I have. In fact, it's the best of the lot. I'd say it's practically perfect.'

Epilogue

Eighteen months later

Lucy hardly dared to ask the question, even though all the faces in front of her were grinning like Cheshire cats.

'Well?' she said. 'Put me out of my misery. What do you all think?'

Lia gave an exaggerated sigh. 'As if you have to ask, Lucy. Honestly, what are you like?'

Oscar closed the book in his hands and turned it over, stroking the cover and turning it back again. '*Lucy's Book Club for the Lost and Found*,' he read. 'Who'd have thought it? But it is, of course, the most marvellous book, Lucy. You've done us proud and I am so very, *very* pleased for you.'

'I think it's flippin' amazing,' said Hattie with a grin. 'I can't believe everything that's happened.'

'*You* can't believe everything that's happened?' echoed Lucy. 'What about me? I still think I'm dreaming.'

Callum took her hand and kissed it, then gave it a gentle pinch. 'Nope, not dreaming,' he said. 'In four weeks' time, you're going to be a published author.'

Lucy looked back at her husband of only two months. Then she turned to Lia, who glowed with vitality. She and Jasper were going to be married in the summer, and whatever else the wedding arrangements involved, Lucy was certain of two things: the first was that Hattie would be making Lia's wedding dress, and the second was that their first dance together was going to be the best first dance in the history of the world – ever.

Next to Hattie sat Oscar, smiling at her, like any proud grandparent. They were still no nearer to finding out the truth about their relationship, but it mattered little. As far as they were concerned, they were granddaughter and grandfather and they didn't need a slip of paper to tell them otherwise. In time, Lucy hoped that Hattie's mum would take the final step on her own very personal journey – but whatever happened, all would be well.

In fact, all would be well for them all; of that she was sure. She glanced up, running her eyes down the length of the library. Who would have thought all those months ago that the members of her little book club would be sitting here today, discussing their dreams – and even holding in their hands the book that had made her *own* dream come true?

Hadn't she always thought that the library was a place where help was just around the corner? She glanced up at the arch of the ceiling above her, its shape just like that of an upturned boat, a vessel which had carried them to a better place.

Oscar cleared his throat, peering intently at the pages of the book he still held in his hands. 'I don't know what to say,' he said. 'Look at this.' He gave Lucy a smile that melted her heart.

She held up her own copy. 'Well who else could I dedicate it to,' she said, 'if not to you all?' And she opened the front cover and began to read.

To Callum, Lia, Oscar, Hattie and Jasper
Five of the best, who not only gave me their stories,
but who also taught me how to write.

Lia held her hand against her chest and sighed. 'Oh, that's beautiful, Lucy, just beautiful.' And then she grinned. 'Utter rubbish of course – I mean, how could we possibly teach you how to write?'

'But you did!' protested Lucy. 'Don't you see? There I was, twenty-four years of age, knowing nothing about anything. Then along all of you came and taught me about everything that was important: love, sadness, friendship, happiness, sacrifice, fear, devotion, loneliness and hope – all the things that make us who we are. How could I ever have written a book without knowing those things? So, you see, I couldn't have done it without you.'

Callum pulled a face. 'Passion,' he said. 'She always forgets about the passion…'

Lucy elbowed him in the ribs. 'Shh! Not in the library,' she said fiercely. But she was laughing, they all were. 'I honestly can't thank you all enough. I just hope everyone loves it as much as you do.'

'Oh, they will, Lucy, they will,' said Hattie. 'I mean, what's not to like? We all turned out fabulous.'

'You did!' Lucy grinned at them all. 'But what a responsibility. I was so worried I wouldn't be able to do it. I mean, what if I didn't do you all justice? Besides which, I don't even know yet how the stories end.'

Lia laughed. 'But that's the best bit, Lucy,' she said. 'None of us do. It's just like life: none of us knows what's going to happen next – we're all just making it up as we go along.'

A letter from Emma

I really hope you've enjoyed reading *Lucy's Little Village Book Club*. Thank you so much! Of course, now that you have it means that I'm already busy with my new series of books, and I'm just as excited about those too! You can sign up to my newsletter here www.bookouture. com/emma-davies and that way you'll be the first to hear all my news.

As Lucy herself says, how can a library not be a special place? Within its books lie so many worlds, so many stories. Whenever you lose yourself in the pages of a book, you are entering these worlds; you can be anywhere you want to be, and anyone you want to be. The fact that all this can happen from a collection of letters on a page is proof of their magic. And that's exactly what happened to me; I lost myself in this book and, in doing so, I hope created something magical. If you loved Lucy's story as much as I enjoyed writing it, it would mean the world to me if you could spare a few minutes to write a review and share some of the love that Lucy and I created. You could even tell all your friends, your neighbours, dental receptionist – anyone who'll listen! – and, of course, your local librarian as well! That would make me very happy.

One of the things I love is hearing from readers, so do come and say hello. You can find me on Twitter and I'm on Facebook too. Or pop by my website where you can read about my love of Pringles among other things...

Hope to see you soon,
Love Emma x

 @EmDaviesAuthor

: www.facebook.com/emmadaviesauthor

: www.emmadaviesauthor.com

Acknowledgements

Lucy's Little Village Book Club is such a special book for me. It was written after a very difficult year for me personally, and the fact that this book exists at all is testament to the love and support from my family and friends, but also to the people who provided the inspiration for it: the staff and customers at my local library, who provided the laughs, the encouragement, the most amazing conversations, and the endless cups of tea and biscuits. There are a few very special people I'd like to single out, but I won't, for their sake. Suffice to say that they have joined the list of my most favourite people on the planet and, I hope, know who they are. This book is my very special thank-you to them.

I've been quite vocal in the past about my love of libraries. Ever since I was a small child they have been a huge part of my life and it breaks my heart to think that in my lifetime I might see the total demise of community libraries, my own included. Our library is so much more than somewhere to borrow books from, or use the computers – for many it is a lifeline to the world outside. We can quantify how much it costs to pay staff and heat the buildings, but I've never met an accountant yet who can put a price on inspiration or knowledge, the comfort and escape provided by a good book, the companionship and care that they find there, or the happiness and laughter that fills the air within the building every single day it is open. It is quite simply, priceless, and we are all forever in its debt.

CPSIA information can be obtained
at www.ICGtesting.com
Printed in the USA
LVOW03s2355260318
571290LV00019B/525/P